10-05 G
15.00

Remember

BARBARA
TAYLOR
BRADFORD
Remember

Random House Large Print

Library of Congress Cataloging-in-Publication Data

Bradford, Barbara Taylor
Remember/Barbara Taylor Bradford.—Large print ed.
p.   cm.
ISBN 0-679-40821-5 (lg. print)
1. Large type books. I. Title.
[PS3552.R2147R45   1991]   813′.54—dc20   91-16353

Manufactured in the United States of America
24689753
First Large Print Edition
Calligraphy by Carole Lowenstein
Book design by Jo Anne Metsch

THIS LARGE PRINT BOOK CARRIES
THE SEAL OF APPROVAL OF N.A.V.H.

*This book is for my husband, Robert,
who fights the good fight, with my
love and admiration.*

Remember me when I am gone away,
Gone far away into the silent land;
When you can no more hold me by the hand,
Nor I half turn to go yet turning stay.
Remember me when no more day by day
You tell me of our future that you planned:
Only remember me; you understand
It will be late to counsel then or pray.
Yet if you should forget me for a while
And afterwards remember, do not grieve;
For if the darkness and corruption leave
A vestige of the thoughts that once I had,
Better by far you should forget and smile
Than that you should remember and be sad.

—Christina Rossetti

ACKNOWLEDGMENT

My very special thanks to my friend Barbara Victor of Paris, for making available some special research and for giving so generously of her time.

CONTENTS

Comrades-'in-Arms

*A friend may well be reckoned
the masterpiece of Nature.*

—Ralph Waldo Emerson

1

Sleep eluded her.

She lay in the darkness, trying to empty her head of every thought, troubling or otherwise, but this seemed to be an impossibility. Bone tired though she had been earlier, when she had stripped off her clothes and fallen into bed, she was now wide-awake. All of her senses were alerted; she strained to catch any untoward sounds from outside. At this moment, though, very little noise penetrated the walls of the plush hotel suite. It was curious, ominous, the silence outside.

That's where I should be, she thought. Outside.

Certainly that was where she belonged,

where her heart and mind were. Outside . . . with her crew: Jimmy Trainer, her camera- man; Luke Michaels, her sound engineer; and Arch Leverson, her producer. They usu- ally hung together most of the time, like any good news team on foreign assignment.

It was rare for her not to be with them, but tonight, over an early dinner, she had been so weary, her eyelids drooping after several nights with little or no sleep, that Arch had insisted she grab a few hours in bed. He had promised to wake her in plenty of time for her to prepare for her nightly broadcast to the States. Common sense plus fatigue had pre- vailed; she had agreed, only to find herself unable to relax and drop off the moment she was between the cool sheets.

She was tense, expectant. Suddenly she knew the reason why. Her intelligence, judg- ment and instinct, combined with her experi- ence as a war correspondent, were all telling her the same thing. It was going to happen tonight. The crackdown that had been in the wind for days would be tonight.

Involuntarily she shivered at this fore- knowledge and turned cold. Blessed with a prescience that was unusual, she knew bet- ter than to doubt herself, and she shivered again at the thought of bloodshed. And blood would be spilled if the People's Army moved against the people.

Pushing herself up against the pillows, she switched on the bedside lamp and glanced at her watch. It was a few minutes before ten. Throwing back the covers decisively, she got out of bed and hurried across the floor to the window. Opening it wide, she stepped out onto the balcony, anxious to see what, if anything, was happening in the streets of Beijing.

Her suite was on the fourteenth floor of the Beijing Hotel, overlooking Changan Avenue, also known as the Avenue of Eternal Peace, which led into Tiananmen Square. Below her on this wide boulevard, illuminated by cluster lights shaded in green, people were moving along steadily in a continuous flow, like trout heading upstream. As they passed through the pools of light cast by the lamps she saw that they were mostly wearing white shirts or tops, and she was amazed that they moved so quietly, so silently.

They were making for Tiananmen Square, that vast rectangle of stone dating back to 1651 in the early Qing Dynasty, built to hold a million people in its one-hundred-acre expanse. She had come to understand that it was the symbolic heart of political power in China, and over the centuries the square had been the site of some momentous events in the country's turbulent history.

She sniffed the air. It was clear, held no hint of tear gas or the smell of the yellow dust that perpetually blew in from the Gobi Desert and was normally all-pervasive in the congested capital. Perhaps the light wind was carrying both smells away from the hotel, or perhaps tear gas had not been used tonight. As she glanced up and down the long avenue quickly, her eyes shifted back to the crowded pavement below her balcony and the people walking toward the square in such an orderly fashion. Everything appeared to be peaceful, and certainly the military were nowhere to be seen—at the moment.

The calm before the storm, she thought dismally, as she turned and went back into the suite.

After switching on the rest of the lights in the bedroom, she hurried into the adjoining bathroom, where she splashed cold water on her face, patted it dry with a towel and began to brush her hair in swift, even strokes.

The face surrounded by the soft blond hair was somewhat wide with a strong jawline, but its individual features were classical, clean-cut, well defined—high cheekbones, straight nose, pretty mouth, chin that was firm and resolute without being pugnacious.

The eyes, set wide apart under arched blond brows, were large and clear, their color a bright sea-blue that was almost but not quite turquoise. The features came together to create a face that was unusually attractive, lively with vivid intelligence and humor, and highly photogenic. In her bare feet, as she was now, she stood five feet six inches tall; slender of frame yet surprisingly strong, she had long legs and possessed a willowy grace.

The young woman's name was Nicole Wells; she was commonly known as Nicky to the world at large. But her family, crew and closest friends affectionately called her Nick most of the time.

At thirty-six she was at the height of her profession, as war correspondent for the American Television Network, headquartered in New York. Renowned as a brilliant investigative reporter as well as an expert chronicler of war, and respected for her spectacular coverage of world events, she had a reputation for being intrepid, and on camera she was very charismatic. She had become a genuine superstar in the media.

Nicky put down the brush, pulled her hair straight back into a ponytail and anchored it firmly before reaching into her makeup kit for a lipstick. Once she had outlined her mouth

in pink, she leaned closer, grimacing at herself. Tonight she looked washed-out, pallid
without makeup, but she was in too much of
a hurry to start applying it. Besides, she was
certain she would not be on camera tonight.
When martial law had been declared on May
20, almost two weeks ago now, the Chinese
government had turned off the satellite; furthermore, television cameras had been
banned in the square. No more live-spot lo-
cation shots without that satellite feed or
Jimmy behind his camera. At least not in
Tiananmen Square, and that's where the
story was—at the center of the action. Once
again, she would have to make do with a
phoned-in report.

Swinging away from the mirror, Nicky returned to the bedroom, where she dressed
rapidly in the clothes she had shed only a
brief while ago: beige cotton trousers, a blue
cotton T-shirt, and a short-sleeved safari-
style jacket that matched the pants. This
was her standard uniform when she was
abroad on assignment in the summer, and
she always packed three identical safari
suits, plus a selection of T-shirts and man-
tailored cotton shirts to add color to the suits,
and for the benefit of the camera.

After she had slipped into soft brown loafers, she went to the closet and took out her

big shoulder bag. This was a commodious carryall made of sage-green waterproofed fabric, and it contained what she laughingly referred to as "my entire life"; she rarely went anywhere without it when she was on foreign assignment. And now, as she always did before going out, she unlocked it, double-checked that her "life" was indeed safely inside the bag. Passport, press credentials, plastic money, real money including U.S. dollars, Hong Kong dollars, English pounds and the local yuan, door keys for her Manhattan apartment, world address book, a small cosmetics bag containing toothpaste, toothbrush, soap, makeup, makeup mirror, hairbrush and a packet of tissues. All were neatly stashed in separate compartments within the interior section of the bag; in the two large outside pockets were her cellular phone, tape recorder, notebook, pens, reading glasses, sunglasses and a packet of gauze surgical masks to protect against tear gas.

As long as she had the bag with her, Nicky knew she could survive anywhere in the world without any other luggage and, just as important, do her job efficiently and effectively. But tonight she needed only a few of its contents. These she now took out of the carryall and locked it. Her passport and press credentials, the cellular phone, reading glasses, notebook and pens, gauze masks, some of the U.S. dollars and local yuan were the essential items, and she popped them into a much smaller shoulder bag made of brown leather.

Slinging the small bag over her shoulder, she pocketed the door key and returned the carryall to the closet. As she left the suite she glanced at her watch. It was just ten-twenty.

Despite her sense of urgency about the need to be outside in the square, Nicky nevertheless headed for the ATN suite a few doors away from her own, just in case Arch Leverson had returned to call New York. The time difference between China and the United States was thirteen hours, and China being ahead, it was nine-twenty on Friday morning back home. This was about the time Arch generally checked in with Larry Anderson, the president of news at the ATN network.

The suite served as a makeshift newsroom-office for them, and when she got there it was her cameraman's voice she heard faintly echoing at the other side of the door. She knocked lightly.

A second later the door was wrenched open and Jimmy flashed a huge grin when he saw her. "Hi, honey," he said, then, walking back toward the desk, added over his shoulder, "I won't be a minute—just finishing a call to the States."

Closing the door behind her, Nicky followed him into the room and stood with her hand on the chair back, waiting.

At fifty-two Jimmy Trainer was in his prime. He was of medium height, slim and spry, with graying dark hair, rosy cheeks in a merry face and a twinkle in his pale-blue eyes. An ace of a cameraman who had won an endless number of awards, he loved his work and being part of Nick's team, and his job was his life, even though he had a wonderful wife, a happy marriage and two children. And, like Luke and Arch, he was totally devoted to Nicky Wells. To Jimmy she was a dream to work with, and he would have put his life on the line for her.

Jimmy resumed his phone conversation, talking fast in a low tone to end the call to his wife. "Nicky just came in, Jo honey. I gotta go. Duty calls." After listening a moment or two longer, he finally said an affectionate good-bye and hung up. Turning to Nicky, he remarked, "This is the best damned phone system. Got to hand it to the Chinese, they certainly installed the most up-to-date equipment. Joanna sounded as if she were in the next room, instead of on Eighty-third and Park, and she—"

"It's French," Nicky interrupted. "The phone system, I mean."

"Yep, I guess I knew that. Jo sends her love."

Nicky smiled at him. "How is she?"

"Sounds fine. But she's watching the news on television, listening to the same news on the radio, and worrying about the four of us. She seems to be handling it well, though, as she usually does." His brow furrowed. "But hey, kiddo, you're supposed to be grabbing a few hours' sleep, not hovering around here obviously anxious to start planning tonight's newscast."

"I know, I know, but I couldn't sleep. I have a premonition something . . . no, *everything,* is going to blow up tonight. My gut instinct tells me there's going to be a crackdown. Probably around midnight, or thereabouts."

Catching the tension in her voice and noting her worried expression, Jimmy looked at her keenly. After five and a half years of working with Nicky Wells in the trouble spots of the world, he trusted her intuition implicitly. Her judgment had rarely, if ever, been flawed.

"If you say so, Nick. You know I'm with you all the way. But look, I gotta tell you this, it *is* pretty quiet out there. At least it was twenty minutes ago."

Nicky focused her eyes on him quizzically. "Nothing's happening in the square?"

"Not really. The kids in the tent encampment were starting to come out of their tents, mingling with each other and chatting, sort of sharing experiences, I suppose, as they appear to do every night." For a moment he was thoughtful, then went on, "To tell you the truth, I was reminded of Woodstock tonight, without the drugs, of course. Or, if you prefer, one of those summer street festivals we have in New York. Everything was very relaxed, friendly, easygoing I'd say."

"It won't be for much longer," Nicky announced with suppressed vehemence, and sat down heavily in a chair. "I've been doing a lot of thinking, and I believe that Deng Xiaoping is at the end of his tether. He's been provoked and frustrated by the students for some time, and I'm sure he's about to make his move. It'll be a bungled move, just as he and the government have bungled the whole Tiananmen Square affair ever since it began. But he'll have no compunction, you know. He'll order the troops to move on the students." She sighed and finished in a low, sad voice, "I'm afraid there's going to be a bloodbath, Jimmy."

He stared at her. "Oh, Nick, surely not! Deng wouldn't go so far. He wouldn't *dare*. He'd hardly risk condemnation from the world and its leaders."

She shook her head. "No, James, I think he'll do it, all right. And I'll tell you something else, I don't think Deng gives a damn about the rest of the world, its leaders, or what they think of him."

The magnitude of what her words suggested struck him, and Jimmy exclaimed, "Oh God, those kids are so young. And so idealistic!" His voice rose as he rushed on, "And they're *peaceful*. All they want is to be listened to—they just want to be *heard*."

"That's never going to happen," Nicky replied. "You know as well as I do what the students call Deng and his cohorts—the Gang of the Old. They're absolutely right. Deng is eighty-five and far, far too old to understand the way it is today. He's completely out of touch with this generation, all he's interested in is clinging to power. We know the students are not making unreasonable demands, and anyway, wanting freedom and democracy is a pretty normal thing, wouldn't you say?"

Jimmy nodded, then took a deep breath. "Okay, so what do you want to do?"

"I want to be out there, right in the middle

of it when it happens. That's why we're here, isn't it? To report the news, to bring the news to the people, to tell the outside world the way it is in China, on this Friday night, the second day of June, in the year 1989.''

"We've still got one big problem, honey. We can't film out there," Jimmy said. "The minute we appear, the police will smash the cameras and the sound equipment. What's more, we could get hauled in for questioning, like some of the other foreign correspondents have been. We could be detained, flung into jail—"

Jimmy broke off when he saw the door open and Arch Leverson walk in.

Nicky's producer did not seem surprised to see her. "And why might we be flung into jail?" he asked the cameraman.

"Nicky wants to try to film in the square," Jimmy answered.

"Don't think we can, Nick. Nothing's changed since yesterday." Arch Leverson went toward Nicky and, putting a hand on her shoulder, gave her a warm smile, which she returned.

Always elegantly attired wherever he was, Arch was tall and thin, with a saturnine face, prematurely silver hair and light-gray eyes behind steel-rimmed glasses. Forty-one years old and a veteran of the television news business, he had been lured away from another network by ATN three years ago. Quite aside from the proposed hike in salary, the most exciting inducement ATN had dangled in front of him was Nicky Wells. The man who had produced her shows for several years had retired, and the job was open. There wasn't a producer in the television news business who didn't want to take over Nicky's newscasts, not to mention the documentaries she was famous for, and for which she had won several Emmys. His agent had negotiated a good contract for him, he had changed networks and had never once regretted doing so. And he and Nicky had hit it off immediately. She was a real professional, who had won both his utmost respect and his affection.

Nicky looked up now at Arch, and said, "There's going to be a crackdown—most probably tonight."

Arch returned her quiet gaze with one equally steady, but he did not immediately respond. After a moment he said slowly, "You're not often wrong, Nicky, and I'm inclined to agree with you. Military intervention does seem inevitable."

"According to Jimmy, it was peaceful in the square earlier this evening. Has the atmosphere changed?" she asked.

"Not really," Arch said. "In fact, I'd go so far as to say it's positively festive out there. Nevertheless, rumors are rife, mostly about troop movements seen in different parts of Beijing again. I just ran into one of the guys from CNN in the hotel lobby, and he told me he'd heard the same rumors."

Arch sat down behind the desk and glanced at Nicky and Jimmy, looking extremely worried. "We'd better prepare ourselves for a rough weekend. Tough in every possible way."

"I'm sure of it," Nicky said.

Jimmy made no comment, nor did he react to the producer's dire prediction. Instead he paced up and down the room, looking preoccupied. Finally he said to Arch, "Since we can't manage any live-shot locations in the square, I'm going to have to film Nick doing her standups in another part of town, the way we did at the beginning of the week."

"I don't think we dare risk that again," Arch said. "The city's teeming with police, and we wouldn't get two steps before we'd be in deep trouble."

"I was thinking of one of the districts on the edge of the city," Jimmy explained, "not anywhere remotely near Tiananmen. It'll be quieter out there."

Arch shook his head again. "*No*. It won't

be safe. It's putting Nick at risk, and need-
lessly so. I'm not going to take that
chance—"

"Oh, come on, Arch!" Nicky cut in. "I'm a
war correspondent, remember. And I've
been in dangerous areas for years. I think we
ought to do what Jimmy suggests—"

"But I don't!" Arch shot back, and rather
sharply for him. "I just told you, I'm not putting you at risk. I'm not going to put *any* of us
at risk, for that matter. Not here in China, for
this story."

"Listen, I'm tired of doing phone narrations with my cellular from the square!"
Nicky exclaimed, "and I'm just as sure New
York's sick of running stills of me to go with
the narrations. Please, let's try to do at least
one newscast live, on camera, tonight, no
matter where we actually film it. I realize we
can't feed it to New York via the satellite,
that it'll have to be shipped, but even so the
network would have it in time to run it Sunday
or Monday." Turning to her cameraman, she
asked, "There's no problem getting the moving film out by courier, via Hong Kong and
Tokyo, is there?"

"The couriers are still operating," Jimmy
assured her. "I suppose we could film you in
your suite, even though you've been dead
set against that, Nicky—" Jimmy broke off

and hurried over to the window. He went out onto the balcony, stepped back inside and stood gazing at the balcony from the room for a moment. He swung to Arch and said, "I think there's a way to film Nick out there, with Changan and Tiananmen in the background. It'll be a tight squeeze, but it's worth a try."

Arch sat up in the chair, looking suddenly more cheerful. "Well, we've talked about it before, but we've always dismissed it. Now we don't have any choices left. Out there on the balcony we'll at least be able to convey a sense of on-the-spot reporting. I hope. Which is what we're about, after all."

"I'll start planning it," Jimmy said.

Nicky went to the open window to survey the balcony, then, pivoting on her heels, she said to Jimmy, "I'm sure it'll work, and I'm all for it."

"Listen, Nick," Arch said, "I'm afraid you *will* have to do a phone narration for tonight's newscast, there's just no alternative. We'll do that first, then shoot out there, so that America can see you live, and in living color, on Monday at the latest."

"Okay. In the meantime, if you don't need me, I think I'll go to the square for a while." Glancing over at Arch, she asked, "Where's Luke? At the Martyrs' Monument?"

"That's where I left him. He's with Clee."

"Then let's make that our meeting place, shall we? Right now I want to walk around, nose about a bit, get a sense of what's really happening. I'll talk to Yoyo and a few of the other students."

"We'll join you in an hour or so," Arch told her. "After I've called the network."

"See you later, then." Her manner efficient and breezy, Nicky picked up her bag, shrugged it onto her shoulder and hurried out of the suite.

Arch sat staring at the door for a few minutes after she left, his thoughts focused on Nicole Wells.

Whenever she went off on her own in a hazardous zone he automatically wanted to caution her to be careful, but he had schooled himself to resist the temptation. He had learned his lesson long ago, having had his head bitten off far too often in the early days of their association. He frequently wished he did not feel so protective about her, but he did, and there was little he could do to change his feelings. In any case, Jimmy and Luke were in the same boat as he was, constantly worrying about her. And she was forever scaring the hell out of the three of them, with the chances she took.

There was no question in his mind about

her courage. She was fearless. Danger did not bother her; she thumbed her nose at it, even seemed to relish it. More than once it had struck him that she behaved as though her life was of little consequence to her. But he knew this was a farfetched idea. Naturally, Nicky cared about her life, even if she *was* sometimes mighty casual about her personal safety.

Reaching into his pocket, Arch pulled out a pack of cigarettes and lit one. Of course it was the story that mattered, that's what it was all about, what *she* was all about. The story came first, it took precedence over everything else, and he understood why, being a newsman himself. Nicky Wells was like most other war correspondents, whatever their gender; she wanted to be at the center of the action, where the excitement was.

She's a chip off the old block, he mused, thinking of her father as he drew on his cigarette. Andrew Wells had also been a renowned war correspondent in his earlier days, and he now was a highly respected columnist for *The New York Times.* And then there was her mother, who could hardly be overlooked: Elise Elliot Wells, Pulitzer Prize winner, former distinguished foreign correspondent, writer of important historical books.

Arch had often wondered what it had been

like, growing up with that formidable duo. Some childhood she must have had, being dragged around the world by two hotshot journalists in search of headlines for their respective newspapers, who nonetheless, by all accounts, had adored their only child. Still adored her, in fact.

Once, in a confiding mood, she had told him that her father called her Nick because he had always wanted a son. That had explained a lot to him, and it had been a definitive clue to her personality, her devil-may-care attitude to danger. She wanted to be the brave "son" while emulating Daddy to the fullest, always seeking his approval.

Kind of a heavy load to dump on a kid, Arch thought, stubbing out his cigarette. Never once had he wished that his daughter, Rachel, had been a boy. He loved her exactly the way she was, didn't want to change her one iota. And not only was she his pride and joy, she had been a great comfort to him after he and her mother were divorced.

As for Nicky, well, she certainly was very different from most people, undoubtedly because she had been exposed to so much at such a tender age, quite aside from having an extraordinary couple for parents. Also, she was well traveled, well educated, intelligent, cool-headed, determined and very ambitious. Awesome combination in a young woman, he had decided long ago.

Her private life, sadly, was a disaster, or so it seemed to him. There were no men around these days. At least, he had not heard her mention anyone special since the last relationship had ended in such an unfortunate way. Tragic, really, when he thought about it, and it had certainly done Nicky in for a while. He wondered if she continued to be hurt, if she was still suffering because of the terrible way it had ended. It was hard for him to tell how she felt because she never discussed her personal problems and always kept up such a good front. Anyway, he did not want to pry. Nicky guarded her privacy fiercely, and so she should, he added to himself. What she does when she's not working is none of my business. Except that I care so damned much about her welfare.

He considered Nicky one of the most decent human beings he had ever met. She was fair, thoughtful, kind and extraordinarily loyal, and she had immense integrity. He wanted only the best for her, the very best. He wanted her to be happy. But what the hell, he thought, who's happy in this crazy world?

He sighed, roused himself from these ruminations and reached for the telephone.

As he picked it up, Jimmy called out, "Arch, before you get involved with New York, could you come over here for a minute, please? I'd like you to stand in for Nicky."

"It'll be my pleasure," Arch replied, putting the receiver down and walking over to the window. "But what exactly do you have in mind?"

"I'd like you to go outside on the balcony, so that I can get my camera angles set properly. It'll save time later. Shooting from this angle, I can get some good close-ups of her," Jimmy explained. "And with my long-range lens, if I position myself here among these plants, I can pick up the end of Chan-gan Avenue and Tiananmen Square. We'll have to film when it's fairly light, unless I can rig up some sort of lighting out there. But it'll work, Arch, don't worry."

"I'm not at all worried, James. Not when you're behind the camera."

2

It was a balmy night, almost sultry.

As Nicky walked along Changan Avenue at a steady pace she had to dodge in and out between the other pedestrians. Everyone seemed to be heading in the same direction.

When she first arrived in Beijing, Clee Donovan had told her that the Chinese always made their way to the square in the evenings and at weekends to demonstrate, celebrate, mark a memorable occasion or simply to while away the time. He had said that they went there to think, to mourn, to stroll, and also that it was a place for Sunday outings.

Lately it had become a place for protests.

Since April, students from every province in China had been peacefully demonstrating for democracy and freedom. It had actually begun at a memorial in the square for Hu Yaobang, a liberal and enlightened member of the government. A special favorite of the young, he had died earlier that month, and they had come to mourn his passing and celebrate everything he had stood for. Unexpectedly the memorial had turned into a kind of sit-in, and then the hunger strikes and nonviolent demonstrations had started.

This had happened over six weeks ago, and the students were still occupying the square—hundreds of thousands of them. Moreover, they were being supported by the citizens of Beijing, who brought them food and drinks, quilts and tents and umbrellas. And they sat with the students, commiserating and airing their own grievances.

At the same time these demonstrations were starting in Beijing in April, Nicky and her crew had been in Israel, where they were doing a special on Mossad, the Israeli intelligence service. But by the end of the month, as they were finishing the special, Nicky had decided they should go to China. Mikhail Gorbachev was due to arrive in the Chinese capital in the middle of May for a state visit, and being fully aware of what the students were doing, Nicky smelled a story developing. A big story. She had phoned the president of news at the ATN network. "Listen, Larry, the students aren't simply going to fold their tents and quietly steal away when Gorbachev comes to town," she had pointed out. "It's my belief real trouble is brewing over there."

Larry Anderson had hesitated momentarily, and she had pushed harder. "Just think of it, Larry. Think of the scenario! How will the kids behave during Gorbachev's visit? Will they continue to demonstrate? Will they embarrass the government? How will Gorbachev react to them? And perhaps more important, how will the Chinese government react to the situation? What will they do?"

These were only a few of the questions she had posed that morning on the phone from Tel Aviv, and she had obviously been persuasive. After talking to Arch, Larry had agreed they should go. He had immediately pulled them out of the Middle East, brought them back to New York for a week's rest, then sent them jetting off to mainland China with his blessing.

She and the crew had arrived on May 9. Ostensibly they had come to cover the state visit of Mikhail Gorbachev, which was due to commence on May 15, but they were really there because of the students—and because of Nicky's anticipation of trouble.

By the time the Russian leader, his wife and entourage appeared, Nicky, Arch, Jimmy and Luke were well ensconced in the Beijing Hotel, along with over one thousand foreign correspondents from every country in the world.

Just as Nicky had suspected, Gorbachev received something of a hero's welcome from the students, but there was a great deal of turmoil during his three-day visit, and the demonstrations continued unabated. As far as Nicky was concerned, the students had totally upstaged the summit meeting between the Russian and Chinese politicians, just as she had predicted they would. She had made a point of focusing on the students and their predicament in her news reports.

One day during Gorbachev's stay, a million demonstrators had converged on Tiananmen, demanding democratic rights, freedom of speech and a government free of corruption and graft. The students had hunkered down in the square, determined to remain there despite a scorching sun, violent thunderstorms and heavy rain.

Arch had made sure that Jimmy got everything on film, and Nicky's daily newscasts had been brilliant, and had been transmitted back to the States via the satellite. For the short time that Gorbachev and the hordes of foreign reporters remained in Beijing, the government turned a blind eye, or assumed an air of tolerance about the students—and the foreign press as well.

But the authorities were quick to make their move two days after the Russians and much of the press had departed. They enforced martial law. Nicky and the crew had stayed on, as had several hundred other journalists. Something extraordinary was happening in China and the news gatherers wanted to be there to do their job, to report unfolding events, history in the making.

Now, as she walked toward the square on this warm June night, Nicky's mind raced. She knew the end was imminent, and she feared the students were going to die. Perhaps even thousands of them. With this terrible thought her step faltered, but only for a moment. She recovered herself, and walked on, even though her heart felt like a lead weight in her chest.

As a chronicler of war, revolution and natural disasters, she was a constant witness to death and destruction, pain and anguish, on every level in many countries. Yet she never grew inured to violence and the horror of catastrophic events.

Over the years, and especially in the last

three, she had come to know the world as a most terrifying and horrendous place to live. Men were no more civilized now than in medieval times. They were still as violent and brutal as they had been then; according to her mother, they always would be. Very simply, those characteristics were part of man's nature.

What she witnessed and reported on bit into her heart like corrosive acid. Yet she had disciplined herself and found a way, especially since the brutal manner in which Charles Devereaux had treated her, to conceal her true emotions, not only from that all-seeing eye of the television camera, but from her crew and friends as well. Not even Clee, the person she felt most drawn to, knew her real feelings about things that affected her.

Her pace quickened as her thoughts settled on Clee. He was in Tiananmen, and she needed to talk to him. His instincts were so good, and he often had a visceral, intuitive response to events, just as she herself did. Moreover, she trusted his judgment. She always had, ever since they first met in Lebanon, when they were both covering the long-running war there. They had been introduced the day after Premier Rashid Karami was assassinated, when a bomb exploded in his helicopter. That was in 1987. She realized she had known Clee for exactly two years.

It was Arch Leverson who had made the introduction. Clee was an old friend of his, and they had bumped into each other in the lobby of the Commodore in West Beirut, the hotel favored by the foreign press corps. Arch and Clee had made a date for drinks that evening, and Arch had insisted she come too.

Cleeland Donovan was something of a celebrity, a legend even. He was considered to be the greatest war photographer and photojournalist since Robert Capa, and, like Capa, he had a reputation for courage and daring. It was a well-known fact that Clee Donovan flung himself into the middle of the action on a battlefield in order to get the powerful images on film for which he was famous. An expatriate American living in Paris, he had founded Image, his own photo news agency, at the age of twenty-five, and seemingly had never looked back. His pictures appeared in every leading magazine and newspaper in the world; he had published several books containing his work, all of which had been best-sellers; and he was the recipient of many awards for his photojournalism. Also, according to Arch, women found him very attractive.

A faint smile touched Nicky's mouth as

she remembered the night they had met. While changing in her room at the Commodore she had gone over what she had heard about Clee Donovan, and instantly she had known what to expect. Obviously he was going to be insufferable—a man who was more than likely conceited, full of himself and certainly egocentric.

She had been wrong; Clee was none of these things.

When he walked into the crowded bar of the Commodore, spoke to some of the correspondents and then headed in their direction, she had thought for a moment that he was someone else, another friend of Arch's, who had been invited to join them. He did not look as glamorous as he did in the photographs she had seen of him, although he was quite good-looking in a clean-cut, all-American way. He had a *nice* face—that was the best way to describe it—a face that was open and honest. His hair was dark, his eyes brown, their expression gentle, and his sensitive mouth was quick to smile. He was about five feet ten inches in height, but appeared to be taller because his body was lean and athletic.

A pleasant, ordinary sort of guy, she had decided, despite all that fame, all that success. He had seated himself at the table, ordered a drink and begun to chat amiably with them.

Within twenty minutes or so she had changed her mind: *Ordinary* was certainly the wrong word to apply to Clee Donovan. He was highly intelligent, very amusing and blessed with a natural charm that was irresistible. He had held them spellbound with his stories, fully living up to his reputation.

She had believed him to be her age, maybe even a bit younger, but later Arch told her Clee was three years older than she. This had surprised her, because he looked so boyish.

The other thing Nicky had discovered at their first meeting was that he was a man with little or no conceit, contrary to what she had expected. He *was* sure of himself, but it was a self-assurance about his work, and it sprang from his talent as a photojournalist. Eventually she had come to understand that Clee's work was his lifeblood.

That night in Beirut they had taken a great liking to each other, and their friendship had grown steadily over the weeks and months that followed. Frequently they found themselves in the same trouble spots, covering the same stories, and when this occurred they always joined forces.

Sometimes they went in different directions, and were on opposite sides of the world, but they managed to stay in touch by phone, or through their respective offices, as a strong fraternal feeling had developed between them. She had come to think of Clee as the brother she had never had. Certainly he was her very good friend, her comrade-in-arms.

3

Cleeland Donovan sat on one of the ledges encircling the Monument to the People's Heroes, also known as the Martyrs' Monument, staring at the Goddess of Democracy. The thirty-three-foot statue had been erected in the middle of the square by the students to face a giant portrait of Mao Zedong that hung above Tiananmen Gate. The defiant white statue, composed of plaster and Styrofoam, had been made by the students and faculty of the Central Academy of Fine Arts and brought somewhat ceremoniously to the square.

It reminded Clee of the Statue of Liberty. It was not so much the face that was familiar, but rather the posture, plus the toga-like robe draped around the body, and the raised arms holding high a torch of freedom. The statue was ugly, but that did not matter. It was the symbolism that counted.

He had been present in Tiananmen when the students had erected the goddess statue and unveiled it three days ago. They had sung the "Internationale" amid much cheering, and shouts of "Long live democracy!" had rung out across the square. The ceremony had been emotional, and had touched him deeply. He had managed to shoot several rolls of film surreptitiously, even though cameras were forbidden in the square; he had had three cameras smashed by the police. Fortunately, he had several in reserve, including the Nikon F4 that was now strapped to his shoulder underneath the loose cotton jacket he was wearing.

The night the statue had been brought to the square the weather had changed in the early hours. There had been strong winds and rain, but, remarkably, the goddess remained undamaged the following morning; there wasn't even a scratch on her. How long she would remain so was another matter.

Clee knew the goddess had irritated and outraged the government more than anything else the students had done, and government officials had denounced it as a "humiliation" in such a historically important and solemn place as Tiananmen Square.

On the other hand, it had been the shot in the arm the students had needed. Just seeing the statue in such a strategic spot had lifted their spirits. To protect the goddess, they had erected tents around her base, and groups of students were always present, ready to defend her.

But the government *will* tear the statue down, Clee thought, sighing heavily.

Luke Michaels, seated next to Clee, looked at him. "Something wrong?"

"I was just wondering how long that's going to be standing there," he murmured, gesturing to the statue.

"I dunno." Luke shrugged, ran a hand through his dark-red hair and turned his earnest freckled face to Clee. "Forever, perhaps?"

Clee laughed hollowly. "I give it a couple of days, at the most, before it's totally destroyed. And I can guarantee you this, Luke—it won't be standing there a week from today."

"Yeah, I guess you're right, it's such a thorn in Deng's side. Well, it's a thorn in all of their sides. The Gang of the Old can't stand the sight of it, and they consider the making of it an act of pure defiance. It was wishful thinking on my part, hoping the statue would stand forever as a sort of tribute to the kids."

"Nobody around here is going to pay *them* a tribute, except for us—the international press. We have to keep telling the world about them and their struggle, do whatever it takes to accomplish that."

Luke nodded, and shifted his position slightly; he leaned back against the stone and closed his eyes. It was photojournalists like Clee and correspondents like Nicky who risked their lives to bring the truth to the public, and he found the two of them inspiring. He especially admired Nicky Wells; she was what his mother called a real trouper. He wasn't married yet, or seriously dating anybody special, but when the time came for him to settle down, he hoped he would find a woman like Nicky. There was something warm and reassuring about her, and she didn't put men down.

He had been part of Nicky's crew for just over a year, and he had seen and learned a lot, working with her. At twenty-seven, he had been in the television business for only five years, and he knew he was green in some respects. But Nicky had been helpful and nice to him right from the start, and had treated him like a seasoned veteran. She was a stickler about punctuality and a lot of other things as well, and a perfectionist, and sometimes she could blow her stack. But she was a pro, and he'd do just about anything for her.

He wished she could find a good guy. Sometimes she looked sad, and her eyes would have a distant expression, as if she were remembering something painful. There were strange rumors about a man she'd been in love with before Luke joined her team. Apparently he'd treated her badly. Arch and Jimmy were pretty closemouthed about it, though, and he didn't like to ask too many questions. Still, it was a shame she was alone. What a waste of a lovely woman—

"Luke! Luke!"

The sound engineer sat up with a jolt, hearing his name. He looked down, and at the base of the monument people were milling about, as they usually were, since this spot was command headquarters for the student movement. The foreign press corps tended to congregate in the area too, and there was always a great deal of activity. His buddy Tony Marsden was beckoning to him.

Luke waved back, and stood up. "I'll go

and see what Tony wants," he said to Clee. "Maybe he knows something we don't, has some new information. I'll be back."

"Take your time," Clee said, gazing out on the square. He knew he would be leaving China soon; the end was in sight. His elbows on his knees, his head propped morosely in his hands, he felt dreadful for the kids—they were so idealistic, so innocent, so brave. When he first came to Beijing almost six weeks ago, he had found them full of excitement and hope. They had spoken stirring words about liberty and democracy, and had sung their songs and played their guitars.

But tonight their guitars were still, and soon their voices would be still too. He shuddered slightly and felt the prickle of gooseflesh; he did not want to think of their fate—he knew they were in grave danger. Although he had not said this to Nicky or to anyone else, he did not have to; they all knew that time was running out for the students.

Suddenly, Clee saw Nicky walking through the square toward the monument. Like Changan Avenue, Tiananmen was extremely well illuminated, with numerous tall streetlamps, each topped with branches of lights, about nine altogether and shaded in white opaque glass. The square was so bright it could almost have been daytime;

everyone was visible, and it was even possible to read a book quite comfortably.

A smile touched his eyes at the sight of
Nicky, and he climbed down off the ledge
and dodged through the crowd, hurrying to
meet her. She spotted him and waved. "I
knew you'd be out here before long," he
said, coming up to her and smiling.

She nodded. "I had to be out here, Clee.
My instinct tells me the situation is about to
blow."

"Wide open," he confirmed. Taking her
arm, he guided her away from the monument. "Let's walk around a bit, I need to
stretch my legs, I've been sitting on that
ledge for about an hour."

"Good, that's what I'd like to do, and perhaps we'll see Yoyo. He's usually with Chai
Ling and some of the other student leaders,
and he might know something new."

"He's constantly in touch with the Flying
Tigers. I've noticed several of them whizzing
around on their bikes in the last hour," Clee
remarked, referring to a motorcycle brigade
of young entrepreneurs who had also been
dubbed Paul Reveres by the American
press. They roared all over Beijing, carrying
messages, monitoring troop movements
and the actions of the police, and in general
acting as lookouts for the students.

"Yoyo's probably in the tent encampment.

Shall we head over there?" she suggested.

"Yes, good idea."

"Where's Luke? Arch said he was with you."

"He just went off with that guy from the BBC, Tony Marsden. They're somewhere around. Do you need him?"

"No, I just wondered, that's all. And speaking of the BBC, have you seen Kate Adie this evening?"

Clee shook his head, and Nicky said, "That's odd, she's usually one step ahead of me."

Clee chuckled. "Your British counterpart *is* often right *in* step with you, and sometimes she's a step *behind* you, but she's never *ahead* of you."

Nicky laughed. "You're prejudiced, which is very nice."

"I guess so. In any event, Kate's probably somewhere in the crowd. There are a helluva lot of foreign press out tonight—no doubt sensing trouble in the wind."

Nicky looked at him swiftly. "I think the crackdown's almost upon us, don't you?"

"Yes. The students and the government have reached an impasse, something's got to give. It'll have to be the students, I'm afraid, and we're going to see a lot of force thrown against them."

Nicky shivered despite the warmth of the evening. "Where's your camera?"

"Under my jacket, strapped to my shoulder. My buddies from Magnum and the Associated Press are doing exactly the same thing, as are most of the photographers."

"Clee . . . It's going to get dangerous out here—real soon."

"I think so too. And before you say it, yes, I'll be careful." A faint smile played around his mouth. "As careful as you are."

"*I* don't take unnecessary chances, even though Arch seems to think I do. I try to minimize the odds against me."

"That's one of the things we have in common," Clee said.

"There's another?"

"Yes. We both have nerves of steel."

"I suppose we do," she agreed, laughing. "We'd *better,* in this business. Just as we have to have a sixth sense for danger."

Clee nodded but did not say anything, and they walked on in companionable silence for a few minutes. As they came to the tent encampment, Nicky turned to him. "You know, this place has really taken on a life of its own, what with the tents and the buses. It's like a small town, and—"

"A shantytown," Clee cut in.

"You're right. Does it smell again tonight?"

"They've probably removed the garbage by now. In any case, there's a nice breeze blowing up."

"The other day when I came looking for Yoyo it stank, that's the only word for it. The stench was disgusting—rotting food, unwashed bodies, heaven knows what else. I felt nauseated."

As they entered the encampment and walked past several buses where some of the students lived, the air was surprisingly fresh, and the area looked as if it had recently been swept and cleaned up. There was no trash in sight.

Nicky was surprised, once again, by the neat lines of olive-green tents, waterproof and commodious, which had been sent from Hong Kong. They were arranged in horizontal patterns, with almost military precision, and lettered signs hung over each group of tents, identifying where the different contingents had come from. There were delegations of students from almost every university in every province of China.

Weeks ago she had discovered that most of the students slept during the day because the action came at night. Now the majority of the tents were empty, although a few late stragglers were only just emerging, getting ready for the rest of the evening and the early hours of the morning that lay ahead.

Vendors hung around on the pavement, selling sodas, bottled water, ices, popsicles and other small snacks.

Clee glanced at her. "Would you like a popsicle?"

She made a face and shook her head.

The young Chinese student, Chin Yong Yu, nicknamed Yoyo, was standing with a young woman in the center of the encampment near his tent. Both of them wore blue jeans and white cotton shirts. The girl was attractive and looked to be about the same age as Yoyo, who was twenty-two. Nicky wondered if this was his girlfriend, whom he had mentioned and who had been visiting relatives in Shanghai for the past few weeks. Yoyo was deep in conversation with the girl, but when he saw Nicky and Clee he broke off and waved enthusiastically; then turning to the girl, he said something and then hurried over to greet them.

Nicky had met Yoyo, an art student, quite by accident, in Tiananmen Square, when she first arrived in Beijing. She had been endeavoring to speak to some of the students that day, hoping to find someone who understood English. Yoyo had approached her with a smile and told her in fairly understandable English that he would be happy to help her if he could. After that, he had been useful in all sorts of ways; he had passed on information, introduced her to other student leaders, such as Chai Ling and Wuer Kaixi, and kept her abreast of developments among the students and the leaders of the movement. He was not only friendly but bright, and she had grown very fond of him, as had the crew, and Clee. They worried about Yoyo, worried about what would happen to him when all this was over.

"Nicky!" Yoyo cried, coming toward her, smiling widely, his hand outstretched.

"Hello, Yoyo," she said, shaking his hand. "Clee and I were looking for you."

"Good evening, Clee," Yoyo said.

"Hi, Yoyo! What's going on?" Clee asked as he took the student's hand.

Yoyo's expression changed, and he said grimly, "Bad things coming. Army drop canisters of tear gas from helicopters. On square. Tonight. You see. You have masks? Also, troops coming."

"*Tonight?* The troops are coming *tonight*?" Nicky probed.

Yoyo nodded. "I hear troops hidden in buildings near square. They come. Very sure. Bad things happen. You tell world, yes?"

"We'll certainly keep telling the world, Yoyo," Nicky assured him. "But do you believe the People's Liberation Army will open fire on the people?"

"Oh yes. *Yes.*" He nodded emphatically. "Some students say no, not possible. The People's Liberation Army our army, they say. Won't kill us. They foolish. Army very disciplined. Army follows orders. I know this."

Nicky stared at him, her clear, intelligent eyes riveted on his face. "You should leave the square. *Now.* While it's still possible, still safe."

"That wise, yes," Yoyo agreed. "But not everyone go, Nicky. Hard get everyone go. Blood tonight."

Nicky shivered and looked pointedly at Clee.

"What about Chai Ling and some of the other leaders?" Clee asked. "Can't they get the students to leave?"

Yoyo shrugged. "Don't know."

"Where are they?" Clee asked.

"Don't see tonight. You like water? Soda?"

"No, thanks," Clee answered.

Nicky shook her head.

The young Chinese looked thoughtful, then he remarked, "Movement lost spirit after martial law declared. Students very depressed. True, they should leave. They won't. End will be bad thing."

"Come with us," Nicky said urgently. "Come with us to the Martyrs' Monument. Find one of the bullhorns you've been using, and relay a message to the students. They'll listen to you, you're one of their leaders. Ask them to leave, beg them, if necessary. And you must leave with them. If you and the other students get out of Tiananmen while there's still time, you'll save your lives. Please, Yoyo, do this. It will be an act of bravery if you lead the students away from the square. It will be a *good* thing to do."

She reached out impulsively, took hold of his arm. "Please, Yoyo, don't stay here. You could be killed."

Her words appeared to reach him. "I come monument. Soon. Bring Mai, my girlfriend. Go, Nicky. I come soon. I promise."

"We'll be waiting for you, but don't be too long, Yoyo. There's not much time left."

When Nicky and Clee got back to the Martyrs' Monument, they found Luke waiting for them, and Nicky told him what had happened with Yoyo. She repeated what the student leader had said about the troops coming that night or in the early hours of the morning.

"Oh Jesus!" Luke exclaimed. "If that happens, those kids don't stand a chance."

"Actually they're sitting ducks," Nicky pointed out. "They're centered in a relatively small area, in relation to the overall size of the square, which is three-quarters empty right now. If the army comes in from the other side, it'll have a clear run straight across the square."

"That's right," Luke muttered.

"Let's hope Yoyo can persuade the students to leave before that happens," Clee said.

Nicky was silent, her expression anxious. Then she brightened. "Here he is now, thank goodness. Perhaps we can get him up on the monument with a bullhorn. He can at least *warn* the kids."

Yoyo and Mai joined them. They were holding hands, and Yoyo said, "This my friend, Mai. *Her* English not very excellent!"

"No need to apologize," Nicky replied warmly. As she looked at Mai she was startled—when she had seen the girl a little earlier, she had not realized how lovely Mai was. Her features were beautiful, her black, almond-shaped eyes enormous in her sweet and innocent young face. She had long glossy black hair, was small and slender, and everything about her was delicate. Nicky thought she was like an enchanting little doll.

Thrusting out her hand, Nicky said with a wide smile, "I'm so pleased to know you, Mai."

The girl smiled back shyly, showing perfect white teeth. Nicky was surprised at the firmness of her hold, as she softly said, "Hi."

Mai shook hands with Clee and Luke, who also obviously appreciated the girl's loveliness.

To Yoyo, Nicky said, "Did you find a bullhorn?"

"Not necessary. *I* don't speak. Chai Ling speak. Later."

"You've seen her?" Nicky asked, her voice suddenly sharp.

"Yes, near goddess. Chai Ling will take bullhorn, tell students to go home. She promise."

"Let's hope she keeps that promise," Clee murmured. "In the meantime, let's sit down."

The five of them found places on the ledges that ran around the base and lower part of the monument, and they sat down to wait for Arch and Jimmy. And, they hoped, for Chai Ling, the respected leader of the student movement, commander in chief of the Tiananmen demonstrators and a graduate student in psychology at Beijing Normal University.

It was almost one o'clock in the morning of June 3 when Arch and Jimmy finally appeared. They came running into the square and as they approached the small group clustered together on the monument, Nicky immediately noticed their troubled expressions.

"What is it?" she cried with raised brows, glancing at Arch and then at Jimmy.

While trying to catch his breath Arch blurted out, "The troops! They're coming down Changan Avenue. We just saw them as we were heading toward the square and—"

Jimmy interjected, "They're being stopped by the people."

"What do you mean?" Nicky cried, looking puzzled.

"The citizens of Beijing have formed a blockade—with their bodies. A human blockade. To stop the army from getting to the students in the square. They're keeping the army out of the square!" Jimmy said.

"Well, I'll be damned," Luke said.

Clee did not wait to hear another word, and neither did Nicky. Simultaneously they jumped off the ledge and began to run toward Tiananmen Gate, which led into Changan Avenue. They were closely followed by Yoyo, who was clutching Mai's hand, and behind them came Luke, sprinting at such a speed he soon caught up with Clee and Nicky. Arch and Jimmy took a few seconds to catch their breath, and then they took off too, making for the entrance onto the avenue.

Nicky and Clee were the first to reach the crowds of people flooding Changan, and almost instantly they were separated from each other by the swirling masses.

She had never seen anything like this in her life. What Jimmy had said was true—the citizens *were* blocking the army, preventing the soldiers from moving forward, literally holding them back with their bodies. They truly were a human shield. Suddenly, she saw that they were actually *pushing* the soldiers back. And what an army it was. Kids, she thought in astonishment. They were just kids; they looked even younger than the students.

Without considering her safety, Nicky moved closer to the crowds; she had to be nearer the action. Within seconds she was surrounded by people and swept forward by the force and movement of their bodies. Everyone was pushing and shoving; several times she swayed and almost went down. At one moment, as people pressed into her from behind, she reached out and desperately clutched at a man's arm; he swung around angrily, but then quickly helped her to regain her balance. A young woman grabbed at her jacket as the crowd surged forward yet again, carrying everyone closer to the troops. Nicky almost fell because the Chinese woman was clinging to her with such tenacity, but somehow she managed to stay upright, and they bolstered each other. The mass of people swept on and on, and Nicky thought she would be knocked over or trampled.

At the precise moment she experienced her first flicker of panic, wondering if she was going to be crushed to death, she felt a hand grasp her elbow roughly. Half turning her head, looking over her shoulder, she saw Arch standing immediately behind her.

"Thanks," she gasped with relief. Then she shouted above the noise, "The troops look unarmed."

"They also look frightened to death."

There was more pushing and shoving and angry shouting before the Beijingers surged onward en masse. They were like a huge tidal wave of immense force, and they propelled Nicky and Arch along with them.

Immediately ahead were the young soldiers, none of whom looked to be a day older than eighteen. They were being mauled and bruised and scratched as the people pushed and berated them. Nicky began to realize that the enraged citizens of the capital were lecturing the soldiers as if they were their children. Most of the troops were milling around in total confusion, and many of them had broken down and were starting to cry.

Clinging to Arch tightly, Nicky exclaimed, "These kids don't know what the hell this is all about!"

"I'm convinced of it," Arch agreed, putting his arm around her waist, determined to keep her safe in this melee.

Unexpectedly, she saw Jimmy pushing his way toward them.

How he had found them in the crowds Nicky would never know. He had sprung up as if from nowhere, and as he took hold of her arm he said, "Come on, we're getting out of this mob!"

Being ruthlessly aggressive, Jimmy and Arch managed to push Nicky and themselves through the seething mass of people until they finally staggered out onto the edge of Changan Avenue. As the three of them stood huddled together under the trees at the side of the wide boulevard, breathing sighs of relief as they straightened their clothes, Arch said, "By the looks of those kids, we weren't in danger of being shot at, but we *were* in danger of being trampled to death."

"Our best bet is to stand here and watch what's happening from the sidelines," Nicky said.

Astonished, Jimmy said, "Hey, that's a new one for you, Nick, when have *you* ever been on the sidelines?" Not waiting for an answer, he rushed on, "But you're right, it's safer here. Being in the middle of that was like being in the center of—a stampede. And what an army it is—just look at 'em. They have camp gear, canteens and knapsacks but don't have any weapons." He shook his head wonderingly.

"I told you they weren't armed, Arch," Nicky said.

Clee joined them a few minutes later. His hair was rumpled, his jacket ripped, but otherwise he looked totally unscathed. His Nikon was slung around his neck and there was a triumphant glint in his dark eyes. "I got some great shots," he said.

"Isn't that a bit dangerous, showing your camera?" Jimmy asked, eyeing the Nikon. "It's liable to get pulled off your neck and smashed."

"Not by this bunch, they're on my side. On *our* side. They *want* their pictures taken, they're chanting the usual thing—tell the world, tell the world."

"But the riot police—" Arch began and

abruptly stopped. "I guess there are no police around."

"It's doubtful," Clee responded. "At this moment, anyhow."

"Maybe I should go and get our cameras, try something live with Nicky," Jimmy suggested, looking at Arch. "We might just get away with it."

"*No,*" Arch said.

"Let's film on the balcony later, Jimmy, as we planned. I'll do a phone narration," Nicky said, knowing it was hopeless to argue with Arch when he was in a cautious mood. She had been in the line of fire on battlefields and he hadn't batted an eyelash or said anything about danger, but ever since they came to Beijing he had been issuing warnings constantly, and she couldn't help wondering why. She would have to ask him later; now was not the time. She glanced around, her eyes seeking Luke, but he was nowhere to be seen; neither were Yoyo and Mai. They had been swallowed up by that mass of people.

Eventually, much to her relief, Luke came into view, with Yoyo and Mai beside him. Mai was limping, had obviously hurt her leg or her foot, and Yoyo was helping her.

"What happened?" Nicky asked, hurrying over to them.

"Not serious," Yoyo said. "Man stand on Mai's foot. She okay."

Nicky put her arm around the Chinese girl's shoulders, and the four of them walked over to join the others.

Luke said to Nicky, "It's surprising the rest of us weren't hurt. You *are* okay, aren't you, Nicky?"

"I'm fine, thanks, Luke."

They sat down under the trees on the side of Changan Avenue to rest and cool off. In spite of the breeze, the air was warm, almost heavy, and both Nicky and Clee took off their jackets. Arch passed around a pack of cigarettes but everyone except Yoyo declined.

Nicky leaned forward and said to Yoyo, "Did you find out anything? Where are those troops from? What's happening?"

Yoyo puffed on his cigarette for a second and then said, "Troops from far away. From outside Beijing. They march many hours. They told go on maneuvers. They told go stop troublemakers. They no understand. They afraid. They young boys. People lecture them. Tell them don't hurt students. Soldiers don't know this Beijing. Don't know where this is. They no fight, Nicky. They too scared."

"Thank God for that, but what an anticlimax!" Nicky exclaimed.

"Where are the helicopters?" Clee asked, looking up at the night sky, then at Yoyo.

"No come now," Yoyo said, sounding as though he knew what he was talking about. "No tear gas."

There was a small silence, which Nicky broke when she said, "The People's Liberation Army came to Beijing to quell the student demonstrators, and were conquered by the citizens. Not a single shot was fired."

And several hours later that was how she began her nightly newscast to the United States.

Saturday dawned bright and sunny.

The young soldiers, still bewildered and now very dispirited, retreated down Changan Avenue, finally, in the middle of the morning.

The Beijingers returned home or went to their places of work. The students retreated to their tents and buses for much-needed sleep, and an air of calm descended over Changan Avenue and Tiananmen Square— suddenly there was a semblance of order and normality.

Nicky was convinced the tranquillity was illusory and that the situation had been contained only for a short while—a dozen or so hours at the most. The way she saw it, the

Chinese government would take a hard line because it would perceive the army's retreat as a humiliation. The officials would automatically blame the students, even though it had been ordinary citizens who had stood up to the troops and prevented them from entering the square. And they would act accordingly, with great force and violence.

After snatching a few hours of sleep, and after her broadcast was finished, she had been in and out of the square all day. Instinctively she knew that belying the atmosphere of calm were tension and fear, and she voiced this thought to Clee as they sat in the Western Dining Room of the Beijing Hotel on Saturday afternoon. Leaning across the table, she added, "The crackdown's still coming. I'm sure."

"Me too," Clee said, and he took a sip of his coffee. Putting the cup down, he went on in a low tone. "The government wants those kids out of the square in the worst way now. They're losing face in the West, and they can't stand that. I'll tell you something else, Nick—when it does happen, it'll be fast. By Monday it'll be all over, and the aftermath's going to be pretty awful. Arrests, trials, repression, and Christ knows what else."

"I'm concerned about Yoyo," Nicky confided. "He's been in the thick of it, and he *is* one of the leaders. I wish we could get him out of Beijing."

"We can," Clee said. "And incidentally, you just took the words right out of my mouth. I was about to tell you that I've been thinking about giving him money for an airline ticket to Hong Kong. We could take him along with us when we leave. He can stay there for a few days and decide what he wants to do."

"I'll split the price of the ticket with you."

"You don't have to," he began, then seeing the determined look on her face, he finished, "Okay, it's a deal."

"There's another problem."

"What?"

"*Mai.* Yoyo won't leave Beijing without Mai."

"So we'll give him enough for two plane tickets. I couldn't live with myself if we left those two kids behind, and I know for sure you couldn't, Nicky. Arch and the others will feel the same way, that it's the least we can do." He smiled at her. "So that's it, then. Mai comes along as well. The more the merrier."

Nicky looked at him. "You're a good guy, Clee Donovan," she said.

"So are you, Nicky Wells." There was a little silence, and then Clee asked, "Where will you go when we leave here?"

"You mean after Hong Kong? To New York. And you?"

"Back to Paris. But I may be in New York at the end of this month. When I spoke to the office last night, or rather, this morning, Jean-Claude told me there's an assignment in from *Life* magazine for me. If I want it. And I'm thinking of taking it—I wouldn't mind a few weeks back in the States."

"Come on," Nicky said, "let's get back to the square, see what's going on. I get nervous if I'm away for very long."

4

The killing began just after ten o'clock on Saturday night.

At that time Nicky and Clee were standing with Yoyo and Mai near the Martyrs' Monument. Arch, Jimmy and Luke were mingling with the other broadcast journalists, mostly American and British, who were assembled nearby. All were comparing notes, trying to predict what would happen next.

Nicky was speaking to Yoyo quietly, earnestly, endeavoring to be as persuasive as possible. "Please take the money, Yoyo. I know how proud you are, but this is not the moment for pride. You must be practical. Listen to me—we *insist* you take the three thousand dollars, it will get you and Mai out of Beijing. Clee and I think you should leave tomorrow, no matter what the situation is here. And the money is from the five of us. We want to help you—after all, you've helped us. We care too much about you to let you stay."

"Too much money," Yoyo said. "Thank you. No." He kept shaking his head. "You, Clee, guys very nice. Very excellent people. But can't take money."

"Come on, Yoyo, don't be stubborn," Nicky said. "Please accept it, if not for yourself, then for Mai. Think of her—of protecting her."

The young Chinese student shook his head again.

Wanting to make it easier for Yoyo, Clee now took charge and said firmly, "I'll tell you what we'll do. I'll go and get the airline tickets for you and Mai. I'll do it tomorrow—"

"Too much money, Clee," Yoyo said, cutting him off. He paused and there was an unexpected change in his voice when he added slowly, "Okay, I think about it—" He broke off and cocked his head, listening intently before he threw Nicky a worried glance. "*Gunfire?*"

"Yes," she said and glanced quickly at Clee; they exchanged knowing looks. He took off without saying a word, with Nicky sprinting behind him, the story uppermost in both of their minds.

Everyone in the vicinity of the monument heard the shots, and there was a sudden rush as the correspondents, photographers and television crews raced after Clee and Nicky. Across the square they ran, heading for Changan Avenue.

On Changan Nicky lost Clee in the chaos. She saw armored vehicles and trucks moving down the wide boulevard; she noted that the troops were armed with AK-47 assault rifles. It was obvious they were making for Tiananmen, and she knew they would enter it by force if necessary. There had been a rumor earlier that Deng had reportedly told the military commanders, "Recover the square at all cost." And there was no doubt in her mind that they would do exactly that.

They had already demonstrated their deadly intentions that very afternoon; at the western end of the square, close to the Great Hall of the People, thousands of soldiers had beaten up demonstrators who had tried to block their entry into Tiananmen. As far as she and Clee had been able to determine, no shots had been fired, but there had been much violence, and at one point the troops had used tear gas. Enraged, the masses had retaliated by throwing bricks and rocks at the soldiers; in turn, the troops had used truncheons and belts in an effort to quell the protesters.

That battle had merely been the prelude to what was happening now. Experienced as Nick and Clee were, and understanding the politics involved, they were aware that the situation could only worsen in the next twenty-four hours.

Now, suddenly, the troops who had been firing shots into the air turned their guns on the citizens and students crowding the side-walks. Unable to believe her eyes, Nicky stood frozen as the people, howling like wounded animals, rushed forward, hurling bricks, rocks, pieces of iron pipes and primitive gasoline bombs at the troops, their anger spiraling into an immense rage. The soldiers replied by firing lethal bursts at them. People fell as they were hit by the bullets, crying out in terror.

The carnage had begun.

Appalled by what she was seeing, Nicky found herself unable to move. She stood staring blankly, as chills shook her. A Chinese woman next to her roused her by grabbing her arm and saying in English, "The People's Army are killing *us*—civilians. They are murderers! Bastards!"

"Don't stay here, go home!" Nicky said to the woman. "It's dangerous here. *Go home.*" The woman simply shook her head, and remained standing where she was.

The drone of helicopters circling overhead made Nicky lift her head and gaze up into the night sky. She remembered what Yoyo had said about tear gas being dropped by the choppers. Opening her shoulder bag with a shaky hand, she pulled out one of the surgical masks and stuffed it into her pocket where it would be handy if she needed it.

Changan Avenue had become a battleground. Tanks and truckloads of soldiers armed with machine guns were rolling inexorably down the avenue, one after another.

God help the students, she thought, moving away from the road.

Fires were beginning to break out everywhere. Overturned buses, which had been used as barricades by the people, blazed at various intersections, and a number of military vehicles were burning on the avenue. They had been set on fire by the infuriated Beijing residents, and orange and red flames shot up into the dark sky, an inferno in the making.

Much to Nicky's amazement, people were continuing to emerge from the apartment buildings and houses that lined Changan.

They were on a rampage, intent on fighting back, using any makeshift weapons they could find—brooms and sticks and bricks. Some of them were armed with Molotov cocktails, which they hurled at the tanks and armored personnel carriers. Gunfire increased and the stench of cordite and blood hung heavy on the warm night air.

Nicky was suddenly overcome by nausea. Bullets were whizzing over her head and it was clear that she had better try to get back to her hotel.

A cart trundled through the crowd, carrying a wounded man and woman. When the people saw it they began to curse and shake their fists at the troops and, in response, the soldiers began to fire again. Nicky dropped to the ground to protect herself as tear-gas canisters exploded close to her. She pulled out the gauze mask, tied it around her face to cover her mouth and nose, but still she began to cough and splutter. Pulling herself up, she inched her way over to the far side of the pavement, where she sought refuge under a clump of trees. Leaning against a tree trunk, coughing and gasping for breath, Nicky groped for tissues in her pocket and wiped her streaming eyes.

Some sixty or so soldiers were advancing with fixed bayonets down Changan. Pessimistic though she had been, she had not anticipated anything quite like this. Then, happily, she saw Arch a few yards away, and she knew that he was looking for her.

Running forward, she cried, "Arch! Arch! I'm here!"

As she reached him, he swung around and grabbed hold of her. "Nicky! You're all right!"

"And you, Arch," she said.

"Have you ever seen anything like this?" he cried grimly. "The way they are killing innocent civilians, and the avenue is so jammed with tanks and trucks, the ambulances can't get through!"

"It's inhuman," she said.

Crouching low, they ran down the pavement under the shelter of the trees and returned to Tiananmen Square.

When they reached the square, Nicky was struck by the curious calm pervading it. The atmosphere seemed peaceful but weirdly so.

They slackened their pace and continued up to the Martyrs' Monument. Some of the press corps had returned and were gathered there. From the expressions on their faces she could see they were as distressed as she and Arch were by what they had witnessed on Changan.

Yoyo and Mai were standing nearby talking with a small group of students. Nicky went over to them and drew them away from their friends.

"There's so much bloodshed out there, I don't know what to say, but I know what you must do," Nicky said tersely. Fishing around in her bag, she found the envelope of money and thrust it into Yoyo's hands. "You must take this, Yoyo."

Yoyo stared at her. "But Clee say he buy tickets—"

"Don't argue, Yoyo, take it," Nicky said. "Tomorrow's going to be worse than tonight, and I'll feel better, knowing you have the money on you. If anything happens and we get separated, or if we have to leave Beijing without you, get yourselves to Hong Kong. We'll be at the Mandarin Hotel. You'll find us there."

Yoyo nodded and put the envelope in his trouser pocket. "Thank you," he said. "I understand. I have passport. Mai have passport. Everything be okay, Nicky."

"I hope so." Nicky glanced around her and then brought her gaze back to Yoyo. "What's been happening in the square?"

"Not much. Very quiet. Wuer Kaixi speak. Say this government oppose the people. Say Chinese must sacrifice themselves. For beautiful tomorrow."

Nicky shook her head. "The students must not show resistance to the soldiers. If you stay, you must be peaceful."

He nodded. "I understand. Chai Ling say this."

"Did she speak also?"

"Yes. She say this peaceful sit-in. Tell students stay seated. No resist army."

Nicky stared hard at Yoyo, then said, "Listen to me, Yoyo, these troops are not young like the others yesterday. They are hardened veterans."

"Maybe Twenty-seventh Army. They tough. Bad. We be okay, Nicky. Don't worry."

"But I do worry," she said under her breath.

"People from Workers' Federation here. They come protect students," Yoyo explained.

"I can't help wishing you'd protect yourselves by leaving," Nicky said, but she knew Yoyo and Mai would stay until the end, even though *he* fully understood they were in peril, if Mai didn't. They were naïve in many ways, like most of the kids in the square.

Clee came hurrying up to them looking disheveled.

"It's horrendous. . . . there are no words, really . . ." he said.

She touched the camera hanging round his neck. "Still undamaged, I see."

"They're too busy shooting unarmed people to be bothered about a camera!"

Arch walked over, and putting his arm around Nicky's shoulders, he said, "Jimmy and Luke are going back to the hotel for a while. Go with them, Nick. You've been out here for hours."

"I think I will," she answered. "I want to make some notes for my broadcast anyway, and prepare my opening. I'll be back in an hour or so."

"Take your time," Arch replied. "I can guarantee you this little shindig is going to last all night."

5

Nicky was in and out of Tiananmen for the next few hours, as were most of the foreign press corps.

The areas surrounding the square were a mess. Soldiers were everywhere and the crowds had not diminished. In fact, it seemed to Nicky that they had increased. Overturned vehicles and abandoned bicycles littered Changan Avenue, and an even bigger number of fires were flaring up as the grief-stricken and angry residents continued to torch tanks and armored personnel carriers.

In the immediate vicinity of the Beijing Hotel the scene was chaotic. The wounded, dying and dead were piling up, and distraught and weeping Beijingers, many of them covered in blood, were desperately trying to move the victims so that they could get them to the hospitals and morgues as quickly as possible. They were using all kinds of makeshift stretchers; Nicky even saw one made out of a door ripped from a telephone booth and tied to two long pieces of iron pipe. Several buses had been pressed into service as ambulances, and so had pedicabs and carts. Most of the injured were being taken to Xiehe Hospital, which was fairly close to Changan, since it was located in one of the streets immediately behind the Beijing Hotel.

In contrast, the square appeared to be peaceful enough when Nicky went back there at three-forty-five on the morning of June 4. Yet after only a few minutes in the square she felt the tension in the air. It was a most palpable thing, and underlying the tension was the smell of fear.

The troops had moved in, and were positioned at the far end.

Near the Goddess of Democracy statue she saw lines of soldiers drawn up. They stood staring at the square, their faces cold, cruel, brutal, with rifles in their hands, ready to charge on their own people when the order was given.

As soon as she reached Clee, who was

hovering near the monument, he told her there were machine guns positioned on the roof of the Museum of Chinese History on the eastern side of the square.

"They're efficient, aren't they?" she said sarcastically. And then she noticed that some of the students on the monument were busy writing, and she tugged at Clee's sleeve. "What are they doing?" she asked.

Clee sighed and shook his head. "Yoyo told me they're writing their wills."

Nicky turned away, swallowing, and felt the prick of tears behind her eyes. She struggled for self-control; the more emotional the situation and the story, the cooler she must be.

Clee had noticed her reaction, and put an arm around her. "It's a lousy world we live in, Nick, and you know that better than anybody."

"Oh, Clee. Some things are really hard to take."

"Yes."

She gave him a halfhearted smile and then said briskly, "Well, our job is to see that the world knows about this. Where is Yoyo?"

"I saw him talking to Arch a little while ago. That singer, Hou Dejian, and a couple of other leaders have been on the loudspeakers, asking the kids to leave in an orderly fashion." Clee stopped short as the lights in Tiananmen Square went out.

"Now what?" Nicky said.

"The worst, I suspect," Clee answered grimly. "Those lights didn't fail, they've been turned off."

In a moment the loudspeakers on the monument began to crackle, a disembodied voice said something, and then the volume increased and music began to play.

"It's the 'Internationale'!" Clee exclaimed. "Christ, I wonder what the kids will do now?"

"*Leave,* I hope," Nicky said.

But as the words of the famous revolutionary workers' anthem rang out across the square, Nicky knew the students would not do so. She could see, even in the dim light, that they simply sat there, listening to the music, motionless, unshakable, proud in their resoluteness. As soon as the record ended it was played again, and it was repeated several more times during the course of the next twenty minutes.

Nicky and Clee conferred quietly from time to time and talked with other journalists; everyone expected the military attack to begin at any moment, and they steeled themselves for the confrontation between the students and the troops. Another half hour passed, nothing occurred—and then, suddenly, the lights in front of the Great Hall of the People were turned on dramatically, flooding that side of the square with the most powerful and brilliant illumination.

Almost simultaneously the loudspeakers came alive once again and several people spoke, but neither Nicky nor Clee could understand what was being said. Then a British journalist standing nearby told them, "The leaders are urging the students to quit the square. They're all saying the same thing— get out before you're killed."

Clee said, "Nicky, I'm going to go get some shots of those guys on the loudspeakers, and of Chai Ling."

Nicky spent the next ten minutes or so strolling in the area of the monument, her eyes scanning the crowds and the ledges hopefully. There was no sign of Yoyo, Mai or the other students she'd come to recognize, and she began to wonder if they had finally left the square.

There was another announcement over the loudspeakers, another short silence, and then a second voice was heard, echoing out.

Nicky walked on, circling the monument one last time. Much to her surprise, a number of the kids were beginning to stand up, climb down off the ledges and walk away. Many had tears streaming down their faces; they had lost their peaceful fight for freedom and democracy, military power had prevailed, and many innocent people had been slaughtered. But at least *some* lives will be saved now, she thought.

Dawn was breaking, streaking the sky with light, filling it with an eerie, incandescent glow. She peered at her watch. It was after five; she could not stay in the square much longer. Sighing under her breath, she left the monument and started to walk to Changan. She would return to the hotel to prepare her newscast and the film segment, shower, put on her makeup and change her clothes. She and Arch had decided that first she would do the filmed piece on the balcony of the hotel, to be sent out by courier later that morning. At eight-fifteen she would do her live phone narration for the seven o'clock nightly news.

Nicky had not walked far when she remembered the small canvas travel bag Yoyo kept in his tent. He had once told her his most important possessions were in it. Was his passport in the bag? Had he gone back for it?

She turned around, dodged through the students who were now leaving, and hurried toward the tent encampment. As she ran she saw to her dismay that an increasing number of soldiers were coming into the square. Suddenly it seemed to her that they were everywhere, and in the distance she heard the clatter and rumble of tanks and armored personnel carriers moving forward across that vast rectangle of stone.

War correspondents were not supposed to be heroic. They had to get the story and get out alive. Her father had drilled that into her. But now she had to go back to look for Yoyo and Mai, and so she plunged ahead through the deserted encampment, shouting, "Yoyo! Mai!"

One or two faces peered out of tents, and she cried, "Leave! Tanks are coming!" Realizing that they did not understand English, she made urgent gestures with her arms, and cried, "Go! Go!" hoping they would somehow get the message. And then she ran on, making for the center of the encampment.

They saw each other at exactly the same moment—Yoyo and Mai, rounding the side of one tent as Nicky came out from behind another. They had both put on jackets, and Yoyo was carrying the small canvas bag.

"Forgot bag," Yoyo explained, holding it up. "Passport."

"Come on," Nicky said. "Troops are here,

everyone's leaving." She swung away from them, ready to return through the encampment.

"This way! Quicker!" Yoyo exclaimed, and he took the lead as the three of them ran down a narrow opening between the rows of tents, and came out into an open area of the square, just to the north of the Martyrs' Monument.

Lines of troops were rapidly advancing in their direction, and behind them came the APCs and tanks intent on destroying everything that stood in their path.

Nicky swung to her right and called, "Follow me!" then ran the opposite way, aiming for the monument and the entrance to Changan just beyond it.

Her heart sank as she heard the sound of rifle fire behind her. Glancing back over her shoulder, she saw that Yoyo and Mai were keeping up, so she continued to race across the square, putting distance between herself and the encroaching army as fast as she could. The sound of the oncoming armored vehicles and the blazing guns was ominous.

Drawing closer to the monument, she saw out of the corner of her eye that the last few students were retreating, trying to escape, just as they were.

"Nicky! Nicky!"

She looked back and to her shock saw that Mai was lying on the pavement. Yoyo was bending over her. Nicky spun around and ran back. "What happened?"

Yoyo looked dazed. "Mai shot."

Nicky dropped to her knees and examined the girl's bleeding shoulder, then touched her face gently. Mai opened her eyes, blinked and then closed them. Nicky slipped her arms under Mai, trying to lift her, but when the girl moaned, Nicky swiftly laid her on the ground again. Her hands felt wet and she looked down at them, and saw they were covered with blood. Her heart tightened; Mai must have been shot in more than one place. She wiped her hands on her pants, straightened and looked up.

The tanks had increased their speed and were almost upon them. There was no time to lose. She said to Yoyo, "Quickly! Take Mai's legs, I'll lift her under her arms, and we'll carry her behind the monument."

These words were barely spoken when she was pulled away from Mai and pushed, almost flung, to one side. She heard Clee shouting, "Hurry, Nick! Move it, Yoyo! The tanks—they're closing in!"

People were scattering in panic and screaming. Struggling to her feet, she spotted Clee running out of the line of fire, carrying Mai in his arms, with Yoyo right behind them. They made it to safety just before the tanks and APCs, their guns blazing, rolled over the spot where, a split second before, Mai had been lying.

Others were not so lucky.

They took cover behind the Martyrs' Monument, an area that seemed to be relatively safe, at least for the moment; there were no troops in sight. Clee placed Mai on the ground, and Nicky sank onto the steps beside her. When Clee came and sat next to her, she said, "Thanks for saving my life."

He put his hand under her chin and lifted her face, staring at her without speaking. He had a peculiar expression on his face, one she had never seen there before.

Finally, he said, "We have to get Mai to a hospital." He took his camera off, hung it around Nicky's neck and said, "Look after this for me, I think I have some good shots." Then he bent down, and lifted Mai up in his arms.

When they reached Tiananmen Gate, they paused to look back at the square.

The Goddess of Democracy was no more, it had been toppled by a tank and demolished, smashed to smithereens. The tent encampment had been flattened to the ground. She found herself praying that the few remaining students had managed to escape before this had happened.

And she felt an immense sadness flowing through her as she hurried after Yoyo and Clee.

Changan Avenue was congested with tanks and troops; the dead and the dying lay in pools of blood, and the anguished residents of the city were trying to do what they could to help.

Nicky and Yoyo walked ahead of Clee, clearing the way for him as he carried Mai.

They had almost reached the Beijing Hotel when Yoyo cried, "Look! Red Cross flag on Number Thirty-eight bus. *Ambulance.* Take Mai to Xiehe Hospital."

Clee nodded, and plowed forward with the injured girl, hoping to God that the doctors could save her.

Nicky stood in the middle of the ATN suite at the Beijing Hotel, concentrating on what she had to say. It was fifteen minutes past eight on Sunday morning in China. In New York it was fifteen minutes past seven on Saturday night.

She held her cellular phone, talking into it

clearly, steadily and without pause, using what she termed her television speed. She was coming to the end of her hard-hitting newscast about the events she had witnessed in Tiananmen, and her final words were dramatic:

"The late Mao Zedong once said political power grows out of the barrel of a gun. The People's Liberation Army turned their guns on ordinary citizens and students today. Innocent people. Unarmed people. It was a massacre. And they did it at the command of aging leaders desperate to hang on to their political power. Mao Zedong seems to have spoken the truth. At least, as far as China is concerned." There was a small beat, before she finished, "This is Nicky Wells saying good night from Beijing."

At the other end of the line she heard Mike Fowler, the ATN anchorman, saying, "Thank you, Nicky, for that extraordinary report from Beijing. And now to the news from Eastern Europe . . ."

Nicky clicked off the cellular and looked over at Arch, who was sitting at the desk, the phone to his ear.

He smiled, nodded several times and held up a bunched fist, his thumb jerking to the ceiling, indicating that she had done a good job.

He was on the wire to the network, talking to the news editor, Joe Speight, who was in the control room at ATN Headquarters in New York. "Thanks, Joe," Arch said, beaming. "We'll ship the film out in an hour. You should have it tomorrow night. Okay. *Ciao.*" He hung up and walked over to her. "Nick, they loved it. You were just great!"

"That's one of the best pieces you've done from here," Jimmy said, "but the moving film we just shot is even better."

"I second that," Luke said.

"Thanks, guys," she said, smiling. Their praise mattered so much to her because she knew they always spoke the truth, and would not hesitate to tell her when she had not been up to her standards.

There was a knock on the door, and when Luke opened it, Clee walked in. He looked awful, drained and haggard; Nicky knew what he was going to say before he said it, she could tell from the empty expression in his dark eyes.

"Mai is dead," he said, his tone flat. "They just couldn't save her. They tried, but she'd lost too much blood."

"Poor kid," Jimmy said.

Luke sat down heavily and Arch looked bereft.

Nicky walked over to Clee, feeling a little

unsteady on her legs. "You look terrible, Clee. Come and sit down, let's get you some coffee."

Clee took a step closer to her, wiped away the tears on her cheeks, which she had not even known were there. "It's all right for you to cry, you know," he said.

"Yes." She took a deep breath. "And Yoyo?"

"He's devastated but unharmed."

She nodded. "Where is he?"

"At Xiehe Hospital, making arrangements to take Mai's body home to her parents—they live on the outskirts of Beijing."

Suddenly all words failed her and she was unable to speak.

Clee put his arm around her and walked her over to the sofa. They both sat there, and then he said, very quietly, "We journalists deal with war and death and tragedy on a daily basis. We get tough, we think we're invincible. But none of us are, not really, Nicky. Not even you."

PART
TWO

Lovers

Come live with me, and be my love,
And we will all the pleasures prove . . .

—Christopher Marlowe

6

It was Cézanne country, van Gogh country. Clee had told her so, and he had been correct.

Colors from the artists' palettes were the colors of the day, the colors of the Provençal earth and sky: rich russet browns and burnt sienna, terra-cotta bleeding into orange and apricot, pink and peach tints balanced by acid yellow and vibrant marigold, and a gamut of brilliant blues and greens so sharp and shiny they resembled glazed enamel. And all were enhanced by a soft golden glow as if they had been liberally soaked in the hot Provençal sunshine.

From the moment she arrived in Provence, Nicky had been entranced by the beauty of the countryside that surrounded the old *mas,* or farmhouse, that Clee owned. A day did not pass without her catching her breath in surprise and delight at one thing or another. In an infinite number of small and grand ways, nature in all its glory was constantly revealing itself to her in this fabled southeastern corner of France.

On this sun-filled afternoon, as she sat near the white-flagstone-edged swimming pool under the shade of a plane tree, sipping a *citron pressé* and daydreaming, she almost laughed out loud at herself. She had been reluctant to come here, but now she realized she would not have missed for anything in the world this brief respite from the business of reporting catastrophes.

And she was grateful to Clee for so generously giving her the use of his home. It was his very private retreat, and she knew that very few people were ever invited here. But then, she realized, that was Clee, always thinking of her well-being; this latest gesture was only one of his many kindnesses.

The idea of her coming to Provence had begun in Hong Kong three weeks ago, when she and Clee were finishing dinner at the Mandarin Hotel. Out of the blue, somehow sensing that her fatigue was especially deep,

Clee had said to her, "Go to my farm in the South of France, Nick. It does me good just to be there, I know it'll take your mind off things to be in that restorative place."

She had balked at first. France had not particularly appealed to her just then, even though in much of the past she had loved it and felt at home there. But for several years now, she had associated it with pain.

Almost three years ago she had gone to Cap d'Antibes with her fiancé, Charles Devereaux, a man with whom she had been very much in love and had been about to marry. Without any kind of forewarning or hint of trouble between them, he had terminated their relationship in the most brutal of ways. No explanations or reasons were given, and it had happened only a couple of months after the idyllic trip to the Côte d'Azur.

She had not set eyes on Charles Devereaux ever again.

And so she had not wanted to upset herself further by visiting a place where they had spent their last days together. There were moments when she still felt savaged by him, and shaken by a fulminating anger. She had lost herself in her work, thrusting aside unwelcome memories.

Of course Clee had no way of knowing any of this, and so he had persisted with the invitation. Just before leaving Hong Kong for Paris, he had said, "I'm afraid I can't be there, Nicky, but my housekeeper will look after you very well. Please go." A confident smile had flashed on his boyish face, and he had added, "She'll spoil you to death, and I guarantee you'll fall in love with her. Amélie's a doll. Listen, the farm's in beautiful country, artists' country—Cézanne and van Gogh both painted in the area. I know you'll relax there. Please go. You need to do something special for yourself, to have a few weeks of peace after the horror of Beijing. You need to be better to yourself, Nick."

Touched, she had relented somewhat and told him she would think about it. And back in New York she had done exactly that. Thoughts of Clee's farmhouse in France and a peaceful interlude there had flitted in and out of her head, and with surprising frequency.

In the few moments she had between filming and editing a television special on Tiananman Square and its aftermath, she had pondered whether or not to take the trip. She had continued to be ambivalent, could not make up her mind to buy an airline ticket, pack her bags and go.

Finally, it was Arch who had helped her come to a decision. Once the TV special was in the can, he had told her she looked awful, more exhausted than he had ever seen her. "Done in" was the way he had put it. "We have no other specials coming up until later in the year, and a good rest would do you good," he had pointed out. "Take a break while you can, Nick. You really need it."

When she had muttered that perhaps something world-shaking might occur, Arch had laughed and said he would fly her back from wherever she was if a war broke out somewhere.

She had laughed too, and had then protested, "But I know I don't look quite as bad as you say I do, Arch. Surely you're exaggerating."

His answer had been pithy and to the point. "*Lousy,* that's the way you look, Nick. Take my word for it."

She had looked at herself in a mirror, and had had to admit that Arch was right. When she had examined her face, she had decided that he had actually understated the facts. She looked positively ill. Her face was unusually pale, even haggard; she had dark rings under her eyes and her hair was lifeless. Much to her alarm, her eyes, always so clear and vividly blue, had seemed dull, faded almost, as if they were losing their color, if such a thing were possible.

Nicky was aware that cosmetics could camouflage a number of flaws for the benefit of the camera, and that she could continue to hide the telltale signs of fatigue with clever makeup tricks. But she had also recognized that afternoon that it would be foolish not to take a rest, especially since the network owed her so much time off. She *had* felt debilitated and emotionally drained, and apparently now the signs were all too evident to others. And so she had put her mirror away, phoned Clee at his Paris office, and told him she would like to accept his offer of the farmhouse in Provence if it was still open. He had been thrilled.

"That's great, Nick," he had said, his energy and excitement echoing down the wire. "I'm leaving for Moscow tomorrow, to photograph Gorbachev for *Paris Match,* but Jean-Claude will make arrangements for you to be met in Marseilles, and then driven up to the farm. All you have to do is get yourself to Marseilles, via either Paris or Nice. Just let Jean-Claude know the day you'll be arriving, and the time. I'll call you from Moscow, to find out how you're doing, after you've settled in."

Within forty-eight hours she was zooming across the Atlantic faster than the speed of sound, a passenger on board the French

Concorde, and landed in Paris a short three hours and forty-five minutes later. After spending the night at the Plaza-Athénée, her favorite hotel, she had taken a plane from Orly Airport to Marseilles the following morning.

Jean-Claude, Clee's office manager, had explained to her that a chauffeur from the car company they used would be waiting for her at the airport. "You won't be able to miss him. He'll be holding up a card with your name written on it in bold letters," Jean-Claude had said on the telephone.

True to Jean-Claude's promise, the chauffeur had been there when she had alighted from the plane and gone to the baggage area. He had introduced himself as Étienne, and he was a pleasant, chatty and informative Provençal, who throughout the drive inland had kept her entertained with rather fantastic folkloric tales of the region. He had also recited more facts about Aix and Arles than she could possibly absorb at one time.

Although she spoke French well, having spent part of her youth in Paris with her globe-trotting parents, Nicky had found the Provençal accent a bit difficult to understand at first. But relatively quickly she had realized that Étienne was adding the letter *g* to many words, so that *bien* became *bieng,* and so

forth. Once she got the hang of this adjust-
ment of the French language and attuned
her ear to the rich and throaty cadence of his
speech as well as to his rapid delivery, she
had discovered that she had no problem
grasping everything he said.

On the way to Aix-en-Provence from Marseilles, Nicky had begun to notice that the
landscape was completely different from
that of the Côte d'Azur, which was the part
of southern France she knew so intimately.
Her parents were Francophiles, and as a
child she had been taken by them to many
of the renowned coastal resorts for annual
holidays and shorter stays. In particular, her
mother and father had favored Beaulieu-sur-
Mer, Cannes and Monte Carlo. And then in
October of 1986 she had spent those two
extraordinary weeks in Cap d'Antibes with
Charles Devereaux, after which he had disappeared from her life altogether and forever.

But Clee's area of Provence was entirely
new to her and, as such, held no memories.
This sudden knowledge had made her feel
suddenly very much at ease. She began to
relax in the air-conditioned comfort of the
Mercedes.

They had passed through a land of flat
plains interspersed with hills and mountains.

There were quaint little towns set in bucolic surroundings and picturesque hilltop villages that looked as if they were propping up the vast unblemished blue sky. Many fields and hillsides were luxuriant with lavender, and dark vineyards and an abundance of fruit orchards stretched for miles. Dotting this fertile landscape intermittently were lines of crooked olive trees and stately black cypresses, which stood like sentinels against the far horizon.

Clee's farmhouse was in the department of Provence called the Bouches-du-Rhône, situated between the ancient university town of Aix-en-Provence and Saint-Rémy. It was on the outskirts of a tiny village close to the lush green foothills of Lubéron, one of the mountain ranges of Provence.

The farmhouse was larger than Nicky had expected it to be. It was sprawling yet had a certain gracefulness, and was obviously quite old. It had looked beautiful in the late afternoon sunshine, which glanced across its red-tiled roof and cast a warm honey-colored glaze over the pale stone walls. Standing at the end of a long straight driveway lined with cypress trees, it was visible for the entire approach to the white front door.

When the car was finally brought to a halt by Étienne, he had exclaimed *"Eh, voilà!"* and waved one hand at the farm with a grand flourish. Then he had turned and smiled at her triumphantly, looking as though getting her here had been a major achievement.

Clee's housekeeper, Amélie, and her husband, Guillaume, had been waiting for her on the doorstep and had welcomed her enthusiastically with warm smiles.

Guillaume had then promptly whisked away her luggage—along with Étienne, who had not needed a second invitation from Guillaume to "come inside the kitchen for a *pastis.*"

With merry laughter, Amélie had ushered Nicky inside the farmhouse and insisted on showing her around before taking her upstairs to her quarters.

They had started out in the kitchen, obviously Amélie's favorite spot in the entire house, and a place she was very proud of. The room was large and painted white, with dark-wood beams on the ceiling and terra-cotta tiles on the floor. A massive stone fireplace took up an end wall; to the side of this stood a big oven, and several marble-topped counters were set under the three windows. Placed on these were flat woven baskets brimming with local produce. One held ap-

ples, oranges, pears, plums, peaches, apri-
cots, cherries and grapes; the other over-
flowed with vegetables—carrots, cabbage,
potatoes, beans, artichokes and peas.
Ropes of onions and garlic and bunches of
the herbs of Provence swung from a ceiling
beam, and wafting in the air was the lovely
aroma of marjoram, rosemary and thyme.

A round table in the center of the kitchen
was covered with a red-and-white gingham
cloth to match the neat little tied-back curtains at the windows. Taking pride of place
on the far wall was an antique baker's rack
made of black wrought iron trimmed with
brass. It was stacked with a variety of copper
pots and pans that glittered and winked in
the sunlight, while on the wall opposite a
series of built-in shelves displayed colorful
pottery platters, plates, soup bowls and dou-
ble-sized *café au lait* cups and saucers.

The dining room opened off the kitchen,
and these two rooms flowed into each other,
as they were visually linked through the use
of the same terra-cotta floor tiles, white-
painted walls and ceiling beams. Here there
was a big old-fashioned fireplace and hearth
made of the local cream-colored stone and
stacked with logs for the winter, and a window at each end of the room filled it with
light. A country feeling had been created by

the long oak dining table, high-backed chairs and carved sideboard. Floating over the table was a rustic black-iron chandelier, and running down the center of the table was a collection of brass candlesticks holding thick white candles. Huge bowls of flowers in the center of the table and on the sideboard brought touches of vivid color to the rather simply furnished room.

Hurrying forward, Amélie had next shown her out into the main hall and opened a door into a small downstairs sitting room. Highly polished cream-colored flagstones gleamed on the floor, the walls were painted a soft butter-yellow, and two sofas covered in cream linen faced each other in front of a small fireplace. Occasional wooden tables were scattered around, and two tall pottery lamps with cream shades stood on antique chests on either side of the chimney. A table under the window held all the latest magazines from around the world, copies of *Life* and *Paris Match* being much in evidence, as well as *Time* and *Newsweek*.

"Now we shall go upstairs," Amélie had said to her, swinging around and guiding her back to the front hall. Nicky had dutifully followed her up a white stone staircase, broad and curved, which stopped on a square landing. On either side of this were the library and the main living room. Both were painted white, had soaring fireplaces, pale wood floors and flat rugs from Morocco.

The living room was decorated with French country furniture in the Provençal style, and the sofas and chairs were uphol- stered in cream, *café au lait* and caramel- colored fabrics. Again, masses of flowers introduced vivid color everywhere, and Nicky had an instant impression of air and light and spaciousness, and the most marvelous sense of tranquillity.

Across the landing, the library was lined with books and furnished with two over- stuffed sofas covered in melon-colored cot- ton. Clee had created an audio-visual center in one corner, using the most up-to-date equipment: a large-screen television, video player, tape deck, compact disc player. Stereo speakers were positioned high on the bookshelves.

"This is Monsieur Clee's room, he likes it the best, I think," Amélie had informed her, nodding her head fondly. Then pointing her finger at the ceiling, she had announced, "One more flight, mademoiselle. *Allons!*"

The two of them had gone out onto the large landing and climbed up a narrower flight of white stone steps to the bedroom floor.

Nicky had discovered that she had her
own suite under the eaves, and it was composed of a bathroom, a bedroom and a
sitting room, which were charmingly decorated, again with lots of white, cream and
caramel, the basic colors in the house. Several good wooden pieces were set against
the walls of the sitting room and an antique
armoire and a chest graced the bedroom;
even a cursory glance had told her that a
great deal of care had been taken and every
comfort provided.

"I will bring up your cases," Amélie had
said after opening the armoire doors and
sliding out drawers in the chest. "And
please, Mademoiselle Nicky, you must tell
me if there is anything else you need. Monsieur Clee will be angry if I do not look after
you properly."

"Thank you very much, Amélie," Nicky
had answered, smiling. "I'm sure I have everything. And thank you for the grand tour."

"Ah, it is a pleasure, mademoiselle," Amélie had answered with a smile before disappearing down the stairs.

This conversation had taken place only four
days ago, but already Nicky was feeling
rested. The farmhouse and the surrounding

grounds had had a soothing effect on her, and she was more tranquil than she had been for a long time. She had slept better than she usually did, and had relaxed completely in this peaceful environment.

Her days were slow, lazy, without pressure, and she had done nothing more complicated than walk around the grounds and the woods close by, and swim in the pool. The fresh air and exercise, plus Amélie's delicious cooking, were restorative. In the evenings she had read, listened to music or watched French television in the library, and, as a news addict, she had found herself tuning into CNN.

According to Guillaume, Clee had recently installed cable to pick up the American news network. "For his work, you know, mademoiselle," Guillaume had found it necessary to add, and she had turned away to hide a small amused smile.

Nicky shifted slightly on the chaise, reached for the *citron pressé* and took a long swallow, enjoying the tartness of the lemonade. It was the last week of June and already hot, although not yet unbearably so. Amélie had told her, only this morning, that July and August were the worst of the summer months in this part of Provence. *Blistering* was the word she had used. Then Amélie had suddenly launched into a little discussion about the mistral, the dry north wind that could blow so furiously even in the summer, bringing havoc. It came whistling down to the south through the Rhône Valley, and it was often the first real warning of mean weather brewing. Amélie, like most Provençaux, blamed a variety of problems and ailments on the mistral.

"Animals can go mad. And people," she had confided somewhat dolefully as she had poured Nicky a second cup of *café au lait.* "It causes migraine. And *la grippe.* And toothache. And earache. And sometimes in winter it can blow for as long as three weeks. It destroys property. Uproots trees and flings tiles off the roofs! *Quel vent!*" And then with a typical Gallic shrug she had hurried off to the kitchen to refill the coffeepot and warm up more milk for Nicky.

Just as Clee had predicted, Nicky had fallen in love with Amélie. The housekeeper was small and stocky, and obviously very strong physically. She was undeniably Mediterranean, with blue-black hair pulled back in a bun, eyes like black olives and a nut-brown complexion. Forever laughing and smiling, and always in high good humor, she went through the farmhouse doing her vast number of chores like a whirlwind—or the mistral perhaps. She cleaned and polished, washed and ironed, baked bread and cakes and tarts, prepared the most wonderful meals, and arranged the beautiful vases of flowers and the decorative baskets of fruit that were all around the house.

Like Amélie, Guillaume was a typical Provençal. He was as brown as a berry, with a face weatherbeaten from being outdoors, jet-black hair speckled with gray and kindly, humor-filled eyes. Medium in height, and very muscular, he tackled every job with the same vigor and enthusiasm as his wife.

He swept the yard, the outdoor dining terrace and the barbecue patio, cleaned the pool and tended the garden and the orchard as well as the little vineyard that stretched out behind the farmhouse for about four or five acres. Guillaume did the spraying, the cropping and the pruning, and he and Amélie, with some local hired help, picked the grapes, kegged the wine and bottled it. "Some of it is sold. Some we keep for ourselves. And for Monsieur Clee, *naturellement,*" he had explained to her when he had taken her around the property pointing out many of its distinctive features.

Amélie and Guillaume had a son, François, who was studying at the Sorbonne in Paris and of whom they were very proud;

Nicky had already heard much about him from his doting mother. Their two daughters, Paulette and Marie, were married and lived in the village, and were pressed into service at the farm on the rare occasions when Clee had extra guests.

When Clee called from Moscow on the night of her arrival, he had described Amélie and Guillaume as the salt of the earth. Now she knew exactly what he meant. They were devoted to him, took care of the farmhouse and the land as if they themselves were the owners. The house they lived in adjoined the main farmhouse and was entered through a door opening off the kitchen. It was built of the same local stone, pale beige in color and weathered by the years, and it had an identical red-tiled roof, heavy wooden shutters and doors painted gleaming white.

Both houses were visible to her from the pool area where she was sitting, and it seemed to her that they appeared to grow out of the earth, as if they were part of the land itself. As in a sense, they were. The farm and its outbuildings were a hundred and fifty years old, so Guillaume had told her, and they did look as if they had been there forever.

Everything about the farm fascinated Nicky, and she was beginning to realize how much she enjoyed being in the country, close to the land. It was easy to see why Clee loved the farm, although he was unable to come here as often as he would have liked. During the two years she had known him he had talked about this place occasionally, and she understood why his voice changed slightly whenever he discussed his home in Provence. It was a very special corner of peace and beauty in the turbulent world.

She stayed outside until almost six o'clock, enjoying the changing light as the sun slowly began to sink behind the rim of the distant dark hills. And then she took her book and glasses and walked slowly up the flagged garden path to the house.

Climbing the two staircases to her rooms under the eaves, she thought of Yoyo, as she did at some moment every day. His whereabouts were unknown, and this worried her. She and Clee had looked hard for him in Beijing before they left for Hong Kong, but he had disappeared. But then so had most of the other student leaders. "Gone underground," Clee had said to her, and she had hoped this was really the case, and that he had not been arrested.

She and the crew and Clee had hung around Hong Kong for several days, hoping Yoyo would show up, but he had not, and in the end they had had no alternative but to leave.

Nicky's only consolation was that Yoyo knew where to find them. She had given him her business card in the first week she had met him, and so had Arch and Clee. She could only hope that he still had them and would be able to get himself out of China using the money they had given him.

At one moment she had thought about writing to him at the Central Academy of Arts, but had decided against it, knowing that a letter from a Western journalist could easily create untold problems for him. The mail was most probably censored these days, and a letter from her might cost him his freedom. Or his life.

Sighing under her breath, Nicky pushed open the door to her rooms and went in, endeavoring to set aside her worries about Yoyo. There was nothing she could do except pray he was still safe and that he would find a way to escape to the West.

7

The scream shattered her nightmare.

It echoed around the bedroom and seemed to pierce her brain, almost as if she herself were screaming.

Nicky sat up with a jerk, instantly wide-awake, her face and arms bathed in sweat. She tilted her head and listened, blinking as she adjusted her eyes to the dimness of the room.

There was no sound except for the faint ticking of the clock on the bedside table, the rustle of the leaves on the tree outside the window as they brushed against the panes of glass.

Had she herself screamed out loud during

her frightening dream? Or had it been someone else? Someone outside? She was not
sure, and just to make certain she climbed
out of bed and went to the window. She
looked out.

The sky was dark, cloudless. A full moon
was slung high above the old stables, and it
cast a silvery sheen over everything in the
yard, throwing into focus the cypress tree,
the old wheelbarrow planted with flowers,
the garden seat, the flight of steps leading
down into the orchard. But there was no one
out there, so it was not possible that anyone
had screamed. Except if she herself had, of
course.

A small shiver passed through Nicky even
though it was an exceptionally warm night.
Turning away from the window, she went
back to bed, troubled by the nightmare that
had so frightened her that it must have made
her scream and woken her up. Slithering
down, she pulled the sheet around her bare
shoulders and tried to go back to sleep.

But she had little success, and when she
was still wide-awake after half an hour she
slid out of bed, slipped into her cotton robe
and went down to the library. After turning on
a lamp and the television set, she curled up
on one of the sofas, deciding that since she
could not sleep she might as well watch
CNN.

Once the roundup of international news was finished and the programming changed to a local American story about farmers in the Midwest, her mind began to wander. And not unnaturally, she focused on the nightmare she had just had. It had been awful, and it remained so vivid it was still dominant in her mind. The nightmare had been about Clee, and she could remember every detail of it clearly.

She was in a vast, empty desert. It was warm, pleasant, and even though she was alone she was not afraid. She felt content. She was walking up a sand dune, and when she was on top of it and looked down she saw an oasis below. Feeling thirsty, she ran down the slope of the dune and began to drink the water, scooping it up in her hands, until she saw that it was streaked with blood. She pulled back, filled with horror, and as she crouched on her heels she noticed a crumpled magazine splattered with mud and blood. It was a copy of Life *magazine. She picked it up, leafed through it and came to a picture of Clee. The caption said he was dead—killed in action while on assignment for the magazine. But it did not say where he had died or when, and there was no date on the magazine. She was frightened and she turned icy even though it was searing hot under the desert sun. She got up and began to run, looking for Clee. She felt sure he was somewhere nearby. And alive.*

She walked for hours and eventually she was no longer in the desert. She was wearing thick winter clothes and it was dawn on a frosty day. All around her were dead men and the bloody signs of war and destruction. Clee walked toward her through the mist and took hold of her hand. He helped her to climb over the dead bodies. Suddenly they saw a jeep in the distance. Clee said, "Look, Nick! We can get a lift back with the retreat!" He leaped forward, running. She ran, too, but she stumbled, and when she stood up he was not there. For a split second she was afraid, and then she went searching for him among the dead soldiers. She could not find him.

There were miles and miles of dead bodies, and everything was so silent she wondered if it was the end of the world. She saw two bodies lying close to each other side by side. She hurried to them, turned their cold dead faces to see if either one was Clee, then she drew back in shock. One of the bodies was Yoyo. The other was Charles Devereaux.

She turned and ran, stumbling and falling against the dead soldiers in her haste to es-

cape the carnage. At one moment she looked down at her hands and clothes; they were covered in warm, sticky blood. A wave of horror and nausea swept over her, and just as she began to despair of ever finding Clee, of ever getting away, she reached the end of the battlefield.

Now she was walking along a white sandy beach, and parked under a palm tree was the jeep she had seen earlier. It was abandoned. She looked toward the dark blue sea. Not far out she saw a body floating. Was it Clee? He beckoned to her. Yes, it was he! He was alive! She rushed into the water. It was icy but curiously thick, like oil, so that swimming was laborious. And then she realized that the sea was not blue but red. It was made of blood.

Clee held out his hand to her; she reached for it; their fingers were inches apart. As she struggled to grasp his hand, his body began to sink, and it disappeared into the sea.

The dream had ended at this moment, and she had awakened to the scream. It had been her screaming, she *knew* that now.

She shuddered, feeling gooseflesh on her arms, and she pulled the robe around her, suddenly very cold. Rising, she went over to the small bar next to the bookcase and looked at the bottles, then reached for the *marc de Bourgogne.*

Some memory registered vaguely, then she recognized the label. Of course, it was one of the brandies Charles had imported from France. She put the bottle down on the silver tray. Then immediately she picked it up again, poured herself a small glass, and taking a sip of it, she walked slowly back to the sofa.

Nicky did not know a lot about dreams, but she was well enough informed to realize that her nightmare was simply a manifestation of impressions stored in her subconscious. Once, several years ago, her mother had told her that one dreamed one's terrors, and that whatever truly frightened a person came to the fore in sleep, when the subconscious rises. And so it did not take her long to analyze her dream. She knew very well what it meant: she was afraid that Yoyo was dead, and she was worried that Clee, a war photographer and in constant danger, might be killed.

It's all very understandable, she told herself, taking another little sip of the *marc.* Both men had been very much on her mind lately, and of course were therefore at the forefront of her thoughts. But why had *Charles Devereaux* been part of the nightmare? Perhaps because she was in France, where they had traveled, and where he had come often to buy wine for his importing company. And where they had spent those two weeks together . . .

The more she thought about it, there was no denying the fact that she had dreamed about those three men because each of them, in his own way, troubled her enormously.

8

Clee stood staring in deep concentration at the dozen or so transparencies arranged on the large light box in his Paris office. After a couple of minutes he turned to Jean-Claude Roche, who ran his photo agency, Image, and nodded. "I think you're onto a winner, and the pictures *are* good, Jean-Claude. Damned good, as a matter of fact. So let's get the guy to come in and see me, and the sooner the better. We can certainly use another good photographer around here, there's more work than we can handle right now."

Jean-Claude looked pleased. "Marc Villier is really terrific, Clee. Very bright, aggressive,

yet sensitive. And he possesses the un-
flinching eye, as you do. You are going to like
him, he is . . . how shall I say—very person-
able."

"Good. And if these photographs are anything to go by, his work is more than excellent. Let's move on. Do you have anything
else to go over with me?"

Jean-Claude shook his head. "No. Everything is under control. The assignment sheet
is on your desk. Everyone is booked out for
the next few weeks. Except for you. I've kept
you free."

"That's *great.* I could use a few days' respite after Beijing and Moscow," Clee exclaimed, his face brightening at the prospect
of some time off. Turning around, he col-
lected the transparencies that lay on the
light box and handed them to Jean-Claude.

"Thanks," Jean-Claude said as he slipped
them into a large envelope. "I shall go and
call Marc, ask him to come in tomorrow
morning. Is that all right with you?"

"Sure. By the way, where do we stand with
my assignment for *Life*?"

"They need you for about three weeks,
late July and early August. They want you to
go to Washington first to photograph the
president and Mrs. Bush, this is their prior-
ity."

"Yeah, that figures. Congress is still in session through July, and Bush is probably going to be gone in August, either to Camp David or Kennebunkport. And who am I doing after the president?"

"They have not said. But they want you for a few specials. I told them I would give them the date of your arrival as soon as possible. They need to confirm with the White House. So, when *will* you go?"

"About the fourteenth, I guess." Clee walked over to his cluttered desk and sat down. "Ask Marc Villier if he can come in early tomorrow, around seven-thirty, eight."

"I will." Jean-Claude went to the door but paused before leaving and looked back at Clee. "There will not be any problem, he will come whenever you wish. He wants nothing more than to work with you, Clee. You're his idol."

Clee merely smiled, made no comment. He knew all about idols and what having one could mean.

Clee's eyes automatically went to the photograph of Robert Capa, which hung on the side wall along with a collection of other pictures. He felt a stab of familiar sadness, as he often did when he looked at Capa. His one and only regret in his life was that he had never met Capa. He had been born too late

and Capa's tragic death had been so un-
timely.

After a moment he dropped his eyes to the
papers littering his desk, shuffled through
them without paying much attention, which
was quite normal for him. Paperwork was not
his strong suit; in fact, it bored him. He
clipped the letters together, scrawled across
the one on top, *Louise, please deal with all
this any way you see fit,* and dropped the pile
into the tray in readiness for his secretary the
following day.

Glancing at the clock, he saw that it was
almost six. If he was going to cancel the
dinner with his friends Henry and Florence
Devon he had better do it immediately.
Henry, a writer, worked at the Paris bureau
of *Time,* and Clee dialed his direct line. It
rang and rang, and then it was finally picked
up and Henry's gravelly Boston-accented
voice was saying, *"Allo, oui?"*

"Hank, it's Clee."

"Clee, don't tell me you're canceling!"

"I have to, Hank. Look, I'm sorry, but it
can't be helped."

"Flo has invited this Lacroix model, what-
ever-her-name-is. Stunning girl. You
wouldn't want to miss meeting *her,* would
you?"

"I wish you two would stop trying to fix me

up!" Clee exclaimed a bit impatiently, and then he laughed and said, "There's really no way I can make it tonight. This meeting just came up and it's important."

"I'll bet it is. Knowing you, I suspect you've suddenly got a hot and heavy date."

Ignoring this, Clee said soberly, "Flo usually hedges her bet and invites a couple of other single guys, so I'm sure the Lacroix lady won't be short of flattering male attention this evening."

"That's quite true. On the other hand, Flo really wanted *you* to meet her, Clee."

"I will. Another time. Tonight I'm stuck. How about lunch tomorrow?"

"No can do. I'm flying to Nice. I'm working on a piece about the Grimaldis of Monaco, and I have to do some interviews in Monte Carlo."

"Then call me when you're back and we'll catch up."

"It's a deal. And, Clee?"

"Yes, Hank?"

"We'll miss you tonight."

"I'll miss being there. Give my apologies to Flo, and kiss her for me." As he hung up Clee made a mental note to send flowers to Florence the next morning. Picking up the phone, he dialed again. A female voice answered immediately. "Is that you, Mel?"

"Hello, Clee. What's wrong?"

"Nothing's wrong. . . . Mel, I—"

"You're canceling our date tonight."

"Listen, honey, I'm sorry, but I have an American picture editor in town, and he—"

"Must see you tonight, because he's leaving first thing tomorrow, and it's vitally important for the agency," she finished for him, sounding as if she knew the words by heart.

"You got it."

"Why don't you come over later, Clee?"

"It'll be too late."

"I don't mind."

There was a small pause. He said finally, "I would prefer to see you at the weekend, Mel. If you're free. We could drive out to the country for dinner on Saturday night. How about it?"

He heard her sigh at the other end of the phone.

She said, after a moment, "Oh all right, then. But I don't know why I let you do this to me, Cleeland Donovan. Most other guys couldn't get away with it."

"Get away with what?"

"Being so elusive."

"Do we have a date for Saturday night?"

"You know we do, Clee."

"I'll call you tomorrow, and I'm sorry about tonight."

He said good-bye and hung up. I'll send Mel flowers from Lachaume tomorrow, he thought, putting his feet up on the desk, leaning back in the chair and closing his eyes.

Clee felt a surge of relief that he had canceled Flo and Hank, and the conflicting date with Mel as well, by telling a couple of harmless white lies. The truth was, he did not have a business date. But he did not have the head for a fancy dinner party at the Devons'; nor was he in the mood to dine alone with Melanie Lowe, bright and lovely as she was, and of whom he was quite fond. He wanted to be alone; he had a lot on his mind and a great deal of thinking to do. This was the other reason why he had been so pleased when Jean-Claude had told him he was free, that he had no other assignments before he left for the States to do the work for *Life*. He was not only going to take it easy for the next week and have the rest he needed, but he would concentrate on a few personal problems that needed sorting out. One in particular had been at the back of his mind for several weeks.

Opening his eyes, Clee stood up and put on his jacket, then walked toward the door.

He paused halfway across the room and stood for a moment looking at the portrait of

Capa. Of all the photographs that had been taken of him, whether in combat fatigues or civilian clothes, this was Clee's favorite. It was of Capa and David "Chim" Seymour, and it had been taken in a leafy Paris square in the early 1950s. The two friends were sitting on metal garden chairs, and Capa was wearing a raincoat over his suit; a cigarette was dangling from his lips. There was a quizzical expression in his eyes and he appeared to be smiling faintly. One hand was resting on his knee, and Clee had always been struck by that hand—the long, sensitive fingers that looked so capable. And how darkly handsome Capa was in this picture; the strong masculine features, the thick black brows and hair, the smoldering dark eyes, the seductive mouth all added up to one helluva knockout of a guy.

Capa had been the possessor of a legendary charm and a debonair personality as well as good looks, and it was not difficult for Clee to imagine why Ingrid Bergman and so many other women had fallen head over heels in love with him.

Everything Clee had ever read about Capa had underscored his courage and daring as a photographer, his compassion and humanity as a man. Once, the British magazine *Picture Post,* now defunct, had run a photograph of Capa, and the headline above the caption had read: *The Greatest War Photographer in the World.* And that was what he had been. It had cost him his life, in the end.

Capa had been killed on May 25, 1954, when he had stepped on a Vietminh antipersonnel mine on a small, grassy slope above a dike, five kilometers outside Dongquithon in Indochina, during the French Indochina war. He had been forty-one years old. Two years older than I am now, Clee reminded himself, thinking of his own mortality and how fragile life truly was in the long run.

In 1955 *Life* magazine and the Overseas Press Club of America had established the Robert Capa Award "for the best photographic reporting from abroad requiring exceptional courage and enterprise."

Clee had won the award for his coverage of the war in Lebanon, and it was his most treasured possession. It came in a box lined with blue velvet and it stood on a shelf next to the Capa photograph, set slightly apart from the other international awards Clee had won for the excellence of his work.

Lifting the lid, Clee stared at the award for a second, and he wondered, as he often had in the past, why he felt so close to a man he had never known and yet missed as if he had been a dear friend. It baffled him, but there was no denying that Capa, a dead man, had been the single most important influence in his life.

Jean-Claude's voice could be heard outside in the corridor. Clee shook off his thoughts about Capa and left the room to see if anything was wrong.

"Hey, guys, what's going on?" he asked, going toward Jean-Claude, who was talking excitedly, and Michel Bellond, a partner in the agency and a photographer of talent and courage.

"*Rien,*" Michel said, and winked at Clee.

"He is right, it is nothing, really," Jean-Claude said and grinned. "We were just discussing the merits of various restaurants, trying to decide where to have the dinner for Steve," he explained, referring to another partner in Image.

"Let's hear the choices," Clee said. "Perhaps I'll cast the deciding vote."

9

When Clee finally left the Image offices on the rue de Berri, it was drawing close to dusk, that time of day when the sky has changed to twilight colors but has not yet turned black.

He lifted his head as he walked toward the Champs-Élysées and looked up at the sky. Tonight it was a deep blue, almost peacock in intensity, and it had a soft incandescent glow to it, as if subtly illuminated from behind.

Magic hour, he said to himself, using the movie term that best described this time of day, which movie directors and cinematographers loved with such passion because it was especially effective on film.

When he reached the Champs-Élysées he stopped and gazed up that long, wide boulevard, his eyes focusing on the Arc de Triomphe in the distance. The tricolor, the French national flag, was suspended inside the arch from the top, and ingeniously illuminated with spotlights. It was blowing through the arch in the wind and looked unusually dramatic at this moment. Clee thought the arch was the most moving and magnificent sight he had seen in a very long time, but then the whole of Paris was particularly glorious right now. A large number of the impressive, ancient buildings had recently been carefully cleaned for the bicentennial celebrations taking place this year.

Turning left, Clee strolled down the Champs-Élysées, enjoying the walk after being cooped up in the office all day; he generally felt somewhat constrained when he was not out on assignment. But, whatever the circumstance, he enjoyed walking in Paris more than any other place in the world.

This was his city. He had first come here when he was eighteen and had fallen in love with it. At first sight. He had wanted to come to Paris because of Capa, who for so many years had lived in the French capital, where he had founded Magnum, his photo agency, in 1947 with "Chim" Seymour and Henri Cartier-Bresson. Capa had been his hero since he was fifteen and growing up in New York. That year, 1965, he had read an article about the late photographer in a photography magazine, and ever after he had searched for anything and everything that had been written about Capa.

Clee had first started taking pictures when he was nine years old, using an inexpensive camera his parents had given him for his birthday. Even when he was a child his pictures had been so extraordinary everyone had been amazed at his talent. His mother and father, and sisters Joan and Kelly, were his willing victims, and had allowed themselves to be photographed day and night doing every conceivable thing, and were his models on special family occasions.

Naturally gifted, sensitive, intelligent, and with an exacting eye, he was completely self-taught. Photography had been his passion, his whole life, when he was a teenager; nothing had changed much in subsequent years.

It was in 1968 that Clee had discovered Paris for himself, and instantly fallen under its seductive spell. That summer he had made up his mind that he was going to live there one day, and he had returned to New York determined to become a great photographer. He wanted to be another Robert Capa if that was humanly possible.

At the time Clee had been working in the darkroom of a portrait photographer in Manhattan, and he had stayed on for only another year. Through a connection of his father's, he had managed to get a job on the *New York Post* as a junior photographer. Very rapidly he had made a name for himself on the paper, and he had never looked back.

During this period he had taken himself off to night school several evenings a week to study French, which he knew was an absolute necessity if he was ever to achieve his ambition and live in Paris. By the time he was twenty-one he was fluent in the language. He was also a far better photographer than some of the most seasoned veterans in the news business.

A staff job on *The New York Times* followed in 1971, but when he was twenty-three Clee left the paper. He had decided to become a roving photojournalist covering Europe, and worked as a freelancer for a number of American and English magazines.

Naturally, he had chosen to base himself in Paris, and two years later, when he was twenty-five, he had started Image. Banding together with two other photographers, he had hired three darkroom assistants, a secretary and Jean-Claude, who managed the agency. Michel Bellond, a Frenchman, and Steve Carvelli, an American of Italian descent, were his partners. Less than a year after Image had been founded, Peter Naylor from London became the fourth and last photographer to join the group as a partner.

Right from the outset, Image had been successful, quickly garnering big international assignments, commanding high fees for the star photographers and soon winning a clutch of awards. After fourteen years it was still going strong with the four original partners and several staff photographers, along with additional darkroom assistants and secretarial help. And it had become one of the most prestigious photo agencies in the world.

Clee was well aware that his family had been dismayed, even distressed, when he had become an expatriate and settled in Paris. At the time, he was regretful of this, but he had never had any intention of changing his life. It was his own to live the way he saw fit. In the early years his parents and sisters had come to visit him frequently, and whenever he had gone back to New York he had spent as much time with them as he could. And he still did, whenever he was there.

Despite the fact that he had defied his father and had not gone to college, choosing instead to plunge into the world of the working photographer, they had remained truly good friends. Second-generation Irish, with an analytical mind, a golden tongue and the gift of gab, his father, Edward Donovan, had been a successful, well-known attorney in Manhattan, and highly respected in the field of criminal law. He had died unexpectedly of a heart attack in 1981, and Clee, like his mother and sisters, had felt the loss acutely. Ted Donovan had been very much a family man, a devoted husband and a loving father.

To Clee's considerable relief, his mother had managed to cope with her grief rather well, and quite bravely, he thought, thanks in no small measure to his sisters' offspring. Both Joan and Kelly were married, and between them they had three daughters and one son. Martha Donovan's grandchildren had become her life, and she appeared to be at peace with herself these days.

Clee's thoughts stayed with his mother as he hailed a passing cab, got in and gave the driver his address. He must call her this weekend and let her know he would be in New York in late July, tell her that they would be seeing each other soon. This would please her as much as it pleased him. They had remained close over the years, and he knew she worried about him a great deal, especially when he was in a combat zone.

This was only one of the many reasons he stayed in constant touch with her wherever he was.

Within a short time the cab was turning into the rue Jacob in the sixth *arrondissement,* that charming part of Paris known as the Latin Quarter. It was here that Clee lived in a fourth-floor apartment of a handsome old building.

Clee sat on the sofa in the living room, the lights dim, the Mozart disc on the player turned low. He nursed a beer, lost to the world as he pondered his personal life.

Nicole Wells. He repeated her name to himself in the silence of his head. She had become a problem. A nagging problem, as it so happened.

For two years they had been *copains*—best buddies in the truest sense. In Beijing he had saved her life. Inside himself, everything had changed.

He no longer thought of her simply as his best buddy. She was a woman he cared about as a *woman.* He had realized this when he had put his arms around her on the steps of the Martyrs' Monument in Tiananmen, after pushing her away from the approaching tanks. In fact, he was so filled with relief that she was safe, for a moment all of his strength had seemed to ebb out of him. Momentarily undone by this surge of unprecedented emotion, he had been incapable of saying a word. Nicky had thanked him, and he had turned her face to his and looked into those cool, appraising blue eyes. Suddenly he was brimming with feelings he did not fully understand.

Ever since leaving Hong Kong he had tried hard to shake off these feelings, but without much success. Off and on, they had continued to both confuse and trouble him, but he was aware of the reasons to some extent. He and Nicky had drawn closer and closer— in fact, had grown to love each other as a brother and sister. Now his emotions were engaged on a different level, and he was not sure what to do about it.

To begin with, he did not want to get seriously involved with any woman because he did not want to care so much for someone that he would feel bound to make a commitment, perhaps get married and eventually have children. For most of his adult life he had believed that this would be unfair, in view of the dangerous life he led as a war photographer. And certainly he was not prepared to give up that life of travel and excitement. Besides, he enjoyed his freedom; he had no desire to be pinned down by marital obligations. If he was honest, he believed himself to be a bachelor at heart.

And then there was Nicky herself. She was perfect as a friend, but hardly the most suitable candidate for a lover. She was too complicated, too complex by far. And then there were the very obvious logistical problems—she lived an ocean away, and she had one of the biggest careers in American television. Hardly the right ingredients for a harmonious love affair.

Also, for a long time Clee had been convinced that Nicole Wells lived out her life on various battlegrounds—the battlegrounds of the wars she covered, the battlegrounds of network politics, the battleground of her damaged heart.

Furthermore, he could not help thinking that she was still in love with Charles Devereaux, as futile as that was, even though she had never made a single reference to him in the entire time he had known her. This omission had always struck him as odd, inasmuch as they were best friends.

Arch Leverson had filled him in, however, and he had a fairly good picture of what had happened. In his opinion, and Arch's, Devereaux had behaved like a louse. But then brilliant and successful women such as

Nicky were not necessarily discriminating when it came to men. Very frequently they picked the wrong ones, the bastards.

The clock on the white marble mantelpiece chimed nine and Clee sat up with a jolt, realizing that he had been thinking about Nicky ever since he returned from the office.

What the hell am I going to do about her?

The question hung there for a while, and then all of a sudden it occurred to him that he did not have to *do* anything. She had absolutely no idea that he was harboring these strange new feelings for her. If he was smart and did not reveal them, she would be none the wiser. Very simply, he would go on treating her as a pal. This was the ideal solution, the *only* solution to his predicament. When he was with her he must behave exactly as he had in the past, and everything would be all right.

Vastly relieved that he had finally solved a problem that had hovered over him since Beijing, Clee got up and went to the kitchen, took another bottle of beer out of the refrigerator and opened it.

As he was crossing the foyer the phone began to ring and he hurried through the living room to answer it.

"Hello?"

"Hi, Clee, it's me."

"Nicky!" he exclaimed, and he was so happy to hear her voice that he felt an overwhelming rush of pleasure, which startled him. He sat down heavily in the nearest chair.

"What's happening down there in Provence?" he asked a bit lamely, glad that she was hundreds of miles away and couldn't see his reaction to her voice.

"It's very quiet here, but it's been wonderful for me these last few days," she said. "So sunny and peaceful, and you were right, I did need the rest. Clee, I love your farm. It's just beautiful, and so comfortable. You made a wonderful job of it."

When he did not immediately respond, she said quickly, "I hope I'm not calling at an inconvenient time."

"No, no," he assured her, finding his voice at last. After clearing his throat, he said, "And I'm glad you like it there, Nick. My sister Joan will be delighted, she's the one responsible for the farm. She restored and decorated it for me."

"And here I've been thinking you've got hidden talents," she said, and laughed her throaty laugh, which suddenly sounded very sexy to him.

He muttered, "How long are you planning to stay in Provence?"

"I don't know. Originally I thought a week, but maybe I'll stay on for a while. Clee, I was wondering if you might come down for a few days? Keep me company. If you don't have anything better to do?"

"I'd love to, Nick, but I'm jammed. The agency's flooded with jobs."

"Oh."

"Look, I'm just in the middle of something, let me call you back later," he said. "Or will you be going to bed early?"

"No, that's fine. Talk to you later, then. 'Bye."

She hung up before he could say another word, and he felt rotten for being abrupt. He had been having erotic thoughts about Nicky, and he had begun to feel self-conscious, ill at ease on the phone with her.

She was a baffling woman in a variety of ways. When he first met her in Beirut two years ago, he had thought she was the classiest-looking woman he had ever seen—beautiful, elegant even in her battered safari suit, and very photogenic. At that time he had categorized her in his mind as a Grace Kelly for the eighties and nineties. She had that very poised, cool exterior that could be so off-putting to some men, but he was sure it concealed great warmth. Eventually he had come to believe that deep down she was romantic and passionate by nature, but that she had been so badly hurt by Devereaux she was frozen cold when it came to men.

None of this had mattered to him before because they were just friends and nothing more. And in any case, when he first met her he had been heavily involved with another woman and had not been interested in Nicky as a lover.

But it mattered now. Everything about her mattered now. But it mustn't. I have to care about her as a friend, and that's all, he cautioned himself.

Jumping up, Clee went back to the kitchen, where he tore a piece off the fresh *baguette* on the table, and made himself a sandwich. Then he paced restlessly around the kitchen, munching on the sandwich and taking an occasional swig from the bottle of beer.

And though he tried his utmost to put her out of his mind, his thoughts continued to turn on Nicky Wells.

At ten o'clock he called her back, and went out of his way to sound warm and friendly. They chatted for about twenty minutes; he told her about Marc Villier and the interview planned for the following morning; they discussed his trip to the States for *Life* magazine. And, as they usually did, they touched on the subject of Yoyo, of whom there was still no news.

Just before he said good-bye, Clee murmured, "I'm sorry I can't come down to the farm, Nick. There's nothing I'd like better than a few days in the sun, a chance to relax with you. But duty calls, I've just got too much work."

"Please don't worry about it, Clee," she said pleasantly. "Honestly, I do understand."

As he hung up he was not so sure that *he* did.

Clee sat for a moment reflecting, with his hand resting on the phone. He had nothing planned for the next few days other than the meeting with Villier tomorrow and the date with Mel on Saturday night. He *could* in fact go down to Provence for a long weekend.

He sighed as he thought of Mel. He was forever canceling dates with her for one reason or another, and that was damned unfair of him. Still, if nothing else, he supposed this told him something important about the status of his relationship with her. She was lovely, but his feelings for her were not particularly intense. If he was truthful, he had to admit he was only mildly fond of Melanie Lowe, and this would never change.

His thoughts veered back to Provence.

There was no real reason why he could not go down there. *Not true.* There was an excellent reason. *Nicky Wells.*

He was also forgetting his decision of a short while ago—to keep his relationship with Nicky exactly the way it had been from their first meeting: platonic. He had absolutely no intention of changing that. Nor did he have any intention of going to the farm this weekend. Why expose himself when he felt vulnerable to her at present? Surely it was better to get a grip on his feelings, wait for them to change, to settle down before he saw her again.

He would be with Mel for the weekend. And for as long as they both wished to continue their pleasant liaison. Mel suited him fine. She was sweet and loving and undemanding. Furthermore, he liked being with her, enjoyed her wry sense of humor, her easygoing ways and her brightness.

And Nicky would remain his comrade-in-arms with whom he shared so much on an entirely different level. She was ideal to have as his best buddy, and he knew he must never do anything to jeopardize their friendship, which he cherished.

10

"What Guillaume told you is true, Mademoiselle Nicky," Amélie said, nodding her head several times for emphasis. "Soon it will be scorching hot. Unbearable. This is not the day to go to Arles." As she finished speaking, Amélie squinted up at the sky and repeated, "Scorching, *oui.*"

Nicky tilted her head, following Amélie's gaze. The sky was so vividly blue it almost hurt her eyes and she blinked. She put on her sunglasses.

"If you think I shouldn't go, then I won't," she murmured, deeming it best to trust the couple's judgment. Amélie and Guillaume were wise in the ways of the Provençal land

and the weather, and in the week she had been staying here they had not been wrong in anything they had told her about the area.

"Too hot to go tramping the streets of the city," Amélie went on, waving her hand dismissively. "Better to be here. Sit under the trees in the shade. Swim in the pool. Stay cool. That is the best thing on a day like this, Mademoiselle Nicky."

"Then that's what I'll do, Amélie." Nicky smiled at her and added, "Thanks for your good advice. I appreciate it."

It was eight o'clock on Friday morning. The two women were standing in the middle of the lawn that stretched from the edge of the outdoor dining terrace on one side of the house to the pool area at the bottom of the garden. The sun was shining brilliantly in that azure sky of dazzling clarity, and the air was already vibrating with intense heat. Nothing moved, not a blade of grass nor a single leaf stirred, and even the birds were curiously silent this morning as they took refuge in the dark green branches of the trees.

Amélie straightened her crisp white apron, peered at Nicky and asked, "What would you like for lunch?"

Nicky burst out laughing. "Amélie! I've only just had *breakfast*! You're going to have to stop feeding me in this way. I'm beginning to feel like a duck being force-fed—fattened up for *foie gras.*"

Shaking her head, Amélie exclaimed, "But, Mademoiselle Nicky, you are too thin!" Opening her arms wide, Amélie threw them around her solid Provençal body and hugged herself. Then she winked and announced, "A man likes something to hold on to, *n'est-ce pas*? That is my opinion."

"Perhaps you're right," Nicky said, laughing. "But please don't make anything too heavy for lunch. It's much too hot to eat."

"I will prepare the perfect lunch for the weather," Amélie reassured her. "Yesterday Guillaume bought wonderful melons in the village, from Cavaillon. They are the best in the whole of France, mademoiselle. So sweet, like honey. *Mmmm.*" Amélie kissed her fingertips, and went on, "So you will commence with the chilled melon. Then you will have a simple *salade niçoise,* and for dessert, vanilla ice cream."

"Thank you, it sounds delicious. But no ice cream, Amélie, iced tea instead."

"As you say, Mademoiselle Nicky." Amélie flashed her a warm smile. "Excuse me, I must go to my kitchen. So much to do. And I must also think about your dinner for tonight. Nothing fattening, no." And so saying she hurried up the steps leading to the terrace and bustled into the farmhouse.

Amused, Nicky looked after her, shaking her head. Amélie seemed to be determined to put some flesh on her bones whatever it took. Turning, Nicky strolled over to the narrow flagged path cutting through the long stretch of sloping green lawn and headed down to the pool area located at the very tip of the garden. This had been skillfully designed to flow into the landscape and it had a lovely natural look to it. The pool was set in a rectangle of lawn, and only a few yards away a cluster of trees formed a small copse, where flowers had been randomly planted to make them look as if they were growing wild.

Under these trees Guillaume had arranged several chaises, old-fashioned deck chairs and low occasional tables, as he did every morning. Nicky had discovered that this was the coolest spot in the garden; frequently, a light breeze rustled through the trees, and it was her favorite place for reading.

She smiled inwardly as she walked toward the copse. Amélie had been fussing and mothering her all week long, and nothing was too much trouble for her or Guillaume. In consequence, she felt rested and spoiled, but she was also beginning to grow just a little bored after a week here alone.

Nicky had said this to her mother last night, when she had called her in New York. Her mother had exclaimed, "Good Lord, darling, how can you be bored in Provence! There's so much to see and do. Besides, it's about time you stayed put for a moment or two. If only to catch your breath. You're never still—forever rushing around the world in search of stories."

Flabbergasted, Nicky had retorted, "Mother, how can *you* of all people say such a thing! You were doing exactly the same as I when you were my age. Not only that, you had *me* in tow."

Her mother had had the grace to laugh. "*Touché.* But to tell the truth, darling, your father and I do wish you *would* slow down a bit. For the past ten years you've been covering wars and uprisings and revolutions, been in the thick of all kinds of catastrophic events, in every corner of the globe. And when I look back, I can't help but shudder to think what you've been through, the risks you've taken. . . ." Her mother had stopped at this juncture in the conversation, and there had been a little pause before Nicky had asked softly, "Mom, are you trying to say that you and Dad want me to stop being a war correspondent?"

Her mother had been quick to deny this.

"Of course not, your father and I would never interfere with your life or your career. But *I* know it must get wearying for you. And it *is* dangerous."

Nicky had laughed dismissively. "Don't forget, Mother, I have a guardian angel."

Elise Wells had chosen to ignore this remark and suggested that Nicky return home to New York for the remainder of her vacation if she was tired of France. "You can always join us in Connecticut, if you wish. Your father and I are going to stay at the house for the rest of the summer, and you know how much we adore having you with us."

They had chatted about the idea of a visit for several minutes, and Nicky had agreed to spend a few days in the country with her parents when she got back to the States.

They were close, the three of them, and they had been for as long as Nicky could remember. She was an only child, and sometimes she felt the responsibility of being one. An only child was expected to excel, since parents generally centered their hopes and dreams in that one child.

Her parents were eminently fair and had never made unreasonable demands on her. She loved them as much as they loved her; they were her champions, her chief supporters in everything she did. They had been especially wonderful to her through the entire Charles Devereaux crisis.

Immediately she pushed the thought of Charles away. She had no wish to remember someone who had caused her pain, however long ago that was.

Reaching the pool area, Nicky put her book down on one of the tables, took off the loose cotton shirt she was wearing over her black bikini and settled on a chaise.

Diffused sunlight trickled through the cool green canopy of leafy branches above her head, and she stretched out her long legs, closed her eyes and for a while drifted with her thoughts, which were still focused on her parents. She knew her mother and father wondered why she had not had a serious involvement with a man since Devereaux, and that at one time they had even believed her to be hung up on him. But she had explained that she was not, and she had spoken the truth. The reason why there was no special man in her life was very simple really. She hadn't met anyone who had genuinely interested her in the past two and a half years, at least not for a long-term relationship.

One day, she thought, one day my prince will come. When I'm least expecting it. And no doubt he'll knock me for a loop. That was the way it was supposed to be, wasn't it? Wobbly knees, palpitating heart and all that stuff. She laughed to herself.

In the meantime, she wasn't unhappy with her life. She had a successful career and she loved her work; whenever she wanted it, there was a family life with her parents, and she had several close girlfriends with whom she shared a great deal. And then there was her friend Cleeland Donovan. He was caring and protective, and she treasured his friendship.

Suddenly Nicky realized how disappointed she was that Clee had not been able to come down for the weekend. It would have been nice to see him, she would have enjoyed his company in these peaceful surroundings. Usually when they were together they were in a combat zone or some other trouble spot in the world. At those times they were under immense pressure, intensely involved in what they were doing, scrambling to do their work properly, to get the story, usually under the most adverse circumstances—they also had to fight the horror of what they were witnessing, plus the fear, which never failed to surface at some point.

What a lovely change it would have been if they could have relaxed together and had some fun this weekend. But he could not get away, or did not want to, or was otherwise engaged, and that was that.

Now that she thought about it, spending a few days with her mother and father in New Milford was a rather appealing idea. If she left the farm on Monday morning, went to Marseilles and then directly on to Paris, she could take the Concorde to New York on Tuesday morning, and drive up to Connecticut on Wednesday afternoon. She would speak to Guillaume later about ordering a car and have the driver Étienne come and get her.

Having made this decision, Nicky pulled her reading glasses out of the pocket of her shirt and picked up her book. It was Richard Whelan's biography of Robert Capa, which she had found in the library upstairs, and it made fascinating reading. From the moment she started it she had understood why Clee had always been so intrigued by Capa.

Nicky began to read and was soon completely absorbed in Capa's life story. An hour slipped by, and then another.

In the middle of the morning Amélie appeared, sailing down the garden path carrying a tray.

"*Eh, voilà!*" she cried, standing next to Nicky's chaise. "I have made fresh lemonade for you, I know how much you enjoy it, mademoiselle." She poured a glass from the jug.

"Thank you, Amélie," Nicky said, taking it from her. "This is just what I need. It's getting hotter by the minute out here."

"*Oui.* The sun can be dangerous, *faites attention,*" the housekeeper cautioned and hurried back to the farmhouse.

Nicky looked up from her book at the exact moment that Clee reached the middle of the garden path leading down to the pool.

He stood perfectly still, smiling at her, and after a second, Nicky's face broke into a delighted smile. She threw her book down and leaped to her feet.

"Clee! How did you get here!" she cried and ran toward him. Throwing her arms around him, she hugged him. He hugged her back, and then they walked back to the pool area.

"How did you manage to get away?" she asked, looking up at him, her smile radiant.

"Jean-Claude reshuffled the assignments, gave my jobs to the other guys," Clee lied. "He thought I looked tired, decided I needed a rest. So I took the last flight from Paris to Marseilles yesterday. When I arrived it was

too late to start driving here, and anyway I
didn't want to disturb the household at that
late hour, so I stayed at a hotel in Marseilles.
Étienne drove me up this morning."

"I'm so glad! It's wonderful to see you!"
Nicky said, her enthusiasm bubbling up. "I
was getting a bit lonely."

He looked at her and nodded, but did not
say a word.

Nicky continued, "I almost drove to Arles
today, but Amélie persuaded me to stay here
because of the heat—" Abruptly she broke
off and shook her head as the truth dawned
on her. "She *knew* you were coming. That's
the reason why she went on and on about
the weather—said it was far too hot to go
into the city."

"As a matter of fact, she was right about
the weather, it *is* murderous in the cities at
this time of year, much worse than out here,"
Clee said. "But yes, she did know I was coming. I told her not to tell you, when I spoke to
her yesterday. I wanted to surprise you."

"Well, you succeeded!" She laughed as
she flopped down on the chaise and stared
up at him. "Why don't you take your clothes
off?"

Startled, he gaped at her, then laughed.
"What?"

"You look so hot, I mean. Don't you think

you'd be more comfortable in swimming trunks?''

''Yes. Yes, of course, I'll go and change. What I need after that long drive is a swim in the pool and a glass of ice-cold champagne. I'll be back in a minute, with a bottle of Dom Pérignon.''

11

"Think of it, Nick, I was only four years old when Capa died in Vietnam during the French Indochina war," Clee said and paused, staring at her for a long moment. Then he added quietly, "He's the only person I've ever really missed not knowing."

Nicky made no comment.

Clee went on in the same quiet voice, "I just wish I'd met him, been a friend. I really do miss not having known him. Do you understand what I mean?" He laughed a bit self-consciously and muttered, "I bet you think I'm nuts."

"No, you've explained it very well. It's a kind of sadness inside, a feeling of regret that you were born too late to meet someone you consider somehow very meaningful to you, even though your lives never crossed."

"Yes."

"Quite aside from being a remarkable photographer, Capa was obviously a fascinating man, by all accounts," Nicky continued. "In the biography I've been reading, the photographer Eve Arnold is quoted as saying Capa had charm and grace and a lightness, that when he came into a room it was as if a light had been turned on. She said you wanted to be near him, that you wanted to be part of that ebullience, part of that zest. He had enormous . . . charisma. I think that's the word for it, Clee. The only word, actually."

"I remember reading that myself. Also there's a wonderful description of Capa by Irwin Shaw that was also quoted in Whelan's biography."

"Yes, I read it, too." Nicky smiled at him. "Capa must have seemed so glamorous to you when you were growing up, and his life must have seemed very adventurous and exciting."

"He did, it did," Clee admitted. "But actually, I'd wanted to get into combat to take war photos long before I'd ever heard of Robert Capa. Still, he was my inspiration in so many different ways." Clee shifted in the chair, crossed his legs and after a moment asked, "When did you decide you wanted to be a war correspondent?"

"When I was little, same as you. I was emulating my father, I suppose."

"Do you think that's really why you do it? I mean now, today, after all these years?"

"Oh no, not anymore. I do what I do because I want to report on history in the making. I want to witness events, to report on them as accurately and as truthfully as I can. I want to bring the news to the people—and with as much integrity as possible."

"I think our reasons are much the same. I just hope my pictures have as much integrity as your newscasts."

"They do." Nicky looked at him probingly. "Do you think you'll ever give it up?"

"I doubt it." Clee shrugged, then grinned at her. "Well, maybe one day, when I'm too old to dodge the bullets. And what about you?"

"I feel the same. It's funny about the fear, isn't it? And how alike we are in that respect. You and I never seem to experience the fear until after the action is over. Do you think all journalists are the same?"

"No, I don't. Some feel the fear at the time they're working, others are like us—get knocked out by it afterward. Joe Glass of the London *Sunday Times* once told me when we were in Lebanon together that he suffers immense fatigue immediately after he's had a very frightening experience in a war zone. You and I are lucky in a sense, Nick, because our emotions don't close in on us until much, much later."

"You take too many risks on the battle-field, Clee."

"Calculated risks. Anyway, you're exactly the same."

"No, not really. I'm much more cautious than you, despite what you and Arch think."

"I should hope you are."

A thoughtful expression settled on Nicky's face, and after a moment, she said slowly, "We broke the golden rule in Beijing, didn't we, Clee?"

"What do you mean?" His brows puckered; he was mystified.

"We became *involved* with Yoyo. That has such inherent dangers, we should never let our emotions become engaged with a subject when we're covering a story. We have to remain a little aloof, a bit removed, to do our job. We have to keep a proper perspective."

"Sometimes it's pretty tough *not* to get involved," Clee responded quickly. "None of us are that hard-boiled, are we? And listen,

Arch and the guys felt exactly the same as we did about Yoyo. How could you not get involved with the kid, he's something else, really special, wouldn't you say?"

"Yes, that's true."

Nicky leaned against the sofa and looked across at Clee. There was a small silence before she asked softly, "What do you think happened to him? You don't think he's . . . dead, do you, Clee?"

"No, I don't. I have a feeling Yoyo is hiding out, that he went underground. I've always said that to you, and I can only reiterate it now. You'll see, he'll turn up, and probably sooner than we think."

"You're not just saying that to make me feel better, are you?" she said focusing her eyes steadily on his.

"No, I'm not," he said adamantly. He leaned forward, intent on what he had to say to her. "Yoyo is bright, enterprising, re-sourceful. He'll make it out of China, I feel very strongly about this—I really do have a lot of faith in him."

Clee rose and went to the door of the library, where they were sitting. "I want to show you something. I'll be back in a min-ute."

. . .

While Clee was gone, Nicky closed her eyes, thinking of Yoyo. Clee had spoken with such conviction, she had to believe that he was correct in his assessment of what had happened to the boy. She had no alternative; she must go on hoping that he would surface eventually, either in New York or Paris or Hong Kong. Practically the last thing she had said to him was that if he arrived in the British Crown Colony and needed help, he was to telephone one of them immediately. Person to person collect. She had promised Yoyo that she or Clee or Arch would take it from there, would get him out of Hong Kong no matter what.

Opening her eyes, Nicky sat up and reached for her glass, took a sip. Knowing it was futile to worry, she put thoughts of Yoyo at the back of her mind.

She glanced around, taking in the peacefulness of the room, and understood why it was Clee's favorite. It had also become hers. Its tranquillity acted as a balm to her troubled spirits.

Decorated throughout in pale colors, primarily white and cream with touches of melon and terra-cotta, it was filled with numerous bowls of flowers and tall pots of leafy branches. Hundreds of books filled the shelves soaring to the ceiling, and there were magazines and big art books arranged on various tables. Some of Clee's photographs, obviously those he liked the most, were framed on the walls, and hanging above the gargantuan stone fireplace was a collection of ethereal watercolors of the area done by a local artist. With the emphasis on comfort, it was a casual room, designed for relaxing, reading, listening to music, and watching television and films.

Today the weather had been extremely hot again, oppressively so. Fortunately, the two large fans on the ceiling—Casablanca fans she called them—circulated the air, and now that the sun had slunk off to the west the atmosphere was pleasant. Outside the windows the summer light was rapidly fading, the sky turning a deeper blue as night fell. It was almost eight-thirty on Sunday evening; earlier, Clee had suggested that they have a picnic in the library and watch a video of an old movie later, and she had agreed.

It seemed to Nicky that the weekend had passed in the blink of an eye. She and Clee had puttered around the farm on Friday after his unexpected arrival, chatting, laughing, reminiscing and catching up with each other's news. As Clee had pointed out to her on Friday evening, in the two years they had known each other this was the first time they had ever had a chance to relax together, to talk in the way they had that day—and about so many diverse things.

On Saturday, because it was so much cooler, Clee had driven her to Arles.

"But don't expect to see many of van Gogh's old haunts," he had warned her on the way there. "There's not much left that's associated with the time he spent in Provence. Even the house he shared with Gauguin has been torn down. But there is the Allée des Sarcophages, which he painted so wonderfully and with such vibrancy. We can go and see that. And of course there are the fields and fields of sunflowers where he used to go and pick bunches for his still lifes. They should be in full bloom now."

Arles, as Nicky had discovered, was a captivating place, very ancient, almost other-worldly in a certain sense. Clee had taken her sightseeing through the old city and she had been fascinated. Her father had always said she made a good tourist, with her curious mind and investigative nature, her desire to know about everything.

The old city was filled with crumbling Roman ruins juxtaposed against strong medieval stonework, and there were numerous monuments and museums, and a lot of quaint things to see. She had been in her element, and Clee had seemed pleased she was enjoying herself so much.

After strolling for several hours through the old city, with its ramparts and air of antiquity, they had gone for a late lunch at a charming bistro Clee obviously knew well. He was greeted with affection and enthusiasm by Madame Yvonne and Monsieur Louis, the owners, who had given them the best table in the house, according to Clee. He had ordered for them both, selecting various local dishes, telling her she would love them and explaining each one to her. He had also insisted she join him in a *pastis,* the popular local drink, an *apéritif* that tasted of aniseed and turned milky in color when mixed with the mandatory splash of water.

After lunch they had wandered around the newer part of Arles, window-shopping mostly, but Nicky had bought a handful of postcards to send off to Arch, her crew and friends in New York. As she pored over the cards in the bookstore Clee had selected a dozen or so magazines and a stack of newspapers, and then they had meandered back to the car.

It was late afternoon when they had set off for the farm, driving along at a leisurely pace. Arriving at the house, they had had icy champagne on the terrace and, a little later, a light

supper. This had been lovingly prepared by
Amélie and served in the garden.

Amélie and Guillaume had departed early
this morning to go to the wedding of a niece
in Marseilles. As much as Nicky appreciated
Amélie, she was glad to have a respite from
all the meals, delicious and tempting though
they were. Clee had not made any comment
when she had refused the cold chicken, fish,
vegetables and various other dishes Amélie
had prepared in advance for their lunch. Instead, she had made herself a small tomato
salad, which she had eaten with a chunk torn
from a fresh *baguette.*

Taking another sip of her drink, Nicky reflected on the day. She and Clee had done
absolutely nothing, mostly because of the
intense heat. In the morning they had taken
it easy under the trees near the pool, reading
magazines and newspapers; in the afternoon they had come up here to the library to
listen to Kiri Te Kanawa's rendition of arias
from *Tosca,* performed with the National
Philharmonic Orchestra and conducted by
Sir Georg Solti.

Nicky had curled up on one of the big,
squashy sofas, closed her eyes and drifted
off into another world, transported by Puc-
cini's music and Dame Kiri's silvery voice.
Yes, she reflected, it has been a special day,
and in so many ways.

. . .

The door opened and Clee entered carrying two large portfolios. He strode over to the long library table, and said, "I haven't told you—but I'm planning a photographic book on Beijing, on Tiananmen. I'd like to show you some of the pictures."

"Oh, Clee, I'd love to see them," she exclaimed, jumping up and joining him at the table.

He pushed aside a pile of magazines, took the photographs out of the first portfolio and spread them out on the table. The collection was a mixture of color and black-and-white.

The pictures were so powerful, had such a sense of immediacy, that Nicky caught her breath; instantly she was carried back to Tiananmen Square. Those tense and turbulent days leading up to the bloody massacre at the beginning of the month were suddenly vividly alive again.

She recognized how accurate Clee's eye was. He had taken very direct and candid photographs of people and events. Each shot had a feeling of intimacy and the people looked so vital.

"These are extraordinary, Clee," Nicky said with sincere admiration. "They're so powerful, and extremely moving."

Her words brought a quick, pleased smile

to his face, and he took another batch out of the second portfolio. "These are more personal," he explained, lining them up, watching her, waiting for her reaction.

Nicky found herself looking down at pictures Clee had taken of her alone in Tiananmen Square and in other parts of Beijing. Some were with Arch and her crew, and others were with Yoyo or with Yoyo and Mai. There were additional shots of Yoyo with the other student leaders, and with Mai, and all of the backgrounds were so familiar to her they brought a lump to her throat: the Martyrs' Monument, the tent encampment, the Goddess of Democracy, Changan Avenue.

"Oh, Clee, they're stunning! That old cliché about one photograph saying more than a thousand words is true, isn't it?"

"I guess so," he said with a shrug of his broad shoulders, and he brought out the last set of photographs. As she stood staring at them she was overcome by a sudden flood of memories. Across the vast rectangle of stone that was Tiananmen Square came the inexorable flow of tanks and armored personnel carriers. Down Changan Avenue marched the implacable, cold-faced soldiers, carrying machine guns that meant death for their own people. Standing at the barricades, defiant and angry, were the ordinary citizens of Beijing, shaking their fists at the People's Liberation Army, and desperately trying to save the lives of the students—the children of China. And blowing in the wind were the giant white banners bearing the students' slogans of democracy and freedom written boldly in bright red paint the color of blood.

Finally Nicky's eyes settled on the pictures of the fallen students, those who had been shot or crushed by the tanks, who lay dead or dying in pools of their own blood in the streets. All at once she could smell the cordite again, hear the sharp crack of rifles and the ominous rumble of tanks rolling across cold stone, the screams of terror; a tremor ran through her.

Nicky was so moved by the breathtaking images Clee had captured on film that tears sprang to her eyes and she brought her hand up to her mouth. She turned to him but discovered she was unable to speak.

Seeing the tears, he reached out for her and pulled her to him. "Don't be upset," he began in a faltering voice.

He had been so conscious of her the entire weekend, and never more than today. He knew it was a mistake to take her in his arms in this way. Her perfume was fragrant in his nostrils, her body warm and vibrantly alive against his.

Reluctantly he let go of her. Nicky had

never looked so lovely to him. Her skin was a golden brown, her blond hair sun-streaked after the week in Provence, and her eyes seemed bluer than ever in her bronzed face. It took all his self-control not to reach out for her again.

She said, "That's what you want, isn't it?"

"What?" he asked, startled, and wondered if she had just read his mind.

"For me to be upset—for everyone who looks at these pictures to be upset. And to be touched and moved and appalled and horrified and angered."

"I suppose so, yes," he admitted.

"They will be. The photographs are so stunning, I feel as if I've been kicked in the stomach. The book is going to be sensational."

"I hope so, darling." He held his breath. The word "darling" had popped out by accident, but if she had noticed this slip of the tongue she did not show it. In fact, she was displaying no reaction whatsoever.

Clee began to put the pictures away and Nicky helped him. At one moment he stopped and said, "You know, Nick, I can write the captions, I'm used to doing that, but what this book needs is some really great text up front. An introduction. I've been thinking . . . well, you're one of the best writers I know. Would you be interested in doing it, in collaborating with me?"

She was taken aback by his suggestion, and her surprise was apparent. "Why, I don't know," she said hesitantly.

"Who better than you, Nick? You were there, you witnessed it all, and you felt it as acutely as I did. You'd bring the right emotions to the writing. The text must back up the pictures. Please say yes."

"Well, all right. Yes."

"Hey, that's wonderful!" He wanted to hug her but restrained himself. Instead he said, "We'll make a terrific team!"

Nicky walked over to the coffee table, picked up her glass and raised it to him. "I think we ought to drink to that."

Clee found his glass and clinked it against hers. "So—here's to our collaboration!"

"To our collaboration!" she repeated, and they both took a sip.

"These need freshening up," Clee announced, walking over to the chest where he had put the champagne and bucket of ice.

Then he said, "Shall we have a swim before dinner?"

"Why not?" Nicky was now smiling.

12

Lying on her back, she floated toward him in the water.

"Oh, Clee, it's so lovely here!" she called out. "I thought it would be warm like water in a bathtub, but it isn't, it's perfect."

"The breeze is cooling everything off," he said.

Nicky made no response and floated closer to the end of the pool where Clee was catching his breath after several fast laps. Suddenly she flipped over and swam toward him.

Clinging to the side of the pool with one hand, she pushed her wet hair back with the other and laughed softly, as if to herself, shaking her head at the same time.

"What is it?"

"I was just thinking how odd it is that we sometimes forget that the simplest things in life can be so wonderful—the best things of all."

"I know exactly what you mean," he said and glanced around the garden. Just before they left the house to come outside for a swim, he had turned on the small spotlights hidden in the foliage, and the shrubs and trees and flowers were now highlighted by circles of pale silver light. Thanks to his sister's remarkable talent, the lights had been strategically placed and there was nothing artificial about the effect she had created. The garden looked as natural as it did during the day, and, to Clee, infinitely more beautiful after sunset.

Overhead the sky had turned color yet again; the mauve and amethyst had deepened to marine blue and a heavy twilight was descending. A peaceful hush had settled over the garden, and the only sounds were the rustling of the trees in the copse, the faint slap of the water as it lapped against the sides of the pool. The air was clear, and much cooler, and sweet with the fragrance of honeysuckle and frangipani, which grew close to the old stone wall running down one side of the garden.

Clee breathed deeply and looked at Nicky.

"What could be better than being in this glorious spot—the two of us here together, enjoying each other's company."

"Nothing could, it's pure heaven," Nicky said, "and it's been such a wonderful weekend, Clee. I've enjoyed every minute of it. And this is a perfect end to an especially lovely day."

"It's not the end yet," he said, looking at her carefully, "we still have the evening ahead of us—" He glanced at his watch. "It's only nine-thirty. We can stay up as late as we wish, since we don't have to be awake early in the morning. Neither of us has a deadline to meet, you know."

"Thank God," she replied with a light laugh. "I must admit, it has been nice to have a vacation. My first in two and a half years, I might add. Thanks for inviting me, and thank you for coming down for the weekend. It's been—well, simply wonderful, Clee. You're so good to me, such a wonderful friend."

She touched his arm resting along the edge of the pool, and he caught hold of her hand, held it tightly. Then before he could stop himself he pulled her to him and kissed her on the mouth.

At first he met resistance, then she hesitantly responded, her body slackening and her mouth becoming soft under his. But abruptly she pulled away and stared long and hard at him.

He could not read her expression; it baffled him. He said rapidly, taking her hand again, "Don't pull away, Nicky. Since Beijing you've become very special to me. Look, it's different now. I don't know exactly what to say."

She made no comment to this; freeing her hand, she swam away toward the far end of the pool.

He followed her, and, getting out of the pool, went to where she stood near the chaises under the trees.

Her head was turned away from him and she was shivering in the light breeze.

He reached for one of the large beach towels on a chaise and wrapped her in it. "You're cold," he said. "Nicky."

She swung her head finally and looked directly at him, but still she did not speak.

They stood motionless, staring at each other, their eyes locked in an intense gaze that neither of them was able to break.

It seemed to Clee that her bright blue eyes were impaling his, and inwardly he flinched, yet he could not look away. And oh God, how he wanted her. He wanted to take her in his arms, to make love to her. He understood something else: he wanted to possess her completely, and be possessed by her. And yet he was unable to make a move in her direction, was momentarily paralyzed; his breath felt strangled in his throat.

She spoke first, at last breaking the silence. She said, "Clee . . . Oh, *Clee . . .*" And then she paused as though she were afraid to finish her thought.

Long afterward he would remember the inflection in her voice quite precisely, would recall the way she had said his name at that exact moment, for it was the inflection that had told him everything. Longing had been implicit in her tone.

"Nicky darling," he said in a voice thickened by desire, and he moved swiftly toward her, even as she rushed forward into his arms.

He wrapped his arms around her, held her tightly. He could feel her heart hammering against his chest, in time with his own. He kissed her deeply, passionately, almost roughly, the way he wanted to kiss her, and she responded with ardor, her lips pliable, yielding, as he moved his tongue against them. Instantly they parted slightly, and he slid his tongue inside her mouth, and their tongues touched, lay still, touched again.

Her hands were on the nape of his neck

and in his hair, then moved onto his shoulders and his back. He loved the feel of her fingers, so strong and supple, on his skin. Pulling her even closer, he slid his hands down her back, molding her body to his body, fitting her into him.

Nicky pressed herself closer, as filled with desire for Clee as he was for her. She was dizzy, her legs were weak, and her whole body trembled as she leaned against him, clinging to him. Clee was tremendously aroused. He brought his mouth to the hollow in her neck, kissed it tenderly, slipped the beach towel off her shoulder, let his mouth linger there, covering her with tender kisses.

Eventually he relaxed his hold on her, took her face between his hands and looked down into her eyes. In the dusky light he saw a look of intense yearning reflected on her face, longing for him. He knew then that she felt the same as he did, and this inflamed him more.

Taking her by the hand, he led her to the chaise. Gently he eased her down onto it and then sat on the edge. Leaning over her, he covered her mouth with his, all the while fumbling with the towel and then the top of her bikini. Suddenly the fastening on the back came loose and he pulled the top away so that her breasts broke free. Cupping them between his hands, he kissed first one and then the other.

"Clee."

Immediately he stopped what he was doing and looked at her. "Nicky?"

"I'm afraid," she said in a voice so low he could hardly hear it.

"Of me?"

"No."

"Of yourself?" he asked, speaking as softly as she had, and reaching out he gently touched her cheek with his fingertips.

"I'm afraid of—of—of making love. It's been so long," she whispered.

"It'll be all right." As he spoke he took her in his arms. "Trust me," he said against her hair. "Trust me."

Releasing her, Clee stood up and offered her both his hands. Taking hold of them, she looked up at him questioningly as he pulled her to her feet.

"Over there," he said, and he nodded toward the copse.

Clee spread the towels on the grass and they slipped out of their swimsuits and lay down together under the trees.

Nicky was shaking inside, filled with desire for him, but a desire tinged with fear—fear of disappointing him, of failing him, she realized that now. She wished she were not so tense, and she endeavored to relax her taut body. She turned her head to look at him, touching his face with one hand, her eyes focused on his.

Clee smiled, again hoping to put her at ease. It was the same lopsided boyish smile he had smiled at her the first time they had met, in the bar of the Commodore in West Beirut, and one she knew so well by now, but tonight it tugged at her heart. A rush of desire for him rose up in her. A curious thought struck her. Had she been emotionally involved with Clee for the past two years without knowing it? Was *he* the reason no other man had interested her in all that time?

Clee was pushing himself up on one elbow, bending over her body, fondling her breasts. He brought his mouth to one of them, kissing the nipple, and instantly it came erect under his lips. He moved his mouth to the other one, kissing it in exactly the same way. A small moan came from deep in Nicky's throat, and she put her arms loosely around him, her fingers slowly trailing down over his shoulder blades until they came to rest in the small of his back.

After a few seconds Clee raised his head, kissed her passionately on the lips, devouring her with his mouth and his tongue, and all the while he continued to caress her breasts. Eventually his hands wandered down onto her flat stomach and her thighs, touching and stroking her silky skin until the tension in her dissipated.

Soon her body was limp, pliable to his touch. He moved his own body so that his head rested on her stomach, and he kissed it as his hands fluttered down onto her inner thighs. Lightly, gently, his fingers caressed, explored, probed, until she opened herself up to his hands and his mouth as a flower opens under warming sunlight. As he savored the velvet texture of her he was consumed by a raging desire. It took all his self-control not to take her immediately.

Nicky looked down at Clee and put her hands on his shoulders; she closed her eyes again, luxuriating in the feel of his strong yet sensitive hands on her body. Her senses were reeling. They had tumbled into each other's arms so unexpectedly, so suddenly she was still shaken. And yet she knew their coming together was right; she felt this deep within herself. He was arousing her fully now, bringing her to the edge of ecstasy, his tongue and his fingers centered on the core of her. Overwhelmed by their mutual sensuality, the erotic feelings he engendered in her, she gave herself up to him completely. She was transported, floating, as he continued to touch and kiss her. And he did so with such sureness and expertise, he might have been making love to her in this way for aeons.

He moved her legs, pushing her knees into a bent position, and then, slipping his hands under her buttocks, brought his mouth to her again, touching her so lightly she could scarcely feel it. An exquisite sensation shot through her and she began to quiver. "Oh, Clee, don't stop, please don't stop," she whispered.

Looking up, he bent over her again and his mouth and hands went on loving her with sensitivity and delicacy, and consummate skill.

Clee was so inflamed by Nicky's mounting excitement he thought he would explode, and he ached to be inside her with every fiber of his being. But she had made it clear to him that she had been celibate for a long time, and he wanted to give her pleasure, to ensure she was totally relaxed and ready for him by bringing her to fulfillment first.

She cried his name again, and her quivering increased, and she gripped his shoulders harder. Her desire for him was acting as an extraordinary aphrodisiac, and he had to bring her to a climax quickly now so that he could take her to him, possess her finally and give himself to her.

The very moment her quivering reached a deep spasm he lifted himself onto her and went into her with a power and force that made both of them gasp.

Nicky clung to him, wrapping her legs around his back, and cried out, "Clee, oh Clee, oh my God," and he brought his mouth down hard on hers and they began to move in unison, instantly finding their own rhythm.

Their passion mounted. He moved against her harder, more urgently, thrust himself deeper inside her, and Nicky was as unrestrained as he, her body arching up to his. And she cleaved to him.

Suddenly Clee stopped abruptly, pushed himself up on his hands and gazed down at her.

Nicky opened her eyes, and returned his gaze. Her look was questioning.

"You're beautiful, Nicky."

"Oh, Clee . . ."

He held her with his eyes, staring deeply into hers, and just as they had been mesmerized by each other a short while earlier, so they were again. Their eyes locked, held fast; they looked deeper and deeper, as if peering into each other's heart and mind and soul.

Clee thought: This isn't only sexual desire, though God knows it's stronger with her than I've ever known it to be with anyone else. I love her. That's what this is all about. I *love* Nicky. I've loved her since Beijing.

As Nicky looked up into Clee's dark and brilliant eyes, her scrutiny fixed, intense and probing, Nicky began to understanding something: she had been waiting for him to come to her as a lover for months, even though she had not realized it until this moment. With a little spurt of surprise, she thought, I'm free of Charles at last. Perhaps I'll be able to love again—perhaps I'll fall in love with Cleeland Donovan.

Clee began to move again, slowly at first, loving her with his eyes. She opened her arms to him, and he devoured her mouth and tongue with his own once more, and she moved against him, picked up his rhythm. He increased his speed, and so did she, matching him all the way.

A sudden intense heat flooded up from her thighs to suffuse her whole being, and she clung to him tighter, her hands digging into his shoulders, his name on her lips. Clee felt her warmth enveloping him, and he plunged deeper into her, moving faster and faster. He murmured, "Come to me, my love, become part of me." And she did, and as he flowed into her they were truly joined, became one.

He called her name, heard her shouting his, and they soared upward together, higher and higher, until he was weightless and floating in a bright blue sky the color of her eyes. Floating into infinity, holding her in his arms as if to never let her go. He never would. She was his love. His only love. There had never been anyone like her before; there would never be again. She was meant for him, just as he was meant for her, just as this was meant to be.

He opened his eyes at last and looked down at her.

In this bosky corner of the garden the light was dim. But several small spotlights were hidden in the leafy bower above their heads, and so he could see her face. It was flushed and filled with happiness. Her eyes were wide, and very, very blue as they looked back at him unblinkingly, and he noticed they held an expression he had never seen in them before. Was it adoration? Did she feel the same way he did? She had to—this joining had not been one-sided.

"Nicky," he began, but before he could say another word she reached up and put her fingertips on his mouth.

"Don't say anything, Clee."

"But, Nicky, I—"

"Sssh," she said and pulled his face down

to hers. She kissed him softly, wrapped her arms around him and held him close to her. And she felt a little more at peace with herself—for the first time since Charles Devereaux had vacated her life.

13

"*Eh, voilà, mademoiselle!* Your American picnic," Clee said, placing the large wooden tray on the coffee table in the middle of the library. With a wry smile, he added, "I'm afraid this was the best I could do."

Nicky jumped up off the sofa, went over to the low table and sat down on the large cushions Clee had arranged on the floor earlier. She scanned the food he had prepared and began to laugh.

"Oh, Clee, how marvelous! You've managed to find some of my real favorites. Chunky peanut butter, *Skippy,* no less. I love that brand. And grape jelly to go with it. Tuna-salad sandwiches, and bacon, lettuce

and tomato on rye. Pickled cucumbers. Hell-
mann's mayonnaise. Where did you get all
this? Especially the rye bread?"

Clee's mouth twitched with laughter. "The
rye came out of the freezer earlier this evening. My sisters bring it when they come to
stay. They also bring loads of other American things for me, stuff I can't always find in
France. Amélie puts some of it in the freezer,
such as the rye bread and the bags of ba-
gels, and the rest goes in the pantry. Now"—
he picked up a can of Diet Coke, pulled the
tab, and went on—"how about one of these
to wash it all down?"

"I'd love it, and come and sit over here
with me," she said, patting the cushion next
to her.

"I will in a minute. Let me put the video in
first." Stepping over to the bookcase, he
continued, "Which movie did you choose in
the end?"

"It's called *Somewhere I'll Find You,* with
Clark Gable and Lana Turner playing foreign
correspondents who . . . get involved with
each other on a foreign assignment."

"Aha!" he exclaimed. A wide grin spread
across his face. "How appropriate. I couldn't
have chosen better myself."

The minute the film started rolling, Clee
sat down on the cushions, leaned over and

kissed the tip of her nose, then picked up a tuna-salad sandwich and settled back to watch.

They laughed a lot during the film. It had been made in 1942 and was somewhat unrealistic. It had a sweetness, an innocence about it, and this made it seem dated to the two tough news veterans accustomed to difficult, often harrowing foreign assignments.

"Hey, Nick, this is really sappy," Clee muttered at one moment, looking at her from the corner of his eye.

"I know. A lot of old movies are."

"Not *Casablanca,* that's held up pretty well."

"You're right, but occasionally this one does have a ring of truth to it, especially when Gable's on the screen." The legendary star was Nicky's favorite, and a few seconds later, when Gable said, "I don't print anything until I've heard it twice and seen it three times," Nicky said, "That's going to be *my* motto from now on!"

He rolled his eyes to the ceiling in mock horror.

"Wait a minute," Nicky said swiftly, "you've got to admit Gable plays a terrific newspaperman, with just the right amount of dash and panache. And he *is* gorgeous."

"True, true." Clee turned her face to his

and kissed her lightly on the mouth. "And so are you," he said softly.

When the movie was over, Clee began stacking the plates and glasses on the tray. "Do you want to watch another film, or shall we go downstairs and have coffee on the terrace?"

"Coffee on the terrace sounds great," Nicky answered, and followed him out.

They sat at the kitchen table waiting for the coffee to brew, and as Clee peeled an apple and offered pieces to her he said, "I'm coming to New York around the middle of July. I have to go to Washington to photograph the president and Mrs. Bush for *Life.* After that I'll be in New York for them until early August. Is there any chance of working on the book together then, do you think?"

"Yes, of course, I'd love to, and I know I'll be there, providing a war doesn't break out somewhere—"

"In which case," Clee interjected, "we'll be covering it together."

Nicky nodded, "I guess so. Anyway, Arch and I will be working on another special during July and August, so I'll probably be writing the script and doing the preparation. But that doesn't prevent me from starting on the book. Do you have a title yet?"

"No, I don't, and any and all suggestions

will be gratefully accepted. That coffee smells great, let's get some and go outside."

They sat on the terrace together, not talking, enjoying the peace and beauty of their surroundings. It was well past midnight. The great arch of the sky was like inky black velvet scattered with tiny crystal beads, and there was a full moon. The breeze ruffled the trees and wafted the scent of honeysuckle toward them.

Clee and Nicky had long understood that conversation was not always necessary, and the silence between them tonight was as companionable as it usually was. Though their relationship had changed radically—and irrevocably—in the space of only a few hours they were completely at ease with each other. Perhaps more than ever, in fact.

Taking her hand at one moment, Clee said in the quietest voice, "We're good together, Nicky, and good for each other. You know that, don't you?"

"Yes, I do," she responded and leaned her head against his shoulder, feeling comfortable, protected with him.

Clee put his arm around her, held her close, and he could not help wondering what would happen to them, where tonight would lead. He had no idea. All he knew for certain was that he had saved her life in Beijing and in so doing had fallen in love with her. Or perhaps he had loved her for a long time before that but had only realized it when he had almost lost her. But no matter—tonight he had become her lover and that was good enough for him right now.

For her part, Nicky was marveling at the way they had come together so naturally— and marveling at herself as well. She had not made love to a man since Charles Deve- reaux had ended their relationship. During the past two years she had built up so many barriers; Clee had made them all come tum- bling down. She was glad she had been with Clee. He had made everything seem so easy and simple, and he had aroused such pas- sion in her she had amazed herself. She smiled in the darkness. Clee had made her feel like a woman again.

Much later, when they were in the kitchen stacking the dishwasher, Clee said, "How long are you staying here with me, Nicky?"

She shrugged lightly, and said, "As long as you'll have me."

"All this week, then," he replied, looking pleased.

"Oh, Clee, I forgot for a minute—I've got to be back in Manhattan a week from to-night, in order to go to work at the network on Monday morning."

"*Oh.*" He looked crushed, but instantly brightened and said, "Tell you what, we'll fly to Paris on Thursday night. You can stay with me at my apartment, and I'll put you on the Concorde on Sunday morning. Does that idea appeal to you?"

"Yes, it does."

"And *you* certainly appeal to *me.*" Putting down the plate he was holding and walking over to her, he took her in his arms. "I don't know whether it's occurred to you yet, but you and I have wasted a lot of time."

"Two years, if you want to be exact."

"I aim to make up for it."

"You do?"

"You bet." Clee covered her mouth with his for a long voluptuous kiss, and then he took her hand in his and led her upstairs to his bedroom.

14

Holding hands, they walked slowly down the cours Mirabeau, the main avenue in the ancient university town of Aix-enProvence.

Nicky glanced around, and she could not help thinking that this was one of the most beautiful boulevards she had ever seen. Long and wide, it had four rows of tall, stately plane trees running down the middle of it, the branches of which intertwined overhead to form an immense, elongated arch. Nicky felt as though she and Clee were walking down a pale green tunnel made entirely of leaves. It seemed endless, since it stretched a good five hundred yards or so, and placed at intervals down the center between the trees were three nineteenth-century fountains that sprayed arcs of crystal-clear water up into the diffused morning sunlight. The sunny side of the cours was lined with sprawling cafés; standing in the shade on the other side were handsome and ancient buildings, many of them private residences.

"Clee, it's extraordinary, and so lovely," Nicky exclaimed, turning to him, her face a picture of delight.

"Isn't it just. I knew you'd be impressed, everyone is. And in my opinion this is the most beautiful main street in any city anywhere in the world. There's a certain elegance about it—the interplay of the architecture, the trees, the fountains, and the way the space has been so brilliantly arranged, and it's always at its best in the spring and summer." He paused, gave her a smile and said, "Now, let's pick a café and have coffee, before we plunge into the old town behind the cours so that you can visit some of the local *ateliers.*"

"You don't really have to come shopping with me," she said quickly. "Perhaps you'd prefer to browse around a bookstore while I pick up a few gifts."

"Nope, I'm coming with you." He tightened his grip on her hand and glanced down at her, the boyish smile playing around his mouth. "I'm not letting you out of my sight for the next three days. I've got to make the most of you, honeybunch."

Nicky laughed. "I haven't heard that term of endearment for years. My mother used to call me honeybunch when I was little."

"Isn't that odd, so did mine," Clee said, and led her toward a lively-looking café close to the Fontaine de la Rotonde, the huge fountain that dominated the western entrance to the boulevard.

Although the café terrace was full of attractive young people, pretty girls and handsome young men who were obviously university students, there were several empty tables. A couple of these were close to the windows in the shade of an awning and slightly removed from the busy sidewalk.

Scanning the area, Clee chose one of the tables near the café's windows, and as they sat down he said, "We can cool off here and watch the world go by at the same time. I love French cafés, they're so convivial, yet they can also be quite private in a certain way." Taking off his sunglasses, he drew close to her and kissed her lightly on the lips. "See what I mean?"

"Yes." She smiled, looking into his eyes.

A waiter was with them almost immediately and Clee ordered *café au lait* for them both, and once they were alone again he relaxed in his chair and turned to face her. "I like most of the titles you wrote down for me last night, but my favorite is 'Children of the Beijing Spring.' I'd love to use that for our book, Nick."

"I'm flattered!" Her pleasure was evident, and she added, "It happens to be my favorite, too."

He leaned across the table and kissed her on the lips again. "Now that we have a title, we're in business, babe."

"With those superb photographs you took, you were always in business, Clee. No question about that, and my text is of secondary importance. After all, it *is* a picture book."

"True. On the other hand, the introduction is pretty damned important—not only to underscore my pictures but to explain China, the politics, the events leading up to the Tiananmen demonstrations, and the massacre. Few people understand how it all came about."

"Yes, I'm well aware of that, and on the plane on Sunday I'll make some notes. I think I'll have a bit of reading to do before I start writing the introduction. Incidentally, I've been thinking—" She broke off as the waiter arrived with the coffee.

"*Merci,*" she and Clee said almost in unison, and then she went on, "What I started to say is that I've been thinking about our working arrangements, and it occurred to me that you might like to spend a couple of weekends in New Milford, at my parents' place, when you're in New York later this month. A few years ago my father built a studio across the lawn from the main house, and I think it's a terrific place to work. We could really spread out there—you know, arrange the pictures consecutively, and in an orderly fashion, even do a pagination. We could leave everything laid out there on card tables, no one would touch it during the week."

"It sounds great, but what about your parents? Don't they use the studio to write in?"

Nicky shook her head and began to laugh. "When Dad built the studio it was actually for my mother, his gift to her. He thought she would enjoy working there. It's airy, spacious, quiet and very peaceful."

"And didn't she?"

"No. I think perhaps it was *too* peaceful, if you want to know the truth. She loved it for only about a month. Then she moved back into the house, into the small room that opens off their bedroom. She told Dad she felt more comfortable writing in a room she'd been using for years. That's true I'm sure, but knowing my mother, she also likes being in the house, in the center of all of that swirling activity. I suppose it is lonely enough writing long, complicated books without being isolated across the garden, away from my father, the housekeeper, the telephones and a busy household."

"Doesn't your father use the studio?"

"Not very often. I suspect he likes being close to my mother, and also in the middle of all that activity just as much as she does. So he pushes his pen, or rather his word processor, in the library, which is where he has always written his column—that way, he's close to the kitchen, can pop in for a cup of tea or coffee and chat with Annie, the housekeeper, or Bert, the gardener. Anyway, the point is we could easily set up shop there, if you want to."

"Will your parents mind?"

"Of course not! Anyway, since meeting you in Paris last year they've been rather taken with you."

"Is their daughter?"

Nicky took off her sunglasses and gave him a long penetrating look. She asked, somewhat coyly, "Is their daughter what?"

"Taken with me?"

"Oh, yes."

"She'd better be."

"She is—definitely—absolutely—taken with Cleeland Donovan."

Clee bent closer to her across the zinc-topped table and took her hand in his. "These last few days have been so wonderful, Nick. It's never been quite like this before, for me. There's something I want to say—about you and me—the way I feel about you, darling, and—"

"Please don't say anything, Clee," she interrupted, her voice as low as his had been. "Please, not now, not yet." She gently extricated her hand and sat back in her chair, looking solemn.

"But why not?" he asked, perplexed.

Nicky was silent for a moment, then said, "I want this, want *us,* to go slowly. . . . I don't want you— No, I don't want *either* of us to say anything now that we might regret—that we might change our minds about later. I want you to be really sure before you say anything at all to me. And *I* want to be sure, too. Sure about what *I* really feel for you."

"But I *am* sure," he began and stopped, understanding that she was afraid of commitments because of the fiasco of her engagement. "I see what you mean, Nicky, and you're right, of course you are. I know how much Charles Devereaux hurt you." The words slipped out before he could stop them. He could have bitten off his tongue, and he stared at her in confusion, appalled at himself.

She gaped at him, her face drained of its vivacity. Instantly it became terribly still, and closed. She did not say a word, merely glanced away.

Clee reached for her hand again, held her fingers tightly in his, wondering how to make amends. He was a clumsy fool and he had obviously upset her. She did not have to utter one word for him to recognize that. He had read it on her face the very second he had spoken.

"Look at me, Nick."

Gradually she turned her head, brought her gaze to meet his.

"I'm sorry," he apologized, "really sorry. I shouldn't have mentioned his name."

"It's all right," Nicky replied after a few seconds and forced herself to smile. "Honestly, it is. I just don't like to talk about him. Whenever I do, unpleasant memories inevitably get stirred up. Anyway, talking about him serves no purpose. He was the past. I prefer to think of the future."

"I couldn't agree more." He took a deep breath, wanting this awkward moment to pass as quickly as possible.

"Clee, you look upset. Please don't be. It

was only natural for you to mention Charles. After all, we *were* engaged."

"I'm pretty dumb though, at times."

"*I* don't think you are." The dark expression that had been clouding her lovely eyes disappeared, and she smiled at him, then picked up her cup and took a sip. "The coffee's gone cold," she remarked evenly. "Shall we order two more *hot* ones?"

Clee nodded, motioned to the waiter and gave the order. Then he said to her, "You told me you wanted to get your mother some Provençal fabric. I know just the right shop in the old town. They'll even send it back to the States for you."

"Wonderful."

Nicky began to tell him about the gifts she wanted to buy and for whom, and much to his relief her voice sounded normal again, and he relaxed.

A short while later they left the café, wandered off into the old town situated behind the cours Mirabeau. They walked through the tiny, narrow streets, stopping to look in the windows of the smart new boutiques as well as the much older establishments selling liqueurs, cheeses, local produce, crafts and fanciful Provençal creations.

Clee took her into the *atelier* Fouque, where *santons* were made. These little figures of local peasants, created from clay or dough and beautifully painted in bright colors, were amazingly lifelike, and Nicky purchased a whole collection of them for her father. After Clee had introduced her to Paul Fouque, one of the great masters of *santon* making, they stood and watched him at work for fifteen minutes before heading to the confectionery to buy *calissons.* This locally made almond-paste sweet was Amélie's favorite, according to Clee, and Nicky wanted to give her a box of it, along with the silk scarf she had bought for her the day before, when Clee had taken her to Saint-Rémy.

A short while later they walked down to the Souleiado shop. Here Nicky selected several bolts of beautiful fabrics in the colorful traditional patterns of Provence, and arranged for these to be shipped to her mother in New York. Then she picked out several address books covered in similar fabrics for girlfriends, and these she took with her, as well as various aprons and other small items.

They continued to meander through the cobbled streets, stepping into all kinds of little shops, sometimes merely to look around and savor the atmosphere. In one shop, Nicky made a few purchases of lavender essence, bags of lavender, and bags of Herbes de Provence.

When the herbs were being wrapped, she turned to Clee and grinned. "You do know I can buy all of this stuff in New York, don't you? At Bloomingdale's, actually. And exactly the same products, too. But it's not quite the same as bringing it from here."

"No, it isn't," he agreed, accepting the shopping bag from the proprietor and guiding her out of the shop. "Come on, I want to show you the place d'Albertas, it's very quaint, and then we'd better be getting back to the farm for lunch."

"Oh God, not another meal," she groaned, and grimaced through her laughter.

Holding her arm, Clee led her toward the ancient square. "Speaking of meals, I told Amélie to make a very light lunch, just a green salad, cold chicken and fruit. I'm taking you somewhere very special for dinner tonight."

"Where?" She looked at him quickly.

"It's quite a famous restaurant, people go there from all over the world, and it's elegant. So if you didn't bring a dress, Nicky, we'd better go and buy one now. There are several chic boutiques around here."

"It's all right, Clee, I packed a couple of silk dresses. And my pearls, just in case. So you can take me anywhere."

. . .

Clee's bedroom was shady and pleasant, the bright afternoon sunlight outside blocked by the wooden shutters, the warm air cooled by the ceiling fan.

They were lying close together on the bed, bodies touching, resting now after their frantic lovemaking. Clee had brought her here after lunch, to rest, he had said, but within minutes the inevitable had happened. Clee had started to kiss her and touch her, and she had responded ardently, as always instantly on fire whenever she felt his hands on her in that particular way. They had undressed each other, and once they were naked he had taken her to him swiftly, and once more their wild ecstasy had begun.

It now struck Nicky how odd it was that they had known each other for two years and had never in that time thought of making love. But in the last few days they hadn't been able to get enough of each other, were unable to keep their hands off each other when they were alone.

Nicky moved her head slightly on the pillow to look at him. Clee was stretched out on his back, as she was. His eyes were closed, his thick dark lashes resting lightly on his bronzed cheeks. He took the sun well, had acquired a tan since he had been at the farm. His whole body was a golden brown, except for the white triangle below his stomach that had been covered by his swimming trunks.

In repose his face had a sweet gentleness to it, and his mouth, so wide and generous, was endearing. She had a sudden impulse to reach out and touch his mouth, but refrained, not wishing to awaken him.

Cleeland Donovan. She said his name to herself. He was a lovely man, a decent man, who did not have one bad bone in his body. He was honest and just and kind and fair. And so very trustworthy. Her mother had a phrase for people who were genuinely admirable. True-blue, she called them. Cleeland Donovan was definitely true-blue.

He was her closest and dearest friend and she had loved him like a brother right from the beginning of their friendship. But now he was her lover. They were sexually involved with each other, and obviously well on the way to becoming emotionally entangled. Perhaps they already were. She wasn't sure what would happen, what would become of them, how long they would be together in this way. But she did know she could trust him implicitly. With her life, as he had proved in Beijing. He was that type of man, courageous and dependable and strong. She felt safe with Clee. She always had, right from the beginning. He gave her a sense of being cared for, of being completely protected.

Clee opened his eyes quite suddenly and caught her studying him. He reached for her and, pulling her into his arms, nuzzled his face in her neck. He whispered against her ear, "You had such a pensive look on your face when I opened my eyes—what were you thinking about?"

"You, actually."

"Ah, I see. And what were you thinking about me?"

"I decided you were—true-blue. That's what my mother calls people she admires."

She felt him smile against her neck.

He said, "Is that a roundabout way of telling me you admire me?" Not waiting for her answer, he added, "I wish you felt something more than admiration."

"I do," she protested, "I feel a lot of things—" She broke off, pulled away and looked into his dark brown eyes, which were dancing with mischief. "Oh, you! You!" she cried, putting her hand against his chest, making a weak attempt to push him away. "You were trying to trap me into saying something I may later regret."

"Who, me? *Never.*" He grinned at her, and brought her back into the circle of his arms. Stroking her hair gently, he then began to smooth his hands down over her back, and found her mouth with his, devoured it, and ever so slowly he began to make love to her.

Instantly Nicky was aflame, hungry for him even though they had made love only a couple of hours ago. She ached to feel the hardness of him inside her, ached to be joined to him, to be part of him.

As if he could read her mind, he was suddenly on top of her, bracing his hands on either side of her body, pushing himself up above her, looking down into her face.

She reached up to touch him, let her fingers trace a delicate line across his mouth, her eyes focused on his, and intently so.

He returned her glaze unblinkingly, and entered her with that same force he had used the first night they had made love in the garden, and it brought a cry of surprise and pain to her lips. He paid no attention, worked against her harder and harder, and the pain eased and she was opening up to him, flowing to him. She wrapped her arms and legs around his body, binding him to her, her skin against his skin, her breath mingling with his breath.

Clee kissed her hard, almost with violence, and then unexpectedly he arched back and away from her, groaning as if in anguish. "I love you, Nicky," he cried. "I love you." She felt him flowing into her as she had flowed into him only a split second before, and at this moment she thought: And I am falling in love with you. But she was unable to say this, and so remained silent, holding him close when he collapsed against her and buried his face in her hair.

15

Clee paused in the doorway of the library and leaned against the doorjamb, staring at Nicky.

"Hi," she said, smiling, and walked toward him.

The dress she wore had a round neck and no sleeves; it was cut loose and full, and fell in folds from ruching on the shoulders. Its color was a delphinium blue that exactly matched her marvelous eyes, and as she moved forward the light silk swirled around her like a cloud. The pearls encircling her throat in a choker and the matching studs on her ears looked unusually luminous against her tan, and with her golden skin, golden hair and brilliant eyes Clee thought there was a special kind of sheen about her tonight.

When she stood in front of him he saw, on closer inspection, that she had the inner glow of a woman who has recently been well and truly loved, and who has loved in return. There was a subtle sexuality about her—a rosy bloom on her skin, a ripeness around her mouth, and a wise and knowing expression in her eyes. It was an unmistakable look, and one that a man always recognizes.

"You look gorgeous, Nicky," he said, taking hold of her bare arm possessively, kissing her lightly on the cheek.

"You don't look so bad yourself," she responded, eyeing him appraisingly, noting the excellent cut of his cream sports jacket, the fineness of the cream voile shirt that set off his tan and dark coloring, the expensive wine silk tie, the well-tailored black linen slacks and highly polished black loafers. After giving him another admiring glance, she added, "Good enough to eat, in fact."

"We'll leave that for later," he quipped, breaking into a chuckle. Moving her forward toward the landing, he went on, "We'd better be on our way. I had a tough time getting a table, and I don't want to lose it."

A few minutes later Clee was pulling his car out of the courtyard and rolling down the driveway.

Nicky asked him, "Where are we going? You've been so mysterious."

"Have I? I didn't mean to be." He glanced at her out of the corner of his eye, then brought his gaze back to the road to concentrate on his driving. Then he explained, "We're going to Les Baux, a town not far from here, just beyond Saint-Rémy. The restaurant is called L'Oustau de Baumanière. It's a charming place and the food is excellent. And I *know,* before you say it again for the umpteenth time, you've had enough meals to last you a lifetime. But you don't have to eat very much, Nick, just a taste. And in any case, I really wanted to take you there because it's a unique spot, and besides, tonight's a celebration."

"What are we celebrating?" She turned to look at him, wedging herself in the corner of the seat, resting her shoulder against the car window.

"We're celebrating our book—which we now have a title for. And a few other things."

"Such as what?"

"I'll tell you later."

Clee turned on the tape player and the car was instantly flooded with Gershwin's *Rhapsody in Blue.* They drove in silence for a long while, listening to the music, and as usual they were at ease with each other whether they spoke or not.

But at one moment, as they were passing through Saint-Rémy, Nicky suddenly said, "Les Baux rings a bell—I think my mother had several references to it in one of her books. But I can't remember *exactly* why, or which book, for that matter."

"Les Baux is very old," Clee told her. "It's a feudal city that's been around for hundreds of years, and it sits on rocky outcroppings high above some of the deep valleys in this region. It's mostly ruins now, a sort of ghost town in a sense. Still, it's quite imposing in its aerie, and it was famous in the Middle Ages, from the eleventh to the fifteenth centuries, when the Lords of Baux ruled the area. They were rather bloody and violent, ferocious men, rough, and yet they gave their patronage to the troubadours—"

"Of course!" Nicky exclaimed. "That's it! *Troubadours.* Now I remember. My mother wrote about Les Baux in her book on Eleanor of Aquitaine, when she touched on Eleanor's patronage of Bernard de Ventadour, one of the most famous troubadours of all. It was at Les Baux that respect for the lady and the ritual of worshiping her beauty began. The first troubadours started writing, singing and playing their lutes there."

"Exactly," Clee responded, "and the Baux fortress in its heyday and at the height of its great splendor was renowned for its Court of Love and chivalry toward women."

"I'm so glad we're going there, Clee. My mother will be fascinated to hear all about it when I get back to New York."

"I'm not planning to take you up to the fortress and the ruins tonight," Clee said quickly, glancing at her askance. "It's far too complicated, not to mention a strenuous climb. You'd never make it in those high heels."

Nicky laughed. "That's all right, I don't feel much like sightseeing, or climbing to great heights this evening."

Soon Clee was pulling up outside L'Oustau de Baumanière, which was set under the white stone cliffs below the ancient town of Les Baux.

After parking the car, he ushered Nicky into the famous restaurant, where they were greeted pleasantly by the maître d', who obviously knew Clee, and who suggested they have an *apéritif* outside on the terrace.

Ten minutes later Clee lifted his flute of champagne, touched it to hers and said, "Here's to you, Nicky darling."

"And to you, Clee." She smiled at him over the rim of her glass, and after taking a sip of the cold sparkling wine, she said, "Now, tell me what else we're celebrating, as well as the book."

He reached for her hand resting on the table, and placed his over it. "We're celebrating being alive, being together, being lucky enough to have lived our lives the way we've wanted to live them—at least so far. And most important, we're celebrating being lovers as well as friends."

"Oh, Clee, those are lovely things to say and to celebrate, and we *are* lucky, aren't we. Most people have so little, really."

"Sadly, that's true."

"And thank you for bringing me here tonight." She looked around her again—the terrace was ablaze with flowers, the gardens were lushly green, the varied species of trees growing under the white stone cliffs were in full bloom. She said, "This is such a beautiful place, Clee. . . ." Sitting back in her chair, she eyed him carefully. "And what with all its ancient symbolism to do with the troubadours and their songs of love, I'm beginning to think you're a romantic at heart, however much you might want to disguise that fact."

"I don't, at least not with you, and I think you're right, I am a bit of a romantic," he admitted, giving her a half smile. Suddenly he became more serious and he glanced down into his drink, looking reflective.

The change in him was almost imperceptible, but Nicky noticed it, and leaning forward she asked, "What is it? Is something wrong?"

"No, no, of course not," he answered, shaking his head. He gazed at her for a long moment, his eyes riveted on hers. "I said something to you this afternoon, and because it was said at the height of passion, you probably think that I didn't really mean it. But I did, and I do, and I'm going to say it again, even if you don't wish to hear it. . . ." There was a small pause. "I love you, Nicky."

She stared at him. Her eyes were huge in her face and glittering brilliantly. There was no question in her mind that Clee was speaking the truth, being sincere; he didn't know any other way to be. "Clee—" she began, and stopped.

"You don't have to say you love me, Nicky. Maybe you do, maybe you don't. We have plenty of time, you and I, to find out about that. One day you'll tell me how you feel about me—when you know yourself. In the meantime I just wanted to tell *you,* here and now when we're not in bed, that I love you. I have for a long time, without realizing it."

Her lips parted and she looked as if she was about to speak.

Clee shook his head. "Not a word, Nicky, not now. It's not necessary," he said, his smile warm and loving.

"But I want to say something." She hesitated a moment before murmuring, "I have all kinds of feelings for you, Clee, not the least of which is my—my physical passion for you." She was on the verge of telling him that she thought she was falling in love with him, and then changed her mind. Instead, she said, "And I do love you, as my dearest friend. . . ." Her sentence trailed off.

"I know you do." He squeezed her hand. "Don't look so worried."

Nicky laughed. "I didn't realize I did." She sighed lightly. "These past few days have been just—*glorious,* Clee, there's no other way of describing them." A wistful expression flitted across her face. "I'm so sorry they're coming to an end."

"But they're not. You'll be with me tomorrow night in Paris, and on Friday and Saturday, before you leave for the States on Sunday." He stroked her arm lightly, traced little lines up and down with his fingertips. "Three whole days and nights, not counting this evening." Bending into her, he kissed the tip of her nose. "And I'm going to make love to you the entire time—circumstances and surroundings permitting."

16

The interior of the restaurant was as eye-catching as the exterior.

An arched ceiling, stone walls and matching floor gave it a medieval feeling, as did the high-backed chairs covered in blue-and-gold brocade velvet, the Provençal antiques made of dark wood and the lantern-style ceiling lamps. Pretty floral cloths covered the tables, each of which had its own three-branch silver candelabra and bowl of flowers, and there were other huge arrangements of colorful blooms scattered throughout.

Because Clee had ordered the dinner while they were sitting outside on the terrace drinking champagne, they were served their first course almost immediately. Nicky had selected melon, Clee one of the specialties of the house, ravioli with truffles and leeks, which he insisted she try.

"Just one piece," he cajoled, "it's delicious. It'll melt in your mouth." Spearing a square of ravioli with his fork, he leaned over the table and fed it to her. He watched her eat it, his dark eyes full of love for her.

"It *is* wonderful," she said, and dug her spoon into the sweet and succulent Cavaillon melon, which Amélie kept insisting was the best in the whole of France. She decided Amélie was correct.

While they waited for their main course, Clee spoke about the book and the various sequences for the photographs that he had been planning since his return from Beijing. When he had explained everything to her, he leaned back and said, "Well, what do you think?"

"It sounds great, and anyway, you know best, Clee, you really do. You've done these books before, whereas I'm just a novice—besides, I'm only writing the introduction."

"Don't say 'only' in that way, the words are just as important as the pictures."

"Not really. But it's nice of you to say so."

"I was thinking of dedicating the book to Yoyo, and to the memory of Mai. How do you feel about that?"

"Oh, Clee, what a good idea. By the way, I've been wanting to tell you, I'm feeling very positive about Yoyo and have been for the past few days. I feel sure he's going to make it."

"We've got to keep on believing that."

The wine waiter was suddenly at their table, pouring more of the white wine with which they had commenced their meal. "It is an excellent wine, is it not, Monsieur Donovan?" he said.

"Marvelous. And I've had this particular Puligny-Montrachet before. In fact, you recommended it to me the last time I was here."

"I believe I did," the wine waiter responded with a deferential smile.

"I hope you like this wine, Nicky," Clee said. "I ordered it because it has enough power to hold its own with the richest-flavored food, and the *daurade* we both chose has a rich orange sauce. Also, the fish itself is flavored with herbs. Anyway, I think this fruity Chardonnay goes well with it." Clee shifted in his chair, turned the bottle around and studied it for a second. "This is a great label—Clos du Vieux Château, Labouré-Roi, and it comes from the world's capital of

Chardonnay, the village in the Côte d'Or where no other type of grape is grown."

Nicky sat gaping at Clee, taken aback by this unexpected display of knowledge about wine. Finding her voice, she said, "I didn't know you were a connoisseur of wine."

"Good God, I'm not, *I'm* hardly an expert!" He looked across at her, and explained, "I just happen to like good wine, and since I live in France, I've made a point of knowing a bit about some of the best vineyards. After all, I can't always drink that plonk we make at the farm." He frowned. "What is it, Nick? You've got the queerest look on your face."

Nicky shivered slightly and a small nervous laugh escaped. "I had a funny sense of déjà vu, as if I'd heard those exact words before, but of course I haven't."

"We've never discussed wine before."

No, but Charles always talked about wine, she thought, and she picked up her glass and took a sip of the Puligny-Montrachet. "It *is* good, Clee. Delicious."

At this moment the main course arrived, accompanied by several waiters. It was served to them with quite a few elaborate flourishes. Nicky caught Clee's eye and winked at him, and he had to swallow the laughter rising in his throat.

When they were finally left alone to eat the

fish, he grinned at her. "That wink and the expression on your face said more to me than a thousand words ever could."

"Isn't that what I keep telling you?"

"And I don't recall disagreeing with you. How's the *daurade,* do you like it?"

"Yes, thank you, and it's one of my favorites. I often had it as a child when my parents brought me down to the South of France. And fish isn't fattening."

"Will you stick around me if I promise to serve you only bread and water?" he said teasingly, but his eyes were serious.

Nicky noticed the expression in them and nodded. "I'll stick around, Clee—"

Putting down his fork, he said, "What are you doing in September?"

"Why?"

"You told me the network owes you a lot of time off, and I thought that you might like to come back here in September. To the farm—to be with me. I plan to take a break then, and it's lovely here at that time of year. The July and August tourists have split, and it's peaceful."

"I'd love to come, if I've finished the script for my fall special."

"*Try,*" he said.

"I will. I'll work like a madwoman through the rest of July and August."

"Promise?"

"I do."

"Don't think I won't hold you to that, because I will." Clee brought his head closer to hers, and said, sotto voce, "I don't want you to turn around, but there's a woman over there who hasn't been able to take her eyes off you since she sat down. I have a feeling she knows you."

"What makes you think that?"

"Because she looked at you several times, spoke to the man she is with, who eventually turned and glanced at you, very discreetly. And in between her conversation with him and bites of food, she keeps looking at you."

"Perhaps she's seen me on television—perhaps she's a fan. Is she American?"

"I don't think so. She looks English to me. Very English, and so does the guy she's with. Okay, she's talking to a waiter, you can look now."

Nicky twisted in her chair and turned her head slightly. She saw the woman immediately, and her breath caught in her throat; she felt a tightening in her chest. She was about to turn back to Clee when the woman looked across the room.

Two pairs of blue eyes met and held.

The woman smiled then, her whole face lighting up with obvious pleasure.

Nicky smiled in return and lifted her hand in a small gesture of acknowledgment.

The woman spoke to her companion, who swung his head, then swiveled around in his chair and beamed at Nicky.

Nicky glanced at Clee and explained, "They're old friends, I must go and have a quick word with them. Please excuse me."

She got up and walked across the room, and Clee could not help wondering who they were. Nicky's voice had sounded odd, breathless, even strained. She's uptight all of a sudden, he decided, and he sat back in his chair, watching, filled with curiosity.

"Anne, how lovely to see you," Nicky said when she came up to the other table.

"And you, my darling," Anne responded, immediately rising, holding her close for a moment.

The man also got to his feet, and a second later he too was hugging Nicky. "You look wonderful, my dear, more beautiful than ever, if I may say so."

"Oh Philip, thank you, you look pretty ter- rific yourself. And so do you, Anne. Please sit down, both of you, *please.*"

They did so, and Nicky leaned against the back of Anne's chair, bending slightly forward in order to speak to them. "You must think I'm very rude, Anne, I haven't been in touch for ages. I have no excuse, except that I've been traveling the world for my work."

"Darling, don't apologize, I understand perfectly. You lead a frightfully busy life. But I must admit, I have missed your phone calls—quite a lot, actually, Nicky. However, I do realize you have another life to lead now." Anne gazed up into her face, smiling faintly. They exchanged a long look, full of understanding, then Anne said, "Who is that awfully attractive man you're with, Nicky?"

"An old friend—a colleague. Cleeland Donovan."

"The famous war photographer?" Philip asked.

"Yes," Nicky said.

"Brilliant chap. I have several of his books, and I recently saw some of the most remarkable pictures that he took in Beijing."

"In *Paris Match,* perhaps," Nicky said. "We were there together, covering the crackdown."

"Nasty business that. Very tragic outcome," Philip said.

"The bloodshed was unbelievable," Nicky told him, and turned to look at Anne. "Are you here on vacation?"

"Yes. We're staying with friends of Philip's at Tarascon, not far from Saint-Rémy. Are you on holiday, too?"

Nicky nodded. "Clee has a farm between Saint-Rémy and Aix, a lovely old *mas,* and I've just spent a week there, resting. Clee came down for the weekend. We were both pretty done in after China."

"I can well imagine," Anne said. "I do wish you would come over to Tarascon with your friend, for lunch or dinner one day. Will you?"

"It's kind of you to invite us, Anne, but I'm afraid I have to be back in New York on Monday. I'm leaving for Paris tomorrow morning."

"What a pity, it would have been so nice to catch up—" Anne reached out and put her hand on Nicky's arm. "I've missed you."

"Oh, Anne, I know, I've missed you too, and it's all my fault. I've been so . . . neglect-ful."

Anne smiled, but made no comment.

Philip volunteered, "Perhaps we can have coffee later?"

"We've almost finished dinner, Philip, and you and Anne are just starting." Her smile was rueful as she explained, "I have to be up at the crack of dawn tomorrow, to drive to Marseilles. I have an early plane to Paris."

"*C'est dommage,*" he said, sounding as disappointed as Anne had only a moment ago.

Nicky took her leave of them graciously

and returned to the table. "I'm sorry. That took longer than I expected."

"Who are they?"

"English friends."

"Is she related to you?"

"No. Why do you ask that?" Nicky's brows drew together in puzzlement.

"You look alike. Same blond hair, blue eyes, and there's even a facial resemblance."

"Oh, really?" Nicky said quickly, dismissing the idea.

"Are they here on vacation?"

Nicky nodded. "They're staying with friends in Tarascon."

"A lot of English people have homes down here these days, and smart Parisians as well. Provence has become very popular. I hope it's not going to get taken over by the rich and the chic."

"I know what you mean," Nicky said. "That could really spoil it."

Clee expected Nicky to say more about her friends, but she made no further comment about them and merely sipped her wine in silence. Eventually he said, "Would you like dessert? That's the one thing I didn't order when we were out on the terrace. *Crêpes* are one of their specialties."

"No, thanks. Just coffee, Clee, please."

"I guess I'll have the same." Clee ordered for them both, and then sat studying Nicky for a few minutes. Without understanding what exactly it was, he knew there was now something different about her. On the surface her demeanor was the same as it had been all evening. Yet there had been a subtle, indefinable change in her.

Convinced that it had something to do with the English couple, he said, "The woman was very affectionate with you, Nicky. Obviously she's extremely fond of you."

"Yes, she is."

"Who are they? I mean, what are their names?"

"Philip and Anne."

"What does he do?"

"He's in Whitehall. You know, with the British Foreign Office. He has some important job, but I don't know exactly what it is."

"How do you know them?" he probed.

"Through my parents, I met them through my parents. My father's known Philip for a number of years. But why are you so interested in them, Clee?"

He shrugged. "I'm not sure, except that you and she have a look of each other, and she was very loving with you. And when you were talking to her I noticed that you appeared to care, and quite deeply, for her."

"I do, in my own way."

The coffee was served, and the wine waiter came back and asked if they wished to have cognac or any other after-dinner drink. Nicky shook her head.

"No, thank you," Clee said.

Once they were alone, Nicky leaned into Clee. "I haven't told you about my fall special," she said. "I decided to call it 'Decade of Destruction,' a title Arch wasn't completely sold on, to tell you the truth. But I'm going to fight like hell for it. It's perfect for my show."

"What's the subject?" Clee asked, intrigued. "As if I didn't know. The last few years of wars and uprisings and revolutions, right?"

"More or less. That's how I'm starting it, but I'm leading right into the nineties, and, in a way, sort of forecasting what's to come— that's the decade I'm referring to—1990 to the year 2000. The decade of destruction."

"Why doesn't Arch like the title?"

"He does, actually, but he thinks the network will balk, that they'll say it's too depressing."

"That figures. Still, you're a big number, and surely your opinion carries some weight."

"Only *some.* About this much," she said,

measuring a tiny space between her thumb and forefinger. "You don't know networks."

"I thought you were going to do a special about the child soldiers, the kids we've seen fighting in Cambodia, Iran and all over the world," Clee said. "The little kids toting guns for their governments."

"I am, but that's for next spring."

They talked for a while about the two programs she was planning, and Clee decided that perhaps after all he had imagined the change in her. She looked and sounded perfectly normal to him now.

A short while later, when they were leaving, Nicky had no alternative but to stop at the English couple's table, and she introduced Clee. "Anne, I'd like you to meet Clee, and Clee, this is Anne."

He shook hands with the Englishwoman and she smiled up into his face; he thought she was one of the loveliest-looking women he had ever seen. He also realized that she did not resemble Nicky facially—they simply had the same blond coloring.

"And, Philip, this is Clee," Nicky went on, and Clee let go of Anne's hand in order to greet her husband.

"We're so sorry you can't come over to see us in Tarascon," Anne said. "But perhaps we'll meet again one day."

"I hope so," Clee replied.

"Keep up the good work," Philip said to him. "I'm a great admirer of yours—of your extraordinary photography."

"Thank you," Clee said. He was about to suggest they meet on the terrace a little later for an after-dinner drink when Nicky took hold of his arm, gripped it tightly and edged away.

"It's been lovely to see you both, but we really must go," she said to Anne and Philip. "I'm afraid I still have to pack."

"Of course," Anne said. "And *bon voyage,* darling."

As they walked to the car, Clee remarked, "She's a really beautiful woman, but her resemblance to you is negligible. By the way, you didn't tell me their name, I mean their surname."

There was a silence.

Finally Nicky said, "They're not married. He's called Philip Rawlings."

"And Anne?"

Nicky cleared her throat. "She's Anne Devereaux—Lady Anne Devereaux."

Clee stopped and swung to face her. "Is she related to Charles?" he asked, surprise reverberating in his voice.

"Yes."

"His sister?"

"No. His mother."

"But she's so young-looking!"

"She's fifty-eight. She had Charles when she was only eighteen."

"Her husband, where's he?"

"He's dead. He has been for years."

"So Philip is her boyfriend?"

"Yes."

"She cares for you a lot, Nick, but then I've already said that."

"Yes," Nicky responded softly. "She thought of me as the daughter she'd never had."

Clee said nothing. He unlocked the car door and helped Nicky in. As they drove off in the direction of Saint-Rémy he decided not to ask any more questions about Anne Devereaux. He knew that Nicky was touchy about Charles, and he did not want to make her uncomfortable.

Nicky hardly spoke on the drive back to the farm. She appeared to be far away.

Clee stole surreptitious glances at her from time to time, and he noticed how rigidly set her face had become. Even in profile this was quite apparent. Eventually he put a tape in the player in the dashboard and concentrated on his driving. He made himself relax and was soon lost in his thoughts.

After a while Nicky leaned her head

against the car window and closed her eyes.

Clee was not sure whether she was dozing or merely feigning sleep. His heart sank. The evening that had begun so wonderfully, so auspiciously, had suddenly fizzled out. He realized that he was vaguely angry, not just distressed, and he was aware that this was because of the change in Nicky, or rather what had wrought it. She had been reminded of the past tonight, and in the strongest possible way. He cursed Charles Devereaux under his breath. That man seemed to have an uncanny way of coming back to haunt Nicky—and now, indirectly, him.

17

"This is one of the best scripts you've ever written, Nick," Arch said, handing it to her across his desk.

"I'm glad you like it," Nicky replied, looking pleased as she took it from him. "But let's not forget that I had some help from Ellen, Sam and Wilma, not to mention you. It was a team effort."

Arch shook his head. "No, it wasn't. Basically, it's all yours. It's definitely got your inimitable stamp on it, and you were in cracking form when you wrote this."

"Thanks," she said, smiling at him.

"Incidentally, we're coming up with some great footage to go with the script," Arch volunteered. "Stuff we found in the archives, as you said we would. The show's going to be a prizewinner, Nick, very powerful." He leaned forward intently. "Listen, I've made a couple of changes, only minor ones, if you wouldn't mind looking them over now. They're on pages six, twenty, and forty-one."

Nicky read the changes he had made, as well as his explanatory notes in the margin of each page. Then she looked up and nodded quickly. "You've really strengthened some of my points. Thanks, Arch. And the changes are fine, I think this does it—let's go with this script. There's nothing else to add."

"You're right, and since you approve, I'll get the script out to retype immediately."

Handing it back to him, Nicky remarked, "I suppose you've spoken to our venerable president of news again—about the title?"

"I sure have, and Larry's with us. He agrees 'Decade of Destruction' is a great title, and appropriate, and he's pushing it through, so don't worry. In any case, you know Larry's never been one to shy away from doom and gloom. In fact, he thinks viewers are fascinated by catastrophes, and I'm inclined to agree with him."

"So we're all set to go?" Nicky asked. "Is that what you're saying?"

"You betcha! I also got an okay from Larry

for your other special—the one about the gun-toting kids. Have you had any thoughts about titles yet?"

"My working title is 'Innocents with Guns.' What do you think?"

"Not bad, Nicky, not bad at all." Arch leaned back in his chair, his expression thoughtful. After a moment he gave her a long, steady look.

Nicky said, "What's wrong? What is it?"

"Nothing's wrong—on the contrary, everything's right. Larry wants to move you in another direction next year, Nick, and he's going to talk to you about it."

"What kind of direction?" she asked sharply, suddenly wary.

"He wants you to do some different stuff, maybe just a fraction lighter than—"

"Hey, wait a minute," she cut in peremptorily. "I've always covered hard news, politics and wars! What are you trying to tell me? That he wants to pull me off my assignment as chief war correspondent for the network?"

"No, no, I'm not saying that at all. Just hold your horses and listen. Don't get so excited, okay?"

"Okay. Shoot. I'm *all* ears."

"Larry's talking about your specials, that's all. He thought that after 'Decade,' which he plans to air in November, and the special on the kids with guns, which he's programming for next year, that you yourself might want a bit of a change. He was thinking of a series of interviews with world leaders—the president, Mrs. Thatcher, Gorbachev. So, how do you feel about it?"

"Not sure, and I'll tell Larry that when we have our meeting." She shrugged. "But it could be interesting, I suppose."

"You don't sound very enthusiastic."

"Don't be misled by my tone, Arch, I'm interested. Very interested, as a matter of fact. But you know me well enough to realize that I've got to have an angle, come up with a strong point of view, for my specials. They can't be wishy-washy. And I'm not averse to change. On the contrary. Actually, I like innovations."

"I know that, and so does Larry, and in any case, he's looking to you, and to me, to come up with some suggestions." He flashed her a wide grin. "You can even interview movie stars, if you want."

Nicky shook her head, though she was also grinning. "No, thanks. I'm not going to try to compete with Barbara Walters. She's the best at that, and we all know it."

"Barbara also interviews political leaders, Nick, and she does a really good mix of celebrities at times. It might be worth thinking about that type of show. Let's not forget that her specials get very big ratings. And I mean *big.*"

"I told you, she's the best. And I certainly don't want to be second best. I'll stick to my formula. Anyway, I prefer to come up with some ideas of my own." She sat back in the chair and sighed lightly. "To tell you the honest truth, Arch, a change might be what I need. I felt a bit exhausted after Beijing. Sort of burnt out."

"I know you did, and you looked it, Nicky. But I guess it was burnout time for all of us in June." There was a little pause before he said, "You're looking great now. I guess Provence did you a world of good—*and* being with Clee, of course."

"It was great," Nicky replied, her voice instantly lighter, happier. "And he's great."

"Do I hear the sound of wedding bells?"

"Oh, Arch!"

"Hey, Nick, it's *me* you're talking to. Arch Leverson. I've known Cleeland Donovan a long time, and I can assure you that he's crazy about you. Hell, honey, it's written all over his face. When we had dinner at 'Twenty-one' last week I knew he had it bad for you." He gave her a penetrating look. "I guess I find it hard to believe that you don't feel the same way he does."

There was a moment's hesitation on her

part. "I do care for Clee," she admitted finally, sounding suddenly shy. "But that doesn't necessarily mean there's going to be a wedding." All of a sudden she walked over to the window and stood staring out, a faraway look settling on her face.

It was a beautiful Wednesday morning in the middle of August. Nicky gazed at a sky that was an intense, vivid blue without a single cloud. The skyscrapers of Manhattan shimmered in the brilliant sunlight, and she could not help thinking how extraordinary the city looked from up here on the forty-ninth floor of the American Television Network building. There's no city like it in the whole world, she thought, and she knew that wherever she lived she would always be a New Yorker at heart. She had been born here, had lived here for the biggest part of her life. It was her city. Just as Paris was her city in its own special way; she had such happy memories of her years spent there as a child. It would be no hardship for her to live there again. . . .

Turning around, Nicky leaned against the wide window ledge and gazed across at Arch. Taking a deep breath, she said in a cool and careful voice, "Are you worried about me marrying Clee and moving to Paris, Arch?"

"Hell, no, Nicky, how could you possibly think a thing like that?" he asked, his voice rising several octaves in indignation.

"Because if you are, don't forget that I have a binding contract with this network, and I would never attempt to break it. *Never.* Nor would my agent let me." Without pausing, she plunged on, "And in any case, whatever happens in my personal life, I have every intention of continuing my career. I love my work. It's a very big part of my life, and it always has been. I've been a broadcast journalist since I left college, as you well know, and it's in my blood. I wouldn't be myself without it."

Arch pushed back his chair and rose; his expression was serious. Slowly he walked over to her and took hold of her by the shoulders, saying, "I don't care about this network or your contract. I only care about *you,* and about what happens to *you.* I want you to be happy, Nicky, and if Clee's the right guy for you, and if you think you can make a decent life with him, then I say go for it, grab it. Listen, honey, life's all too brief and difficult and painful, so if you have a chance of making it work with a good guy, then for God's sake do it. Don't think about anything, or anybody, only yourself."

Nicky hugged Arch to her, touched by his

concern for her. Then, pulling away from him, she smiled up into his face. "Thanks for that, Arch. Your affection for me means such a lot, and I appreciate the moral support you've always given me, that you're giving me now." Clearing her throat, she added, "And he *is* a good guy, isn't he?"

"And then some, Nicky, there's no man I know who is a better man than Cleeland Donovan. As my mother would say, he's a real *mensch.*"

Holding his arm, she led him over to the sofa, where they sat down together.

Nicky said, after a moment, "I must admit, I have been worrying a bit. I mean worrying about how I would work it out—my career and Clee and living in Paris, if we ever did decide to get married. Mind you, let me hasten to add, he hasn't proposed to me."

"Give him half a chance and he will."

"I'm not as certain as you are about that, Arch. Clee has always been reluctant about settling down, and for several good reasons. He—"

"I know the reasons," Arch interjected a trifle impatiently, "he's told me often enough. He doesn't want to expose a wife and family to grief and pain, should he get himself killed in the line of duty, and he doesn't want to give up the challenge, excitement and danger of being a war photographer. Isn't that what you were going to say?"

"Yes."

Arch began to laugh. "That was all very easy for Clee to say before you came into his life—at least, before you became his lover. Because, in my opinion, he'd never really been head over heels in love before. But he is with you, Nick," Arch pointed out. "Take my word for it. He loves you very *deeply.* I know this because I know the man so well. And I'll tell you something else—Clee would turn his life upside down for you."

Nicky had listened carefully and now she bit her lip. "Oh, I don't know. . . ." She let the sentence trail off. A second later she exclaimed, "In any case, Clee thinks of himself as a bachelor at heart! You know, in the same way Robert Capa was."

"It's often struck me in the past that Clee has patterned his life on Bob Capa's, but I'm not so certain of that anymore," Arch answered. "Oh sure, Capa's been his idol since he was a kid, and he's always striven to be as great a photographer as Capa, especially on a battlefield. But I think that's where the identification stops, deep down inside himself."

"Maybe."

"Listen, Nick, Clee's coming from a different place than Capa was, this is a different time, a different world we live in today, and we're talking about a different man. I truly believe Clee will marry, but only someone he considers to be the right woman for him, the *only* woman, and in my opinion, that's you."

Nicky remained silent.

Arch said, "Tell me something, honey, what would you say and do, if he did ask you to marry him?"

"I'm not sure, and I'm being absolutely honest with you, Arch, I'm just not sure."

"If you're worrying about the network, *don't.* We can work it out. You're contracted to make between two and four specials a year, and those you could easily plan from Paris, or anywhere else in the world, for that matter. If you think about it, that's what you've been doing all along—coming up with ideas for specials while covering the news. So, all you would have to do, once the planning stage was over, would be to fly in here for two or three weeks, a month at the most, to do the taping, or the live broadcast, depending on the type of special it was."

"I know, Arch, I realize that. But I'm also this network's war correspondent. How could I possibly be based in Paris?"

"I'm not sure, I'd have to give some

thought to that, work something out with you, your agent, Larry Anderson and Joe Speight. The network doesn't want to lose you, Nicky, I can assure you of that, so they'd be willing to be—well, accommodating, to say the least. Also, don't lose sight of the fact that ATN has a big Paris bureau, and I don't see why you couldn't work out of that bureau, operate from there, if you had to, Nicky."

"I guess it might be a viable proposition," she agreed.

"You and Clee could cover wars together, you know. You certainly have an advantage over most women in that respect—Clee wouldn't have to give up that side of his career for you."

"That's true, yes. But do you know something, Arch? There are days when I wonder if I want to go on being a war correspondent for the rest of my life."

If Arch Leverson was startled by this statement, he did not show it. He merely nodded, and said, "It gets to everybody one day. You've certainly had *your* bellyful of wars and revolutions these past eight years or so. I also know that one day Clee will be turned off, too, even though he thinks otherwise right now. Burnout is not uncommon when you've seen as much killing and death as we have. It's deadly. But"—he eyed her carefully—"keep your options open for the moment, and don't make any hasty decisions about your career."

"No, I won't . . . about anything."

"I'd like to ask you something." He raised a brow quizzically.

"Go ahead."

"I know you don't like to talk about Charles Devereaux, but if I remember correctly, you weren't planning to give up your career after you'd married him. Nor were you going to move to London. So, how were you intending to swing it?"

"Charles was eventually going to open a branch of his wine-importing company here in New York, and he was going to live here most of the time, except when he had to travel to Europe to buy wines. And, of course, he planned to keep his office and the flat in London. We were going to straddle the Atlantic, so to speak."

"I see. I guess it's a bit different with Clee, because of his photo news agency. Although, come to think of it, he could start an Image office here in New York, couldn't he? Base himself here, perhaps?"

"Everything's possible," Nicky admitted, and then shrugged lightly. "Maybe Clee doesn't want to do that."

Arch nodded. Several other questions were on the tip of his tongue, but he decided not to ask them at this time. They could wait.

Settling back in the corner of the sofa, he remarked, "Clee told me before he left for Paris that you're going to be spending September with him at the farm. I'm glad about that, honey. You've not taken enough time off in the past few years."

Nicky reached for his hand and squeezed it. "Thanks for caring."

"I worry about you," he admitted with a wry smile. "A *lot.*" Then he glanced at his watch, and exclaimed, "It's time for lunch! I've booked a table at your favorite spot—the Four Seasons. So come on, let's get going. And on my way out I'll give the script to Hildy to be sent out for a retype."

They both rose.

Nicky said, "I'll give it to her, Arch. I've got to go back to my office to get my bag and some other stuff." She picked up the script from his desk and said, "If you don't need me this afternoon for further discussions on the special, I'm going to take the rest of the day off."

"I'm glad to hear it, you work far too hard."

"So my parents keep telling me," she responded and grinned at him. "Very conveniently they forget that they set an example for me years ago, and are still setting it, in fact."

"Speaking of your parents, I hear on the

grapevine that they're as crazy about Clee as he is about you."

"Grapevine! What grapevine? Surely you mean Clee told you."

Arch laughed.

Nicky said, "But yes, it's true, they all got on very well when we were up in Connecticut working on the picture book. They think he's—well, wonderful."

Arch laughed again and said, "I told you once and I'll say it again, Clee is everybody's favorite, folks just love him."

"You don't have to tell *me.* My parents haven't stopped raving about him." Nicky hurried over to the door. "I'll pick up my things, and alert Annette that I'm not coming back after lunch, then I'll meet you at the elevators. Okay?"

"Okay, see you in five."

18

After lunch at the Four Seasons, Nicky went shopping at Bergdorf Goodman. Here she bought several pairs of cotton pants, a selection of cotton shirts and three summer dresses, items she needed for her vacation in Provence in September.

Then she walked across town slowly, heading back to her apartment, which was located on Sutton Place, overlooking the East River and part of downtown Manhattan.

It was a stifling hot afternoon, somewhere around 100 degrees, and even though she was wearing a lightweight cotton suit she soon felt damp and sticky. She was glad when she finally arrived at her building and stepped inside the cool, dim lobby.

After picking up her mail, she took the elevator to the top floor, where she had a large and airy penthouse. Gertrude, her maid, who came every day whether Nicky was in town or not, had closed all the blinds at the windows and turned up the air-conditioning before leaving for the day. In consequence, the apartment was beautifully cool and shady, and it was a relief to Nicky to be inside after tramping through the boiling hot streets of Manhattan.

Nicky dumped the Bergdorf shopping bags on the floor of her bedroom with its sea-green walls, matching carpet and French country furnishings, and went back through the hall to the kitchen. She took out a bottle of carbonated water from the refrigerator, poured a glass, drank some of it thirstily and carried it back to the bedroom. Shedding her smart little summer Trigère, she hung the black-and-white suit in the large walk-in closet, then slipped on one of the loose cotton caftans she had bought on a trip to Morocco some years before.

Several minutes later Nicky was seated behind her desk in her book-lined library-den. This had a magnificent view of the river, the Empire State and Chrysler buildings, and the other soaring skyscrapers that stretched from midtown down to the twin towers on the tip of Manhattan Island.

Taking a long swallow of the water, she glanced at the carriage clock on the English Victorian desk, and was surprised to see that it was almost six o'clock. The folder in front of her was marked *Children of the Beijing Spring;* she opened it and glanced at the first few pages of her introduction to Clee's book. Annette, her secretary, had sent it to him by courier several days ago, and he had phoned her very early this morning from Paris to tell her that it was perfect, that he loved it. Nicky was delighted he had been so pleased, and that he had not minded the length. It was only fifty pages of typescript, and Clee had said she had told everything succinctly but movingly. "I'd rather have it short and brilliant than long and boring," he had said before hanging up.

Nicky now put the folder away in one of the deep drawers of the desk, and began to sort through her mail, which she had brought in with her from the bedroom. There was nothing of consequence—a few bills, post-cards from several friends away on summer vacations, and a letter from her lawyer about Nickwell, her own production company. But not even this was of any great importance, so she put the mail in the black lacquer Japanese tray on her desk to be dealt with another day.

On her way back to the kitchen, carrying

the empty glass, she paused in the doorway of the living room, looking at it with a keen and critical eye. There was no question that it was beautiful; nobody could deny that. It was large, with a huge picture window that also looked downtown, and was furnished with English antique pieces and decorated throughout in light colors. Primarily she had used varying shades of peach and apricot, pale greens and blues, and it was a room that was especially effective at night, warm and mellow and inviting.

Nicky loved her apartment floating high in the sky. Light-filled, airy and cheerful, it was a joy to be in, whatever the time of day or night, and whatever the weather was like outside. It was sunny and lighthearted when the weather was good; it was highly dramatic in a thunderstorm or blizzard. After dark it became part of the fairyland that was Manhattan when the lights came on and glittered brilliantly outside the apartment's many windows.

Her parents had persuaded her to buy the apartment four years ago, and she was glad that she had. It was a real home, and something of a refuge for her between her travels and foreign assignments.

In the kitchen, which was white and blue, sleek and modern and convenient, Nicky poured herself another glass of water and returned to the library.

Flopping down on the sofa, she propped her feet on the coffee table and focused her thoughts on Clee and their affair, ruminating on everything that Arch had said in the office and, later, over lunch.

Of course, he had made it sound easy; but in her opinion he had oversimplified the situation. She still wasn't so sure she could handle Clee, marriage, living in Paris *and* her career in American television, which necessitated her being here in New York part of the time, at least.

Oh, yes, you can, a small voice inside her head told her.

Maybe I can at that, she thought, and laughed out loud. Like most other modern young women, she wanted it all. And then some. Was that possible?

Also, if she and Clee did marry, he might want to have a child. Did she? Some days, the answer was yes. Others, it was no, and most especially when she reflected about the horrors she reported on, and on a daily basis. Who would want to bring a child into a terrible world like this? Only a madwoman, surely?

Her mother, the historian, kept saying that the world had always been a pretty lousy place—since time immemorial, in fact.

"You mustn't, indeed you *can't* have these attitudes," her mother had recently said to her. "If over the centuries everyone had thought as you do and decided not to procreate because of the evil and horror in the world, then the human race today would be extinct." Well, there was no denying her mother was a wise woman. Still . . .

Nicky let these thoughts go, sighing heavily. Leaning her head against the chintz cushions on the sofa, she closed her eyes and drifted with her complex reflections about her life.

In a sense, what it finally boiled down to was her feelings for Clee. She *was* emotionally involved with him, and her physical passion for him knew no bounds. But was she really in love with him? And sufficiently enough to make a life with him? Forever? Might she not be merely infatuated? She wasn't sure. Anyway, although he had twice told her he loved her, once in bed and once at the restaurant at Les Baux, he had not said those words to her again. Furthermore, he had never ever mentioned marriage. And did *she* want to marry Clee? I just don't know, she answered herself.

Nicky sat up and opened her eyes, feeling suddenly irritated with herself. Why was she so ambivalent? She had no answer, at least not exactly. However, she *was* fully aware of the importance of her career. It was her life-blood, in all truth. Was that at the root of it? Was that the stumbling block? The fact was, Clee lived in Paris and liked living there, and obviously did not want to return to the States to take up residence. She lived in New York and needed to, because the network was here and she was a big number in American television. Maybe *that* is the reason I'm so uncertain, she finally admitted, and grimaced wryly to herself. She obviously wasn't pre-pared to jeopardize her brilliant career.

A few minutes later Nicky automatically glanced at her watch. It was ten minutes to seven and time to put ATN on, to catch the evening news on her own network with an-chorman Mike Fowler, to whom she was close.

She stepped over to the bookshelves, where the large television set was housed, turned it on and went back to the sofa.

The initial coverage was the local New York news, and Nicky paid scant attention to this. She picked up *Time* magazine from the coffee table, flipped the pages to the section on the press and began to read, listening with only half an ear.

A short while later, at the sound of the familiar music, the splendid, rather grand theme that heralded ATN's nightly national and international news, Nicky lifted her head.

There sat Mike looking as wonderful and as reassuring as he always did. Like Peter Jennings of ABC, Mike was extremely good-looking and glamorous, but also a superb journalist. Peter and Mike were two of the best in the business as far as she was concerned. First-rate reporters who got the point, were informative and reasonable, and for those reasons they took all the ratings.

Only vaguely listening to Mike giving the headlines of the world news, she continued to read the *Time* piece, and went on reading it as he gave more in-depth details of the national news.

But when she heard the voice of her channel's Rome correspondent, Tony Johnson, Nicky looked up, suddenly more attentive.

She listened carefully as he told of a shooting incident at a political rally outside Rome. Several people had been hit when a gunman had gone berserk and fired a machine gun into the crowd. Tony said there was speculation that the incident had really been an assassination attempt by the opposition party.

As the camera moved away from Tony, and slowly panned around, it lingered for a moment on a group to the left of the speakers' platform, then settled briefly on a face in the crowd.

Suddenly Nicky sat bolt upright, and stared in shock at a face on the screen. "Charles!" she said. "It's Charles!" But how could it be? Charles Devereaux was dead.

Charles Devereaux had killed himself two and a half years ago, just a few weeks before their wedding. How could he be in Rome, larger than life? No, it can't be Charles, Nicky thought. Charles had drowned off the English coast.

It was true, however, that his body had never been found.

Suddenly Nicky knew; yes, it *was* he. Charles Devereaux was alive. But how could that be? Why had he disappeared from her life? And what was she going to do about it, if anything?

PART THREE

Conspirators

*False face must hide what
the false heart doth know.*

—William Shakespeare

19

The house where Anne Devereaux lived was old, very old, a venerable place of historical significance as well as of singular beauty.

Pullenbrook was its name, and it stood on a low plateau of parkland in a dell beneath the rolling hills of the South Downs. Cradled deep in the heart of the Sussex countryside, it was unusually secluded for a great house of its kind. Because it was hidden in the folds of the pastoral land, the tips of its chimneys became visible only at the very last moment of approaching it. Then, unexpectedly, the manor could be seen through the lush green foliage of the high trees that fringed the edge of the park, and the view never failed to take one's breath away.

Built in 1565 by an ancestor of Anne's, it was a Tudor house of exceptional distinction, typical of the Elizabethan period, with its gray stone walls, half-timbered gables, soaring leaded windows, square-cut bays and many tall chimneys. Clustered around the main house were the outbuildings, the stables, a small church and two walled gardens; flaring out on either side and running along the front façade was the lovely park where fallow deer grazed as they had for centuries.

A house of unchanging appearance, it had remained much the same since it was built by one Sir Edmund Clifford, a magnate and warrior knight in service to Elizabeth Tudor, the queen of England. The lands of Pullen were granted to Sir Edmund by the queen in gratitude for services rendered to the Crown; later she showered him with more royal favors when she elevated him to the peerage by creating him Earl Clifford of Allendale, and giving him Castle Allendale and additional lands in Sussex.

Edmund, his eldest son, Thomas—who became the second earl—and his subsequent descendants divided their time between the manor and the castle. But by the end of the seventeenth century the Cliffords were residing permanently at the castle, which had grown in size and magnificence over the years, and in consequence the manor house was used only part of the year. However, it had always been kept in good repair and its outer structure and interiors were unimpaired over the centuries.

Fortunately, because the Clifford family lived mostly at Castle Allendale for the next few hundred years, Pullenbrook had been saved from certain and perhaps excessive modernization, and so it had retained its purity of architecture and Tudor character.

It was Anne's grandfather, the ninth earl named for the first, who preferred to live at the manor rather than at the great castle, and thus, in 1910, Pullenbrook once again became the main residence of the Cliffords. His son, Julian, the tenth earl and Anne's father, followed this tradition and resided at the manor house until his death.

Anne Clifford Devereaux's entire life had been spent at Pullenbrook. She was born there on April 26, 1931. As the daughter of an earl she had the honorary title of lady, a title that was retained even after marriage. She was raised in the ancient house, married from it in 1948, and three years later she had returned to live there as a young widow with a small son. At this time in her life she had needed to be in the bosom of her family, rather than alone in the grand London town house her late husband, Henry Devereaux, had left her.

When her brother, Geoffrey, had inherited the Clifford earldom, estates and lands, after their father's death in 1955, he had chosen to make Castle Allendale his home. And understanding how much his sister cared for the manor in West Sussex, he had suggested she continue to live there for as long as she wished, and whether or not she remarried.

Thirty-four years later she was still in residence, *châtelaine* of the house for her brother. To say that Anne loved Pullenbrook was something of an understatement. In a sense, she revered it, and much of her life revolved around it, because it gave her constant succor and comfort. She felt safe and protected within its familiar walls, and derived much pleasure from its ancient and stately beauty, its timelessness, the continuity of family line and history it represented. There were times when she wondered what she would have done without the house, for it had seen her through many hours of unhappiness—sadness, loneliness and heartache, grief, sorrow and illness. Its very existence over so many centuries seemed to reassure her that she too could, indeed *would,* survive.

Now on this Saturday morning in August Anne came into the Great Hall, her step light, her high heels clicking sharply against the stone floor. Carrying a bowl of roses, she stood poised in the doorway, marveling at the hall's peaceful beauty, as she so frequently did. It never failed to cast a spell over her.

Thousands of dust motes rose up in the shafts of trembling light that slanted in through the leaded windows, but otherwise there was no motion whatsoever in the room. It was all stillness, filled with bright sunlight that burnished the ancient wood pieces, gave them a mellow glow and brought into focus the old paintings of her ancestors by such master portraitists as Lely, Gainsborough and Romney.

A fleeting smile crossed her face. Every aspect of the house gave her immense pleasure, but this room in particular was a special favorite. Moving toward the long refectory table, Anne placed the roses in the center of it; stepping back, she eyed them critically. The head gardener had picked the flowers earlier that morning and they were beautiful. In various shades of pink, they looked perfect in the silver bowl engraved with the family crest that gleamed against the ripe old wood of the table. The roses were full blown, and several petals suddenly fell off. She was about to pick them up, but changed her mind—she left them lying where they were, thinking how natural they looked next to the silver bowl.

Anne went back through the heavy carved-wood door leading into the private quarters of the house, which were not open to the public.

The flower room, where she had been working, was off to one side, across a small stone-flagged foyer, and Anne went in, lifted the last vase of flowers from the old deal worktable and took it down the corridor to the drawing room. This was a wonderfully spacious room with a series of soaring leaded windows set in a square-cut bay, a huge stone fireplace and a high coffered ceiling. The room had been decorated mostly in shades of green, such as celadon, which were repeated in various upholstery fabrics and in the Aubusson carpet on the floor; some of the greens were so pale they were almost a silvery gray. Fine Georgian antiques and paintings graced the room, which, like the Great Hall, had an air of time-lessness and tranquillity about it.

After placing the tall crystal vase of white

roses on an antique fruitwood table in the
center of the room, Anne hurried out to the
small parlor she used as an office. Cozy and
comfortable, this seemed full of sunshine
because of its yellow walls; a raspberry-col-
ored carpet stretched across the floor, and
a loveseat covered in a raspberry-and-white
striped fabric was placed in front of the fireplace. The most important piece of furniture
in the room was the Georgian walnut desk
where Anne now sat going through the
morning mail. After reading it all, she picked
up the menus she had written out for Pilar,
the cook, and glanced at them again. Then
she looked over the list of things to do, which
she had scribbled the night before, and sys-
tematically began to check off those chores
she had already accomplished.

At this moment a shadow fell across the
doorway, and lifting her head, she smiled
warmly when she saw Philip Rawlings standing there.

"Am I disturbing you, Anne?"

"No, darling, not at all. I've just been
checking my list, and I'm happy to tell you
that I've done everything I had to do. I'm now
as free as a bird—and all yours."

"Well, I'm certainly glad to hear that," he
said and sauntered into the room. A slender
man of medium height, with intelligent gray

eyes in a pleasantly attractive, somewhat boyish face, Philip looked much younger than his fifty-six years, despite the silver wings in his dark hair. This morning he wore a wine-colored paisley-patterned cravat with an open-necked pale blue shirt, dark gray slacks and a gray-checked sports jacket, and his appearance was more like that of a country squire than an important member of the British Foreign Office.

"I thought we might have a stroll before lunch," Philip went on, smiling.

"And why not? Actually, I'd rather like it," Anne said. "I was going to come looking for you, to suggest the very same thing. So, come along, let's go to the coat room, where I'll change these shoes, put on a pair of flats, and then we can stroll up Sweetheart Hill. That's a pleasant walk, and not too long, either."

"Splendid," Philip said.

Anne glanced at her watch as she rose, and went on, "We have about an hour. Plenty of time for the walk *and* a drink before lunch. Inez is going to serve Pilar's cheese soufflé promptly at one. She's making it especially for you, you know."

Philip put his arm around Anne's shoulders as they walked out into the corridor together. "The problem in this house is that you all spoil me," he murmured genially, kissing her cheek.

Anne looked at him and began to laugh. "You're worth spoiling, my darling," she said, her pretty eyes mirroring the love and affection in his.

Sweetheart Hill rose behind the house, and it was an extraordinary vantage point with spectacular views of the countryside for miles around.

Several hundred years before, in 1644, during the ill-fated reign of Charles I, one of Anne's female ancestors had climbed the hill every day for months. Lady Rosemary Clifford had hoped and prayed to see her sweetheart returning from the Battle of Marston Moor, during the bloody Civil War that had racked England at that time. A stone bench had been built on top of the hill for Lady Rosemary so that she could sit and watch and wait in comfort. She had waited in vain, as it turned out. Her Royalist sweetheart, Lord Colin Greville, had been killed by the Roundheads—Cromwell's men—and had never returned to claim her as his bride. Eventually she had recovered from her sorrow and had married some other young nobleman, but the place where she had so devotedly waited had been known as Sweetheart Hill ever after.

Anne and Philip now sat on that bench, enjoying the mild air, the splendid views of the great Tudor house and the surrounding country on this glittering summer's day.

"You're glad Nicky is coming for the weekend, aren't you?" Philip said, breaking the silence that had settled between them after their climb up the hill.

Anne turned her face to his, and nodded quickly, her blue eyes lighting up. "Oh yes, very happy, Philip. I've missed her terribly— but then you know that. I can't wait to spend these few days with her. Nicky has always been unusually special to me."

"I know, and I'm delighted she phoned from London, and that she more or less invited herself down here." He smiled at Anne and remarked, "Actually, I have to admit I'm looking forward to seeing her myself. There's no one quite like Nicky Wells."

"Wasn't it lucky we went to Tarascon?" Anne did not wait for an answer, but hurried on, "And to think that we almost didn't go to stay with the Norells."

"Not only that, if we'd listened to them we wouldn't have gone to Les Baux for dinner that evening. Remember how they kept telling us it was a tourist trap in the summer months?"

"Yes. But it was meant to be—that we ran into Nicky the way we did."

Philip did not say anything. He put his arm around her and brought her closer to him, and after a moment he said softly against her hair, "There is something else that is meant to be, Anne."

She swung her head to look at him, her eyes questioning.

"Marry me, Anne. *Please.*"

"Oh, Philip," she began, and was about to reject him, but her voice faltered as she looked into his face. There was such an earnest plea in his eyes, and his expression was so loving, she felt her breath catching in her throat. As far as she was concerned, there was no one who could hold a candle to Philip Rawlings. He was a man of great kindness and generosity, and he had been inordinately loyal and a source of great strength to her over many years. He had asked her several times to marry him during the past six or seven years, and always she had refused. Now, suddenly, she realized how cruel she had been, and was continuing to be to this truly good man who cared so much about her and her well-being.

She took a deep breath. "You simply want to make an honest woman of me, that's what this is all about, isn't it?" she said, adopting a light tone, one echoing with gaiety, and she laughed.

He shook his head very slowly and emphatically. "No, that's not it at all, Anne. I don't care what the world thinks of me, or of you, or of us, or of the fact that we've been living together for years. I want to marry you because I love you very much indeed—and I thought you loved me in the same way."

"But I do! Oh, darling, you know I do! But marriage seems so . . . well, to be honest, *irrelevant* at our age. As far as I'm concerned, we *are* married. What difference does a little bit of paper make in the long run?"

"It makes a lot of difference to me. You see, I want you to be my wife, and it's important to me that you bear my name, that we are . . . married." He began to laugh as lightly as she had a second before, even a bit self-deprecatingly, and added, "Having just said I don't care about the world, perhaps I really do, after all. Maybe I want the world to know that I belong to you, and that you belong to me. I believe I *need* us to be married, Anne. We've been together an awfully long time, darling, and marriage seems to me to be the natural, logical and most wonderful culmination of our relationship."

Anne nodded, but found she was unable

to say anything for a moment. She averted her head and gazed out across the landscape, her eyes reflective. Everything Philip said was true, of course. They had known each other for fifteen years, and had been deeply involved with each other for fourteen of those years. They had met in 1974, just after Philip had left his wife, and what had begun as a friendship had eventually developed into a full-blown affair of the heart. She had dropped the man she had been seeing at the time, and Philip had become her lover, and for them both it had been a relationship made in heaven. They were ideally suited to each other, temperamentally and sexually, and they had quickly bonded. Philip's divorce had taken four years, and by then they had settled into a perfectly happy, congenial and contented routine, seeing each other every weekend when Philip came down to Pullenbrook and during the week whenever she was up in London.

Philip's children, Vanessa and Timothy, had been quite young in the seventies, and he had not wanted to marry until they were older. She had not minded this; marriage had always been somewhat irrelevant to her, in the sense that her love for Philip existed without it, and would always exist, no matter what. The kind of deep and abiding love she felt for him did not need a marriage license to give it validity, make it stronger or more real. Besides which, her first marriage had been such a mockery she had been quite cold about the idea of matrimony ever since.

Obviously, though, Philip needed marriage for them at this time in their lives. Hadn't he just said as much? If she truly loved him, and of course she did, then his happiness had to be important to her. And it was. Thinking about it, she realized there was no truly good reason why she should not marry him. Quite unexpectedly, she discovered she rather liked the prospect of being his wife, especially since it would give him such enormous pleasure.

Bringing her gaze to meet his, she said quietly, "Yes."

"Yes, what?"

"Yes, I'll marry you, Philip. I will be happy and honored to marry you. As you said a moment ago, it's only right and proper that we get married at this particular time."

"Oh, darling, that makes me so very, very happy." He kissed her gently on the mouth, took her in his arms and held her very tightly. He had never loved a woman the way he loved Anne Devereaux—and there had been plenty of women in his life before he had met her. Anne had known such hurt and pain, and the only thing he wanted was to love and cherish her, protect and safeguard her all the days of his life and hers.

Finally releasing her, Philip said, "Let's set a date for our marriage here and now, before you change your mind. That way I can have my secretary send an announcement to *The Times* first thing on Monday morning."

"Never fear, I'm not going to change my mind," she responded, her face radiant, her eyes shining. "And I'll be glad to work on the announcement with you over the weekend. But let me think for a moment about the date. . . . I believe we should get married in December, Philip."

"But that's months away," he protested.

"After all these *years* of living in sin, surely a few more *months* don't matter!" Anne exclaimed, her ready laughter surfacing. "And I'm suggesting December for a very good reason—*Geoffrey*. I would like my brother to give me away, and I know he's going to be abroad quite a lot between now and the end of November."

"Very well, darling, December it is."

"A Christmas wedding in the little church here at Pullenbrook will be very pretty—

rather picturesque, actually, don't you think?"

"Indeed it will. Anne?"

"Yes, darling?"

"I do hope you're going to allow me to give you an engagement ring."

"What a lovely idea! And of course I am. Every girl likes to have a ring, Philip."

A huge smile spread across his face, and he reached into his pocket and brought out a small leather box. "I went to Asprey's earlier in the week, looking for a ring for you. You see, I was determined to propose this weekend, and equally, I was absolutely determined you would accept me this time. Anyway, I found this, and I hope you like it." As he finished speaking he handed her the box.

Anne lifted the lid and gasped when she saw the deep blue sapphire set within a circle of diamonds nestling in the velvet. "Oh, Philip, it's simply beautiful."

"I selected this particular ring because I know how much you like antique jewelry," he explained. "Anyway, the color matches your lovely eyes, my darling."

"Thank you, Philip, for the ring—and for everything."

"Here, let me do that," he said, as she fumbled with the box, and took it away from her. As he slipped the sapphire on her finger, he added softly, "There, we are now properly engaged, and what more appropriate place to pledge our troth to each other than here on Sweetheart Hill."

20

Nicky had not been in this house for almost three years, and two days ago in New York, when she had made the decision to come to see Anne Devereaux, she had dreaded the thought of being within its walls once again.

But now that she was here at Pullenbrook most of her fears were evaporating. This was due in no small measure to Anne's warmth and her loving demeanor, as well as to Philip's avuncular kindness and his special brand of geniality.

When she had arrived from London an hour ago the two of them had greeted her with much affection; she knew this to be very genuine on their part, and it was an affection she fully reciprocated. Instantly she had begun to relax because they made her feel so welcome and had put her completely at ease.

And then there was the house itself. The minute she had stepped over the threshold into the Great Hall she had felt its peacefulness most forcibly. This was something she had never quite forgotten, but she had resolutely pushed it to the back of her mind in recent years, and for the most obvious of reasons. But there was no denying that there was a special kind of tranquillity within the boundaries of Pullenbrook; it was an almost palpable thing that enfolded itself around her, seemed literally to envelop her like a cloak. In fact, she now recalled what a soothing effect the old manor had had on her in the past, and she understood why Anne thought of it as her safe haven, why she never wanted to leave it—at least, not for very long.

Suddenly it struck Nicky that this ancient Tudor house had seen so much, witnessed so much over the centuries, that if its walls could talk they would reveal some incredible secrets.

She shivered involuntarily. What dark secrets about Charles Devereaux did this house hold? *Was* he alive, as she believed? And if so, *why* had he faked his own death?

She shivered again and pushed these disturbing thoughts away—for the moment, at any rate. She had come here to tell Anne that she had seen Charles on American television four days ago, and that she had good reason to think he was living in Rome. But now she realized this was not the right time to broach the subject. She would have to wait for a more opportune moment later this evening.

Nicky and Anne were sitting in the drawing room, and Anne was busy pouring tea. Nicky could not help thinking how exquisite this room was with its interplay of pale greens. They made a perfect backdrop for the mellow antiques and the fine paintings, most of them English landscapes, several of them priceless masterpieces by Constable and Turner. She had always marveled at Anne's extraordinary taste, her skill at decorating and the way she kept up this house, undoubtedly a gargantuan task for anyone.

Surreptitiously Nicky looked across at the fruitwood table in the center of the room. A vase of white roses stood in the middle of it and was surrounded by a collection of family photographs in silver frames. There were several of her—alone, with her parents, with

Anne and Philip in the gardens here at Pullenbrook and, of course, with Charles. She swung her head to look at an end table next to the sofa near the fireplace. On this stood their engagement picture, taken by Patrick Lichfield, which was framed in gold. Her gaze was riveted on it for several seconds and then she averted her eyes. But within seconds she managed to be calm, and totally in control of herself again.

"You're awfully quiet, Nicky darling," Anne remarked as she rose and brought her a cup of tea.

"Thanks," Nicky said, accepting it. "I didn't mean to be rude, sitting here like an idiot and gaping so avidly at everything, as if I'd never been here before. I was savoring the room, admiring it—I'd forgotten how beautiful it is—how beautiful the whole of Pullenbrook is, actually, Anne."

"You always did love this house," Anne murmured, looking down at her, a faint smile touching her mouth. "And in the same way I love it. At least, that is what I've believed for years now. You have a true *feeling* for Pullenbrook, and I realized this the first time you came here. I couldn't help noticing that you were—well, emotionally drawn to it. That's the best way for me to describe what I thought your reaction was to my home. And the house accepted you, welcomed you, Nicky."

Anne went back to the sofa, continuing, "It doesn't always do that, you know. It *can* reject people." Quite suddenly she started to laugh a bit self-consciously. "Good Lord, that does sound bizarre, doesn't it? You must think I've turned into a dotty old woman, talking in this strange way about a house."

"No, I don't. You're making perfect sense to me. And *you,* of all people, a dotty old lady! Never. Why, Anne, you're fantastic."

"Thank you for saying so." Anne leaned over the silver tea service on the table in front of her, and confided, "I was fifty-eight in April, but I must admit, I don't feel it, not one little bit. Anyway, getting back to what I was saying, I know you know what I mean about the house, the way it made you feel as though you belonged in it from the very first moment."

"And that feeling came rushing back today," Nicky told her quietly. "And you know something else, I happen to think of houses as *living* things. They do have atmospheres and vibrations, some good, some very bad. This place has good vibes to me."

Anne nodded. "We're an odd couple, you and I, Nicky. But then we've always under-

stood each other extremely well." Anne took
a sip of tea, and a second later exclaimed,
"Oh dear, I've been so busy chattering to
you about the house, I forgot to offer you a
tea sandwich, or would you prefer sponge
cake?"

"Nothing, thanks, Anne. I'm trying to
watch my weight, especially after that fattening trip to France."

"Oh gosh, yes, I know exactly what you
mean." Anne laughed.

At this moment Philip came back into the
room, having been summoned to the phone
a few minutes before. He said to them both,
"Sorry I took so long," and then glanced at
Anne. "It was Timothy, darling. He's just arrived in London. He sends his love, by the
way."

Anne nodded and smiled up at him. "I'm
glad he's safely back home."

Philip took the cup of tea Anne had just
poured for him, and went and sat down on
the chair next to Nicky. Turning to her, he
explained, "My son's just started working as
a journalist on the *Sunday Times,* and he's
been in Leipzig. There's a lot going on there,
all sorts of political situations on the bubble,
as I'm sure you're aware."

"Yes, my friend Cleeland Donovan, whom
you met in Les Baux, leaves for Germany

tomorrow. He wants to photograph the Berlin Wall—while it's still standing, he says."

Philip looked at her alertly. "Does he think it's about to come down?"

"He's been saying it would for the past two years, but, of course, he was never certain exactly when—who could be certain of that? At one point he thought it would take another twenty or thirty years, perhaps even longer. But recently he's been muttering that the wall will be dismantled imminently."

"Has he now?" Philip put his cup and saucer on a nearby table and sat back in his chair, his attention still focused on Nicky. "That's very interesting to know, especially since I happen to agree—as do a number of my colleagues, actually." Philip shook his head, and went on somewhat acerbically, "However, only six months ago, East Germany's President Erich Honecker vowed that the Berlin Wall would remain standing for another hundred years. But I'm inclined to believe that that was an idle boast on his part."

"Or wishful thinking," Nicky volunteered. "And in any case, let's hope Honecker is wrong and Clee is right."

"I couldn't agree more," Philip murmured, and asked, "And is Cleeland going anywhere else in the Eastern bloc?"

"Yes, after Berlin he intends to roam around for a few days, and he wants to go to Leipzig, too. He plans to cover the demonstrations that keep erupting all over the place."

Philip nodded. "Those demonstrations are going to be on the increase, I think. And I have a strong suspicion we're going to see any number of Communist regimes come tumbling down this year."

Nicky was thoughtful for a few seconds, and then she said slowly, with some deliberation, "Only the other day I told Arch Leverson that we're going to see the tectonic plates of history shifting under our feet in the not too distant future. There's going to be a lot of movement, a lot of changes, especially in the Iron Curtain countries."

"Very astute of you to say so, Nicky. You're right on the button," Philip exclaimed.

Nicky smiled at him; she was pleased to get his confirmation of her opinions on world affairs. After all, Philip Rawlings was an important man at the Foreign Office.

When they had spent time together in the past, Philip and Nicky had inevitably become embroiled in political discussions, and this afternoon was no exception. They went on chatting about the state of the world for the next ten minutes or so, until Philip finally cut short their conversation. Shaking his head, he said, "Here we go again, Nicky, boring poor Anne with all this dry stuff about politics and politicians, which she couldn't care less about. Sorry, darling," he apologized, and looked at Anne affectionately.

"But that's not true!" Anne spluttered. "I'm not bored. You seem to have forgotten that I grew up with politics, and that my father was quite a statesman in his day."

"I hadn't forgotten, but I do know that's not where your interests lie, not really." Philip pushed himself up out of the chair and went to sit with Anne on the sofa. Taking her hand, he said, "And now, on to more important things—have you told Nicky our happy news?"

Anne said, "I haven't had a chance yet, and in any case I thought it would be much nicer if we told her together."

"Told me what?" Nicky looked from one to the other, filled with curiosity.

"Philip asked me to marry him today—"

"For about the twentieth time," Philip cut in.

"And I accepted him," Anne added, her face radiant.

"*Finally,*" Philip said. "Anne has finally agreed to become my wife and she's even set the date. We're going to have a Christ-

mas wedding here in the little church at Pullenbrook."

"Oh, Anne, Philip, this is wonderful news!"
Nicky exclaimed, jumping to her feet to offer
congratulations.

21

Nicky sat in the window seat in her room, staring out across the formal gardens of Pullenbrook. But she was not really looking at them. Her gaze was turned inward.

How she wished now that she had not come down here today, that she had delayed her visit until Monday, as she had originally intended when she had set out from New York yesterday.

When she arrived in London last night, the first thing she had done, after she had checked into her hotel, was telephone Pullenbrook. Anne had been overjoyed to hear from her, and so soon after their chance meeting in France. They had chatted for a few minutes, and then she had more or less invited herself down for the weekend, telling Anne that she was in England for only a few days and would love to see her.

Anxiety had prompted her haste; she had a desperate need to talk to Anne. Who else was there in whom to confide her terrible suspicions about Charles?

But to her dismay she found she had walked into this house on a very special day in Anne Devereaux's life. How awful it would be if she ruined it by revealing to her that her only child, the son she had adored, might not have drowned after all, as they believed, but that he might have faked his own death. In doing so, she would be branding Charles dishonorable, duplicitous, a liar and a cheat—and a savagely cruel man who had caused his mother untold suffering and grief, as well as herself, Philip, his uncle Geoffrey, and everyone else who was close to him. Of course, he *was* all of those things if he was alive and living under a new identity. But she couldn't drop that bombshell tonight, as she had planned.

Nicky leaned her head against the windowpane, turning things over in her mind. She might not even be able to tell Anne tomorrow either; she might well have to stay over until Monday and talk to her then. It was not that she was afraid to speak out; it was just that she didn't want to spoil Anne's weekend. It was going to be very difficult, keeping up a calm front, putting on a good face for the next few days. Still, she must conceal her nervousness and anxiety for Anne's sake. She was such a wonderful woman, so straightforward and honest, she deserved a little happiness at this stage in her life. No, she couldn't dump this on her at the moment; she had to let her have this chance to celebrate with Philip.

For another half hour Nicky sat on the window seat, mulling everything over in her mind. Then she let her eyes wander over the vast room. Full of pale lavender tints, soft pinks and light grays, it was a feminine room with pretty watercolors on the walls and painted-wood pieces that were elegant and graceful.

With her usual tact and thoughtfulness, Anne had chosen a bedroom for her that she had never occupied before, in an effort perhaps to ease the burden of unhappy memories. But every corner of Pullenbrook held memories for her—yet not all of them were bad. In fact, some of them were positive and happy.

The four-poster with its lavender silk hangings and matching eiderdown looked inviting all of a sudden, so Nicky took off her shoes and lay down on it. She pulled the eiderdown over her, hoping to have a nap before getting ready for dinner, but her mind kept running.

Not unnaturally, Nicky was thinking of the last time she had been in this house—that particular visit had been heartbreaking, one of the saddest times in her life, and the memories of it were very bad indeed.

October 1986. A Saturday in the middle of the month. She had arrived at Pullenbrook in the morning. She and Anne had talked for hours, and had hardly noticed when Inez had brought the tea into the drawing room promptly at four o'clock, automatically observing that traditional British ritual. They had been far too devastated to care about the tea, and it had gone untouched.

Her own pain had begun the day before, when Philip had shown up in New York unexpectedly, ringing her doorbell just after ten o'clock. He had stepped off the early-morning British Concorde into a waiting limousine, and had ridden into Manhattan to break the bad news to her in person, at Anne's request, rather than doing so on the telephone from London.

Philip had not wasted any time. He had

told her as gently as he could that Charles was believed to be dead, that he had apparently drowned off Beachy Head on the Sussex coast several days earlier. His pale-blue Jaguar had been found parked nearby, late on Wednesday afternoon. In it were his raincoat and a locked briefcase bearing his initials with a leather luggage tag on the handle. The name on the tag read Charles A. C. Devereaux, and, of course, the local police had known at once whom to contact: his mother, Lady Anne Devereaux of Pullenbrook Manor.

When the locks of the briefcase had been prised open by the police, in front of Anne, the only item they found inside had been a letter addressed to his mother. And that letter had told them everything they needed to know—Charles Devereaux had taken his own life. Everything had been spelled out precisely and explicitly, and he had made his intentions very clear. But there would have to be a police investigation; that was the law. However, the police had agreed to keep the matter under wraps until Charles Devereaux's fiancée in New York had been informed. Again, this had been one of Anne's requests, which the local police chief, Superintendent Willis, had said they would be willing to accede to, out of deference to her ladyship and her standing in the county.

Philip had recounted all this to her on that horrendous Friday, when her whole world had fallen apart with such abruptness and finality. She had been shattered, and in shock, when she had phoned Arch at the network, and told him in a shaky voice that she had to fly to England immediately because Charles had committed suicide. She had been trembling so excessively, as the facts had truly begun to sink in, she had been unable to continue and had handed the phone to Philip. Carefully he had given the pertinent details to Arch and promised to be in touch with more news as soon as possible.

Not long after this she had thrown a few clothes into a bag and packed her toilet articles and makeup, with the help of Gertrude, who had arrived to clean the apartment in the middle of it all. And then, just before they set off for Kennedy Airport, Philip had attempted to reach her parents, who were staying at the Cipriani in Venice, but they had been out. Philip had left his name and the number at Pullenbrook, along with an urgent message for them to telephone Anne as soon as they could.

By one-thirty she and Philip were on board the French Concorde, taking off for Paris. Philip had pointed out that this was the easiest and fastest route to London. They would be flying for just under four hours, would spend the night in Paris and be on the first plane to London on Saturday.

She had wept for almost the entire journey across the Atlantic. Philip had done his level best to console her, but with little success. Yet, from time to time, she had had her moments of calm, during which they had asked each other the same question. *Why?* Why had Charles done this terrible thing? There seemed to be no valid reason to either of them, and therefore no explanation.

Upon arrival at Charles de Gaulle Airport they had taken rooms at one of the hotels, and on Saturday they had been on the seven o'clock flight to Heathrow. From there they had driven directly to Pullenbrook, where Anne, grief-stricken, still suffering from shock, was waiting for them.

Later that day Nicky had asked Anne if there had been any mention of her in Charles's letter. Anne had shaken her head sadly. Nicky had been stunned to hear this. *Charles had killed himself without one last word to her.* And she couldn't quite get over that.

Her parents had arrived from Venice via London on Sunday. They were full of compassion and concern for her, and they had both done their best to help her. But in the end it was she and Anne who had helped each other the most, had given each other the most sustenance and support.

She had stayed with Anne for several weeks, the two of them inseparable and moving between Pullenbrook and Anne's flat in Eaton Square. And during this difficult and painful time for them both, things had become crystal clear. Charles had been quite deliberate in everything he had done before his suicide. He had meticulously put all his affairs in order. His flat in Knightsbridge had been sold; the shares he held in his privately owned wine-importing company in London had been sold to his partner; his shares in the European end of the business had been bought by his Spanish partner. And, finally, he had made a new will a few weeks before his death. In it he had left everything to his mother.

Ever since then, for almost three years now, Nicky had asked herself why he had killed himself, and she had never been able to come up with an answer. At least, not one that was acceptable.

At one point, anger had replaced her initial grief, and this had troubled her. On several occasions, when she was in New York and not on foreign assignment, she had gone to see a psychiatrist, one who had been recom-

mended by Arch. Her aim had been to understand the anger and to come to grips with it.
The psychiatrist, Dr. Alvin Foxgrove, had pa-
tiently explained that most people who had
been close to, or emotionally involved with,
suicides inevitably experienced great anger,
and that it was a perfectly normal reaction.
This knowledge had helped her somewhat,
especially since Dr. Foxgrove had told her
that the anger would eventually go away. But
in her case it had not fully evaporated. The
awful truth was that there were times when
the anger blazed again inside.

After a while, Nicky managed to pull her
thoughts away from the past and concentrate on the present. It had always bothered
her that there was no body, but then Charles
had slipped into the English Channel and
been washed away to sea. Or had he?

Her plan now was to find out exactly what
had happened. After she had spoken to
Anne she would return to London, and from
there she intended to fly to the Continent.
She was going to use her investigative skills
as a journalist to solve the mystery of
Charles Devereaux's death, to find out the
truth about him.

22

An hour later, at about seven o'clock, having changed from her tailored safari suit into a navy silk dress and pearls, Nicky went downstairs for drinks before dinner. Neither Anne nor Philip was anywhere in sight when she looked inside the drawing room, but as she glanced toward the windows she spotted Anne outside. Nicky crossed the small foyer and went through the side door that led to the terrace. This ran along the back façade of the house, and faced Sweetheart Hill and the South Downs.

Anne half turned and looked over her shoulder at the sound of Nicky's step, and her face lit up with pleasure. "Ah, there you are, darling, I was just thinking about you, thinking how glad I am that you're here with us this weekend."

"It's wonderful to see you, Anne, to visit with you," Nicky responded, truly meaning what she said. Ever since running into Anne in France, she had felt guilty about the way she had neglected her, and had planned to stop off to see her en route to Paris and Provence in September. Then when Charles Devereaux's face had suddenly stared out at her from the television set the other night, she had suddenly had more reason than ever to come to Pullenbrook to talk to Anne. And so she had revised her plans and moved them up by two weeks.

Clearing her throat, Nicky said slowly, "I realize I've been rather unkind to you for the past year and a half by not being in touch, and I'm sorry for that, Anne. I've no excuse. Of course, it's true that I've been away on foreign assignment consistently, covering some pretty lousy wars and other disasters, but I'm not going to hide behind my work. I often do that, but I won't now, not with you. The truth is, it was easier not to see you. Easier for me."

"I know that," Anne replied softly. "And I understand perfectly. Seeing me, whether here or in London, or even in New York, would have only prolonged your agony about Charles. Under the circumstances, I think it was wise of you to go on with your life the way you did. It enabled you to start afresh.''

"Yes, that's true. But still, it *was* selfish of me." There was a little pause before Nicky ventured cautiously, "How . . . how did you manage to cope these past couple of years?"

"I had a great deal of support from Philip, and from my brother and his family. And the house helped me—" Anne broke off and shook her head. "Oh dear, here I am, talking about the house in a strange way again. What I meant, actually, is that I got involved with a project to do with the house, and that has kept me very busy. It's been quite absorbing, and I'm still working on it."

"What kind of project?" Nicky asked, curious.

"The library. I decided to impose order on chaos, and to have the thousands of books cataloged. There are some very rare ones, including some special first editions, and naturally I had to engage a professional to help me. Anyway, in the first few months I fell upon the diaries of the Cliffords, which had been kept by the women of the family over the centuries. I'd vaguely heard about them from my grandfather, but I'd never read them. Needless to say, I became fascinated with them. And at my worst moments I would suddenly pull myself up short and remind myself about those generations of Clifford women who had gone before me, who had been through so much themselves, lost so much and so many loved ones: husbands, sons, fathers, brothers . . . daughters and mothers and sisters. Just think about it—my ancestors lived through the invasion of the Spanish Armada, the Civil War, the Great Plague, and so much else—subsequent wars, extraordinary changes in England and family tragedies as well. Yet they went on stoically, and they survived. I suppose I simply refused to give in to my grief, or to feel sorry for myself, out of pride. You see, the Clifford women of the past set a great example for me."

Nicky nodded, and was about to ask her more about the diaries when Anne sighed heavily and glanced away. A look of such intense pain crossed her face, Nicky wanted to reach out to her and put her arms around her but refrained.

After a moment Anne said, "Losing a child is a terrible thing—one never expects that, you know, Nicky. You always believe that you'll die first, for that really is the proper order of things. . . ." Her voice floated away on the heavy evening air. Again, she stared off into the distance, and then, almost to herself, she finally murmured, "I have always believed that a child, that children, are the justification of life—that they make life worthwhile, worth living."

Nicky found she could not speak. She acutely felt the other woman's overwhelming sadness, and her eyes filled with tears. Swallowing hard, she impulsively took Anne's hand and held it tightly in hers.

When Anne finally turned her head to look into Nicky's face, a slight smile quavered on her lips. She said in the same quiet voice as before, "I was so pleased when I saw you with another man in Les Baux, Nicky. It lifted my heart, to tell you the truth. It meant you had recovered from Charles. I hope you won't think I'm prying too much when I ask whether it's serious or not?"

Nicky hesitated only momentarily before saying, "I'm not sure, I think it could be. Clee *has* told me he's in love with me."

"And what about you? How do you feel?"

"I've known Clee for two years, and he's my best friend, and very dear to me. But it's only in these past few weeks that we've become romantically involved, and nobody was more surprised than I when it happened. And yes, to answer your question, I think I'm falling in love with him."

"I'm so happy to hear that. There was certainly no doubt in my mind how Clee felt about you. It was obvious just from the way he looked at you." Anne squeezed her hand and then said, "Nicky, he adores you."

"But love isn't always enough to make a relationship work as a marriage, though. A lot of other things are tremendously important—if you're going to spend the rest of your life with someone."

"That's very true," Anne agreed. "But you appeared to be comfortable with each other, obviously compatible, and, of course, you do share the same kind of work, so that must be quite a plus, surely." A blond brow was raised, and she looked at Nicky questioningly.

"It is. On the other hand, my career might present a few problems in the long run, and I—"

"There's nothing in the world that can take the place of a good man," Anne interjected, and then she laughed quietly, as if to herself. "Who am I to talk? I've certainly kept a good man dangling on a string for years."

Leaning closer to Nicky, she added, "Take my advice, don't do what I did. Take the plunge. I only began to realize today that I should have married Philip years ago." She gave Nicky a piercing look, and in a much stronger voice she said, "You must reach out for life, Nicky. Grab it with both hands.

Live it to the fullest. Because before you know it, years will have slipped away, and you'll be middle-aged, and then old, and it will be too late. Far, far too late."

"After the age of thirty time does seem to pass very quickly. I've begun to notice that recently."

"And there's another thing," Anne continued. "Don't sacrifice a good relationship, one that works well, because of your career. You might end up being alone if you do. And believe me, Nicky, loneliness is the most terrifying thing. It's another kind of death, actually."

Anne leaned her elbow on the balustrade and fixed her gaze on the South Downs. Watching her, Nicky thought she had never seen her looking lovelier than she did this evening. She wore a deep-rose-colored silk dress that enhanced her fine English complexion, a double strand of pearls and pearl earrings. In Nicky's opinion, Anne Devereaux could easily pass for a woman in her mid-forties; aside from her beautiful blond hair and incomparable skin, she had a slender figure and beautiful legs with finely turned ankles.

Suddenly Anne straightened up and, looking at Nicky, said a little sadly with a rueful smile, "Oh, Nicky, I was such a stupid fool years ago. Fairly early on in my widowhood there was a man I loved, and I should have married him. He wanted me to do so, but there were certain obstacles. And so I rejected him, and in some ways I lived to regret it. And then about twenty years ago, when I was thirty-eight, another man came into my life. I cared for him deeply, as he did for me, but I rejected him as well, because of— Well, never mind *why,* that's not really important. In both instances I chose to be by myself, and as a result I had some pretty dreadful years of loneliness until I met Philip."

"Do I hear my name?" Philip demanded in a jocular manner as he strolled out onto the terrace.

The two women turned around to face him, and Anne said, "Oh, hello, my darling. I was simply telling Nicky what a lot of lonely and very unhappy years I spent before you came into my life."

Philip seemed touched by her words, although he did not make any comment. He simply nodded, but when he came up he put his arm around her waist and held her close to him.

Anne's expression was affectionate as she glanced at him and said, "I was talking to Nicky about Cleeland Donovan, telling her how happy I am that she's involved with him. How happy we both are, actually."

"And relieved," Philip said, offering Nicky a warm smile. "We've been worried about you, my dear." Turning back to Anne, he went on, "I have champagne waiting in the drawing room. Shall we go inside?"

Anne nodded, smiling, and took his arm. "Yes, let's do that."

Much later, after the champagne had been consumed, the three of them sat around the circular table in the small family dining room, which Anne used for more intimate dinners. Inez served the light supper Pilar had prepared, and between the vichyssoise, the grilled sole and the summer pudding, Philip and Anne plied Nicky with questions about her work.

Nicky talked about her sojourn in Beijing, and recounted some of the things that had happened there. They seemed particularly moved when she told them about Yoyo and Mai, Mai's death and Yoyo's subsequent disappearance.

"Clee and I, and Arch and the crew, just hope and pray he's going to show up, and that he used the money we gave him to advantage," Nicky confided. "Clee thinks he'll make it to Hong Kong, and so do I."

"That's the most likely place," Philip remarked, nodding thoughtfully. "And there *is* an underground operating between Beijing and Hong Kong, so I've been told. If Yoyo has *guanxi*—that is, *connections*—he might slip through."

"As my father would say, from your mouth to God's ears, Philip. Yoyo's pretty smart; if anyone can get out, he can."

"How terribly tragic that the young woman was killed," Anne murmured. "From the way you tell it, Nicky, the Chinese army sounds very harsh."

"They are brutal, murderous, and cruel beyond belief. Clee has much proof of that on film. He was able to take hundreds of photographs because they were so busy killing their own people, innocent people, they didn't have time to grab his camera. Mind you, the authorities smashed three of his other cameras in the days before the crackdown. In spite of all that, he's created an amazing book about Tiananmen with those photographs, and I've written the introduction. It's called 'Children of the Beijing Spring,' and it'll make your hair stand on end when you see it. I'll be sending you a copy when it's published next year."

"Thank you," Anne said.

"We watched a lot of the Kate Adie coverage of the student demonstrations on the

BBC," Philip said. "And at the time, Anne and I were utterly appalled by the brutality, the bloodbath. China has a very large black mark against it, and the world is already making its disapproval and abhorrence known. The PRC has been pretty shortsighted."

"Yes, its violation of human rights has been, and still is, horrendous," Nicky pointed out.

Philip nodded, and took a sip of the Pouilly-Fumé. Giving Nicky a probing look, he changed the subject when he asked, "And why are you in England, Nicky? Holiday or business?"

"A bit of both," Nicky answered quickly, and she had to exercise the most enormous control not to blurt out something about Charles. "I'm hoping to do an in-depth interview with the prime minister," she improvised, and rushed on, "Next year, not now. And Arch wanted me to start talking to a few people in advance. You know, sort of get the lay of the land."

"So how can I be of assistance?" Philip asked.

"I'm not sure yet. I'll let you know later. Right now I want to formulate my ideas for the special, think about it in visual terms as well as content." Nicky sat back, filled with relief that she had not said the wrong thing.

"Well, just give me a shout if you need my help," Philip said. "You know I'll do anything I can."

"Thanks, Philip, I appreciate it. You're very kind."

"Shall we have coffee in the drawing room?" Anne said, pushing back her chair and rising.

Anne slipped her arm through Nicky's as they left the dining room and walked across the foyer. "Your work is very dangerous, Nicky, and you're quite intrepid—at least, so it seems to me. Aren't you ever afraid, darling?"

"Not when I'm actually reporting, only afterward," Nicky admitted. "That's the way it is for Clee, and a lot of other journalists as well, Anne. I guess we're so concentrated, so busy doing our jobs during the action, we don't have time for fear."

23

"Anne, I'd like to talk to you about something," Nicky said, hovering in the doorway of the library on Sunday morning. She had changed her mind after a sleepless night and wanted to talk to Anne now. She could not wait until Monday.

Anne stood next to a long mahogany table, picking up fallen rose petals; she looked across at Nicky, and with a little frown, she said, "You sound awfully serious. Is something wrong?"

"Yes, I think so," Nicky murmured as she came into the room. "Where's Philip? I'd like him to hear what I have to say."

"Here I am," Philip said from the depths of

a leather wing chair positioned at the other end of the room.

Nicky heard the rustle of newspaper before his head appeared around the side of the chair. He pushed himself to his feet, folded the paper and dropped it on the floor with the others piled up near the fender.

Anne deposited the handful of rose petals in an ashtray and joined Philip, who stood in front of the fireplace. The two exchanged glances, then sat down together on a Chesterfield sofa; Nicky seated herself on the identical one facing them.

Anne and Philip both focused their attention on her, and Anne said, "You look strange, Nicky. What is it?"

"Before I tell you, I'd like to explain something," Nicky began. "After we ran into each other in Provence, I decided I wanted to come and see you—to make amends, really, for neglecting you—and I'd planned to do so at the end of August, on my way to join Clee in Paris. Then the other night, in New York, something happened that caused me to change my plans. I decided to come a couple of weeks earlier, because I needed to talk to you urgently, Anne. And to you, Philip."

"Please tell us what this is all about," Anne said.

Nicky took a deep breath and plunged in. "Four days ago, on Wednesday night, I was at home in my apartment watching the world nightly news on television. Our Rome correspondent was reporting a shooting incident at a political rally outside Rome—"

"I read about that in Thursday's *Daily Telegraph*," Philip cut in. "There was a suggestion that it might have been an assassination attempt—by a member of the opposition party. Isn't that so?"

"Yes, that's correct," Nicky answered. "But to continue, as Tony Johnson, our Rome correspondent, was finishing his report, the camera moved away from him and panned around the immediate area. It picked up a face in the crowd." Nicky leaned forward, clasping her hands together, and finished quietly but with some intensity, "*It was Charles. The face in the crowd was Charles's face.*"

Anne drew back, and stared at Nicky. She was so stunned she was unable to speak.

Philip exclaimed, "How could it possibly be Charles, Nicky? Charles will have been dead for three years in October. We know he drowned off Beachy Head."

"But did he?" Nicky gave Philip a hard look. "There never was a body, and that has always troubled me, frankly." To her surprise, her voice was perfectly steady, and she continued calmly, "I don't blame you for being disbelieving, I couldn't believe it myself when I saw his face staring out at me from the television set. Nevertheless, I know it—"

"If you believe Charles is alive, then you must think he faked his own death," Anne interrupted, her voice rising, her sudden agitation showing. "Why would my son do such a thing?"

Nicky said, "I don't know, Anne."

"And how would he have done it?" Anne demanded.

"I've kind of figured that out—it would have been quite easy for him."

"It would?" Philip said, eyeing her with some curiosity. "Tell us how."

"Charles could have had an accomplice," Nicky said, returning Philip's direct gaze. "Someone who helped him to rig his death, then disappear afterward. That person, whether a man or a woman, could have done one of two things. He, or she, followed Charles to Beachy Head; Charles parked the Jaguar where it would be easy to find, and then his accomplice drove him back to London. From there, Charles would have had no problem leaving immediately for Europe, whether by plane or train, using a forged passport," Nicky pointed out. "Alternatively, the accomplice could have been waiting in a boat just off the coast, near Beachy Head. Charles could quite easily have swum out to the boat, been picked up and ferried across the English Channel to a French port."

"This sounds a bit farfetched to me!" Philip exclaimed. "As Anne just said, why on earth would Charles do such a thing?"

Nicky shook her head, then shrugged. "I've racked my brains, and I can't really come up with a good reason." She hesitated fractionally, and volunteered, "Well, that's not strictly true. I have thought of one."

"What is it?" Anne leaned forward alertly, her eyes riveted on Nicky.

"That he wanted to start a new life," Nicky said.

"But that's ridiculous!" Anne cried. "He was in love with you, about to marry you, and to all intents and purposes, Charles was a happy man, with everything to look forward to."

"What you say is true," Nicky acknowledged, "but only on the surface." It was her turn to give Anne a long, knowing look, then she said pointedly, after the briefest pause, "Because whether Charles killed himself, *or* did a disappearing act, he wasn't happy with his life. If he had been, he wouldn't have done *either* thing. Therefore, we must assume that he was discontented with everything in his life, including me."

Anne looked as if she was about to say something, and then obviously had second thoughts. She pursed her lips, sat staring at Nicky in silence, twisting her hands in her lap nervously.

"Nicky does have a point there, darling." Philip turned to Anne and took her hands in his. "In fact, we agreed three years ago that Charles must have been excessively troubled and unhappy, even temporarily deranged perhaps, for him to take his own life." Now Philip glanced across at Nicky, and announced in a very firm voice, "*Which is what I believe he did.* You know, my dear, it's often been said that we each have a double, someone who looks exactly like us, living somewhere in the world. Isn't it just possible you saw a man on television who resembled Charles very closely, but that's all?"

"Philip is right," Anne interjected. "He really is, Nicky darling. My son committed suicide while the balance of his mind was disturbed—about something."

"I wish I could truly believe that."

"You really *must,* for your own good," Anne told her, and leaned forward again. Choosing her words carefully, she went on,

"It's a well-known fact that young women who are widowed frequently feel guilty when they become involved with another man. Even though you weren't married to Charles, you were about to be. Perhaps you feel guilty about Clee, and in believing Charles is now alive you're giving yourself a reason to break off with Clee. Isn't that a—"

"No, Anne! It's nothing like that!" Nicky shot back fiercely. "First of all, I don't feel guilty about my relationship with Clee. Not at all. Secondly, it is *not* wishful thinking on my part—believing that I've seen Charles alive on television. I know what I saw. Or rather, who I saw."

"People who do disappearing acts and assume new identities have to be awfully devious by nature," Anne retorted. "My son wasn't like that. Nor would Charles be cruel to me, or to you—why, he loved us both."

Nicky fumbled with the flap of her handbag and brought out an envelope. "On Wednesday night I was as stunned, shocked and disbelieving as you and Philip are now, Anne. But once I'd recovered my equilibrium, I raced down to my network, where I had one of the studio technicians rerun the Rome segment of the nightly world news. He froze the frame with Charles in it. In other words, he stopped the film at that juncture, so that

I could study the man's face. Which I did, and very intently, I might add. And I took a photograph with my Polaroid. Then the technician also took a picture for me with his own camera, which he developed that night and gave to me the following morning. In the meantime, I went back home to my apartment, and I compared my Polaroid shot of the man in the network's film with a photograph of Charles." Nicky opened the envelope and took out several photographs.

Handing one of them to Anne, she explained, "This is my Polaroid of the man who was on television. As you can see, he has darker hair than Charles, and a mustache." She immediately passed a second photograph to Anne, continuing, "And this is Charles in the South of France the year of his—death, or disappearance. What I did was darken his hair and give him a mustache, like the man on television. Look at the two pictures closely, Anne. I'm convinced they are one and the same man."

"Oh I don't know," Philip said somewhat dismissively after looking at the photographs Anne was holding in her hands. "Rather flimsy evidence, wouldn't you say?"

Anne was silent. She sat studying the pictures, her face thoughtful.

Nicky said, "Here is the other photograph,

which the studio technician took for me. It's much larger than my Polaroid, and a bit clearer. Surely the man in Rome is Charles— Charles with a slightly altered appearance. Look at it closely. There's no denying it, Anne."

"There *is* a resemblance," Anne admitted quietly, "but I'm still not convinced it's Charles. How could it be?"

"Why are you telling us this, Nicky? What do you want us to do about it?" Philip asked, sounding slightly put out, even irritated, all of a sudden.

"I'm not sure," Nicky confessed. "But I had nobody else to talk to except you and Anne. And after all, the two of you knew Charles best."

"I'm very concerned for you, my dear," Philip murmured, shaking his head sadly. "And I'm sure Anne is, too."

"I am," Anne concurred.

Philip went on, "It's obvious to me that this whole incident has truly upset you. Certainly you still seem to think that Charles is alive. I wish you wouldn't persist in this belief, Nicky, you're only going to make yourself ill if you do. Once and for all, let me say that *I* do not believe that Charles Devereaux is alive. And *you* don't, do you, Anne darling?"

"Absolutely not. Look here, Nicky," Anne

said, adopting a loving tone, "Charles cannot be anything else but dead. Please take my word for it. I'm his mother—I'd know instinctively, deep down within myself, if he was alive. You mustn't let Charles haunt you in this way, darling. Please put him to rest again, for your own sake. And for Clee's. You have a new life to lead with him. Charles is the past. Let him *be* the past."

Nicky looked from Anne to Philip, and she saw their sympathetic expressions, the anxiety reflected in their eyes. It suddenly dawned on her that they thought she was off-the-wall. Therefore there was nothing else she could say to them about Charles.

A long sigh escaped her. "I brought the photographs to you because I thought you would see what I see—I suppose I was looking for corroboration, and neither of you can give me that. I guess I understand . . . sort of . . ."

Anne rose and sat next to Nicky on the sofa. She took Nicky's hand, and her expression was a mixture of love and concern. After a little while Anne said slowly in a gentle voice, "Let's examine the character of the man for a minute. Charles was the kindest, most thoughtful person, and very loving. You know this from your own experience of him, without my having to tell you. And he had such immense integrity. Good Lord, honor was his byword. Everyone who knew Charles said his word was his bond. He was a true gentleman in the best and most noble sense of that word, and he never did a shoddy thing in his life. That would have been quite alien to his nature."

Anne paused, and her light blue eyes filled with tears as she remembered her son, the qualities he had had and all the things he had stood for. "Charles was such a good man, Nicky, a decent man, and he didn't have a bad bone in his body. He certainly wasn't duplicitous, and he couldn't have dissembled if his life had depended on it. I bore him, brought him up, and I knew my son exceedingly well, especially as a single parent." Her voice began to tremble with emotion as she went on, "*Nothing, no one,* will ever be able to persuade me that Charles contrived his disappearance. Very simply, I *know* he didn't. He couldn't have, not the Charles Devereaux who was my son." Anne swallowed hard and blinked back her tears.

"Oh, Anne, the last thing I wanted was to cause you pain, please believe that," Nicky said with dismay at Anne's increasing distress. "But I *had* to come and tell you. I suppose you think I'm crazy—"

"No, I don't," Anne replied in a shaky voice. "And I know Philip doesn't."

"Of course I don't!" Philip exclaimed, smiling at Nicky. "But I don't think Charles is alive either. The whole idea is quite far-fetched, Nicky, as I said before. Preposterous, in fact."

"But people have disappeared, and they have often done so most successfully," Nicky pointed out, still unable to let go. "There was Lord Lucan, for instance, whose body has never been found. Surely, you remember that case? For all we know, Lucan could be alive and well and living *somewhere* in the world. South America. Bora Bora. Darkest Africa. Under a new identity, of course."

"I doubt it." Philip shook his head vehemently. "I'm positive Lucan is dead—that he drowned, as was generally believed at the time of his disappearance."

"What about that British Member of Parliament—John Stonehouse? *He* did a very clever disappearing act in the seventies," Nicky was quick to add.

"Ah, but he was eventually found," Philip countered swiftly.

Anne said in a voice reverberating with sorrow, "Nicky, it is *not* Charles in these photographs. Truly, it isn't. My son is dead."

24

Nicky went for a walk through the grounds of Pullenbrook on Sunday afternoon.

Earlier, she and Anne and Philip had struggled through lunch, the three of them carefully avoiding the subject of Charles. Only Philip had shown any interest at all in eating. She and Anne had picked at their food, and she had been glad to escape after the pudding, politely refusing coffee and then excusing herself.

She had felt the need to be alone. Now that she was outside in the sunlight she breathed a little easier, and she endeavored to shake off the tension that had held her in its grip for the past few hours.

Unexpectedly the past tugged at her, drew her toward the rose garden, so she swung around and began to walk in that direction. When she arrived at the ancient wooden door set between the mellow stone walls, she turned the wrought-iron handle and pushed open the door. Six stone steps led down into the garden, and when she got to the bottom she stood marveling at the loveliness of the scene before her.

There were a number of gardens at Pullenbrook, but to Nicky this was the most beautiful of them all. Enclosed by high gray stone walls, the sunken rose garden was large but most effectively laid out, with different sections devoted to individual species of roses and other flowers.

Nicky knew from Anne that its intricate design dated back to the eighteenth century, including the parterres, those ornamental areas where flower beds and paths formed a distinctive pattern. There was a small green lawn in the center of the garden, and this was bordered by shrub roses; the parterres were laid out on all four sides of the lawn, beyond the shrubs.

Rambling and climbing roses covered the ancient walls with a mélange of pink and red, bleeding from palest blush to brightest crimson. Under the walls grew hybrid tea roses

and floribunda, including cool white Iceberg
roses, which Anne had surrounded with lavender. Beds of other old-fashioned plants
were set in the parterres, as well as such
herbs as hyssop, savory, thyme and rosemary, mingling with pinks, pansies, violas
and cistus. The idea of combining herbs in
among the roses and other flowers was very
much in the manner of the Tudor and Stuart
gardens of the past—at least, this was what
Anne had told her once.

But quite aside from its beauty and fragrance, the rose garden held a very special
meaning for Nicky. She had first met Charles
here, and later it was in the garden that she
had realized she was in love with him. Also,
he had chosen to propose to her while they
were strolling along its paths one evening.

Now Nicky moved forward, breathing in
the heady scent of the roses, and was almost overcome by it today. Automatically
she headed for the old wooden garden seat
that stood in a bosky corner under the walls,
shaded by a sycamore tree. Sitting down and
leaning back, she closed her eyes and allowed herself to drift with her thoughts. But
after only a short while she opened her eyes
and looked up.

The sky was cloudless and that perfect
blue Charles had always called the color of

speedwells, which he had said exactly matched her eyes. The scent of the roses was more intoxicating than ever, and somewhere nearby a bee buzzed and hummed as it danced in the balmy air. It had been on such a day as this that she had first encountered Charles Devereaux.

Innumerable memories assailed her. Four years fell away. It was suddenly that Friday afternoon in June of 1985 when Charles had walked into her life. She closed her eyes once more, reliving that day all over again, remembering . . . remembering . . .

A perfect rose, Nicky thought. The most perfect rose I've seen in a long time. It was large, a pale pearly yellow, and it had opened fully, but was not yet overblown and fragile, ready to fall. She leaned forward, touched a velvet petal of the rose lightly with a fingertip and breathed in its lovely scent.

It was then that she heard the crunch of footsteps on the path and turned. A man was strolling toward her, a young man, obviously in his thirties. As he drew closer, she saw that he was not much taller than she, about five foot eight in height, and slender and compact of build. He was naturally fair in coloring but she noticed how tanned he was, and his light brown hair had been streaked blond by the sun. He was good-looking in a lean and hungry way, with high cheekbones, sharply chiseled, somewhat gaunt features and a thin aristocratic nose.

"You're Andrew's daughter," he said, staring at her with intensity, not even bothering to conceal his curiosity and interest in her.

Thrusting out her hand, she nodded. "Nicky Wells."

"Charles Devereaux," he responded as he grasped her hand in a firm grip.

Nicky found herself looking into a pair of green eyes, the clearest green eyes she had ever seen. They continued to stare at each other, their hands still clasped. Nicky was experiencing an overwhelming and spontaneous attraction to him.

His scrutiny was intense, and she knew that he was as taken with her as she was with him. Her face grew warm and she felt the color rising from her neck to suffuse her face.

"You're blushing, Miss Wells. Are you not accustomed to having a man look at you with undisguised admiration?"

Nicky gaped at him, feeling suddenly tongue-tied and at a loss. He was certainly direct, and not in the least impeded by social conventions. He got straight to the point.

Very brash, especially for an Englishman, and an aristocrat at that, she thought and smiled inwardly. She rather liked his directness; it was refreshing, if a little unnerving. And she found his upper-class English voice a joy to listen to. It was beautiful, the voice of a Shakespearean actor, full of color and cadences and rhythms. Richard Burton, she thought. He sounds like Richard Burton.

Charles said, "You're very silent—oh dear, I'm afraid I've embarrassed you, Miss Wells."

"No, you haven't, and please call me Nicky."

"I will. And please, do excuse my bad manners. But you are very beautiful, you know. Undoubtedly the most beautiful woman I've ever met."

"Beware of a suave Englishman paying lavish compliments." Leaning back, she eyed him carefully, with a certain amusement.

"I meant what I said. Look here, will you have dinner with me on Monday evening? In London. Just the two of us. I want to get to know you better."

"Yes, I'll have dinner with you, I'd love it," Nicky found herself saying.

"Excellent. We'll have an intimate dinner in a quiet little restaurant. Leave it to me, I

know the ideal spot. Are you staying at Cla-
ridge's with your parents?"

"Yes."

"I'll pick you up at seven o'clock. Please
be prompt. I can't bear to be kept waiting by
women. And dress simply, even casually.
The place where we'll be dining is not very
fancy."

"Are you always this dictatorial, Mr. Deve-
reaux?"

"Call me Charles and no, I'm not. I do
apologize. I didn't intend to sound so insuf-
ferable."

"You didn't, not really."

"I have a confession to make."

"Oh. So soon in our relationship?" Nicky
quipped, raising her brows.

Charles chuckled. "Ah, a sense of humor,
I see, as well as a perfect face. Almost too
good to be true." He chuckled again, and
told her in that mellifluous voice of his, "A
week ago today I went to fetch your parents
from the hotel, to drive them down here for
the weekend. In their suite I saw a photo-
graph of you." He took a deep breath, and
finished with some deliberation, "I was ut-
terly bowled over by you."

Nicky could think of nothing to say.

Charles went on, "Your mother caught me
studying your photograph, and she told me

all about you." He paused and there was a very direct look in his green eyes when he added, "I'm afraid I haven't been able to get you out of my mind since then."

"This is the best line I've heard in a long time," Nicky said, her tone teasing.

Charles had the grace to laugh. "But I really mean what I say. When I arrived at the house fifteen minutes ago, the first thing I did was ask my mother where you were. And when she told me, I came straight out here to find you."

"Charles," Nicky began and stopped abruptly. It suddenly struck her that he was in earnest, that he was being quite serious, and she murmured, "I honestly don't know what to say, how to respond to you. You're so outspoken, so blunt, even a bit aggressive. You knock the breath right out of me."

"And you take my breath away."

Very gently, Nicky extricated her hand and glanced down at it. He had held it so tightly there were red marks on her skin and her hand felt sore.

Charles followed her gaze, and said, "I'm so sorry! Sometimes I don't know my own strength. My grip can be far too strong." As he finished speaking he gently caught her hand in his, brought it to his mouth and brushed his lips across it.

Nicky thought she was going to jump out of her skin. His touch was like an electric shock. Swiftly she pulled back her hand and glanced away, conscious of those cool green eyes watching her so intently.

There was a silence, then Charles asked, "And tell me, what on earth were you doing, lingering out here?"

"Looking at the roses." Nicky turned to him, and striving to sound normal, she said, "In particular, I was studying this one. It's the most perfect rose of all." She touched the yellow bloom and said, "Isn't it?"

Charles glanced at the rose, and then at her and exclaimed, "Your eyes are the exact color of speedwells."

"What are they?"

"Little flowers of the brightest blue."

Suddenly taking firm hold of her elbow, Charles steered Nicky toward the wooden door at the other end of the garden. "I think we'd better go in for tea. That's the safest thing for us to do right now."

Charles stayed close by her side for the next hour or so, disappearing for only about ten minutes toward the end of tea, which was being served in the drawing room. Nicky was acutely conscious of his eyes on her for most of this time, and so were her mother and Anne, who kept exchanging knowing *and delighted glances. Her father was too busy talking to Philip about Margaret Thatcher and the British political scene to notice anything. The two older men sat off to one side of the room by themselves, and were so engrossed in their conversation they were oblivious.*

Later, when she went upstairs to dress for dinner, the first thing Nicky noticed when she entered her room was the yellow rose she had admired in the garden. It was in a crystal bud vase on her bedside table. Propped next to it was an envelope with her name on it. The note inside was written in a neat, precise hand. It said very simply: "I didn't mean to embarrass or offend you. Think kindly of me. C.D."

She dropped the note on the bed, picked up the vase and pressed her face into the center of the rose, breathing deeply of its scent. She felt overwhelmed by Charles Devereaux. He's going to be my undoing, she thought and sighed, knowing she was incapable of doing anything about that now. It was already too late. She had fallen for him in the space of a few hours, captivated by his looks, his voice, his charisma and even his somewhat domineering manner. He had charm and panache and the most extraordinary nerve. He is unique, she decided, as she dressed for the evening. I've never met anyone like him.

A little while later, when she ran into him in the foyer outside the drawing room, she thanked him for the rose. He said with a slight smile, "Perfection deserves perfection," and for the rest of the evening he hovered over her so solicitously, so constantly, even her father became aware of his attentions to her. He even remarked about it to her privately, when they went up to bed. As her mother hurried along the corridor to their bedroom, her father lingered outside hers and finally followed her inside. "I don't want you to think I'm interfering, Nicky," he said quietly, putting his hand on her shoulder affectionately. "But I've known Charles for several years, and he's quite the man-about-town. And used to getting his own way with women."

"I can well imagine that, Daddy," Nicky said, looking into a pair of eyes as blue as her own, noticing immediately their worried expression. "Hey, Dad, relax! I can take care of myself!" She laughed and kissed him lightly on the cheek. "I'm a pretty tough journalist, remember, and the independent, feisty, capable woman you brought me up to be."

Andrew Wells nodded. "I know that your

mother and I instilled the best and bravest instincts in you, angel face. And I know you can look after yourself. You've been facing danger for years in your work. But this is not your work, and Charles Devereaux is a special breed of man. He's Eton, Oxford and the British Establishment, very much the aristocrat with an august lineage and an impeccable background. Don't forget, his grandfather was a peer of the realm, his uncle is the present earl and his mother has a title in her own right."

"I'm not quite sure I know what you're getting at, Dad."

"The British aristocracy is a world unto itself, very snobbish, and inbred. And closed to most."

Nicky burst out laughing. "I can't believe I'm hearing you say this, Andrew Wells! Are you suggesting that I may be viewed as "not suitable," quote unquote, for Charles Devereaux, because I'm an American?"

Andrew laughed with her. "Not really. As far as I'm concerned, you're good enough for anyone, my dearest girl. And probably far too good for most men."

"Spoken like a true, devoted, adoring father."

"I'm simply trying to say that he comes from a different world than you. And I merely

want to caution you, and to explain that Philip once told me Charles was a bit of a playboy, that's all."

"I can handle myself, Pops, honestly, I can."

"I know. Just watch your step."

"And keep my eyes open. That's what you used to say when I was little. Watch your step and keep your eyes open, Nick. And that's what I always did, and I've never forgotten any of your instructions, Daddy," she finished with a small grin.

Andrew hugged her to him. "You're the best, Nick. The very best there is, and the apple of my eye. I just don't want you to get hurt unnecessarily. Now, good night, darling."

Nicky and Charles spent the entire day together on Saturday; they got to know each other better as he drove her around Pullenbrook estate in his Land-Rover. She soon discovered he was well read, knowledgeable, informed about world politics, extremely intelligent and erudite. And she found herself liking him as a person, quite aside from being attracted to him as a man.

Anne gave a dinner party on Saturday night and invited several local couples; it was a pleasant evening. Once again, Charles was assiduous in his attentions to her and *scarcely seemed to notice his mother's guests or anyone else except her. And she was equally engrossed in him, although she played it a little cooler than he, conscious of her father's eyes on her for a good part of the evening.*

By the time she went to bed she was euphoric, floating, and after she had undressed, she sat on the window seat dreamily gazing out at the moonlit grounds. Her thoughts were only of Charles. There was a sudden, light tapping on the door. She went to open it and was not in the least surprised to see Charles standing there. Without a word he came into the room quickly, closed the door behind him and leaned against it.

"Forgive the intrusion at this late hour," he said. "But I couldn't sleep. I had to come and see you, if only for a moment."

He took a step forward, reached for her hand, and pulled her toward him. "I had the most pressing and desperate need to—kiss you good night." He peered at her closely, and smiled a quiet little smile. Without another word he kissed her fully on the mouth. Her arms went around his neck, and immediately he drew her even closer. After a moment he loosened his hold and said against her hair, "I want to make love to you, Nicky.

Let me stay with you tonight—don't send me away."

She was silent.

He kissed her again, more passionately than before; she could not help responding, and clung to him.

"Oh, my darling," he said, and brushed his mouth against her cheek. "Please let me stay."

"But I hardly know you," she began, and then let her voice trail off uncertainly. She was unnerved by him, and afraid. Charles Devereaux was having a potent effect on her. He was lethal, and she suddenly understood that she could quite easily be devastated by him.

Charles took her face in his hands and looked deeply into her eyes. His voice was tender when he murmured, "Oh Nicky, Nicky, don't let's play games with each other. We're both adults, we're mature, intelligent people." Again the faint smile played around his mouth, and he added, "And do you honestly think you'll know me any better on Monday? What difference does it make whether we make love tonight or wait until then?" He brought his mouth to hers, kissed her long and hard and then released her, leaving her standing in the middle of the floor.

Pivoting, he went to the door and locked it. As he walked back to her he took off his silk dressing gown and threw it on a chair, and began to unbutton his pajama top. When he stood in front of her, he said in his low-pitched, seductive voice, "You know you want me as much as I want you, Nicky. It's written all over your face." Unfazed by her continuing silence, very sure of himself and entirely in command, he took her hand and led her toward the four-poster bed.

Nicky sat up on the garden seat and reached into her pocket for her sunglasses. As she put them on she felt dampness on her cheeks, and she realized with a little jolt that she had been crying. But she was not going to shed any more tears for Charles Devereaux. She had used them up years ago.

Pushing herself to her feet, she walked down the path between the parterres, endeavoring to shake off the past, to quench the memories. Climbing the steps, she turned the handle of the old door and went out of the garden.

Pullenbrook soon came into view. She could not help thinking how extraordinary it looked, bathed in the late afternoon light. The sunshine brought a warmth to its old gray stone, the many windows glittered and winked, and it was like a living thing to her. Anne had spoken the truth when they had discussed the house the other day; she *had* loved Pullenbrook from the moment she had first set eyes on it.

On that fateful Friday I've just been remembering, she thought, gazing up at the great Tudor edifice so steeped in English history and the history of the Cliffords, I was snared by a man, by a woman and by a stately family home. Yes, she had fallen in love with them all. Instantly. She still loved Anne and the house. As for Charles, her love for him had died three years ago.

Inside the house, the Great Hall was eerily quiet and filled with pale sunshine when she entered a few minutes later. The family portraits that hung on the fireplace wall caught her eye, and she stood staring up at them thoughtfully. Then she scrutinized the others as she traversed the length of the huge room.

Suddenly, she thought: Charles Adrian Clifford Devereaux was descended from a great line of noblemen, magnates and warrior knights in service to the Crown of England. He was a true aristocrat, and in the best sense of that word. Honor and nobility were bred in the bone; justice and fair play were inculcated from birth. He *was* a good man, a decent man. I could not have loved him the way I did had he been otherwise. Certainly I could not have loved a man capable of shoddy behavior, a man who could cold-bloodedly fake his own death for reasons of his own, a man who could callously bring pain and heartache to me, the woman he loved, and to his mother. I would never have wanted to marry a man like that. Never. Never.

The sound of footsteps caused Nicky to swing around.

Anne was walking toward her with a look of concern on her face. Coming near, she took hold of Nicky's arm. "Are you all right, darling?"

Nicky nodded and gave her a half smile.

"You rushed off, were in such a hurry to escape, I've been worried about you. I hope you're not angry with me, or with Philip?"

"Of course not, just the opposite." Nicky cleared her throat before continuing, "I've been thinking about Charles, remembering things this afternoon, and I've come to a conclusion. You're right, Anne, I don't think he faked his death. Very simply, he wasn't capable of being devious. I recognize that now. I agree with you and Philip that the man my network filmed in Rome merely bears a remarkable likeness to Charles."

Anne appeared startled, but quickly recovering herself, she said, "This is quite an about-face—you're not just agreeing with us to make *me* feel better, are you?"

"No, I'm not. Surely you know me better than that. I'm my parents' daughter and a stickler for the truth, just as they are. Not only in my work but in my private life. In all things, in fact."

Anne began to walk toward the door leading to the private quarters of the house without answering. Nicky caught up with her and slipped her arm through Anne's. She said, "I'm sorry if I've upset you, truly, truly sorry. It was never my intention to cause you pain by coming here—with my story and the photographs."

"I know that, and you did the only thing you could, under the circumstances."

"I hadn't meant to blurt it out today," Nicky said, shaking her head. "I really hadn't. I was going to tell you tomorrow, because I didn't want to spoil your engagement. But I was so terribly worried this morning, after a restless, sleepless night, and unfortunately the words came out before I could stop them."

"No harm has been done, and I'm glad you had the confidence to come to me . . ." Anne smiled. Her face was full of love. "At least it's brought you back into my life, Nicky."

"Yes, that's true."

Now Anne said softly, "I feel absolutely certain Charles committed suicide. *Why* he did we will never know, he had everything to live for. Over these past few years I've come to believe that he must have been ill. Physically ill, I mean, with some sort of fatal disease—cancer, a brain tumor, leukemia, something dreadful like that, and which he never told us about, of course. I think he took his life in order to save us the pain of his eventual suffering and death from that fatal disease. To me, this is the only possible explanation."

"Charles's death will always be a mystery," Nicky murmured, almost to herself.

After Nicky had gone upstairs to rest before supper, Anne returned to the Great Hall, where she locked and bolted the front door. Retracing her steps across the hall, she hurried through into her own wing of the house.

Earlier, she and Philip had had tea in the drawing room, and she had left him there when she had gone in search of Nicky. Glancing through the open door, she saw that he was no longer sitting there.

Perhaps he's also gone to his room to rest, she thought, and she headed down the corridor. She was making for the library, wanting to rescue the magazine sections of the Sunday newspapers before Inez scooped them up and threw them out.

The door was ajar, and faintly she heard Philip's voice. He was obviously speaking on the telephone, and she increased her pace, anxious to tell him about Nicky's unexpected about-face.

Pushing open the door, she saw that Philip was sitting on the edge of the desk with his back to her. Before she could announce herself, she heard him say, ". . . and won't let go. Like a dog with a bone . . ." There was a short pause as he listened, and then he exclaimed, "No, no! *Rome.*"

As Anne entered the room she exclaimed, "Philip, I've something to tell you."

Startled, he swung around, and she knew from the expression on his face that she had caught him unawares.

He gave her a little nod of acknowledgment and said into the receiver, "Look, I've got to go now. I'll talk to you tomorrow— better still, I'll see you tomorrow," then he hastily hung up.

Anne walked over to the desk, frowning slightly. "You were obviously talking about Nicky, Philip. Who were you speaking to?"

"My son. I was speaking to Timothy, my

dear," Philip said with a smile, and without missing a beat.

"About Nicky?" Anne sounded incredulous.

"Yes. When I was on the phone with Tim the other evening, just after he'd returned from Leipzig, I sort of half promised I'd go back to town tonight. To have supper with him. I just begged off. He wanted to know why I wasn't coming up, and I was simply explaining about Nicky, and her weird story about the man in Rome."

"Why did you beg off? You didn't have to, you know. You could have gone up, I wouldn't have minded."

"Darling, don't you see? I didn't want to leave you alone this evening," Philip said. "You've been somewhat upset by all this—fuss. I felt I ought to be here with you, *wanted* to be with you. I can see Tim tomorrow."

"I see," she murmured, and gave him an odd look.

25

On Monday night Nicky caught the last flight to Rome.

Once the plane was airborne and she was well settled in her seat, she took out her notebook and scanned the notes she had made in her suite at Claridge's Hotel earlier in the day. After a couple of seconds of studying them, she slipped the notebook back into her handbag, then reached for the glass of white wine that the flight attendant had brought to her a short while before. She took a few sips, endeavoring to relax, but her mind continued to turn as rapidly as it had for the last few days.

Despite her discussion with Anne and

Philip at Pullenbrook this past weekend and their opinions, her gut instinct told her that the man accidentally captured on the ATN news footage was none other than Charles Devereaux. And because her father had always said she should rely on her gut instinct, this was *exactly* what she was doing now.

Putting her wineglass down on the flat section of the armrest, she reached into her bag again. This time she pulled out the photograph taken from the news footage by Dave, the studio technician. Frowning, she gazed at it intently, as she had done quite frequently since last Wednesday. However many times she tried to convince herself she was wrong, she always came back to her first conclusion: the man *was* Charles Devereaux.

Yesterday, at Pullenbrook, she had begun to waver in this belief, no doubt influenced by the house and the history it represented, by the prestige of the family and, not unnaturally, by Anne Devereaux herself. If Anne said that the man in the picture was definitely not her son, then who was to argue otherwise with her? And so on Sunday afternoon she had done that sudden and unexpected volte-face, had agreed with Anne, somewhat to her own surprise as well as her friend's.

But then this morning, when she arrived at

Claridge's, she had reversed herself and come back to her original opinion.

I suppose there's nothing quite like the cold light of a drizzly Monday morning in London to bring one to one's senses, Nicky now thought, putting the picture away. Anne and Philip had said that the man in Rome merely had a *look* of Charles. She could not agree; the resemblance was much stronger than that. If the man in the picture was not Charles after all, then he was his identical twin.

This morning at the hotel in London, as she had sat ruminating on everything that had happened, she had asked herself how his partner would react if she showed *him* the photograph. Christopher Neald and Charles had been friends for years, as well as being in business together, and they had always been exceptionally close—since their twenties, in fact.

On the spur of the moment, she had picked up the phone and called Chris at Vintage Wines, only to be informed by his new secretary, Michael Cronin, that Chris was away on holiday. She had pressed for more information, had been told that Mr. Neald was "island-hopping in Polynesia," and was therefore quite unreachable, and would not be back in England until the middle of September. Disappointed, she had said she would phone again next month.

It was then that she had decided to go to the source of the film footage—the ATN bureau in Rome. Maybe Tony Johnson, the Rome bureau chief, could help her in some way; perhaps there was additional footage, which had not been transmitted by satellite to New York, footage that might give her some leads.

In any case, here she was on a plane en route to Rome, and she could not help wondering if she was on a wild-goose chase. How did you go about finding a man who had so cleverly and effectively disappeared three years ago? A man who obviously did not want to be found, and whose presence in Rome was known to her now only because of a fluke, an accident, chance, fate, call it what you will. If the ATN cameraman covering the story with Tony that night hadn't picked up a face in the crowd on film, and if she hadn't been watching the news intently at that precise moment, she would have been none the wiser. A million-to-one chance, she thought, remembering how that face was on and off the screen in a flash, in a matter of seconds. How easily she could have missed it if she had gone to the kitchen for a glass of water, or if she had been on the phone and not paying attention. But then life was like that—full of flukes and coincidences. It was meant to be, she said under her breath, and shivered involuntarily. But looking for Charles Devereaux would be like looking for the proverbial needle in a haystack.

Nicky shifted in her seat, glanced out the window at the dark night sky and wondered, suddenly, why she was continuing to pursue this matter, why she was persisting with it. Naturally, she came up with the answer immediately: given who and what she was as a person, as well as a journalist, she simply had to know the truth, needed to know it. That trait had been nurtured in her since childhood. Also, there was another thing— she wanted to finally close that chapter of her life that had once been centered on Charles Devereaux. It was not that she harbored any emotional feelings for him; those had been well and truly killed off long ago. But she certainly had no desire whatever to continue to be haunted by the specter of him.

After all, there was Cleeland Donovan now, a very special man, one who had grown more and more important to her in the last couple of months. Clee represented a new beginning for her. There was the most wonderful chance to make a life with him if they could work it out, given all the logistics involved. Lately she had come to believe that they probably could, with a little give-and-take on both sides.

Clee was the future. Her future. Therefore, she must not permit any shadows from the past to hang over her or them. The fact was, she wanted and needed to be truly free in her heart and mind and soul—to be free for Clee, with no encumbrances from the past.

As often happened these days, her thoughts now settled on him, and as always she felt a lovely warmth spreading through her. Having Clee in her life, knowing he loved her, made her feel good, even when he wasn't with her. Fortunately, she had managed to reach him at the Kempinski in West Berlin late this afternoon, before setting out for the airport. She had wanted to tell him she was off to Rome on business for a few days.

Because of the nature of their work, he had not been unduly surprised, nor had he found it unusual that she was suddenly flying off somewhere.

"What's cooking?" he had asked, laughing, and had then added, "I guess you've just had a brainstorm, Nick, dreamed up some sort of exotic special."

Quickly, concisely, she had explained that it was not one bit exotic, that she was considering doing a piece on the European Common Market and the changes that would take place when all the frontiers came down. "Later I'll have to interview politicians in every country, but right now I want to poke around, get a feel for things in Rome, since I've done that in London," she had said, resorting to a few harmless white lies.

He had understood; they had gone on to chat about his impending trip to Leipzig, and arranged to stay in touch by phone or through the Image office in Paris if necessary. And they had agreed they would still meet in Paris in a week's time, as they had originally planned to do.

"*Ciao,* Nick," Clee had said. "I can't wait to see you on the twenty-eighth." And she had answered, "Neither can I, darling," before breaking the connection.

Nicky closed her eyes, feeling unexpectedly drowsy and blaming the wine. She missed Clee very much, more than she had ever missed anybody. It suddenly struck her that he might be rather annoyed with her if he knew the reason why she was really going to Rome, and she sat up with a start. Then she asked herself whether she would tell him when she saw him. She wasn't sure.

But by next Monday she was bound to have all the answers about Charles Devereaux. Or none at all, perhaps. The decision about confiding in Clee would be made then, and not before. She would only tell him in person, not on the telephone. And in any case, if she had told him earlier he would have dropped everything and flown to Rome. She did not need him to hold her hand as she looked for Charles; nor did she want her past colliding with the present.

Two and a half hours after the flight had left Heathrow it was landing at Rome's Leonardo da Vinci Airport exactly on time. When Nicky had cleared customs, she went through into the terminal, and within the space of a few minutes she spotted the limousine driver holding up a card with her name printed on it.

Forty-five minutes later the car was pulling up outside the Hassler Hotel, near the church of Trinità dei Monti at the top of the famous and very beautiful Spanish Steps. Her parents had first brought her here as a child, and whenever she came to Rome she invariably stayed at the Hassler. The night manager recognized both her name and her face, and after she had registered, he escorted her to her suite, chatting amiably.

Once she was alone, Nicky went to the windows, parted the curtains and looked out. The view of Rome was spectacular, and it was a sea of flickering lights under a star-strewn inky sky. Was Charles Devereaux living somewhere out there in the Eternal City? And if so, what were her chances of finding him? With a little stab of dismay, she had to admit that the odds seemed against her.

The following morning, as soon as she had had her simple breakfast of tea and toast, Nicky telephoned the ATN bureau. After asking for Tony, she sat back, waiting. The woman who had answered had not bothered to ask her name, and she had not given it; when the bureau chief came on he said, "Tony Johnson here. Who is this?"

"It's Nick, Tony. How're you doing?"

There was a startled silence, and then he exclaimed, "Nicky Wells? Is this *that* Nick?"

"Of course it is! What other woman do you know called Nick?"

Tony chuckled, obviously delighted to hear her voice. "Hey, Nicky, how are you? And more important, *where* are you?"

"Around the corner."

"You mean *here*? In Rome?"

"I most certainly do."

"Good God! The entire network seems to be descending on me today."

"What do you mean?"

"A friend of yours just arrived, Nicky. Now he's trying to grab the phone from me, itching to talk to you, it seems. But before I pass it over, let's make a date. For lunch. Today. Is that okay?"

"More than okay, it's wonderful, Tony. But who wants to speak to me?"

Again Tony's deep chuckle echoed down the wire. He said, *"Ciao,* Nick."

"Hi, Nicky, what are you doing in Rome?" Arch Leverson asked, his tone jocular but curious.

"I could ask the same of you, Arch," she said, completely taken aback, but keeping a cool head as usual.

"You're slipping, honey. Or rather, your memory is. I told you last week that I was going on vacation to Capri. I just stopped off here for a couple of days, to break the journey and see my old buddy Tony."

It was true, Arch had told her, but somehow she had not associated Capri with Rome. And anyway, she had been so preoccupied last week. Now she said swiftly, "Yes, you're right, I did forget."

"Last I heard from you, Nicky, you were off to London to investigate the possibilities of doing a special on Margaret Thatcher. So why *are* you in Rome?"

"To buy shoes," she said, improvising, not knowing how to answer him at this moment.

Arch guffawed. "Hey, come on, it's me you're talking to! You're about as much into shopping as I'm into fly fishing. Come on, Nicky, what gives?"

"I can't go into it now," she answered, wanting to buy time.

Her answer seemed to satisfy Arch, who now said, "Fine, fine. Is Clee with you?"

"No, he's in Berlin today, Leipzig tomorrow, Paris on Sunday night. I'm meeting him there on Monday, and we're going down to Provence sometime next week."

"That's great, Nick. I guess I'll be seeing you for lunch with Tony. Right?"

"It's the best offer I've had all day. Where shall we meet? At the bureau?"

"Good idea. Where are you staying, by the way?"

"At the Hassler, as usual. And you?"

"The Eden. Listen, Nicky, I've got another offer for you. Dinner tonight. I'm leaving for Capri very early tomorrow morning, to join Patricia and the Grants at the villa they've rented for the season. Hey, wait a minute, here's a thought. Come with me. You don't really have anything better to do, do you?

And they'd love to have you for a couple of days."

"Thanks, but I can't, honestly. However, I will have dinner with you tonight."

"It's a date. Now, why don't you plan on picking us up at the bureau around one-thirty?"

"You've got a deal."

26

After she had hung up, Nicky sat staring at the telephone for a few minutes, a frown lingering on her face.

Arch Leverson was the last person she had expected to find at the Rome bureau, and she had been taken aback to say the least, although she had quickly recovered herself. She nonetheless had no idea what she would say to him when she saw him later. She would have to think of something, since she did not want to tell him the truth. He worried and fussed about her far too much already, and instinctively she knew he would try to dissuade her from her purpose. When she left for London, she had been able to put him off with a few words about the Margaret Thatcher special; she doubted he would buy a story about her being in Rome to do research for a possible Common Market piece.

She sighed. Unfortunately, because Arch was at the ATN bureau with Tony, she could not go over there this morning and start asking leading questions about the news footage transmitted last Wednesday. The questions would have to wait until Arch left for Capri; there was no alternative but to talk to Tony tomorrow.

In the meantime she now had nothing to do until she met Arch and Tony for lunch, and she felt a sudden surge of frustration—she loathed the thought of having to kill time until then.

Rome was a familiar place to her; she had visited it many times in the past, and, in any case, she was hardly in the mood to go sightseeing. Besides which, she had done that years ago, and had had the best guide there was—her father, Andrew Wells.

Her father loved Rome in much the same way she loved Paris—he felt a spiritual affinity for it—and so as a child she had seen the Eternal City through his eyes. "Rome is the cradle of civilization," he had told her when she was twelve, and old enough to understand one of his history lessons as they had tramped around the city. He had taken her down the Spanish Steps below their hotel, to the Trevi Fountain, the catacombs, the Borghese Gardens, Saint Peter's Church, Vatican City and the Sistine Chapel. There was not much she had been allowed to miss as a child; her father had seen to that on their different visits over the years.

Sometimes, when she returned to places she knew well, she enjoyed visiting old haunts that held a special meaning for her, but not today, not on this trip. The mystery surrounding Charles Devereaux filled her mind, as it had for the past five days, and she recognized this was the way it would be until she arrived at the truth.

Once again letting out a sigh of frustration, Nicky went through into the bathroom to take a shower, deciding as she did that she would buy some shoes. Her mother had a favorite boutique on the Via Veneto, and she would stop by there before heading over to the ATN bureau.

As it turned out, Arch did not ask any questions when she arrived at the bureau at one-thirty, carrying a shopping bag of shoes. He merely glanced at it and winked at her knowingly.

Tony was as tanned and handsome as

ever, and his usual exuberant and affectionate self. After hugging and kissing her, he
introduced her to his new secretary, Jennifer
Allen, and other members of the staff she
had not met before. Then she, Arch and
Tony retreated to the latter's private office to
chat and catch up.

Nicky and Tony were old friends from the
early days, when she had started at the network and he had been based in New York.
The men dated back even further than that,
to the time they had both been in their first
jobs at another network.

"It's like old home week," Tony said as the
three of them trooped out of the office and
went around the corner to lunch at Tony's
favorite trattoria. "The best in Rome," he
explained as he ushered them inside. Over
drinks they continued to catch up with one
another's news, and lunch was a wonderful,
breezy affair, full of warmth and camarade-
rie, plenty of laughter, joking around, shop
talk and industry gossip.

Much to her relief, Nicky found herself
relaxing completely with Tony and Arch. She
felt at home with the two men; they were
colleagues and were all on the same wave-
length, and she enjoyed every minute of
being with them. So much so, she actually
forgot about the Devereaux problem for a

short while. For the first time in several days she felt like her old self.

But thoughts of Charles came rushing back to trouble her soon enough. The minute she was alone in her suite at the Hassler, in fact. And that evening, as she was getting ready for dinner, she made a decision. She was going to confide in Arch after all. She needed a sounding board, someone to whom she could unburden herself, and someone who would bring both an open and an analytical mind to the problem.

"Well, aren't you the beauty," Arch said as he strolled into her suite in the Hassler at a few minutes past eight.

"Thank you," she said and gave him a smile.

After kissing her on the cheek, Arch stepped back and nodded approvingly as he regarded the cream silk suit she was wearing. "Now *that* little number is the epitome of elegance," he said, and nodded again.

"Pauline Trigère made it for me."

Arch glanced down at her feet, appeared to be studying her high-heeled cream silk pumps, before saying in an amused tone, "And tell me, Nicky, did Miss Trigère also make your shoes?"

Nicky had to laugh. "No, she didn't. I bought them this morning. On the Via Veneto."

"Pretty expensive shoes, I guess, when you take into consideration the price of the air ticket from London to Rome."

"You know very well I didn't come to buy shoes," she shot back. "Although shoes I did indeed buy. I'll tell you why I came here in a minute. Now, would you like a glass of white wine? I ordered a bottle, just in case. But if you don't, I can easily order something else from room service."

"Thanks, the wine'll be great."

"Why don't you sit down over there, and I'll bring you a glass," Nicky said, walking over to the console near the window. She poured wine into two crystal goblets and carried them back to the seating arrangement.

Arch, who had remained standing, touched his glass to hers silently, took a sip and seated himself on the sofa.

Nicky took the chair opposite him, and after a quick swallow of wine, she put the goblet on the table and leaned against the cream brocade of the chair back.

Arch said, "So, why *are* you in Rome, Nick?"

Nicky did not at first respond. After taking a deep breath, she said, "I think Charles

Devereaux is alive, and in Rome. I must know if I'm right."

Arch sat up on the sofa with a jerk, almost spilling his wine as he did. He was so thunderstruck his jaw dropped—he was speechless. Then finally he said, "I know you wouldn't say that unless you had some real evidence. What is it? What've you got? Shoot."

"Last Wednesday night I saw someone who looked exactly like Charles Devereaux on television," Nicky began, and then slowly, precisely, leaving nothing out, she told Arch everything that had happened since then.

When she had finished, Arch muttered, "I tend to agree with Philip Rawlings. It's just not enough for me, Nick, I'd—"

"I'll show you the pictures," she interrupted, getting to her feet and hurrying into the bedroom. She returned at once with the photographs and, seating herself next to Arch, spread them out on the coffee table.

Pointing to one of them, she said, "This is my Polaroid of the man in the news footage." Moving on to the next, she continued, "And this is the larger photograph that Dave took. The third is the one of Charles, which I doctored up—I darkened the hair and added the mustache."

Arch studied all three photographs very

carefully. "There's a strong likeness, a very strong likeness, in fact. Yes, I think you're right about that, Nicky. These three pictures could be of one and the same man." He turned to her and finished, "The guy on our news footage could very easily be Charles Devereaux, no doubt about it."

Relieved to hear him say this, Nicky exclaimed, "Thank God you agree with me, that you don't think I'm imagining things!"

Arch said, "Never, honey, you're one of the sanest people I know."

"Thanks, Arch." She touched his arm lightly, affectionately. "I appreciate your saying that. I began to feel a bit peculiar at Pullenbrook this weekend."

Bringing his hand up to his face, Arch rubbed his chin, looking thoughtful. "Answer me this, Nicky. Why would Charles want to fake his own death and disappear?"

"I've no idea."

"Usually people do that only if they're in some kind of trouble. You know, financial trouble, for instance."

"Charles didn't have money problems. I know that from his will. Anyway, people do disappear for other reasons."

"Such as?"

"If they're depressed—which he wasn't. Or if they've done something criminal, or if they are criminals."

Arch exclaimed, "Jesus Christ! You're not suggesting Charles was a crook, are you?"

She shrugged. "I don't know whether I am or not—but I am giving you reasons why people melt into thin air and start a new life . . . people who are murderers, drug traffickers, arms smugglers, big-time swindlers . . ." Nicky rose, and walked over to the window, where she stood looking out. Eventually she turned around and said, "How well does anyone know another person? Truly *know*, I mean. There are secret parts to all of us, parts we don't always know well ourselves."

"Yes," Arch murmured and lifted his glass to his lips, at a loss for words.

Nicky said, "Maybe he was a homosexual, and wanted to escape me and our marriage."

Arch stared at her. "Only you have the answer to that!" he exclaimed, and asked, "Do you think he was?"

"No, I don't. Not at all."

"No indications?"

"No."

"That was a very weak *no,* honey."

She was silent as she slowly walked back to the chair, where she sat down. "It *was* a weak no, that's true, but it didn't mean anything, I wasn't implying anything. You know as well as I do that there are men who have hidden their homosexuality even from themselves for years, and then they suddenly come out. . . . That's all I meant when I brought up homosexuality. And if you're asking me if Charles showed any homosexual tendencies in our sex life, the answer to that is a categoric *no.*"

"Still, he could have been—in the closet?" Arch lifted a brow questioningly.

"Anybody can be anything, I suppose, but I believe Charles was straight."

"I have to agree with you. I didn't know Charles well, but he struck me as being a pretty tough sort of guy, maybe even a bit ruthless. He wasn't the sort to vanish without a trace just because he was afraid to break off his engagement. He'd have done that no matter what the reason, Nicky, if he'd wanted to. If he did disappear, it was for a reason that had nothing to do with you."

"I've finally come to that conclusion myself.

"*Why?*" Arch muttered. "Why would a man like Charles drop off the face of the earth?"

"Don't you think I've asked myself that a thousand times since last Wednesday?" She shrugged wearily. "I just don't know."

"Perhaps it *wasn't* him on our news footage. It seems to me Charles Devereaux had no possible reason to walk away from his life. Therefore, he must have committed suicide."

"I don't believe he's dead," Nicky said quietly but vehemently, looking at Arch intently. "Not here, not inside." She paused, pressed her hand against her stomach. "My gut instinct tells me that he's alive, and that he dropped out of sight for a very, very serious reason. A reason so bizarre that you and I couldn't possibly imagine what it is. And that's why I haven't been able to come up with an answer. Why no one else has."

Arch looked at her keenly but made no comment.

Nicky now spoke slowly, to give even greater emphasis to her words. "We're lacking some information, Arch, there's something about Charles that we don't know. And that's why we're at a loss. He vanished for a reason that's not *apparent,* that's not in the least obvious. Not to us, anyway. And believe me, it's no ordinary, everyday reason."

"Do you mean he had, *has,* some sort of secret?"

"Yes, maybe. But whatever it is, neither his mother nor Philip has an inkling of it, and I certainly don't."

"Hell, Nick, I don't know what to say . . ." Arch shook his head and lifted his shoulders helplessly.

Bending forward, her eyes leveled on him

earnestly, Nicky said, "Listen, Arch, Charles came to Rome, to continental Europe. He didn't go to Australia or Africa or—Polynesia. So obviously he wanted, or needed, to be in Europe, had to stay here."

"There's another point. If he *is* alive, what's he using for money? How's he living?"

"He could have been stashing money away in Europe for years. He did a lot of business in France and Spain—wine business—and even here in Italy from time to time," Nicky explained. "He probably had a Swiss bank account. In fact, that's more than likely. Yes, I'm certain he did."

"I see what you mean."

"You never knew this, but Charles was always something of a financial genius, even when he was very young," Nicky confided. "Of course he inherited money, but aside from that he made his own fortune, and in a variety of ways. Stocks and bonds, and real estate, to mention only a few things. And he turned his wine-importing company into a real gold mine. Money and its management and manipulation were never problems to him."

"He left everything to his mother, didn't he?"

"Everything that was visible, and in England. How do I know what he got out over the years? Or the deals he made in Europe?" She nodded, as if confirming something to herself. "Charles would have no problem living, and living pretty damned well."

"I guess you're right. Do you think Charles had, and still has, a secret life?"

"Again, I don't know—but the indications are there, aren't they? A man doesn't do what he did without a truly compelling motive."

Taking another tack, Arch asked, "When you came to Rome, what was your plan, Nicky? I mean how did you aim to find him?"

"I didn't really have a plan, Arch. I just decided to come to the source of the film. I was going to talk to Tony about the footage, show him those pictures." She gestured to the photographs on the coffee table. "I intended to ask Tony if he'd ever seen that man knocking around Rome, and if he had and knew his haunts, I was going to go and look for him. If Charles *is* living here, he's obviously doing so quite openly, quite freely. The reason he was captured on film is that he was *outside* in the square with the crowds that night—not hiding somewhere."

"Yes, that's true. On the other hand, you've so little to go on, honey. Does Clee know that you're here?"

"Yes, of course."

"Did you tell him *why*?"

"No. When I spoke to him on the phone, I said I was here on business."

"I don't think Clee would be too happy if he knew you were roaming around looking for Charles Devereaux. I think he'd be pretty damned mad. After all, you two seem to be very involved."

"Yes, we are. But that doesn't mean he runs my life, or that I have to ask his permission about anything," Nicky said in a firm voice. "I'm a very independent woman, nobody tells me what to do, or when or how to do it. I'm my own person. That's the way I was brought up, as you well know. What I'm doing in Rome is my business, Arch, and only mine."

"All I meant is that I'm not sure Clee would relish the thought of you investigating Charles's disappearance. Hasn't it ever occurred to you that it might be dangerous? Charles Devereaux doesn't *want* to be found, honey. I'll bet my bottom dollar on that."

She nodded. "Maybe."

"Tell me something. What are you going to do if you do find him, Nick? Take him to task for running out on you? Chastise him and walk away? Turn him in to the authorities?"

Nicky's mouth tightened but she said nothing.

"Are you still in love with Charles Devereaux?" he asked, deciding to confront her with the big question. "Is that why you're hell-bent on tracking him down?"

"No, it isn't. I'm not in love with him. I haven't been for a long time."

"Then why *are* you doing this?"

"Because I have to get to the truth, Arch, to know what really happened. And why. I'm a reporter, remember, and training will out, as they say. Besides, I want to close the chapter on Charles Devereaux, and get on with my life—with Clee."

"Close it now, Nick. Stop this. It's a waste of time, in my opinion."

There was deep anxiety in his voice and she saw how serious he was. He was worrying about her again, as she had guessed he would. "Perhaps I should do as you say," she murmured, wanting to pacify him, to put his mind at rest. "I suppose it would be wise to let it drop. There's only the remotest chance that I might find Charles. And as you said, even if I did, what then?" She sighed lightly. "You're right, Arch, as you so often are."

He smiled at her, and a look of immense relief flooded his face. "Go to Paris, Nick. Promise me you'll go to Paris tomorrow."

"Yes, I will," Nicky said, and reached for her glass of wine. What did one more white lie matter in the scheme of things?

"Let's go and sit in Tony's office, it's more comfortable there," Jennifer Allen said, ushering Nicky into her boss's inner sanctum. "Can I get you anything, Miss Wells? A cup of coffee, perhaps?"

"Nothing, thanks, Jennifer, and please call me Nicky."

The young woman smiled at her. "Thanks, I will."

"So Tony won't be back until late this afternoon?" Nicky said, lowering herself onto the low-slung Italian leather sofa.

"He said about five or six o'clock," Jennifer answered, taking a chair next to Nicky. "He went to Vatican City, and after the meeting there he has a lunch. And after that he's got to go to the dentist."

Nicky pursed her lips and nodded, wishing now that she had spoken to Tony on the phone earlier.

"Can I be of help in any way?" Jennifer asked, eager to please one of the superstars of the network.

"No, not really. I'd hoped to speak to Tony about a piece of news footage that was transmitted from here last Wednesday, a week ago today, in fact."

"Oh, the segment on the shooting incident at the political rally," Jennifer exclaimed. "That's the footage you're referring to, isn't it?"

"Yes, I was wondering if all of it was sent, or whether there might be some spare footage left over?"

Jennifer shook her head. "No, there isn't, Nicky. We passed everything to New York."

"I see."

"Are you sure I can't be of help? You look worried."

Nicky forced a laugh. "I'm not. Only curious, actually. And maybe you can help after all." As she spoke, Nicky opened her handbag and took out the three photographs; she handed only two of them to Jennifer. "The man in these pictures was caught on that news footage, just a face in the crowd. I had the frame frozen at the network and these pictures taken of him, because—"

"Why? Is he important or something?" Jennifer cut in.

"In a way, but only to me. About a year ago, in New York, I was working on a piece. This man was one of the key figures involved," Nicky said in a cool voice, having worked out a suitable story in advance. "Then he disappeared, and I've not been able to pull the special together without him. I've been wanting to contact him ever since. To interview him. Seemingly he's living in Rome. I thought Tony might know him, that he might be a local character, one who mixes with the international crowd. I was hoping Tony might suggest a few places I could look for him. Bars, restaurants."

Jennifer had listened carefully, and now she glanced down at the photographs she was holding. She shook her head after a few seconds, and handed them back. "No, I don't think I've ever seen him around. But—" She paused, looking thoughtful, then shook her head. "No, I don't know him."

"But *what*?" Nicky pressed. "You were about to say something."

"I thought, for a minute, that he looked slightly familiar, but no . . . no, I can't place him."

Putting the photographs back in her handbag, Nicky smiled at her and said, "A pity. Well, never mind."

The two of them walked through into the outer office, and Nicky headed for the door, realizing there was no point in hanging around the Rome bureau. "Tell Tony I'll call him later, and thanks, Jennifer."

"Sorry I couldn't be of more help."

Nicky went down the corridor to the elevator, pressed the button and stood waiting. The elevator arrived, and she was about to step inside when she heard her name being called. Pivoting, she saw Jennifer rushing down the corridor toward her.

"I'm glad I caught you!" Tony's secretary cried as she came to a halt. "I've just realized why that man's face seemed a bit familiar to me. Could I look at the photographs once again, please?"

"Yes, of course," Nicky said, her heart skipping a beat as she opened her purse and took out the pictures.

Jennifer peered at the larger one, which Dave had taken, and nodded her head. "I'm pretty sure this guy was on the same plane as I was last Thursday."

"A plane? To where?" Nicky asked.

"Athens. I went there for the weekend. This guy was standing next to me at the carousel, waiting for the baggage. He helped me get my bag off." She passed the pictures back to Nicky.

"Are you sure it was the same man?" Nicky's voice was suddenly an octave lower, very quiet.

"Yes. He was very polite. Gentlemanly. And he had a beautiful voice."

Hardly daring to breathe, Nicky asked, "What nationality was he, do you think, Jennifer?"

"English. He was an Englishman."

27

That afternoon Nicky flew from Rome to Athens.

The flight time was only an hour and a half, and around five o'clock the plane landed at Ellinikon Airport. As soon as she had cleared customs, Nicky found a porter to help her with her luggage and within minutes they were standing outside in the suffocating heat, waiting in line for a taxi.

The drive into Athens did not take long, just half an hour, but by the time she arrived at the Grande Bretagne hotel in Syntagma Square Nicky felt exhausted. The cab had not been very well air-conditioned, and August was a stifling hot month in Greece.

Her suite overlooked the Acropolis, and it was large and roomy. To her immense relief, the air conditioning was turned on full blast when she walked in, and she soon felt cooler. After taking a few clothes out of her hanging bag, Nicky showered, redid her makeup, brushed her hair and then dressed in a pair of white cotton pants, a pale-blue cotton shirt and white flat sandals. Her aim was to be as cool and comfortable as possible. Slinging her white leather handbag over her shoulder, she left the suite and took the elevator down to the lobby.

Walking over to the reception desk, she leaned against the polished wood and smiled at the two dark-suited young men standing behind it. They both returned her smile, flashing teeth that looked very white in their tanned Mediterranean faces.

"I'm Nicky Wells of the American Television Network in New York," she said, focusing on the smaller of the two young men, who was closest to her.

"Yes, miss, I know. I am Costa Theopopoulos, and this is my colleague, Aristotle Gavros. How may we be of assistance?" he asked politely.

Nicky gave a little nod of acknowledgment, and said, "I'm trying to locate someone, a friend, and I'm not sure whether he's staying here or not." Opening her bag, she took out the photograph of Charles that had been taken by the studio technician, since this was the best one in her opinion. She showed it to the young man.

After studying it for a few seconds, Costa looked her right in the eye and shook his head. "I've never seen this gentleman before." Glancing at his colleague, he asked, "Have you, Aristotle?" and handed him the photograph.

While the other desk clerk eyed the picture, Costa said, "What is this man's name, miss?"

"Charles Devereaux," Nicky replied. However, knowing full well that Charles would not be using his own name, she added, "But Mr. Devereaux frequently travels incognito, and so he may well be registered under a different name—that's the reason I showed you the photograph of him."

"Oh," Costa said and stared at her in the oddest way. "Why would he do such a thing?"

Nicky had her story ready, and she said pleasantly, "Mr. Devereaux is a famous writer. Very, very famous, actually, and he seeks anonymity much of the time. Hence the various names he hides behind."

"And what would *they* be?" Costa asked, his eyes now nailed to hers.

"*Smith* is one of them. *Charles Smith,*"

Nicky invented. "Another one is *Charles Dixon*."

Costa had been writing the names down on a pad as she spoke, and lifting his head, he said, "I will look at the register," and then he stepped away.

The other desk clerk, Aristotle, came to her and handed her the photograph. "I have seen this man," he said quietly, "or someone like him."

Nicky gave him a swift glance, and exclaimed, "So I was right! I *was* fairly certain my friend would be staying here."

Aristotle shook his head. "I bumped into a man who looked like this when he was entering G. B. Corner last Saturday. I do not believe he was a guest in the hotel."

"What's G. B. Corner?" Nicky asked.

"It is a restaurant for light meals and snacks to the right, off the hotel lobby," he explained.

At this moment Costa walked over to them. He said, "None of the names you gave me are listed in our hotel register, miss. I am sorry."

"Thanks, anyway. Aristotle says he saw my friend going into G. B. Corner last Saturday. They bumped into each other. Did *you* happen to see him, by any chance?"

Costa said, "I was not here. It was my day off."

Nicky shrugged her shoulders lightly. "I see. Well, anyway, I do have another question—regarding hotels. Aside from this one and the Hilton, what are the names of the other big hotels in Athens?"

"There aren't any," Aristotle said, suddenly taking charge as Costa sidled away. "There are many small hotels, of course, but—" It was his turn to give a shrug. "I doubt this gentleman would stay in any of them. But there are some beautiful hotels out at Vouliagmeni. You could try those."

"Where is Vouliagmeni?"

"Oh, not so far away. Only about forty-five minutes by car," Aristotle told her.

"Perhaps you could arrange a car and driver for me, for tomorrow," Nicky said. "I think I'd better go out there."

"What time would you like to leave?"

"Midmorning, I think."

"That is wise, miss. It will not be too hot then." Aristotle smiled, pulled a notepad toward him and began writing.

Nicky leaned against the desk and plied him with questions about Vouliagmeni.

So engrossed was she in her discussion with Aristotle she did not notice Costa. He had retreated to the small office behind the front desk, and was busy dialing a number, almost furtively. After a brief moment of waiting, he muttered rapidly into the receiver. His expression was anxious, and as he spoke he did not take his eyes off Nicky.

Aristotle handed her the piece of paper. "This is the name of my brother-in-law, miss. He is a good driver. Careful. He speaks English. I will arrange for him to be here at ten o'clock tomorrow."

"Thank you very much, you've been most helpful."

He leaned closer and murmured, "His price is fair, and much less than some of the other drivers would charge."

She smiled at Aristotle, then looked around for Costa, spotted him on the phone in the office and raised her hand in a half wave. "Thank Costa for me," she said to Aristotle.

"I will, miss."

Next, Nicky found her way to G. B. Corner, which opened off the lobby, and went inside. She spoke to one of the waiters before showing him the picture. The waiter shook his head, but went off with the photograph, quite obviously trying to be of help. He passed the photo around among the other waiters. When he returned to Nicky a few minutes later he said in a most regretful voice, "Cannot help, miss. We have not seen this man. If he was here on Saturday no one noticed him. No one. Sorry."

. . .

She took a cab to the Hilton Hotel and went through the same routine all over again, asking questions of the three clerks at the reception desk and the cashier, and showing them the picture of Charles.

It was exactly the same story once more. No one had seen this man, and none of the names she mentioned showed up on the hotel register. Of course not. She had not expected them to be there. Asking the desk clerks to check was just a ploy, one she hoped would help to give her story the ring of truth. It would seem odd, to say the least, to be looking for a friend if you didn't know his name. And the men on desk duty always asked his name.

As she left the Athens Hilton, Nicky's sense of frustration was now so enormous she almost went back to her hotel in disgust, but she suddenly changed her mind and took a cab to the Plaka. This was the oldest part of Athens, full of quaint little streets, shops, bars, restaurants and cafés. She strolled through the narrow streets for an hour or so, alertly looking around, keeping her eyes open as her father had taught her to do when she was a child. She knew only too well that life was full of strange coincidences; there was always the odd chance she might just spot Charles sitting outside at one of the open-air cafés or restaurants.

The Plaka was crowded, jammed with tourists, as it usually was in August, and Nicky soon grew weary of being pushed and jostled; also, it was unbearably hot tonight. And so in the end she gave up her search. Deep down, she was beginning to admit to herself that it was futile, a waste of time, looking for Charles in the streets like this. Finally, she took a cab back to the Grande Bretagne hotel, deciding she might as well be frustrated in comfort.

Once she had cooled off in her air-conditioned suite, she dialed room service and ordered grilled fish, fresh fruit and a bottle of carbonated water for dinner. Then she strolled over to the window, where she parted the curtains and stood looking out at the Acropolis.

She knew the temple on top was called the Parthenon. Her father had explained that to her when they had once come here for a family vacation. This evening it was dramatically illuminated, as it usually was in summer, and the ancient ruins looked extremely impressive, even heart-stopping, and incredibly beautiful, thrown into relief as they were against the darkening night sky.

She suddenly realized that a performance of Light and Sound was in progress at this very moment. The lights were constantly changing as a story of ancient Greece was being narrated to the audience seated on the hill opposite the Acropolis. For a moment Nicky was transported back in time; she remembered attending such a performance with her mother and father years ago, and it was something she had found very moving. It had held her in its grip, and she had never forgotten it.

Her knowledge of Greece was limited to what her father, that inveterate traveler, had told her. These were mostly stories from Greek mythology; she had also garnered some knowledge from the wonderfully vivid novels of Mary Renault. She had read Renault's book *Fire from Heaven* when she was sixteen, and had been unable to put it down. This, too, had been another of the writer's novels about ancient Greece, and she wished, all of a sudden, that she had one of the Renault books with her right now. She suspected it was more than likely that she would have another sleepless night.

. . .

The driver's name was Panayotis, and he was a cheerful young man with a deferential manner, a fairly decent command of English and a brilliant smile that seemed to be permanently pasted on his face.

He picked her up at the hotel promptly at ten o'clock the following morning. She was delighted to see the relatively new-looking Mercedes and even more delighted to discover it had an efficient air-conditioning system. It was already steaming hot in the streets, and the cool interior of the car was welcome.

"Aristotle tell me you want to go out to Vouliagmeni, to see the Astir Palace Hotels," Panayotis said as he pulled out of Syntagma Square.

"Yes, I do. He said there were three altogether."

"It is—how do you say—a complex. Yes. There are the hotels, bungalows. Very nice place. Very beautiful. Forty-five minutes we get there. Okay? You comfortable, miss?"

"I'm fine, thank you." Nicky leaned back against the soft leather.

"You like music, miss?" Panayotis asked, half glancing over his shoulder. "You like I put on radio?"

"Why not," she said, not really caring either way. Turning her head, she looked out the window, and asked herself if she had been foolish to come to Athens. Yesterday had been a genuine waste of her time, and although Aristotle had said he had recognized Charles, had seen him going into the snack restaurant, what did that mean in the long run? Athens was a big city, just as Rome was, and if she were honest with herself, she had to acknowledge that she really had very little chance of finding Charles, even if he *was* here.

Perhaps she should have done what Arch had suggested and gone to Paris. Instead, she had been determinedly stubborn and intent on doing her own thing, following her own instincts. So she had rushed here just because of Jennifer Allen's story. But for what? And what was her ultimate goal if she found Charles? She wasn't too sure about anything anymore, and she sighed heavily. Seemingly she was unable to let go of the idea that Charles Devereaux was alive. At least, she wasn't ready to just yet.

As they approached Vouliagmeni, Nicky realized that it was a resort area. There was a marina with yachts; a long, curving road led up to the top of high cliffs, where the hotels were located at intervals. The area was actually a large and rather beautifully laid-out compound, with the three hotels built at varying levels on the sides of the cliffs. The bungalows were situated to one side of the hotel that stood on the lowest level; there were various restaurants, a tennis court, swimming pools and beaches. The setting was extraordinary, breathtaking, perched high above the Mediterranean. Homer's winedark sea, Nicky thought, glancing out of the car window. This morning it was intensely, brilliantly blue, glittering like a sheet of glass under the golden sun, and the reflection it threw off was almost blinding.

Panayotis finally brought the Mercedes to a standstill in front of the hotel that was located on the highest point of the cliffs.

"I wait over there," he said with his huge smile, and took a piece of paper out of his trouser pocket. "From my brother-in-law, Aristotle. Ask for this man."

"Thank you," Nicky said, looking down at the piece of paper she was holding. It was a short note from Aristotle. He had written: *Demosthenes Zoulakis is Assistant Manager. He is friend of my father. He will help if he can. A.G.*

Within moments of asking for him at the reception desk in the hotel, Mr. Zoulakis was grasping her hand in his, smiling broadly and telling her in impeccable English that Aristotle had telephoned to explain everything.

"Would you please show me the photograph of the friend you are seeking, Miss
Wells," he said, taking out a pair of horn-
rimmed glasses and slipping them on.

"Yes, of course, right away," Nicky said,
and reached into her bag for the famous picture.

Mr. Zoulakis took it from her, studied it
intently, frowned slightly, looked at it more
closely, then shook his head. "This man was
never a guest at any of the hotels. I always
make a point of knowing everyone, and I
have a good memory for faces."

"But you were frowning, and you looked
as though you *did* know him," Nicky pointed
out, having carefully observed the man's initial reaction.

"Yes, that is so, Miss Wells. For a split
second he *seemed* familiar, but that is all. It
is possible that I saw him briefly in one of the
restaurants or in one of the other hotels. Perhaps I got a glimpse of him at the pool, or on
the beach. However, if I did see him, it *was*
fleeting." He smiled at her and ushered her
across the lobby. "But come along, Miss
Wells, we will visit the hotels on the lower
levels, and talk to the staff. Maybe they will
have some information."

"Thanks, Mr. Zoulakis, you're being so
very kind. I appreciate it."

"It is nothing, Miss Wells, truly it is nothing," Demosthenes Zoulakis said, wishing he could help this beautiful American woman who was apparently so important.

Two hours later Nicky was being led to the Mercedes by the affable assistant manager, who had genuinely put himself out for her, but to no avail. "I am so sorry we have not been able to help you, Miss Wells," he said. "Perhaps your friend merely passed through Athens, en route to another destination."

"That is a possibility," Nicky agreed, and thanked him again.

Nicky was halfway across the lobby of the Grande Bretagne hotel when she stopped dead in her tracks. A second before, she had passed the newspaper and magazine kiosk, and it suddenly struck her that Clee's photograph had been on the cover of one of the magazines being prominently displayed.

Clee was the most famous war photographer in the world today, and the only reason he would be on the cover of a magazine was if something had happened to him. He was in Leipzig, and that wasn't a battlefront, but there were demonstrations going on in East Germany, and there *were* places to die other than a war zone. But she knew he was all right. She had spoken to him only last night. Perhaps he was on the magazine cover because he had won an award for his coverage of the demonstrations in Beijing. That was a possibility. But if so, why hadn't he mentioned it? Modesty? Clee was one of the most modest people she had ever met.

Nicky swung around and walked back to the kiosk. She opened her purse, took out some money and handed it to the vendor. Then she lifted the magazine off the rack and held it up for the vendor to see what she was buying.

The man nodded his head, understanding, counted out the change and dropped it in her outstretched hand.

Turning away from the kiosk, Nicky took a few steps, and looked down at the magazine. It was called *Tachydromos* and it was a news magazine similar to *Life* or *Paris Match.* And there was Clee on the cover, smiling faintly and wearing an open-necked shirt and his worn, brown-leather bomber jacket. Except that it *wasn't* Clee, it was Kevin Costner, the actor! It was true that they did bear a striking resemblance to each other, and it had been an easy mistake to make.

Once she was inside her suite, Nicky threw the magazine down on the coffee table and went to the mini-bar. Taking out a bottle of Coke, she opened it and poured herself a glass. After a long swallow, she carried the drink over to the sofa and sat down.

My God, Kevin Costner really does look like Clee in this shot, Nicky thought, eyeing the magazine cover facing her. He's the spitting image of him. He could be his twin. In the back of her mind a voice suddenly echoed. It was Philip's, and she heard his words again: *They say we all have a double living somewhere in the world.*

Nicky sat bolt upright with a start. It had just dawned on her that if she could mistake Kevin Costner for Clee Donovan, then perhaps she was mistaking some other man for Charles Devereaux.

Damnation, she muttered to herself, maybe I *am* on a wild-goose chase. She leaped to her feet, suddenly impatient, irritated with herself, and walked over to the window; she stood looking out, her mind racing.

It was quite possible that the man filmed in the news segment originating in Rome was a total stranger. Certainly that was what Anne and Philip believed. Who could argue with them, really. She had no one who could endorse her opinion that the man was

Charles. What a pity Christopher Neald was on vacation. Charles's English partner would have agreed with her, she was certain of that. A small sigh escaped her, and she leaned her head against the pane of glass. Admit it, there's no point continuing with this search, she muttered, and then she straightened as a thought suddenly struck her. There *was* one person who might back her up if he was shown the photographs: Don Pedro Alejandro Pérez, Charles's Spanish partner.

One last shot. I'm going to give this one last shot, Nicky thought as she hurried across the room to the desk and her address book. Within the space of ten minutes she had found Don Pedro's number, telephoned Madrid and spoken to a receptionist at Don Pedro's wine-exporting company. The woman had told her that Don Pedro was out of town until Monday, that she should ring again after lunch, at five o'clock, in order to speak to Don Pedro's secretary, Señorita López.

Nicky sat at the desk for a short while, hesitating, wondering what to do next. She could stay in Athens until Sunday and fly to Madrid that morning, but it was unbearably hot in Athens; also, she didn't know a soul here. Whereas ATN had a decent-sized bu-

reau in Madrid, and although Peter Collis, the
bureau chief, was not a close friend, he was
at least an acquaintance of long standing.
Madrid it is, she thought, making a snap decision to leave immediately. She would go
today, if that was possible.

Years of traveling with her parents as a
child had taught her one thing: If you want to
get something done, and especially in a
hurry, ask a concierge to help you. They
knew everything; they also had a network
that stretched from hotel to hotel across
Europe. And so now she dialed the desk
downstairs to enlist the head concierge's
help. The line was busy, so she left the suite
and went down to the lobby, feeling more
impatient than ever to move on.

Yannis, the head concierge, greeted her
pleasantly and asked how he could be of
assistance.

"I need to get on a flight to Madrid today.
Any airline, it doesn't matter which, and I
need a suite booked at the Ritz. Can you do
that for me, please, Yannis?"

"Yes, immediately, leave it to me, Miss
Wells. I will telephone your suite as soon as
I have news." He glanced at his watch. "Are
you packed, miss?"

"More or less."

"It is almost three. I think you should be

prepared to leave for the airport soon. I know there is a late-afternoon flight to Madrid. I will try to get a seat on it for you."

"Thank you, Yannis." She smiled at him and walked across to the reception desk, making a mental note to call Jean-Claude at the Image office, to leave her number in Madrid. Aristotle was nowhere in sight, but Costa was on duty. She had felt his eyes on her all the time she had been talking to the concierge.

Nicky said, "Hello, Costa. Thanks for trying to help me yesterday."

He inclined his head with his usual politeness, and asked, "Did you have any luck out at Vouliagmeni?"

"No, unfortunately, I didn't. Would you please arrange for my bill, Costa."

"You are leaving, miss?"

Nicky nodded.

"Back to America?" he asked.

"No, I'm going to Madrid, as a matter of fact."

"*Madrid,*" he repeated, sounding slightly startled.

Nicky stared at him curiously. He had such a look of consternation on his face she could not help wondering why. She said, "What's wrong with Madrid?"

The young desk clerk seemed baffled for

a split second. Then he murmured, "Excuse me, I don't understand."

"You sounded so surprised when I said I was going to Madrid."

"Not at all," he responded, sudden denial on his face. He offered her a faint smile, and added, "I will have your bill prepared, miss. Immediately."

She reached into her bag, pulled out a handful of drachmas, and pressed them on Costa. "Thank you," she said.

"Thank *you,* miss," he answered, pocketing the money.

Costa watched her walk across the lobby to the elevators. When she had entered one and disappeared from sight, he left the reception desk and went over to speak to the head concierge. "Do you think you can get Miss Wells a seat on a plane to Madrid?"

"I am sure I can," Yannis said somewhat sharply, frowning at Costa, obviously puzzled by his interest.

"And the hotel? Did you get her a hotel?"

"The head concierge of the Ritz is an old friend. I will have no problem when I speak to him," Yannis boasted. "And what's it to you?"

Costa grinned and winked. "She's nice. She tips well. I want to be sure everything goes smoothly for her."

Yannis nodded, and turned away to answer one of the shrilling telephones.

Costa walked back to the reception desk, where another colleague was speaking with a guest. He hurried into the back office, which was empty, and made a quick phone call.

"She's leaving," he muttered into the receiver. "She's going to Madrid. What could she have found out at Vouliagmeni? She must know *something.* She'll be at the Ritz. Tell him."

28

It occurred to Nicky that she really was being followed only when she came out of the Prado Museum early on Friday evening and stood for a moment under its shady portico. She was debating whether or not to go directly back to the Ritz Hotel when she noticed the man with the black cigarillo again.

He had first sprung to life that morning, had suddenly appeared by her side while she was speaking to the concierge. The man had been puffing hard on his little black cigar, and the smoke billowing around her had caused her to splutter and cough. The concierge had said something politely but firmly in rapid Spanish, and the man had immediately moved away from her, stepping to one side. Once she had finished her business she had hurried across the lobby, glad to be away from the man with the cigar, who was deep in conversation with the concierge. On her way up to the suite in the elevator she had silently cursed him because she was still coughing behind her hand.

Then later, on her way to lunch with Peter Collis of the ATN Madrid bureau, she had stopped to wander along the Galería del Prado, a shopping arcade under the Palace Hotel. As she had left a boutique she had seen the man with the cigar gazing in its window. Immediately he had glanced away, looking somewhat self-conscious, and had swung around and darted into a shop on the opposite side of the arcade.

Now, here he was once again, only a few yards from her. He stood near the statue located between the steps and the small park just beyond, and he was with another man. In his mouth was the usual black cigarillo—his trademark.

The man had not seen her. Not yet, anyway. And the only reason she had spotted him so quickly and so easily was because of the screaming children. They were toddlers flanking a young woman; they were clinging to her hands and bawling at the top of their lungs. Their harassed mother had stopped to speak to the two men near the statue, and the man with the cigar was saying something, apparently in response to a question. He was pointing and gesticulating, and it was obvious that he was giving her directions.

Suddenly a group of young German students came out of the museum, surrounding her and laughing and chattering, and Nicky fell in with them. She stayed close as they trooped through the little park and into the Paseo del Prado.

Within a few minutes Nicky was entering the Plaza de la Lealtad, where the Ritz stood in its own lovely gardens. The man with the cigar was nowhere in sight. Not that it mattered, in point of fact, since he knew where she was staying anyway.

After collecting her door key and several messages, Nicky went up to her suite, preoccupied with thoughts of the strange man and the possibility that someone was having her movements monitored. *Someone?* If it was anybody, it was Charles Devereaux.

The minute she walked into her suite Nicky was conscious of the smell of an unfamiliar perfume. She stood in the small foyer, frowning and glancing about, the door key clutched in her hand. She sniffed several

times. There was no mistaking it—a pungent
odor clung to the air. It struck her then that
it smelled more like a man's cologne than a
woman's perfume, so this eliminated the
maid. Had the valet been here? But for what
reason? She had not sent out any clothes for
pressing. Had the strange man gained entry
to her suite? If so, how? That's a stupid
thought, she muttered; he could very easily
have bribed a member of the staff. As her
father always said, money talked. And certainly he would have had the opportunity.
She had seen him in the shopping arcade
around eleven o'clock that morning, before
going to the ATN bureau to pick up Peter.
They had gone to lunch at the Gran Café de
Gijón around one-thirty, and from lunch she
had strolled off to the Prado. Once there she
had spent several hours raptly gazing at the
paintings by Goya and Velázquez, and she
had been out of her suite for most of the day.

A worried frown wrinkled her brow as she
went into the sitting room and put her key,
the messages and her handbag on the coffee table. Her suspicions now fully aroused,
Nicky walked through into the bedroom,
went immediately to the wardrobe and pulled
open the door. Her big carryall bag, which
she never traveled without, looked oddly
askew, yet she knew that she had placed it

neatly in the corner before leaving to meet Peter.

Reaching for the carryall, she dragged it out and carried it over to the bed. Inspecting the lock on the front, she noticed at once that it had been tampered with; when she touched it with her finger she realized that it was very loose. Seemingly someone had picked the lock, then had been unable to close it properly afterward because it was badly damaged. Certainly the bag had been secure when she had left earlier, so someone had definitely been in her suite, poking around.

Nicky inspected the carryall. Nothing was missing. Her notebook, tape recorder and all of the other items were intact. She had her passport, press credentials, credit cards and Spanish money in her white leather shoulder bag, but she had left a wallet containing foreign currency in the carryall. Pulling this out and examining it, she saw that none of the money had been taken. But she was positive the bag had been searched, and very thoroughly at that. Quite aside from the broken lock, her things were not as neatly placed inside as they usually were. And her tape recorder was not in the corner of the carryall, where she invariably put it for easy access.

Closing the bag and returning it to the

wardrobe, Nicky hurried over to the chest on the other side of the bedroom, and began to open the drawers one after another. Again she knew that someone had riffled through her things, for the simple reason that she always stacked everything carefully. They were now rumpled and, like the carryall, slightly askew. There was no doubt that someone had handled them.

She shook her head, a concerned expression settling on her face as she closed the drawers and walked back into the sitting room. Flopping into a chair, she closed her eyes, endeavoring to concentrate on the problems at hand. Was it just a coincidence that the man with the black cigarillo had been underfoot several times today? Or was he actually following her? If he was, then it certainly proved one thing: *Charles Devereaux was alive.* There was no question in her mind that her rooms had been searched and her carryall tampered with; the evidence was there. Obviously this also reinforced her theory that her former fiancé was flourishing here on the Continent.

Suddenly Nicky snapped her eyes open and sat up jerkily. If Charles was having her followed in order to know what she was doing, who she was seeing, and if he had had her room searched, then he must be aware that she was in Madrid. But how did he know that? Did he have a contact here in the Ritz? Or one in the Grande Bretagne hotel in Athens, perhaps? More important, why was he doing it?

There was only one answer to that: he wanted to know what she was up to, and very badly.

It struck her then that he might possibly think she was doing an investigation on him for a story. After all, he knew full well that she had been an investigative journalist before she became a war correspondent, and was still one, in fact. But if he believed this, then he must be involved in something that merited an investigation. Something illicit. Something immense, maybe. What was illicit and immense and made big money? Arms smuggling. Drug trafficking. But why would Charles want to make more big bucks? He was already a rich man. Still, she kept coming back to the idea that whatever he was doing involved money.

Unless it was something else, something quite bizarre, as she had suggested to Arch in Rome. But what could that be? . . .

The telephone rang and interrupted her thoughts; she went to the desk to answer it. "Hello?"

"Nicky, Peter here. I called before and left a message. Did you get it?"

"Oh, Peter, I'm sorry, I just came in and I haven't opened any of my messages yet."

"No problem. Amy and I want you to have dinner with us tonight. Are you free?"

"Yes, and I'd love to meet your wife. But look, Peter, you don't have to feel obligated to look after me, really—"

"We want you to join us," he interrupted. "We've invited a few friends. We're going to the Jockey Club, it's quite famous."

"I've heard of it."

"I'll pick you up around eight-thirty, and take you home for drinks. Dinner won't be until ten, even ten-thirty, I'm afraid. When in Madrid do as the *madrileños.* See you later, Nicky."

"I'm looking forward to it, Peter. 'Bye for now."

Immediately after she had hung up the phone rang again. "Hello?"

"Hi, Nick, it's me," Clee said. "Jean-Claude told me you called."

"Clee! Oh darling, hello. And yes, I did, just to touch base. How are you? Where are you calling from?"

"I'm terrific, and I'm in Berlin—at the Intercontinental. Didn't you get my message?"

"Yes, but I only just got back. I haven't really had a chance to look at it."

"Nicky, I've got great news! The greatest!" he exclaimed.

She could almost feel his excitement flowing down the wire. "What is it? Tell me!"

"Yoyo! I've had a message from Yoyo, Nick."

"Oh, Clee, thank God. He is all right, isn't he? And where is he? Is he in Paris?"

Clee laughed. "Whoa, I can only answer one question at a time. He's fine, he's in Hong Kong, but he'll be in Paris soon. Hopefully in a few days, another week at the most."

"That's wonderful," she said, and unexpectedly her eyes filled with tears of relief and gratitude that the boy was alive and well. She was unable to speak for a couple of seconds.

Clee said, "Are you there?"

Swallowing hard, Nicky replied, "Yes—I felt very emotional for a moment or two, that's all."

"I know what you mean. I had the same reaction when I heard the news from Jean-Claude."

"Oh, so you didn't actually speak to Yoyo yourself?"

"No, he called the office from Hong Kong, and said he'd be in touch the moment he arrived in Paris."

"Clee, it's just wonderful. Perhaps we'll be able to have a reunion on Monday."

"Maybe. And, yes, it's the best news we could have. What time will you be arriving in Paris, Nick?"

"Late afternoon, I think."

"Then it's dinner that night. Just you and me. Or Yoyo, too, if you like, and providing Yoyo has arrived, and is feeling up to it."

"I can't wait to see him," Nicky said. "Or you."

"And I can't wait to see you, darling."

They talked for a few more minutes and then they said good-bye and hung up. Nicky stood with her hand resting on the receiver for a moment. Clee had been so excited about Yoyo, he had not asked her why she had moved on to Madrid. He had simply assumed she was there on business, much to her profound relief.

Later that evening, when she was putting the finishing touches to her makeup, the phone began to shrill. Going into the bedroom, she picked it up and said, "Hello?"

No one answered.

For a second time Nicky said, "Hello?" and did so somewhat sharply. There was a click and the phone went dead. Immediately, she dialed the operator. "This is Nicky Wells in suite 705. My phone just rang. I answered, but no one spoke. *Did* you have a call for me?"

"Yes, Miss Wells. I put it through myself," the operator answered.

"Who was calling? Do you know?"

"I'm sorry, no, I don't. But it was a man who asked for you."

"Thank you." Nicky put the receiver down and returned to the bathroom to do her hair. Suddenly she stopped brushing it and for a moment stood staring into the mirror but without seeing herself. Her mind was elsewhere. She could not help wondering if someone was checking on her movements again. And then she remembered something Arch had said to her in Rome. He had pointed out that a man who disappears does not want to be found. Not ever. He had also said she could be putting herself in danger. Was she?

Her brain focused on Charles Devereaux. Arch had remarked that Charles was tough, ruthless. And all of these things were true. She had spotted those characteristics in him herself.

A look of comprehension flashed in her eyes. Yes, she could be in danger.

29

The news about Yoyo had lifted Nicky's spirits, and it had completely overshadowed the Devereaux problem and her search for Charles.

Last night she had felt a great sense of buoyancy and lightness when she had gone out to dinner with Peter and Amy Collis and their friends. Even the troublesome thought that Arch might be correct, that she could be in danger, had been diminished considerably. Now, on this lovely, warm Saturday morning, all of the demons had fled, chased away by her happy mood and the bright sunlight, the incredible turquoise sky and the thin, dry Castilian air that gave that sky its extraordinary clarity. Not only that, the brisk bustle of this elegant and imposing hotel was reassuring, as was the atmosphere of normality that pervaded it.

Ever since the phone call from Clee, Yoyo had been on Nicky's mind. The fact that he had escaped from China to Hong Kong, and was safe in the British Crown Colony, did much to ease the anxiety she had lived with lately; she felt as though one of her burdens had been lifted. She could not wait to see Yoyo, to find out what had happened to him since they had last seen each other three months ago.

Just as important, she wanted and needed to see Clee, to be with him. They had not been together for several weeks, and this separation had only made her appreciate him that much more. She longed for his warmth and intelligence, his love and affection and understanding.

Nicky picked up her cup and finished her coffee. Then she sat back in the chair and glanced around, absorbing her surroundings. She was having a late breakfast in the restaurant set in the midst of the trees in the hotel gardens. In some ways it was these gardens that helped make the Ritz so special. The hotel was situated in the very heart of Madrid, and the gardens surrounded it with tranquillity and loveliness—they were an oasis of calm in this busy, noisy and hectic metropolis.

She looked up at the sky, which was a phenomenal blue, like none she had ever seen anywhere, and it was cloudless. The sun was high, and by noon it would be unbearably hot, as torrid as it had been yesterday. But it was shady here under the trees and pleasant; nonetheless, she was glad she was wearing a loose cotton dress and flat sandals. Keeping cool was a major consideration in this city.

"Señorita Wells."

Nicky looked around and found herself staring into the scrubbed young face of a bellboy. "Yes?"

"For you." He was holding a small silver tray on which lay an envelope, and he thrust this at her, smiling.

Nicky took some pesetas out of her handbag, dropped them on the tray and picked up the white envelope. "Thank you," she said.

The bellboy eyed the money, smiled at her and pocketed it. "*Gracias, señorita.*"

Nicky examined the letter with curiosity, wondering whom it was from. Peter? The *madrileños* she had met last night? They were a lovely young couple who had wanted to take her out over the weekend. Her name was neatly printed across the front, along with the hotel's name and address, but the sender's name was missing.

Tearing it open, she took out the note, and the moment she saw the handwriting she froze in the chair. That beautiful script was unmistakable—the note was from Charles Devereaux.

Dear Nicky: she read. *Since you are looking so hard for me, I believe it has now become imperative that we meet. The man who delivers this note will wait in the lobby for you. I have sent him to fetch you to me. C.*

Nicky stared out at the gardens, a stony expression settling on her face. She clutched the note in her hand, and swallowed several times. Her throat had gone very dry. Then she looked down at the note and read it again. There was no question in her mind that it was from Charles. Quite aside from the recognizable handwriting, only Charles would use the word *fetch.* He had done so frequently in the past, and it was very English.

So, I was right all along, she thought, sitting up straighter in the chair. *I just knew I was.* And from the very moment I saw Tony's newscast from Rome. And yet she realized she derived no satisfaction from this knowledge, only a sense of immense dismay and a terrible feeling of sadness. But the sadness was more for Anne Devereaux than herself.

As she sat holding the note, her mind focusing on the man waiting to take her to Charles, a thought struck her. Last night, remembering Arch's words, she had wondered if she was in danger. If she truly believed she was, how could she possibly go off with Charles's messenger? For most of her working life as a war correspondent, she had been in harm's way and she had never flinched. And long ago she had accepted the fact that she was fearless by nature. On the other hand, she was not going to let her overriding curiosity and her quest for the truth be her undoing now. Certainly she was not going to do something foolhardy and put herself at risk.

But I won't be at risk. Whatever Charles Devereaux is, he is not a killer. Deep down in her heart she knew that Charles would never hurt her, not one hair of her head—she was absolutely convinced of that. Still, it would be prudent to be a bit cautious.

She wished Peter Collis were available to accompany her. They could have taken his car, and he could have waited outside for her while she had her meeting with Charles. Unfortunately, Peter and Amy were away visiting friends who lived outside Madrid.

She was on her own. So be it.

Nicky walked across the lobby to speak to Enrique, the head concierge.

"Good morning, Señorita Wells. Can I be of some help?" he asked with his usual geniality.

She nodded. "I need a car and a driver. Immediately. And I'd like a driver who speaks English, please."

"No problem, señorita, I'll arrange it right away. How long will you need the car?"

"I'm not sure. Several hours, at least, maybe the whole day. How soon can it be here?"

"It is already here, Señorita Wells. We have cars and drivers standing outside, in readiness for the hotel guests."

"How convenient. A short while ago someone delivered a letter to me. I believe he's waiting."

"Yes, he's over there," Enrique told her.

Nicky followed his gaze. She saw a youngish man, well dressed, at the other end of the lobby. "Thank you," she murmured to the head concierge, and hurried away from the desk.

Coming up to the young man, she said, "I'm Nicky Wells. Do you speak English?"

The young man nodded. "Yes."

"What's your name?"

There was a slight hesitation, and then he said, "Javier."

"All right, Javier." She showed him the envelope. "You brought this letter to me. Correct?"

"Yes."

"And you're supposed to take me to the man who sent it, aren't you?"

"Yes. He waits for you."

"Very well, I'm coming with you now. But I'm using my own car and driver."

"I don't understand. I have car. I take you, Señorita Wells."

Nicky shook her head. "No, absolutely not, I prefer to come with my own car, or I don't come at all," she said firmly, and her expression was suddenly tough, determined.

Javier could not fail to notice her attitude, but again he hesitated, looking uncertain and at a loss. Then he said, "Okay. Wait, please. I make phone call."

"Oh, I'll wait," Nicky answered coolly, understanding that he was now going to put through a call to Charles. Her eyes followed him as he crossed the lobby in search of a telephone.

Within minutes he returned. "Okay. We go now. Your car follow mine."

Her driver's name was José, and once she was settled comfortably in the car he went to speak to Javier.

Nicky sat watching them through the car window. It was open and she could hear their voices. However, since she spoke no Spanish, she did not understand a word they were saying.

A second or two later, José got into the driver's seat, released the brake and turned on the ignition.

As they slid smoothly away from the hotel and into the street, Nicky said, "Did Javier explain where we are going?"

"Yes, señorita. We are going out to the area near the ring."

"The ring?"

"*Sí, sí.* Yes, the bullring of Madrid, the famous Plaza de Toros de las Ventas. It is not too far, twenty minutes, maybe half an hour, depending on the traffic."

"Oh yes, that's right."

"Do you know the ring, señorita? Have you been to a *corrida*?"

"Yes, I have, some years ago," she said, remembering the time she had met Charles in Madrid, just a few weeks before they had become engaged. Don Pedro had taken them to a bullfight on the Sunday afternoon.

"Did you enjoy it?" José asked, half glancing over his shoulder, smiling at her.

"Yes, I did, thank you."

Leaning back against the car seat, Nicky cast her mind back to that long weekend. She and Charles had stayed in Madrid for four days, and now she suddenly recalled how taken with it Charles had seemed to be. Well, it *was* affluent, fashionable and vibrant. Life was lived to the hilt here, and he had appeared to enjoy that, and the night life, as well as everything else. She wondered if he lived here permanently. Perhaps he did, maybe he had only been visiting Rome. *Drugs,* she thought, seizing on the South American connection, the common bond of language and heritage. And for all its glossy façade, she knew that Madrid had its problems like anywhere else. Recently she had read that heroin was responsible for a death every two days in Madrid.

Was Charles somehow involved in drug smuggling? Was that what it was all about? Was that the reason he had faked his death and fled abroad to start a new life? Soon she would know the answers to everything, she presumed.

Half an hour later, José was pulling up behind Javier on a side street, and parking in front of a brownish-colored brick apartment building. He helped her to alight, and she said, "Please wait for me here, José, however long I am."

"*Sí, sí,* yes, I understand. I will not go away. I will stay here all day if necessary."

Nicky nodded. "But I probably won't be much longer than a couple of hours," she added, and walked over to join Javier, who was already standing near the front door.

"This is the place, is it?" she asked, staring into his face.

"He waits here," Javier said as he pushed open the door and stood back to let her enter the building first.

As she strode across the small foyer, following Javier to the lift, Nicky steeled herself. She had no idea what to expect, and her mouth had gone dry again.

30

Javier opened the door of the apartment with his own key and ushered her inside.

Nicky found herself standing in a small, dark foyer that was rather nondescript. It had an Oriental rug on the floor, a console table holding a vase of bedraggled artificial flowers, and framed posters of bullfighters on the walls. She glanced from side to side, intensely curious, and saw several closed doors, as well as a long corridor leading off the foyer. The living room was straight ahead, through an arched entranceway.

Everything was quiet. There was no sign of life, and Nicky could not help wondering where Charles was. She glanced about again, straining to catch the slightest noise.

"Please, go in there," Javier said, indicating the living room, and as she walked forward he hurried down the corridor.

Her eyes swiftly scanned the room she had just entered. It was as ordinary and unprepossessing as the foyer, with more Oriental rugs on the wood floor, another and larger collection of bullfight posters on the white walls and several dark wood pieces. A sofa and two chairs were covered in drab olive velvet, and arranged around a cheap metal coffee table with a top made of decorative tiles.

Half expecting to find Charles waiting for her, Nicky was disappointed when she realized the room was empty. Stepping over to the window and looking out, she saw that the bullring, the famous Plaza de Toros de las Ventas, was only a stone's throw away. Whoever it was that lived here, and she knew it was not Charles, was undoubtedly an aficionado. Charles must have borrowed this apartment for our meeting, she thought, he wouldn't live in a place like this. It would offend not only his sensibilities but his sense of taste.

"Hello, Nicky."

She almost jumped out of her skin on hearing his voice and swung around. She stared at Charles, who had entered the room through another door at the far end. And it was indeed Charles Devereaux she saw before her, although he looked very different. His hair and the mustache he had grown had been dyed black, and his deep tan served to underscore an unexpected look of swarthiness about him, one that was quite alien to her. He was naturally fair like his mother, and had always been extremely Anglo-Saxon in appearance. He was wearing a pair of navy blue cotton pants and white shirt, open at the neck; she had never seen him dressed quite as casually as this.

Nicky discovered she could not speak. She had not anticipated the shock of coming face-to-face with him; the impact was enormous, and she felt as though she had been punched in the stomach. Actually seeing him alive and well and obviously in good health, after believing him for a long time to be dead, was overwhelming. She was shaking inside, and her heart was pounding at an alarming rate.

"You look very well, Nicky," Charles said at last, breaking the silence between them, walking toward her. "And thank you for coming." He stopped about a foot away from her and offered her a faint smile.

She did not return it. Her face was cold,

her eyes blue ice. Finally, she said in a voice that was glacial, "Let's cut the small talk, shall we? That's not why I came here."

"I was merely attempting to put you at ease, my dear," he answered, and once more the faint smile flickered.

On hearing those words and observing that superior little smile again, something in Nicky snapped. Grief, anguish and pain had long ago coalesced and become a simmering anger. And now that anger became an unmitigated rage and she exploded. "You rotten son-of-a-bitch! Why did you do it? Why did you do such a terrible thing? To me, to Anne. How could you hurt your mother, and me, be so horribly cruel? You caused us both so much heartache and suffering. We *grieved* for you, you callous bastard! I'll never understand how I could ever have loved you! I hate you for what you did!"

Charles visibly flinched at this torrent of angry words and her venomous tone, and a small muscle twitched in his clenched jaw. But he said nothing to defend himself, he merely stood watching her, his gaze perfectly steady.

Tears of outrage ran down Nicky's face, and unexpectedly she leaped forward, her anger propelling her toward him. She began to pummel his chest and face fiercely with her fists, showing surprising strength.

Her sudden and violent behavior took Charles by surprise, and he staggered under her incessant blows, but he swiftly regained his balance. He began to struggle with her and at last managed to grab her wrists.

"Stop it, Nicky! Do you hear me, stop this at once! This ridiculous display will not get us anywhere. I had you fetched here to tell you something, to explain—"

"You had me followed!" she shouted.

"I certainly did not!" he shot back.

"You had my suite searched, you bastard!"

He hesitated only fractionally, then obviously decided to admit to this. "Yes, that is perfectly true, I did. But followed?" He shook his head. "No, no. Most decidedly not. I did not have you followed."

She ignored this denial. "You faked your death and ran away to start a new life, " she cried. "That was despicable and cowardly. *Unconscionable.* I don't know what your reason was, but nothing you could tell me now will ever justify—"

"I had no choice," he cut in peremptorily, in a voice that was icily calm and controlled. "I did what I did because I had no choice."

"Everybody has a choice!"

"In this instance, *I* did not. It was a question of duty."

"*Duty!*" she exclaimed shrilly. "That's hard for me to believe! Duty to what?"

"I want to explain why I did what I did, and then perhaps you'll understand and go away and leave me alone."

When she did not respond, Charles added, "You're putting me in jeopardy, Nicky."

"What do you mean, jeopardy?"

"You're putting me at risk, putting my life at risk, running around the world asking questions about me, showing my photograph to people," he said, his voice suddenly low, almost conspiratorial, and he pinned her with his eyes. "No one must know I'm alive. Not even my mother."

Although she was thrown off-balance by this statement, Nicky made no comment, she simply gave him a curious look. Her eyes were full of skepticism as she weighed his words.

Charles said, "Come and sit down, and try not to be so angry."

"It'll take me a long time to get over my anger!"

"Just so," he murmured, nodding. "But won't you endeavor to calm yourself sufficiently in order to listen to me quietly, and in a reasonable fashion? Your anger is only getting in the way."

"Good God, Charles, you expect too much!"

Unexpectedly, he let go of her wrists, and her arms fell to her sides.

Nicky lifted them immediately, looked at her wrists, and began to rub first one, then the other. They were red and sore. "Look what you've done."

He said apologetically, "I'm so sorry, Nicky. I never did know my own strength, did I? Would you excuse me for a moment, I'll be right back." He went out through the side door.

Nicky leaned against the wall, feeling weak in the legs. She was still shaking, and the anger seethed inside her. But that was the only emotion she experienced; there was nothing left but anger, and perhaps hatred for Charles Devereaux. Otherwise she felt absolutely nothing for him. She was numb.

When Charles returned a few seconds later, he was followed by another young man, not Javier. The man carried a tray with a bottle of water and two glasses on it, and as he walked past Nicky and placed it on the coffee table, she caught a whiff of a pungent cologne. It was one she recognized instantly, and she stiffened.

Immediately Charles noticed this, and when they were alone again he said, "Why did you react to Pierre like that?"

"Because he's the one who searched my suite," she replied in a hard voice.

"How do you know that? Did you see him leave?"

"No, but I smelled him." She glared at Charles.

Charles frowned. "What do you mean?"

"His cologne. My suite smelled of his cologne!"

Charles frowned once more. "He's too young," he muttered, almost to himself. "Too inexperienced. He was very careless." Charles did not say anything else for a second, looked thoughtful, then murmured quietly, "Pierre didn't find anything."

"That's because there wasn't anything to find," Nicky said. "Except the photographs, and I had them with me."

Charles made no comment about the pictures, but said, "Now come, sit down, Nicky. Your temper hasn't helped us thus far. Please, do try to be calmer so that we can talk in a sensible, civilized manner."

Nicky remained standing where she was, her eyes focused on Charles intently. She knew her anger was justified; it was an anger that had bubbled in her for three years now. And she did not regret her outburst or anything she had said. But he did have a point. She would not find out anything if she did not control herself and let him speak, tell his tale.

"Come, Nicky," he said again, waving his hand at the chair nearest to her. "Please, do sit down, won't you?" As he spoke he lowered himself into the other chair, reached for the bottle and poured himself a glass of water. He glanced up at her. "Would you care for a glass of this?"

She nodded. "Thanks, it's very hot in here."

He jumped up at once, went to turn on a fan standing on a table in a corner and returned to the chair. After pouring water for her, he picked up his own glass and drank.

Nicky continued to watch him. This was a man she had loved and adored, whom she had been intending to marry, and to whom she had been wholly committed. She had slept with him, been intimate with him on every level, shared so much with him, but at this precise moment he seemed like a total stranger to her.

She sat down, took a drink of water and said, "I'm calmer now, Charles. Talk."

"What I'm about to tell you is extremely confidential. You cannot tell anyone. Not ever. And not even my mother."

When Nicky remained completely silent, he said, "Promise me that you won't reveal that I am alive, or repeat what I'm about to tell you to anyone, least of all my mother."

"I don't know that I can do that."

"Then I'm afraid I cannot tell you anything."

"Why mustn't Anne know anything?"

"Because she would want to see me if she knew I was alive, and that's impossible. It could be dangerous—for her," he said.

"*Why?*"

He did not answer this question; instead, he said to her, "If you give me your promise, swear on your honor that what I say will remain absolutely confidential, then I will tell you everything. Well, at least I will tell you why I faked my own death and disappeared."

"Okay, I promise. I won't tell Anne or anyone else that you're alive. Nor will I disclose what you now say to me in confidence."

"No other living soul, Nicky. Say it."

"I won't tell another living soul. I promise."

"I sincerely hope you mean that. I think you do. It's not in your nature to break your word. But let me just add this—what I'm involved in has to do with national security. British national security."

Nicky leaned forward, her eyes narrowing. "I told you I wouldn't say a word, and I won't."

"All right." He sank back in the chair, and after a moment said in a low voice, "I am a British agent."

This was the last thing she had expected to hear, but thunderstruck though she was she kept her expression neutral. Whyever didn't I think of the intelligence business? she wondered, but she said in a cool, very steady voice, "You're with MI6, is that it?"

"A special branch of SIS, actually."

"What is SIS?"

"The Secret Intelligence Service, which is the same as MI6, more or less. And I faked my suicide and disappeared because it became necessary for me to assume a new identity."

"Why?" Nicky asked, leaning forward again.

"I needed a new identity in order to infiltrate a foreign intelligence service."

"Are you telling me that you're a mole?"

"That is correct, I am."

"Which foreign intelligence service have you infiltrated?"

"Now, you know damn well I can't reveal that to you, Nicky. Come on, use that intelligent head of yours," he said in that mellifluous voice of his.

She nodded. "I understand. How long have you been an agent?"

"For years. Fifteen years, to be exact. Since I was twenty-five."

"So you were working for British intelligence when you met me," she said, twisting her hands together, suddenly understanding there was a part of him she had never known.

"I was indeed," he confirmed.

"But we were going to be married. How did you ever hope to keep that a secret from me?"

"Very easily. First of all, you were heavily involved with your career, and to the exclusion of all else, except for our relationship, of course. And you traveled a lot as a war correspondent. Quite frankly, I didn't think you would be too nosy, prying into what I was doing all of the time. It wasn't in your nature to do so. And in any case, my secret had been safe from everyone for years. I had the perfect cover, you see. My wine-importing company."

"But it was so successful," she exclaimed, sounding surprised. "Most cover operations are just that, *a cover.* They don't necessarily make money."

He smiled. "That was always one of my problems, Nicky. Whatever business I became involved with prospered. My immediate boss, my spymaster, said I had the golden touch. That's why I dropped my other businesses in the early years. I then started the wine company, and although this too flourished, at least it was a splendid cover."

"I can see that it worked very well for you."

"It truly was ideal. I could travel anywhere I wanted, anytime," Charles said. "But you know that. Once I'd brought Chris Neald in as my partner, I wasn't tied to a desk at all. Chris ran the business, and I went around the world, doing what I had to do whilst purchasing wine for the company."

"It always seemed so legitimate to me," Nicky murmured with a small frown.

"Oh, but it was. In the end, of course, it was really Chris's company, inasmuch as he was doing most of the real work. Naturally, that suited me very well. I gained more and more freedom."

"Did Chris know you were an agent?"

"Good God, no!"

"But you did have an accomplice, didn't you? I mean someone who helped you to fake your death and get out of England."

"Yes, I did."

"Who was it?"

"You know very well I can't tell you that."

"Another agent?"

He nodded.

"Why did you have to do a vanishing act

at all? You just said you had the perfect business cover, and that I didn't pry too much.
Why couldn't you have married me and then
just continued as before, Charles?"

"That's what I had always intended to do.
But a few months before our marriage I
found out I had to go away for a long time.
You see, it had become imperative for an
SIS agent to infiltrate a particular foreign intelligence agency and to go under deep
cover in order to do so," he explained. "And
we all understood that the deep cover would
last for years—many years, perhaps, if it was
to be effective. And so it seemed kinder to
disappear before we were married than afterward."

"I see. But why *you,* Charles? Why not
another British agent?"

"Because of my special talents, my expertise in certain areas, the foreign languages I speak perfectly. I was the best
person for the job. And it was vital for British national security that I infiltrate as soon
as possible. You don't do that overnight,
you know. It takes time to gain people's
confidence and trust, to be accepted." He
took a sip of the water, and continued, "As
I said, we all knew that I would be working
undercover for many, many years. That's
the gist of it, really."

"And so you sacrificed our life together," Nicky murmured softly, looking at him closely.

"I had to—for my country, my beliefs," he replied, gazing back at her, his eyes suddenly very soft. There was a regretful look on his face.

She was quiet, sitting extremely still in the chair.

He said gently, "If it's any consolation, I did love you very much." He wanted to add that he still loved her, but he did not dare, and, anyway, it would be inappropriate.

She said slowly, "You caused me a lot of pain, Charles."

"I know I did. Can you ever forgive me?"

"Under the circumstances, I suppose I can. I do already." Now she gave him a penetrating look. "Your mother was as devastated as I was."

"Yes . . ."

"She's much better now. She's become engaged to Philip Rawlings."

"I know, I saw the announcement in *The Times.* He's wanted to marry her for years. He must be very happy."

"They both are."

"I'd like to ask *you* something now, Nicky. How did you discover that I was actually alive? And how on earth did you get that photograph of me, I mean the photograph of me as I look today?"

"It was a fluke," she said, and proceeded to explain.

When she had finished, he shook his head. "And I never knew that that damnable television camera was even focused on me. I'd been dining with a friend, in a restaurant near the square where the rally was being held, when we heard the hullabaloo. It was the shooting. My friend and I dashed out to see what was happening. I saw the television camera, of course, and I should have followed my instinct and left the scene at once. I'm usually much more careful."

Nicky nodded. Then she remarked, "You changed your appearance by growing a mustache and dyeing your hair. But you didn't change your eyes, they're still green."

"I have brown contact lenses, which I usually wear," he confided. "But I didn't think it was necessary to do so for you. But not to digress. Tell me what led you to Athens, Nicky."

"After I'd spent the weekend at Pullenbrook two weeks ago, I decided to go to Rome, which was the source of the film. I was hoping I would come across something that would lead me to you. By a curious coincidence, our bureau chief's secretary recognized your photograph. She'd seen you at the airport in Athens."

"Ah, yes, the lovely American girl I assisted with her luggage, I've no doubt."

"That's right."

"And so from Rome you went to Athens," he asserted. "And started asking questions at the various big hotels."

"You *had* been there, hadn't you? I mean, you weren't merely passing through, were you?"

"No, I wasn't. I spent two days in Athens, in point of fact."

"You stayed out at Vouliagmeni, didn't you?" Nicky said, leaning back in the chair, studying him again.

"Actually, I didn't. But I did spend some time there with one of my contacts. I had several luncheons there and dinner. But I was living in a safe house in the city."

"Is this a safe house?"

"Yes, it is."

"But you don't live in this apartment, do you?"

He shook his head. "No."

"Did you find out I was in Madrid when I got here, or did you know I was coming before I arrived?"

"Before. I knew of your presence in Athens the moment you started inquiring about me, and I knew when you left for Madrid. I was always one step ahead of you, Nicky, so to speak."

"Someone at the Grande Bretagne told you, didn't he? Was it Costa? Aristotle? Or Mr. Zoulakis out at Vouliagmeni?"

"I can't tell you that. And incidentally, *why* did you suddenly come here? What led you to me?"

"Nothing led me to you, Charles. I didn't even know you were here. I wanted to see your former Spanish partner. I hoped Don Pedro would agree with me that it *was* you in the photograph. Or tell me I was wrong."

"But you said my mother didn't believe it was me!" he exclaimed. "Wasn't that enough for you?"

"Not really. In any case, deep inside myself I felt you were still alive. Call it gut instinct."

"Yes, you always were very strong on that. I'm curious about another thing—once you decided I was alive, what did you think my motive had been for slipping off the face of the earth?"

"To be very honest, I wasn't sure. After your so-called suicide, there'd been no scandal in England, so I knew you couldn't have been involved in a big financial swindle. Therefore, I thought it must be some kind of illicit operation, and that you'd decided it was wiser to disappear and start a new life."

"What kind of illicit operation did you think I was caught up in?" Charles asked, his brows coming together in puzzlement.

"Arms dealing or drug smuggling," she said in a low voice.

"Good heavens, Nicky, you didn't think very highly of me, did you?"

"How could I?"

He rose, walked over to the window, paced up and down for a second or two and then came back to his chair. After a moment he said, "It perturbs me enormously that you believe someone followed you in Madrid. Are you sure of this?"

She shrugged. "Not absolutely certain, no."

"Tell me what leads you to think this?"

"There was a man who was hovering around me when I was speaking to the concierge yesterday morning. I almost stumbled over him again in the shopping arcade underneath the Palace Hotel a short while later. Then when I came out of the Prado, early last evening, he was there too, but he was preoccupied momentarily, and I slipped past him."

"I see. Can you describe him to me?"

"Of course. He was definitely Spanish, of

that I'm quite sure. Medium height. Well dressed, dark hair slicked back. About forty years old or thereabouts, and always smoking a black cigarillo."

"What makes you think he's Spanish?"

"He looks it. Also, he spoke Spanish to the concierge, I heard him as I was walking away from the desk."

"Do you think he might have been a guest in the hotel?"

"I don't know."

"He may not have been following you. He could have been a local Lothario who likes beautiful blondes," Charles pointed out. "A man who was simply trying to pick you up. That's not so unusual."

"Are you worried that I might have led him to you?"

"No, I'm sure you didn't do that," he reassured her.

"There's one other thing. My phone rang last night, but when I went to answer it, no one spoke. However, I checked with the operator and I did get a phone call. Someone did ask for me."

He nodded. "I did."

"Why didn't you say something?"

"I was going to ask you to meet me last night, and then I changed my mind. I thought I might frighten you off, and I decided it was better to wait until this morning."

"Do you live in Madrid?"

"No."

"Where do you live?"

"Everywhere. Nowhere. I sort of—float around. I'm never in one place for very long."

"For security reasons?"

"That's about it."

"I'm sorry that I might have put you in danger, Charles, showing your photograph and asking questions about you. That foreign intelligence agency would have you killed if they knew you were a mole, wouldn't they?"

He laughed lightly. "Oh yes, they'd have no compunction. But that's the intelligence business. No one ever said it was safe."

Nicky opened her handbag and took out the photographs of him. "I want you to have these," she said and handed them to him.

"Thanks, Nicky." He tore them into shreds and dropped the pieces on the tray.

"You *do* know I won't tell a soul that you're alive, or discuss what you've told me, don't you?"

"Yes. I know you'll be my fellow conspirator, and keep my secret."

"I could have blown your entire operation," she began, and stopped, biting her lip.

"You could have, that's true," he agreed. "And that could have been quite horrendous, because it's taken several years to set up. However, don't look so worried, I'm positive you haven't. If you had, I'd know by now. I probably wouldn't even be around to have this conversation with you. I would have been taken out."

This thought chilled her to the bone, and she fell silent. But after a short while, she said, "About the man I thought was following me . . . Shall I ask if he's a guest in the hotel? You could call me later, to find out what the concierge said."

"Oh no, Nicky, I don't want you to be involved in anything I do. It's far too dangerous. Please don't worry, I'll find out who the man is. I have my ways, my contacts. Just leave everything to me. Please leave everything alone. *Do you understand me?*"

"Yes."

"Nothing is ever as it seems in the world of intelligence and counterintelligence. You might say that everything is upside down in the clandestine world that I live in." He let out a small breath. "You never really know who anyone is." He straightened in the chair, and added, "I want you to leave Madrid as soon as possible."

"I will. I intend to go tomorrow."

"That's good, Nicky. I'll feel better knowing that you're nowhere near me."

Suddenly Nicky understood there was nothing more to say, and she pushed herself to her feet. "I think I'd better be going." She —

began walking toward the archway that led into the foyer.

Charles also rose and followed her.

She turned, waited for him to draw closer, and then she said, "I'm glad that we had this meeting, Charles. So much has been clarified for me."

"Yes, I'm glad we saw each other, too, Nicky." He studied her for a moment, his head on one side, and then the small smile touched his mouth and he said, "You're as beautiful as ever."

She nodded, but discovered she could not speak.

He went on, "You're obviously still flying around the world, covering disasters and the like. But you're not married, I see. Or rather, I should say you're not wearing a ring. Are you married, by any chance?"

"No, I'm not married."

"There's no special man in your life?"

"Yes, there is, as a matter of fact, but only recently."

"Are you in love with him?"

"I think so—I'm not sure."

"Are you going to marry him?"

"He hasn't asked me."

"He's a fool if he doesn't. And if he does ask? Will you?"

"I don't know."

"I wouldn't have done you any physical

harm, you know," Charles remarked, changing the subject. "However, I can't say that I blame you for wanting your own car and driver to come out here to see me."

"I was being cautious."

"And independent. That was one of the many things I always loved about you."

She turned to walk into the foyer and he caught hold of her arm, pulled her to him and held her tightly, held her very close to him.

Nicky was taken by surprise, but she did not resist him. She let him hold her in this way, understanding that he needed to do this, needed to be close to her. She could feel his heart hammering under his thin shirt, and with a sudden flash of insight, she thought: Oh God, he still loves me. Swallowing hard, she gently pushed him away.

"It's better that I leave now," she murmured softly, and then against her own volition she reached up and touched his cheek. "Please don't worry, I will never betray you, Charles."

"I believe you, Nicky," he said, taking her arm, walking with her to the front door. "I trust you. With my life."

Once she was back at the Ritz Hotel and in the privacy of her suite, Nicky broke down.

She lay on the bed and cried bitterly, sobbing as if her heart would break. Her tears were for Charles and the dangerous and lonely life he had chosen to lead, for herself and what they had once had together, and for what might have been.

But eventually she calmed down and took control of herself. She lay for a long time propped up against the pillows, thinking of everything that had happened in the past few weeks. And not unnaturally, she felt a sharp stab of guilt when she considered some of the dreadful things she had ascribed to Charles. How could she have ever thought that he was some sort of criminal— an arms smuggler, a drug trafficker? She should have known better.

Yes, he had sacrificed her, their love, their future, the future of the children they might have had together. But he had done it for a noble cause. He had done it for his country. And yes, she ought to have known it was something like this, not some grubby deal. After all, his mother's family, the famous Cliffords of Pullenbrook, had always been in service to the Crown of England, and since time immemorial. Honor and duty and loyalty to country had been inculcated in him since birth. He was simply following in the footsteps of his ancestors.

PART
FOUR

Enemies &
Friends

*In thy face I see
The map of honor, truth and loyalty.*

—William Shakespeare

*For I have sworn thee fair,
and thought thee bright.
Who art as black as hell, as
dark as night.*

—William Shakespeare

31

It was that time of the year when Parisians have fled to summer resorts for their annual vacations and the tourists have invaded. Paris was awash with foreigners, but Nicky did not care; she was both relieved and glad to be here.

Madrid was not a city she knew well, and she had visited it only once before this last trip, but she had no desire to return. The past forty-eight hours had left their mark on her, particularly the confrontation with Charles yesterday, and she knew that thereafter Madrid was always going to hold unpleasant memories for her.

She had managed to get a flight out of

Madrid late on Saturday afternoon, and had checked into the Plaza-Athénée when she arrived at night. Clee was not returning until Sunday evening, and was not expecting to see her until Monday. And, in any case, she needed some time alone, time to sort out her turbulent thoughts, to come to terms with all that had happened since she had last seen him in New York at the beginning of August.

On an urgent quest for Charles Devereaux though she had been, the unexpectedness of suddenly coming face-to-face with him had been an enormous shock, as indeed was the news that he had a secret life as an agent with British intelligence. She had not slept well last night, even though she had been bone tired, and after restlessly tossing and turning for hours she had finally fallen asleep as dawn broke.

When she awakened around ten, she had felt out of sorts with herself, and by noon a heavy sadness had settled over her. It was a sadness so acute it verged on depression, and in an effort to throw this off she had dressed and left the hotel.

Optimistic by nature and generally upbeat, Nicky was not accustomed to being down in the dumps, and she loathed the feelings enveloping her now. So she hoped that being outside in the sunshine, walking the familiar

streets and visiting favorite haunts, would
help to lighten her mood.

For as long as Nicky could remember she
had felt a spiritual affinity for Paris. It was her
city in so many different ways, and the childhood years she had spent here in the sixties
had been extraordinarily happy. And so it
was that she tried to recapture some of that
youthful joy as she walked along energeti-
cally; perhaps the happy memories of the
past would help to chase away the demons
of the present.

Nicky was not sad for herself but for
Charles. Long ago, long before he had
known her, he had clearly set himself upon
a deadly course that was now irrevocable.
He had made a choice, one that had ulti-
mately led him to that safe house in Madrid,
where they had met yesterday. In deciding to
serve his country, he had elected to live in
the covert world of espionage, a dangerous
netherworld of secrets and spying, duplicity
and double-dealing—and, more often than
not, death.

A chill ran through her, despite the warmth
of the day and the radiant sunlight. Such a
life had little to commend it, or to offer a man;
she knew Charles could never marry now,
never have children, never lead a normal
existence. The loneliness and fear he had to

contend with must be excruciating, and the specter of betrayal, or discovery, unnerving. That kind of terror must strike close to the bone, she thought, and she shivered involuntarily.

Nicky walked on at a steady pace, but her mind raced. All manner of different thoughts jostled for attention, and one, in particular, took precedence over the others: Charles had admitted to being a British agent since the age of twenty-five, and since he was so obviously deeply committed, then why on earth had he ever become involved with her in the first place?

She wished she had asked him this; she also wished she had asked him why he had not left one last word for her, as he had for his mother. Maybe he had not known what to say to her, or had had nothing to say, perhaps; certainly the letter to Anne had been brief and to the point, a bleak little epistle, if ever she had read one. Well, she would never find out now. It was too late, the chance had gone.

Having come down the avenue Montaigne from the hotel and turned onto the Champs-Élysées, Nicky now struck out across the vast place de la Concorde, and was soon entering the Jardin des Tuileries. She slowed her steps and glanced around. It was years since she had been here in the gardens, but there were so many good things to remember, so many lovely memories of her childhood associated with them.

Quite unexpectedly she thought of Marie Thérèse Bouret, the *au pair* who had looked after her. She had been seven years old, Marie Thérèse seventeen, when the young French girl had come to live with them, being more like a big sister than a nanny. Vivacious, loving and joyful of spirit, Marie Thérèse had brought Nicky to the gardens to play almost every day in summer. And she had taken her to so many other places as well, during the six years her parents had been based in Paris for their respective newspapers. It was with Marie Thérèse that she had gone to the Louvre for the first time to see the *Mona Lisa* and other great paintings; together they had gone up the Eiffel Tower to view Paris from on high, and, as the young nanny had explained, for her to see how the Arc de Triomphe resembled the hub of a giant wheel, with the great avenues and boulevards designed by Baron Haussmann stretching out from it like long spokes.

And when her mother had taken her to Fontainebleau, Versailles and Malmaison on her "historical outings," as she called them, Marie Thérèse had always accompanied them. She, too, had been treated to her mother's unique lessons in French history, which were never dull and boring but intriguing and fascinating. And it was Marie Thérèse to whom she had clung when her parents were away, doing their work as journalists, and to whom she had said her first halting words in French. Yes, she had been indispensable to her when she was little, had loved her dearly, taught her so much about the language, about Paris and the French way of life.

They had stayed in close touch over the years, and saw each other from time to time, whenever Nicky was in Paris. Marie Thérèse had married at twenty-three, and had had a son a year later. Sadly, her husband, Jean-Pierre, had been killed ten years ago in a car crash in Mozambique, where he was working on an engineering job. Her son, Paul, now twenty-two and an engineer like his father, had recently married.

I must call her, Nicky thought. I'll do it later when I get back to the hotel and take her to lunch tomorrow. I hope she can make it. The thought of seeing the woman she held in such affection, and who had played such an important role in her life when she was a child, cheered Nicky; a little of the sadness evaporated.

After walking in the gardens for a while, Nicky finally went on her way, past the Jardin du Carrousel and across the Pont des Arts. This was the only metal bridge in Paris, and one she knew well, since her father had a very good painting of it by Jacques Bouyssou, the official painter of the French navy.

When she came to the quai Malaquais, Nicky hesitated; she looked up and down, wondering whether to wander along the Seine to Notre-Dame or to plunge into the streets behind the quai. The apartment she and her parents and Marie Thérèse had lived in had been on the two top floors of an eighteenth-century house on the Île Saint-Louis. It stood in the shadow of the ancient cathedral, and she loved that particular part of the city. She decided to wander up there later.

Striking out down the rue Bonaparte, she headed for the place Saint-Germain-des-Prés. "Napoleon Bonaparte," she murmured under her breath, recalling how that name had been a familiar one in their home for years. She had learned it young, and at once it evoked another rush of memories. Her mother had been fascinated by Bonaparte, and after years of scholarly research had finally written a masterly biography of the great general and France's first emperor.

To Nicky the book had been extraordinary,

and she still believed it to be her mother's best. It was a portrait that was extremely fair and well balanced, and her mother had made the man accessible in modern terms. He had been all too human, and so had Josephine, his grand passion, the only woman he had ever really loved. But their love had foundered on the rocks of his overweening ambition; he had had their marriage annulled in order to beget an heir to his empire with a younger woman.

According to her mother, this heartbreaking decision had ruined their lives. Without Josephine at his side, Napoleon's luck turned bad, and Josephine died of a broken heart just after his first abdication and exile to Elba in 1814. "They never stopped loving each other," her mother had said to her time and time again when she was writing the book. "And that was the tragedy of it all."

Nicky sighed. The anguish men and women caused each other, the terrible things they did to each other in the name of love never failed to amaze her. Nothing has changed and it never will, she thought, because human beings are exactly the same as they were hundreds of years ago. And we've learned nothing over the centuries. What Charles had done to her was cruel, unconscionable, however important his cause might be. It had been wrong of him to even contemplate marrying her under the circumstances. He had been selfish. But then who isn't? she asked herself.

By the time she reached the place Saint-Germain, Nicky was damp with perspiration, tired from the heat and footsore. Heading in the direction of a café on the shady side of the square, she took a table and ordered café au lait, bread, a tomato salad, sliced chicken and a bottle of water. She had not eaten much in the last few days, and she discovered she was starving.

The waiter brought the bottle of water immediately. She thirstily drank a glass straight down and then leaned back in the chair. The long walk had done her good, and she felt certain she would sleep tonight, and tomorrow she would be with Clee. This prospect filled her with warmth and pleasure. She could hardly wait to see him.

Taking off her sunglasses, Nicky blinked and looked around. The area was busy. People were strolling around or sitting at cafés as she was, whiling away the time, enjoying the nice weather on this pleasant Sunday afternoon. The noise of people talking and laughing surrounded her, and as her eyes scanned the place Saint-Germain she could not help thinking how ordinary and normal everybody looked and sounded. This was reassuring, and she pulled her thoughts away from Charles Devereaux and the treacherous and cynical world he occupied. Suddenly it struck her that he had done her a favor by vanishing when he did. How terrible her life might have turned out to be if she had married him.

Marie Thérèse lived on the opposite side of Paris, just off the boulevard de Belleville. Since this was quite a distance from the Plaza-Athénée, Nicky allowed herself a good half hour to get there by taxi on Monday. Even so, she was a bit late when she finally arrived, because of the distance and the heavy traffic congesting the streets at this busy time of day.

As she climbed the long flight of stairs to the apartment she could not help wondering why her friend now lived in this section of the city. Belleville—pretty town—certainly did not live up to its name.

It was an odd area, totally lacking in elegance and even a bit scruffy. It struck her that it was rather off the beaten track for a woman like Marie Thérèse, who was used to so much better.

But after she had hugged and kissed the

Frenchwoman in the small foyer of the apartment, Nicky glanced around and saw that the living room ahead was large and nicely appointed. Also, there was a happy feeling about the place; it had a pleasant atmosphere.

As for Marie Thérèse, she was as pretty and vivacious as she had always been, her large, dark eyes dancing, her generous mouth twitching with hidden laughter, just as it had years ago.

"Now you can see why it is difficult for me to get around," she said and pointed to her left leg encased up to the knee in a plaster cast. "The stairs are hard for me—with this."

Nicky nodded sympathetically. "I was sorry to hear about your accident, and sorry that I couldn't take you to lunch at the Relais Plaza. But it's great to see you, and you do look wonderful, Marie Thérèse."

"I feel it, *ma chérie,* except for this silly thing." She tapped the cast with her cane and grimaced.

"This is for you," Nicky said, giving her the black shopping bag she was carrying.

"Nicky, you shouldn't have! But how wonderful—something from Chanel."

"I hope you like it. I went across the street this morning to their boutique. They said you can exchange it, if you wish."

"I am sure that I will adore it, thank you. But come, let us not stand here, let us go and sit down so that I can open your *cadeau.* You are so generous, *ma petite.*"

They sat in wide armchairs opposite each other, and within a few seconds Marie Thérèse had opened the Chanel box and pulled out a beautiful red-and-white silk scarf. It was obvious from her expression that she loved it, and Nicky was delighted to see this.

"Thank you, Nicky, you are such a darling." Pushing herself up, she went to kiss her and then added, "I have a bottle of white wine ready for us, and a little of the country pâté you always liked."

With a chuckle Nicky said, "I hope you've got *cornichons* to go with it."

"*Bien sûr.* I wouldn't dare to serve pâté to *you* without them. I have not forgotten how much you love them. Why, you and your little friend Natalie used to eat them like candy!"

Nicky burst out laughing. "And I've never lost the taste for them. Neither has Natalie."

"And where is the beautiful Natalie these days?"

"Living in Los Angeles, and being very successful in films."

"She was certainly beautiful enough to be a movie star when she was a child."

"And she's still a beauty. But she works in

production, behind the scenes, not in front of the camera."

"But you are in front of it, my Nicky, and you are fantastic. One of the French networks recently showed a documentary you had done for ATN on the women of Beirut and their point of view about the war. It was very touching, and I was so proud of you."

"Thank you," Nicky murmured. "As I recall, they dubbed me in French."

Hobbling across the floor of the living room, Marie Thérèse said, "Yes, they did. I will get the wine from the refrigerator so that we can have a drink."

"Let me help you!" Nicky said, jumping up.

"*Merci, chérie.*"

Nicky followed her through the foyer and down a short corridor to the kitchen, where she opened the wine and put it on the tray along with the loaf of pâté, a plate of toast and a crystal dish of *cornichons.* Marie Thérèse placed several paper napkins on the tray, which Nicky carried back to the living room.

Once they were settled in their chairs and had clinked glasses, Nicky let her eyes roam around the cheerful room. "Your things look beautiful here, and the apartment seems to be large, but why did you move? You were comfortable on the Left Bank, weren't you?"

"I was, Nicky, this is true. But my apartment had only one bedroom. It was too small for three people."

"*Three?* Are Paul and his wife living with you, then?"

The Frenchwoman shook her head. "*Non, non, chérie,* they have their own apartment. I live here because of Marcel, my friend. He is a widower, with a son, and he already had this place. It was so much easier to move in here with them. Marcel and I did it up a little, and brought my things. . . ." She shrugged. "We are content here."

"I'm glad," Nicky replied. She suddenly realized that her former nanny looked far younger than her forty-six years. The short curly hair was still dark, untouched by gray, the rosy complexion youthful, and those warm brown eyes she remembered so well from her childhood shone with happiness. "Why, Marie Thérèse, I do believe you've fallen madly in love with your friend Marcel! I can see it in your eyes!"

Marie Thérèse blushed slightly and nodded, looking shy and girlish.

Nicky said, "I think Marcel must be very good for you."

"Oh, he is, Nicky, I have not been so happy in years. Marcel is a nice man, very kind, and we are happy together."

"Are you going to marry him?"

"Yes, perhaps. There is no hurry." She lifted her shoulders in a shrug. "When we feel like it, we will." Marie Thérèse leaned forward slightly and asked, "But what of you, Nicky? Last night, on the telephone, you said you had a boyfriend in Paris. Is that why you are here? To be with him?"

"Yes, it is. He's a photographer. We met in Beirut two years ago. And then just after we came out of China, where we'd been covering the demonstrations in Tiananmen Square, we . . . well, we became involved. That was at the end of June."

"I never thought you'd be interested in a Frenchman. You were such an all-American girl when you were small."

"I guess I still am," Nicky laughed. "And my friend is an American, even though he lives here. His name's Cleeland Donovan, Clee for short, I'm sure you've seen his photographs in *Paris Match.*"

"*Oui, oui!*" Marie Thérèse exclaimed. "I have! And are you going to marry him?"

"Maybe," Nicky said.

"That would be wonderful for me, if you came to live in Paris . . . perhaps we could see each other more often than once every couple of years," Marie Thérèse said, sounding wistful.

At this moment the doorbell rang, and Marie Thérèse said, "Nicky, could you go to the door, please? It is the lunch arriving, I ordered it from the restaurant next door."

Nicky hurried into the foyer, and Marie Thérèse, struggling to her feet, called after her, "Everything is paid for, all you have to do is put the dishes in the oven for me. It is already turned on."

"Okay," Nicky said over her shoulder and opened the front door; taking a large tray from the waiter standing there, she said "*Merci beaucoup.*" Marie Thérèse hobbled toward her, saying "*Merci,* Olivier, *merci*," and the waiter inclined his head. "*De rien,* Madame Bouret," he replied before disappearing down the stairs.

In the kitchen, Marie Thérèse leaned against the doorjamb while Nicky put the dishes in the oven. "I ordered *couscous,* they make it with chicken. It is delicious," she explained.

"It certainly smells good," Nicky replied as she straightened and pushed her hair out of her face.

Marie Thérèse continued, "Now, let us go back to the salon and have another glass of wine, and you can tell me all about your friend Clee."

"I'd be delighted to do that." Nicky flashed

her a wide smile, and added, "I'll begin now if you like by telling you that he's absolutely wonderful."

"Aha! I think you too are in love!"

"I just might be at that," Nicky said.

32

Nicky felt her mood changing the minute she opened the door to Clee on Monday evening. The last vestiges of her sadness, that awful feeling of melancholy, dissipated instantly, and her spirits lifted. All of the things that had troubled her for the last few days were pushed to the back of her mind. The only thing that mattered was Clee.

He stood there, saying nothing, a huge smile spreading across his face, radiating warmth, his love shining from his dark eyes.

She smiled back, her face filling with radiance, opened the door wide and stepped to one side so he could enter.

"I've missed you, Nick," he said, entering

the suite. He grabbed hold of her and wrapped his arms around her, pushing the door closed with his foot. "It's been too long, babe," he went on, brushing her cheek with his lips. "Far too long. For me."

"And for me," she said, holding him tightly. "I've missed you terribly."

"I'm glad," Clee said, kissed her lightly on the mouth, and then, with his arm around her shoulders, walked her into the small sitting room.

Pausing, he held her away from him. "Nicky," he exclaimed, "God, it's so good to see you! I've longed for you."

"And how I've longed for *you*!" Nicky responded, taking herself by surprise with this fervent admission. She was usually more cautious in what she said to him, yet now she ached to escape to Provence, to obliterate everything that had happened since she had arrived in Europe, and most of all to be with Clee and to forget about Charles Devereaux.

"Well, I guess I'd better dump my problems on you now," he announced with a grimace.

"What kind of problems, Clee?"

He didn't immediately answer this question. Instead, he asked, "Is that a bottle of champagne in the ice bucket over there?"

"Dom Pérignon. Your favorite."

"Let's have a glass, darling, and then I'll explain."

Nicky sat down on the sofa, experiencing a pang of anxiety, hoping the problems he had mentioned were not insurmountable. She couldn't bear it if he had to go away on another assignment. All she wanted was to be with him. She needed him, needed his gentleness and affection.

Clee went over to the coffee table, opened the bottle of champagne with efficiency and filled the two crystal flutes on the tray. After clinking his glass against hers, he took a long drink. "Mmmm, that's good," he murmured, and walked over to the fireplace. "It's been a rough day at the office."

"The problems, Clee, what are they?" she pressed.

He put his glass down on the mantelpiece, and said, "Okay, here goes. First, I've got a leak in the bathroom. I came back last night to find a flood. Bathroom *and* bedroom under water—well, almost. I called several plumbers today, but in typical French fashion, not one was available until tomorrow. Anyway, my housekeeper has done her best to contain the deluge, but there's no way I can move you into my apartment tonight. So—"

Reaching into his jacket pocket, he pulled

out a toothbrush and banged it down on the mantel. "I have to sleep here tonight. I can camp out in the suite with you, can't I?"

"Of course you can!" she cried, laughing, filled with relief. "I'd love it, and I'd hardly call that a problem. I mean, staying here isn't, but I am sorry about your apartment."

He grinned at her. "It needed redecorating anyway." His face sobered as he went on. "Also, we can't leave for the farm on Wednesday as we'd planned, Nick. I've got problems at the office—"

"Such as?" she cut in.

"Two of my partners have to be away for various reasons. Pete Naylor and I have been splitting their assignments between us. Do you mind if we stay in Paris for another week or so?"

"Oh, Clee, you know I love Paris. Besides, I don't really care where I am, as long as I'm with you."

"Nicky, that's the best news I've had in weeks," he said, smiling broadly. But his eyes were fastened on hers intently. He was very sensitive to every nuance of her behavior, and he realized that her feelings for him had deepened since they were together in Provence and in New York.

Taking a sip of champagne, he continued, "There's another thing, although it's more of a disappointment. Yoyo won't be arriving in Paris until the end of the week. So I'm afraid our celebration tonight will be private."

"Oh, Clee, I'm sorry we won't be seeing Yoyo right away," Nicky remarked between sips of champagne. "But the main thing is that we're together, and he's on his way here, not rotting in a Beijing jail. Have you actually spoken to him yet?"

"No, but he phoned the office on Saturday, and Jean-Claude says Yoyo knew you would be in Paris today. Apparently he spoke to your secretary in New York."

"Last week, he phoned the network."

Clee nodded, finished his champagne and poured himself another glass. "A refill, Nicky?"

She shook her head. "No more for me just now, thanks."

Leaning against the mantel, Clee asked, "How did your research go in Rome, Athens and Madrid?"

"Fine, thanks. And how did you get on in Berlin and Leipzig?"

"Not bad, not bad at all. I have a feeling I might go back there in the not too distant future. A lot's happening—we've seen nothing yet." He began to talk about the political situations now existing in East and West Berlin, Leipzig, the Eastern European bloc in general and, most especially, Russia.

Nicky sat back, listening attentively, respecting his judgment, as she always had. But at the same time, part of her mind was focused on him personally. She could not help thinking how marvelous he looked, his face lightly tanned from being outdoors so much, his brown hair lightened by the sun. He wore a dark-blue silk suit, a pale-blue shirt and a navy tie, and she had never seen him looking smarter. But although he had long ago acquired that inimitable stylishness of the French, and looked European in a certain sense, his face was wholly American, boyish and open, a nice face. The brown eyes were full of candor and sincerity, his wide Irish mouth was generous, also very gentle. Yes, Cleeland Donovan was a quietly handsome man, and very appealing.

Unexpectedly, her feelings for him seemed to engulf her, overwhelm her. For the first time she truly understood how much this man really meant to her. There was no one in the world who was more important than he was, and she was startled by this sudden realization.

Lost for a few seconds in her contemplation of him and of her feelings for him, she wasn't aware that he had stopped speaking until he let out a low whistle, startling her. With a jolt she sat up straighter and blinked.

"Hey, Nicky, where are you drifting off to?"

he asked and broke into laughter. "Am I boring you?"

"Oh, no, Clee, certainly not, honestly,"
she said.

"What's wrong?" he demanded. "You've
got a peculiar expression on your face."

"I love you," she said.

He gaped at her. "What?"

"I love you."

He crossed the floor in three strides and
sat down on the sofa next to her. He held her
hands tightly and peered into her face.
"Nicky, would you mind repeating that one
more time?"

"I love you, Clee. I love you."

"Oh, Nicky," he said, and then he took her
face between his hands and kissed her; he
leaned against her and eased her down onto
the cushions. Moving a strand of blond hair
away from her face, he said, "I love you
too—I've told you that before. And it's been
painful not having you with me."

Nicky touched his mouth and traced its
shape with a fingertip. "I know, it was the
same for me, darling."

He kissed her more passionately this time,
his tongue finding hers, grazing it, lingering
against it. Abruptly he stopped and whispered against her hair, "Let's go to bed. I
want you."

Clee stood up, offered her his hand and together they went into the bedroom. They flung off their clothes and wrapped their arms around each other. They stood for a long moment without saying a word, without moving, just happy to be close and intimate and together again.

At last he said, "It's never been like this before for me."

"It hasn't for me either," she said, and she knew now that this was the truth. She had not loved Charles in the same way that she loved Clee; each man had brought out something different in her.

There was another moment of silence as he buried his face in her hair and his hands moved down over her back, sliding onto her buttocks; he pulled her against him so that their pelvic bones touched.

Nicky became aroused, as he already was, and now it was she who took the lead, pushing him gently away from her and pulling him over to the bed.

They lay on their sides, facing each other, gazing into each other's eyes, saying nothing. But neither of them needed words. Each could read the other's face, which was eloquent with love and desire.

"Ah, Nicky, my lovely Nicky," he whispered, and he brought her closer, his right hand on the nape of her neck. "I want to possess you completely, take all of you to me. . . ."

"I know . . . I want that too."

Their mouths came together again, and he slipped on top of her, pushed his hands under her back and pulled her against him. His mouth became insistent, demanding; ardently she responded to him, her passion mounting as his did. He entered her unexpectedly, without any foreplay, as he had several times in Provence, and she gasped in astonishment. And then as he eased deeper into her, her legs went around his back and she cleaved to him, became part of him. At once they found their own rhythm, as they always did, moving faster and faster.

"Oh God, Nicky, oh God," Clee cried as he lifted his mouth from hers. His breathing was labored; he gasped as she was gasping.

She stiffened under him, began to quiver. "Clee! I love you!" She opened her eyes and looked up into his face. "I love you," she moaned softly. Her quivering intensified and she gave herself up to him, came to him swiftly.

As always, her passion for him brought Clee to the very height of excitement, and he began to lose control. Before he could stop himself, he was flowing into her, calling her name as she had his, telling her that he loved her as he had not loved any woman ever in his life.

He fell against her, breathing heavily, then lifted his head, bent over her and kissed her face. Her cheeks were damp; he tasted the salt of her tears.

"You're crying," he said in surprise, wiping the tears away. "Nicky, what is it? Why are you weeping?"

"I don't know," she murmured, looking up at him. Half laughing, she added, "Because I'm so happy, I guess."

He merely smiled that lopsided smile of his, which she knew so well, and saying nothing, he simply took her into his arms and held her.

"This is a much better picnic than the one we had that night at the farm," Clee said between bites on a chicken leg.

"I don't agree!" Nicky looked at him and shook her head. "That was the best picnic I've ever had in my entire life. You made such wonderful things, including the greatest peanut butter and jelly sandwiches I've ever eaten."

Clee threw back his head and laughed. "If that's all it takes to please you, I can see I'm going to have an easy time with you."

Nicky laughed and reached for her glass

of white wine on the bedside table. "I can be very tough about some things, you know."

They sat cross-legged in the middle of the large bed, wrapped in the hotel's white toweling bathrobes. There was a plate of chicken and the bread basket between them; on the room-service table nearby, which Clee had wheeled in from the living room, there was a bowl of green salad, a basket of fresh fruit and the bottle of Montrachet in an ice bucket.

"Do all the girls mistake you for Kevin Costner?" Nicky suddenly asked, eyeing him appraisingly.

"Heavens, no, why?"

"Well, he's your look-alike, you know."

He made no comment and drank his wine.

"*I* mistook you for him, in fact."

"What are you saying, Nicky?"

Then she told him about the mistake she had made in Athens, how she had bought a magazine because she thought it was he on the cover.

"It must be wishful thinking on your part," Clee said dismissively. "Is that what you really want? A movie star?"

"No, Clee. I want you."

"You've got me, babe, in case you hadn't realized it."

Nicky smiled and said, "I'm glad."

"And what about you, Nicky? Do I have you?"

"You know you do, my darling."

He grinned and blew her a kiss.

Reaching for her wine, Nicky took a sip, then sat nursing her glass in both hands, looking thoughtful. After a moment or two she said slowly, "Clee, when I was in London and called you in Berlin, just before I left for Rome, I told you I'd been to see Anne Devereaux at Pullenbrook—"

"You went to make amends, right?"

"Well, yes, that's true, in a way. But I also had another reason to go and see her."

Nicky cleared her throat and plunged in. "I had decided that Charles might be alive. That he might very well have faked his own death, to vanish, for his own reasons."

Clee stared at her dumbfounded for a second, then put the chicken leg back on the plate and exclaimed, "You can't be serious!" He shook his head and began to laugh. "Come on, Nick, it's me you're talking to—stop kidding around."

"But I'm not kidding, I'm serious, dead serious."

Her sober tone had its effect, and he looked grave, carefully weighing what she had said. Finally, he asked, "What happened to make you think that, after all these years?"

Nicky told him the story, reciting most of the pertinent details, but stopping short once she had filled him in about the events in Rome and Athens. She said nothing at all about Madrid.

When she had finished, Clee said in an oddly subdued voice, "Why the hell would you want to traipse all over Europe looking for a dead man? Well, a supposedly dead man. Hadn't he caused you enough pain? Or do you still have feelings for him, Nick? Is that it?"

"No, I don't. I'm emotionally free of Charles Devereaux, and I have been for a long time. Long before I fell in love with you, in fact."

He simply looked at her more closely, his eyes pinning hers. Then he said quietly, "If you say so . . . Yes, I believe you, Nick. Just tell me why you went looking for him."

"I wanted to get to the truth. Listen, Clee, I was stunned, shocked, disbelieving, when I saw that face on our newscast from Rome. But he did look so much like Charles that I felt I had to go and talk to Anne. I just couldn't get that face out of my mind. And I'd always been a bit dismayed, sort of troubled because Charles's body was never found." Nicky paused, then shook her head. "I suppose it's human nature to want to have a funeral, to bury the dead. . . . I think I wanted to get to the truth so that I could close that chapter of my life."

"Is it closed now? Really and truly closed? Or is he going to haunt you?"

"No, I've just told you, it's closed."

"Tell me something else, Nick. Why are you now so sure he committed suicide, that he's really dead? What made you change your mind?"

"Because I kept coming up against brick walls wherever I went. There was no trace of him in Rome or in Athens."

"Why did you go to Madrid?" Clee frowned slightly before reaching for his drink. "What did you hope to find there?"

"I wasn't sure what I'd find, actually. I wanted to show the pictures to his former Spanish partner. I guess I was seeking a confirmation or a denial from Don Pedro."

"And what did the Spanish guy say?"

"I didn't see Don Pedro, he was away. As I told you on the phone this morning, I took a flight out of Madrid late on Saturday afternoon and checked in here."

"Why the sudden change of heart?"

"It hit me that if I could so easily mistake Kevin Costner for you on the cover of a magazine, then perhaps I could have mistaken another man for Charles Devereaux—with a slightly altered appearance, of course."

"Photographs *can* be very deceptive and

misleading. Let me see them, Nicky, I'd like to take a look."

"I got rid of them. . . . I hope you're not angry with me, Clee."

"No, not angry, just startled, and troubled. I wish you'd told me immediately, the day after you'd seen the newscast. I'd have understood, Nick, once I'd gotten used to the idea that the guy might be alive—and giving me competition."

"You have no competition, Clee. I love you."

"I'd also like you to trust me—I'm a pretty intelligent guy, and I respect you, your emotions, your mind, your professionalism. And your independence. I would never interfere with anything you wanted to do, unless I thought you might get hurt in some way. For God's sake, you're a mature woman, a seasoned broadcast journalist, a war correspondent that I've worked side by side with for two years. Do you think I don't know you and trust you? Anyway, I'd never treat you like a child."

"Thanks, Clee, and yes, you *do* know me, perhaps better than anyone else. I'm glad you trust me, and I do trust you, you know."

There was a sudden silence, and after a couple of minutes, Clee said, "So his mother didn't think the photographs resembled him?"

"No, she didn't. She was adamant, in fact. And so was Philip Rawlings, her boyfriend. You know, the man she was with in Les Baux."

He nodded. "I remember. What's the legal situation in England? I mean about Charles Devereaux."

"He was listed as a missing person because there was no body. A suicide note doesn't make any difference when there's no body. I'm not sure whether the police have closed their files on him yet. I never thought to ask Anne."

"You've never ever discussed Charles Devereaux with me—what little I know came from Arch Leverson. But he was pretty closemouthed about the whole thing, didn't say very much, out of loyalty to you. I didn't even know Devereaux had left a suicide note. Was it addressed to you?"

"No, to his mother."

"What did it say—do you know?"

"Yes, she showed it to me when I flew to England a few days after the suicide. It was only a couple of lines, very brief, almost cold. He said in the note that he didn't want to live any longer, that he was doing the only thing he possibly could—taking his own life—and that he hoped she would forgive him."

"Has she?"

"I don't really know—she still grieves for

him, I'm certain of that, although she keeps up a good front."

"Was there a letter for you?"

"No."

"Didn't you find that strange?"

"Yes, I did. But maybe he didn't have any last words for me."

"Why do you say that?"

"Because in the months before he killed himself he did everything very deliberately. He sold his shares in the wine-importing company to his British and Spanish partners, he sold his flat, made a will and put all of his affairs in order. It was all done very, very methodically, Clee. So if he *had* had anything he wanted to say to me, he would have written me a letter, don't you think?"

"I suppose so," Clee murmured. "Who got his money?"

"Anne is the beneficiary under his will, but of course she hasn't inherited it yet, because Charles is not considered to be legally dead. Under British law, Anne can go to court for a legal declaration of death only after seven years, not before. She's got four more years to wait."

Clee leaned forward, a frown furrowing his brow, his eyes thoughtful. He said slowly, "When a man melts into thin air to start a new life with a new identity, he usually does so for a helluva good reason. When you thought Devereaux might be alive, why did you think he'd faked his own death? For what reason, Nick?"

"I wasn't sure. I told Arch when I saw him in Rome that it might be a reason so bizarre no one could even imagine it. But actually I thought Charles was involved in something illegal."

"Such as?"

"Arms smuggling or drug trafficking."

"Yeah, I guess I'd have come to the same conclusion," Clee agreed. "Especially in view of the world we live in today."

"I brought all this up tonight because I wanted you to know, Clee," Nicky said, gazing at him earnestly. "I didn't want anything to be between us."

"I'm glad you told me, and I'm not angry." Clee's boyish smile flashed, and he went on, "I just feel a bit protective of you, that's all. . . . I love you."

"And I love you."

"Let's not discuss this guy Devereaux anymore. Let's bury him once and for all, shall we?"

"He's already buried," Nicky said as she slipped off the bed. She went around to Clee's side, and hugged him hard. "Thanks for being so wonderful, and for understanding," she murmured. Then she said, "I'll be back in a minute, don't go away."

"I'm *never* leaving," Clee said, and smiled.

Nicky went into the bathroom, closed the door and leaned against it. She had wanted to tell Clee as much of the truth as she possibly could, but she had known all along that she must not tell all of her story. Thankfully she had managed to tell it without a hitch. No one must ever know that Charles Devereaux was still alive. She had given her promise and she would not betray him; his life was in her hands. And her secret did not harm Clee. Besides, she would never see Charles Devereaux again. That chapter of her life was finally closed.

33

"After Mai die in Xiehe Hospital I take her body to parents," Yoyo said, looking from Clee to Nicky. "Friends help me. We find two pedicabs. They take us. We go to Mai's house. Her parents weep. They very sad. I very sad." Yoyo shook his head, and he mournfully added, "Mai such young girl—" His voice quavered, and he stopped speaking.

Nicky reached out and touched his arm in sympathy and with deep affection. It was hard to believe that Yoyo was with them in Paris at last, and looking so well, almost prosperous, she thought. He wore a neat, dark suit, a white shirt and a red tie, and seemed totally in command of himself and the situation.

Clearing her throat, she said, "Clee and I know how terrible it was for you, how grief-stricken you must have been, and still are. It is so tragic. We were all upset and so very sorry when Mai died."

Yoyo tried to smile without much success. "I know, Nicky." He turned to Clee. "Thank you, Clee, for carrying Mai so far. Trying to save Mai. Taking her to Xiehe. You a good man, Clee. You a good friend. And you a good friend, Nicky."

"I just wish we could have saved her," Clee said, his heart going out to the young Chinese student who sat with them in his apartment on the rue Jacob. It was early on Friday evening, on the first day of September. Yoyo had come over to the sixth *arrondissement* on the Left Bank to visit with them, tell them how he had escaped from Beijing and share his news. Later they were going out to have the long-awaited celebration dinner together, as the guests of his benefactor, a Mr. Loong.

Yoyo suddenly said, "Mai's death bad joss."

"Yes, it *was* bad luck," Clee agreed. He and Nicky glanced at each other, and in an attempt to change the subject, Clee went on,

"Nicky and I have been terribly worried about you all these weeks, Yoyo. So have Arch and the guys. We didn't know what had happened to you after we left Beijing. We waited in Hong Kong for you, as we promised we would, and for several days, you know."

"Sorry I did not come. It was hard for me, Clee."

Nicky said, "Don't apologize, Yoyo, we understand. It's just that we were so concerned for your safety. We hoped nothing bad had happened, that you weren't locked up in a Beijing jail." She squeezed his arm again, gave him a warm smile. "Thank God you're all right."

"Many things happened to me. But I lucky. Really."

"Tell us everything, how you got out of Beijing, how you came to Paris," Clee said.

"I begin at beginning. Yes?"

"Okay, Yoyo, shoot," Clee replied, smiling at him.

Yoyo nodded, took a deep breath. "After you leave, police everywhere in Beijing. I go Mai's house. Mai's parents hide me. Police asking many questions about students. Many arrests. Many students go to jail. At Qinghua University very bad things happen. It dangerous. I stay Mai's house one week.

Mai's parents worry police find me. Arrest me. Mai's father take me house of friends. They hide me for ten days. It difficult. Dangerous. Necessary I leave Beijing."

"Is that when you left the city? In the middle of June?" Nicky asked.

"No. No. I stayed in Beijing. I move many times. I go to friends of Mai's parents. They hide me. Mai's mother say she help me escape. She have *guanxi*—"

"That means connections," Nicky interrupted, looking across at Clee. "Philip Rawlings told me when I was at Pullenbrook."

"How would he know a thing like that?" Clee asked, frowning.

"I told you before, he's got an important job at the British Foreign Office. Hong Kong is a British Crown Colony and under British protection and government until June 30, 1997." Nicky thought a moment. "Who knows, maybe he's on the China desk or the Hong Kong desk at the Foreign Office. He's always been very cagey about what he actually does there."

"I understand," Clee said, then turned to Yoyo. "Sorry for the interruption. Keep going, Yoyo."

"Mai's mother have many connections. She sent me to southern China. Mai's father give me money. I have your money. I keep it safe. Mai's mother say I need much money. For bribes. They very important."

"How did you get to Hong Kong?" Nicky asked.

"Many people help me. Ordinary people. They hate government. They hate what government did to students. They sorry for students. They like democracy movement. Many different people help me. Mai's mother help me go to Shenzhen—"

"That's adjacent to Hong Kong," Clee cut in, looking at Nicky and explaining. "It's an economic zone, something like Hong Kong, and it became a sort of boomtown overnight.

Yoyo nodded. "You know Shenzhen, Clee?"

"Yes, I did a story there about a year ago." Once again he glanced at Nicky. "It's kind of honky-tonk, full of criminals and lowlifes, as well as legit businessmen and entrepreneurs. But continue with your story, Yoyo."

"I needed papers to go to Shenzhen. All Chinese citizens need special certificate. Mai's father have friend. This friend have *guanxi*. This man buy certificate for me."

"But how did you get to Shenzhen from Beijing, it's a long way," Nicky said.

"Mai's father take me to Shanghai. In car. His brother help. He pass me along. To many friends. It is network, Nicky. They help students. I cannot say more. Okay? You understand?"

"Yes, of course I do," she said. "You don't want to divulge too much about the network, because other students may have to use it as an escape route."

"That is correct, Nicky. I arrive Shenzhen beginning of August. I have special connection. Friend of friend. I stay two weeks. Friend in Shenzhen take me to Zhong-Ying Street one day. It busy shopping street. One side China. Other side Hong Kong. Many tourists. We bribe police. They look other way. I go over border."

"But there are Hong Kong police stationed on the other side of Zhong-Ying Street," Clee said. "On the Hong Kong side. I know that area because of the story I did on Shenzhen. How did you manage once you'd crossed over?"

"I run. I slip through back streets. Alleyways. I hide. I get to water. Hong Kong on other side of bay. Mr. Loong have boat waiting. Every day boat wait for me. Until I come. I go to Hong Kong on Mr. Loong's boat. Mr. Loong look after me in Hong Kong. He good man."

"Who exactly is Mr. Loong, Yoyo?" Nicky probed.

"He brother of Mai's mother. He very im-

34

Nicky had been thinking of Anne Devereaux ever since Madrid, and on Sunday
morning she decided to phone her at Pullenbrook.

"It's lovely to hear your voice, Nicky,"
Anne said.

"And yours, Anne. I'm here in Paris with
Clee, and I thought I'd call to say hello."

"I'm so glad you phoned—I didn't know
where to find you—I've been wanting to talk
to you."

Nicky caught something odd in Anne's
tone; she shifted in the chair and sat up
straighter. "What about?" she asked carefully.

"Charles. Nicky, I—"

"Oh Anne, I'm so sorry I came to see you at Pullenbrook two weeks ago, with that story, I know how much I upset you, and it was wrong of me. I acted impulsively, without really thinking things through. Charles *did* commit suicide three years ago, I know he did. It wasn't Charles in the news segment, I was wrong about that."

"I'm not so sure anymore," Anne said.

Nicky stiffened, gripped the phone tighter. "What do you mean?"

"I've been thinking—mostly about the two photographs you had. When you first showed them to me I *did* see the resemblance. In fact, I thought it was quite striking. But then I immediately convinced myself that they couldn't possibly be of Charles, for the simple reason that my son would never do anything shoddy like fake his own death. But in the last two weeks those photographs have haunted me."

"Forget them, Anne, it wasn't Charles. Honestly, it wasn't."

"I'd like to see the pictures again," Anne said quietly. "Would you be kind enough to send them to me?"

"I don't have them, I destroyed them. There was no point in keeping them."

"You really don't have them?"

"No, I told you, I got rid of them, they were torn up and thrown away."

There was a silence at the other end of the phone. Nicky waited for a moment, and then she said, "Anne, are you there?"

"Yes, I'm here, Nicky."

To Nicky her voice sounded very faint, and she exclaimed, "Are you all right?"

"I haven't been sleeping much lately, to tell you the truth. I suppose my mind has been on Charles. So many memories coming back . . ."

"Oh, Anne darling, don't do this to yourself," Nicky said softly, aching with compassion for her friend. "This is all my fault. I don't know what to do to help you, to put your mind at rest, to make you feel better." When there was no response at the other end of the line, Nicky said, "Is there anything at all that I can do?"

"Could you come to England, Nicky? I would like to talk to you—*need* to talk to you—there's no one else. Perhaps if I saw you I'd feel less alone . . ."

Nicky's heart dropped, and she was about to refuse, but knowing she was responsible for this woman's pain and heartache, she said, "I could try to come over tomorrow, Anne, for the day. I wouldn't be able to come to Pullenbrook, could you meet me in London? For lunch?"

"Of course, that would be marvelous!" Anne's voice sounded stronger, more cheerful, and she hurried on, "Why don't we meet at the flat? It's quiet and private, and so much more comfortable than a restaurant."

"Yes, that'll be fine, Anne. All right, then, I'll see you tomorrow—let's say between noon and twelve-thirty."

"I'm so looking forward to it."

"Give my best to Philip."

"I will. He's out taking a walk at the moment, otherwise I would have put him on. I know he would have wanted to say hello. Well, I'll see you tomorrow, darling, and thank you."

After Nicky had hung up she sat in the chair at Clee's desk in his small den, pondering her conversation with Anne. Anne had sounded wan and low-spirited at the beginning of their conversation, and she knew it was her fault. She was the one who had ripped open a wound that had partially healed during the past three years, and in so doing had caused new suffering.

The past had come rushing back to torment this lovely woman, who deserved so much better. Nicky experienced a flash of sudden anger, thinking of Charles and what he had done to his mother when he had vanished, and then she instantly pushed this to one side. He no longer played a part in any of this, and certainly not in Anne's life. She was going to find a way to stop the bleeding, to help Anne's wound to heal again. In order to do this she had to go to London, and so she would fly over in the morning. It was only an hour's flight, after all, and when she got there she was going to convince Anne Devereaux that her son was dead. As indeed he was—to all intents and purposes.

The front door banged and startled her; she jumped up and went into the small entrance foyer. Clee was standing there, his arms laden with shopping bags. Two *baguettes* poked out of one, vegetables out of another, and flowers were balanced on top of a third.

"Hi," he said, grinning at her over the top of them. "Come on and talk to me while I unpack this stuff."

She followed him into the kitchen. "It looks as if you bought enough food to feed an army!" she exclaimed. "What are you intending to make for lunch?"

"Donovan's famous farm omelette, for one thing," he replied, dumping the armful of bags on the kitchen table.

"And what's that, may I ask?"

"You'll have to wait and see. It's my specialty, and it's delicious. You'll love it." Whipping the bunch of flowers out of the bag, he spun around and handed it to her.

"For my girl," he said, leaning forward, kissing her on the cheek. "And the top of the mornin' to you, mavourneen," he added in a strong Irish brogue.

"Oh, Clee, how sweet of you, thank you," she said, taking the bouquet and pressing her face into the blooms. Then impulsively she threw her arms around him and hugged him close. Her face next to his, she whispered, "I love you."

"I love you too, Nick." He lifted her chin with one hand, looked into her eyes and added, "And you'll never know how much—I'll just have to try and show you. In the meantime, I've got to get started and make brunch, otherwise we'll be eating at four o'clock this afternoon."

"What can I do to help?"

"Once I've moved the groceries over to the countertop, you can set the table, open the bottle of champagne, pour us two glasses, and add a dash of orange juice to them. Then you can sit here and talk to me while I make the omelettes. Okay by you?"

"Okay by me," she said, laughing, and helped him to carry the grocery bags to the other side of the room before putting the flowers in a vase of water. Once she had spread the cloth on the table, and added the plates and knives and forks, she busied herself with the bottle of champagne. Her father liked mimosas, the mixture of champagne and orange juice, and now she made them with great expertise.

"Here's to the girl I love," Clee said, clinking his glass against hers. *"Santé."*

"Santé, darling," she murmured and smiled at him.

Clee strode to the long countertop under the window, began emptying the bags and then started to prepare the meal.

Nicky sat watching him, thinking how fast and efficient he was as he handled the vegetables, all of which were obviously intended as ingredients for the omelette. Looks to me as if he's making a Spanish omelette, she thought, and bit back a smile.

"Are you still going to Brussels tomorrow?" Nicky asked after a moment.

"Yep, sure am. Why?"

"I called Anne Devereaux while you were out, and I was a bit upset when I heard how depressed she sounded. That's the wrong word, I thought she was troubled actually, Clee."

He turned around and looked at Nicky

thoughtfully. "I guess you think you've opened a can of worms. Or, perhaps more appropriately, Pandora's box. Is that it?"

"Yes. And it really is my fault, Clee. I was very stupid, rushing to see her the way I did. It was far too impulsive on my part. I should have waited, thought things over, and spoken to you."

"You most certainly should have done that, and I would have told you to forget it. But never mind. No use crying over that now." He turned back to the counter, and began to peel the three large potatoes lying on the chopping board. "What do you want to do about her, Nicky? Is there a way to help her?" he asked as he worked.

"She wanted me to come and see her. Asked me to, in fact. She says she has no one else to talk to but me."

"What about Philip? Isn't he sympathetic to her needs?"

"I'm sure he is, but she and I have always been extremely close, and anyway, I was..." She let her sentence trail off.

"And anyway, you were engaged to Charles," he finished for her, glancing over his shoulder. He smiled at her. "You don't have to tiptoe around me—about Charles Devereaux, I mean. You *were* engaged to him, and you did have a relationship with him, and none of us is without a past, a history, at our age. We all carry a certain amount of baggage with us."

"Thanks for understanding. Anyway, I did agree to go to London tomorrow, to have lunch with her at the flat in Eaton Square. Since you'd said you were going to be in Brussels for two or three days I thought you wouldn't mind."

"I don't, and I wouldn't have minded even if I were going to be here. You have to do what you have to do, and I'm not going to try to put a leash on you. I'm not that kind of guy." He turned to face her, and leaning against the countertop, he added, "And I hope you're not going to put a leash on me either."

Nicky shook her head. "Never! That's *verboten,* for sure. Besides, you're a bachelor at heart, remember? You cast yourself in the same mold as Robert Capa years ago, when you were still a boy. And I know that you want to take your camera and roam the world as he did. I understand."

He put the knife he was holding on the countertop and walked over to her. He took the glass out of her hand, placed it on the table and pulled her to her feet.

"Listen, honeybunch, I might want to roam the world taking photographs, and I might want to be footloose, but I certainly don't want to be fancy-free. I want you at my side." He kissed her hard on the mouth, then held her away from him, and the lopsided smile flickered.

He touched her face lightly with one finger, and said, "Shall we get married?"

Nicky was caught off guard, and she stared at him. "You've taken me by surprise—do I have to decide today?"

"No, you don't have to decide today." He grinned and kissed the tip of her nose. "You can decide tomorrow or next week, or whenever you want. Just as long as you say yes."

35

Like Pullenbrook, Anne's flat in Eaton Square was beautiful, and impressive in its own way. It had been decorated years before by the great English interior designer John Fowler, and it was one of his last assignments before his death.

The living room was spacious and high-ceilinged, its walls painted a peculiar faded pink, which the late interior decorator had named Ointment Pink. The taffeta draperies at the two tall windows were slightly deeper, and this soft shade, used throughout, helped to give the room its rosy glow. Georgian antiques, an Aubusson rug on the floor and several large horse paintings by Stubbs added to the room's quiet elegance. As she always did, Anne had put her inimitable stamp on it; there were skirted tables laden with family photographs in silver frames, pots of tall white orchids, vases of flowers everywhere and slow-burning scented candles.

On this sunny Monday morning, Anne and Nicky sat on a small sofa in front of one of the windows overlooking Eaton Square and the leafy green bower of trees in its central gardens.

Anne was more at ease with herself than she had been since Nicky's last visit, and this showed in her face. The tight lines around her mouth had all but disappeared, and her body was less taut. In fact, most of the tension had gone, and she was relaxed and smiling.

Nicky, relieved that she had succeeded in putting Anne's mind at rest, was also feeling more comfortable, and she was pleased she had come to London. The trip had been worth it just to know that the wounds she had opened would quickly heal now. Anne was already looking and sounding more like herself.

These two women had always been compatible, and after their intense, hour-long talk this morning there seemed to be an even deeper bond between them.

"You don't know what it means to me that you came," Anne said, reaching out for Nicky's hand, taking it in hers. "You made me see sense, helped me to put myself back together again, and for that I'm very grateful, darling. I had become rather depressed, and sad." She paused, made a moue and shook her head. "I think I was even beginning to feel sorry for myself, which is not like me at all. I can't abide self-pity, it's such a sign of weakness, and I'm very intolerant of it in others. Anyway, thank you, Nicky, you've worked wonders."

"You don't have to thank me, Anne, I was glad to come," Nicky said, squeezing her hand. "Quite aside from loving you, and caring about your well-being, I feel very responsible. It was I who opened Pandora's box and let all the horrors out. I wanted to put things right, make you feel better, if I could."

"Well, you did, so don't fret anymore, and the lid is firmly closed." Anne looked deeply into Nicky's eyes, and added in a loving voice, "You always were very special to me, Nicky, like the daughter I never had—and you've brought me such enormous comfort today, helped me to draw on my inner strength again." A smile touched her mouth. "You've put me back on the track, so to speak."

Nicky smiled back at her. "That makes me

feel good, Anne, it really does. I was so worried about you yesterday, and I could feel your pain. I knew what you were going through." There was a slight hesitation on Nicky's part, and then she said slowly, "Two weeks ago at Pullenbrook, you begged me to put Charles to rest again—I have, and I hope you can do the same."

"I think so—now. Yes, I'm sure I can, darling."

Nicky said, "Anne, I have some great news. Yoyo, the young Chinese student we met in Beijing, has managed to escape. He showed up in Paris last Thursday, and Clee and I had dinner with him on Friday. He's in terrific spirits, looks wonderful."

"I'm thrilled he escaped, that he's safe," Anne exclaimed, her face lighting up, suddenly growing animated for the first time in days. "Do tell me about him."

Nicky did so, and she was just finishing recounting the details about Yoyo's journey to Hong Kong, their celebration dinner at the Ritz with him and Mr. and Mrs. Loong when the doorbell rang.

"Oh, that must be Philip," Anne said, rising, crossing the floor. She paused halfway and turned her head. "I was rather surprised when he called at eleven and asked if he could join us. He usually lunches at his club.

Then I realized he wanted to see you. He's so very fond of you, Nicky."

"I'm glad he's having lunch with us, I'm fond of him, too," Nicky said, genuinely meaning this. "He's a lovely man."

A moment later Philip Rawlings was striding into the room, embracing first Anne, and then Nicky. "I thought you were supposed to be in Provence," he said, eyeing Nicky curiously.

"We were," she answered. "But Clee has problems at the office. We hope to leave sometime next week."

"Nice time of year, down there," Philip murmured. He went to a tray of drinks on a chest, and proceeded to mix himself one. He usually did not drink at lunch during the week, and today was an exception. In fact, this was not his first scotch and soda. On his way here he had done something he had not done in years—stopped off at a pub. He had gone to the Grenadier, which was the only pub he remembered in the Belgravia area, and downed a quick one before walking over to Eaton Square.

False courage, he thought, as he dropped a piece of ice into his crystal tumbler and turned around to face Anne and Nicky, who was about to sink into a chair next to the sofa where Anne had already seated herself.

He lifted his glass to his mouth, said, "Down the hatch," and took a long swallow. No use putting it off, he thought, and taking a deep breath, bracing himself, he went over to sit next to Anne.

"I'm afraid it's not a very fancy lunch, Philip," Anne remarked. "I left Pilar and Inez in the country when I came up to town this morning. So I stopped off at Harrods and picked up a few cold meats, and I made a salad."

"Don't worry about it, I'm not very hungry," he said.

"I'm feeling so much better, darling," Anne continued, smiling at him. "Being with Nicky, talking to her, has been a wonderful tonic."

"I can see that."

"I'm really all right now, Philip. *Truly.*"

"Yes," he said.

"I was just telling Anne about Yoyo," Nicky volunteered. "You know, the Chinese student who was so helpful in Beijing. He managed to get to Hong Kong, and finally to Paris, and we saw him this past week."

"One of the lucky ones." Philip shook his head. "Sadly, quite a few of the students who were involved in the democracy movement, and who escaped, were sent back to China by the Hong Kong government. God knows what their fate has been."

"How terrible!" Anne exclaimed. "How could we do a thing like that!"

Philip did not answer. He took another long swallow of his drink, almost gulping it down, and then he put the glass on the antique lacquered tray table in front of him. Again steeling himself, he said, "Anne, I have something to tell you, and I'm glad Nicky is with us. She has a right to hear this too."

Both women looked at him, noting his serious tone, the grim expression settling on his face.

"It's about Charles—"

"Charles?" Anne interrupted, her voice rising.

Nicky stiffened in the chair, and apprehension stabbed at her.

"This morning some information came across my desk at the Foreign Office. It's restricted, classified information, but I felt, under the circumstances, that I was morally obligated to take both of you into my confidence. However, because it is a privileged communication, is top secret, actually, I must warn you that what I tell you must never be repeated. It cannot go beyond these walls. I count on your confidentiality. I must have your word on this, Anne. And yours, Nicky."

"You know I would never discuss anything you told me about the office, confidential or otherwise," Anne said, looking at him slightly askance.

"I give you my word," Nicky murmured. She was worried, wondering what this was about, what Philip was going to tell them.

Philip nodded, and then he reached for Anne's hand. "When Nicky came to see us at Pullenbrook in August, she was correct in everything she said, Anne. It *was* Charles on that ATN newscast from Rome. He *had* faked his death three years ago."

Anne gasped, her eyes wide with shock. She was speechless for a moment, and then she exclaimed, "Are you saying he's alive? Is my son alive?"

Philip did not immediately answer.

Nicky held herself perfectly still, clasping her hands together in her lap. She knew she must be careful in her reactions, that she must not betray anything.

Anne repeated, "Is he alive? Philip, please answer me! Is Charles alive?"

Philip took a deep breath, and very gently he said, "No, Anne, he's not. Charles is dead."

"I don't understand!" she cried, her agitation increasing. "You just said Nicky was right, that Charles did fake his own death, and was alive. Now you're saying that he's dead. How can that be? Are you sure?"

"I'm positive."

Nicky, who was as shocked as Anne, was doing her best to control herself. Now she said in the steadiest voice she could muster, "But how do you know Charles is dead, Philip?"

"My friend Frank Littleton told me this morning. Frank and I were at Harrow together, and Cambridge, and we've been close friends since those days, for donkey's years. Frank's with the Secret Intelligence Service—MI6—but he's not an agent out in the field. He has a desk job. He sent me a note this morning, asking me to come and see him. I did, and he told me that Anne's son had been killed."

"Oh God, what are you saying?" Anne looked at him frantically. "MI6. Agents. Intelligence. Was Charles involved in something dangerous?"

"Frank didn't go into too many details," Philip responded quietly, wondering how he was going to help her get through this new ordeal.

"You just said *killed.*" Nicky stared at Philip. "So he didn't die of natural causes. Nor in an accident, presumably. Are you saying he was murdered?"

Philip nodded. He put his arm around

Anne as she let out a strangled cry. She began to tremble.

"When was Charles killed?" Nicky demanded.

"Late last week," Philip said.

"*Where?*" Nicky clasped her hands together, hardly breathing.

"In Madrid. He was in a plane that blew up at Madrid airport, a small private plane, a Falcon."

"Oh my God!" Anne pressed her hands to her mouth. "My son! Charles!" She turned to Philip, pleaded, "Please tell me what this is all about, Philip. *Please tell me.* I don't understand."

Nicky cut in, "Was his body recovered?"

Philip paused, then said in a low voice, "It was a very bad explosion."

Anne was sobbing quietly, leaning against Philip's shoulder. He held her closer, desperately trying to comfort her.

"You said the information came to you through your old friend with MI6," Nicky continued. "That implies Charles was an operative, working in the covert world of intelligence. And if he was, then he was probably killed by foreign agents. Is that the case?"

"I think so, Nicky."

"You're not sure?"

"Frank gave me the barest details, he's

not supposed to tell me anything. But he knows Anne, is aware we're going to be married, and he wanted me to have the information. He stuck his neck out for me. But he certainly wasn't going to breach security. That's more than his job's worth."

Leaning forward, Nicky said, "But didn't he give you any clue at all about the killer, or killers?"

Philip hesitated. "I got the impression they might have been Israeli agents."

"*Mossad!*" Nicky was startled. "Why would Mossad want to kill Charles Devereaux? From what you've just told us, it sounds as if he was a British agent. The British and the Israelis don't bump each other off. They're on the same side."

Philip said nothing.

"He *was* working for British intelligence, wasn't he?" Nicky probed, all of her journalistic training coming out.

Philip shook his head. "Perhaps not. Frank told me—" He broke off, and changing his mind, he finished, "I think that perhaps I ought not to say anything else. Not that I know much more than I've already told you."

"Just one thing," Nicky pressed. "If Charles wasn't working for the British, he must have been working for someone else. *Who?*"

"Frank didn't actually say, Nicky. However, he implied Charles was involved with an organization based in the Middle East."

Nicky gaped at him. "A terrorist organization? Is that what you're saying?"

Philip nodded.

"Do you mean he was a terrorist?"

"It's possible," Philip said.

"Did he work for the PLO? Abu Nidal? The PFLP-GC? *Who?*"

"Frank didn't mention any of those groups, but he did indicate that Charles was working for the Palestinians."

"I don't believe it!" Nicky exclaimed incredulously. "I don't!"

"The Palestinians," Anne repeated, suddenly pulling away from Philip, sitting up straighter on the sofa. She looked from Philip to Nicky and back to Philip, as if bewildered. "Did you say Charles was working for the Palestinians?"

"That is what Frank implied, yes."

Anne's face went as white as chalk. Her eyes glazed over, were suddenly devoid of all expression. She sat staring ahead, appeared to be gazing into some far distant place; it was as if she saw something Nicky and Philip could not see. There was an extraordinary remoteness about her, and she was silent, utterly still, as if she had fallen into a trance.

Philip glanced at Nicky worriedly.

Nicky nodded, then looked across at Anne. Drawing on the information she had been given by Charles in Madrid, she said slowly, "Perhaps Charles wasn't a traitor to the British. Maybe he was a *mole.* A British agent who had assumed a new identity and gone undercover."

"I don't know," Philip replied. "But it's possible, of course. Sometimes these things are done at a very high level. Often others in an agency don't even know, for security reasons. Maybe Frank doesn't have all the information."

"Exactly," Nicky exclaimed. "And if Charles was a mole, that would make him a *counterfeit* traitor, wouldn't it?"

"Yes," Philip agreed, and glanced at Anne, hoping she had heard what Nicky had just said. And it was a possibility. A very strong possibility. Certainly Nicky's theory made sense.

Nicky sat back in the chair, rapidly turning over in her mind all the facts she had and suddenly she found herself thinking, Is Charles really dead? Or has he faked his own death a second time?

He just didn't trust me not to betray him, she thought. He was afraid—afraid I would put him in jeopardy. Yes, that's got to be it.

Somehow he's faked his death a second time, in order to continue to work as a mole for the British!

Her heart tightened. What, really, was she to think? Was he dead this time? If he was, then had Mossad killed the wrong man? Had they assassinated a British agent?

There was no noise in Clee's apartment. Everything was perfectly still, not even the ticking of a clock disturbed the silence. It was late, almost midnight. Nicky was alone; Clee was still in Brussels on assignment for *Paris Match.* She had spoken to him on the phone earlier, and had managed to limit discussion about her day in London. Now she sat in the living room, finishing a bowl of soup and reflecting on the events of the day.

Philip's extraordinary revelations had not startled her as much as they had Anne—for obvious reasons. After all, she had seen Charles ten days ago, had heard his story, and it was a story she fully believed. She also believed he was still alive. The Charles Devereaux she had known, been engaged to, had always been exceedingly clever, a brilliant man. And so it was reasonable to assume that he was a superlative agent and the best mole in the business. Therefore, he had not been blown up in that plane at the airport in Madrid. Somehow he had managed to make it look as though he had, because he wanted her and everyone else to think he was dead. She was certain another man had been in the Falcon in his place.

But whether he was alive or dead, she was positive that he had not worked for the Palestinian cause; he had simply infiltrated a terrorist organization as a mole. Deep within herself she wished she could have told Anne what she knew, if only to make her feel better about her son. But for Charles's sake, just in case he *was* alive, she had not dared to do this.

Eventually Anne had roused herself from her trancelike state, and Nicky had had the opportunity to repeat her theory that Charles was a counterfeit traitor, a double agent, a mole. And she had expounded on the idea that Frank Littleton, Philip's friend, did not have all of the facts at his disposal.

All of this had seemed to give Anne a measure of comfort, and after a while she had excused herself and retired to her bedroom, explaining that she needed to be alone.

Nicky and Philip had talked for another hour, before she left for Heathrow and her plane back to Paris. At one moment he had started to worry out loud that he had made a terrible mistake. "Perhaps I shouldn't have told Anne anything at all, Nicky," he had said. "I ought to have kept it to myself, don't you think?"

Nicky had reassured him that he had done the right thing, and he had appeared to be heartened when he heard this. Then he had confided, "I love her very much, Nicky, I've loved her for years. I couldn't believe my good fortune when she finally agreed to marry me. And I told her about Charles because I respect her, and because there's never been anything but honesty and truth between us. She and I have never dealt in lies. Anne's a mature, intelligent woman, and I thought she was entitled to know absolutely everything that I knew about her son, to know what Frank had told me out of friendship. And I thought you should know the truth, too, Nicky."

If it's really the truth, Nicky had thought at the time, but she had said: "Yes, you're right, Philip, and you really did do the best thing. No woman wants to be treated like an imbecile by a man."

Marie Thérèse said, "Ah, Nicky, *ma petite,* you are being evasive. How can you say you don't know if you are going to marry this Clee of yours—you must have some idea what you intend to do."

"But I don't," Nicky protested. "He only asked me on Sunday morning—"

"But it's *Thursday* today!" Marie Thérèse exclaimed, laughing. "You should know how you feel by now. Anyway, I think he will expect an answer when he returns to Paris tomorrow. *N'est-ce pas?* In my opinion, you must say yes, *chérie.* What else is there to say?"

Nicky smiled at the Frenchwoman, her dear old friend from childhood. "Ah, Marie Thérèse, you are an incurable romantic. I could say no, you know."

"Mmmm, that's true. On the other hand, why would you want to do that when you are so very much in love with your Clee."

"And what makes you say that?"

"I see it in your eyes, *ma petite,* and when you speak about him your face glows with love."

Nicky sighed. "We'll see. I guess I'll make up my mind in Provence—I haven't had time to think straight in the last few days." Glancing at her watch, Nicky exclaimed, "I've got to go! I promised Yoyo I would have dinner with him tonight, and I've so much to do this afternoon. Thanks for another delicious lunch. Hopefully, you'll have your cast off by the time I get back from Provence, and then I'll take you for that fancy lunch at the Relais Plaza.''

"With Clee, I hope."

Nicky nodded. "With Clee."

"And if we can't have lunch, you will phone me before you go back to the States at the end of September, won't you, Nicky?"

"Of course I will—but don't worry, we'll be having our lunch, I promise." Bending forward, Nicky kissed Marie Thérèse on the cheek. "Don't get up, I can let myself out."

"*Au revoir, chérie.*"

"*Au revoir,* and take care."

Nicky closed the door of the apartment behind her and ran down the steep flight of stairs. Dashing out of the front door and into the street, she turned right, hoping to find a taxi—and ran into a group of men leaving the restaurant next door to Marie Thérèse's apartment building.

"*Oh, pardon!*" she exclaimed as she bumped into one of them.

"*De rien, mademoiselle,*" the man said, and swung around, smiling.

Nicky's jaw dropped: she was staring at Charles Devereaux.

"Oh my God!"

Stepping forward, Charles took hold of her

arm and propelled her into the car waiting on the curb. "*Au revoir,* Bernard, Haji," Charles said as he got in behind her.

"What's happening, where are you taking me, Char—"

"Be quiet," he hissed, cutting her off. "Don't say another word."

36

They stood facing each other in the living room of the drab apartment to which he had just brought her.

"What in God's name were you doing in a disreputable district like Belleville?" Charles asked. "I could hardly believe my eyes when I saw you. What were you doing there?"

"Before *I* answer any questions," Nicky cried, "I'd like to pose a couple myself."

He nodded. "All right. I'll respond if I can."

"First of all, you bundle me into a car, which shoots across Paris and turns into a side street, the name of which I don't see, then you drag me out and into this building. I haven't the slightest idea where I am. Where are we, I'd like to know!"

"This apartment is on the rue Georges Berger, northeast of the Arc de Triomphe, behind the Parc de Monceau, just off the boulevard de Courcelles."

"Why did you push me into the car?"

"I didn't know what you were going to say, what you would blurt out. It was much easier to come here. Now, tell me why you were in that area. Belleville is not a pretty place. Are you on to some sort of story there? Interviewing people in Belleville?"

"No, but what do you mean? Is there a story in Belleville?"

He shrugged. "How should I know."

"But *you* just brought it up!"

"I can't imagine why you would be there, that's all. It's the Arab area—a lot of North African immigrants live there. But surely you knew that."

"I was visiting Marie Thérèse Bouret, the Frenchwoman who was a sort of nanny to me when I was little. I'm sure I told you about her, once."

"Yes, I think you did."

"She moved to Belleville because her boyfriend lives there. She's moved in with him."

"Is he Moroccan, Tunisian, Algerian?"

"I don't know—I've never met him." Immediately Nicky remembered the *couscous* Marie Thérèse had ordered for lunch the previous week, and the name of the restaurant: Café Tangier. She exclaimed, "That restaurant you were leaving—it's North African, isn't it?"

"Moroccan."

Nicky went on, "Why did you bring me here?"

"I didn't want to talk to you in the middle of the street."

"Do we have anything to say to each other?" She paused, looked at him closely, and added, "You could've trusted me. I wouldn't have betrayed you. I gave you my word of honor in Madrid. So you see there was no need for you to fake your death a second time."

"I didn't! And I did trust you—do trust you—Nicky."

"You were thought to be in that private jet, that Falcon, that blew up in Madrid late last week. I was told you'd been killed in the explosion."

He was startled by this statement, and threw her a keen look. "Who told you about the plane?"

"Philip Rawlings."

His eyes fastened on hers intently. "Did you see Philip?"

"Yes. I went to London earlier this week, on Monday. I went to visit your mother, she was depressed, upset. And she was wavering in her belief that you had committed suicide three years ago. I met her at her apartment for lunch. I wanted to convince her that you were dead—"

"Why did she have a change of heart?"

"The photographs—of the man in the newscast. Of you."

"Yes, I understand. Go on."

"I talked to your mother for about an hour, and I succeeded, I brought her back to believing you were dead. Then Philip arrived. He broke the news of your death, and explained to your mother that I had been right all along." Nicky now repeated everything Philip had told them, although she omitted Frank Littleton's name.

When she had finished, Charles nodded, his eyes reflective. "I suppose Philip learned about the plane in Madrid from an old friend in intelligence. I know all about the British Establishment and the old-school-tie network." Now he motioned to a group of chairs and said, "Let's sit, shall we? I think we will be more comfortable."

Once they were settled, Charles continued, "Contrary to what you believe, I didn't fake my death by having that plane blown up. In fact, I would have been on it, if not for a last-minute change in plans. I had to stay on in Madrid unexpectedly—an assignment. Because there was an extra seat available— my seat—Javier took it. The destination of the plane was Gibraltar, where his sister lives. He was going for a weekend visit."

"Are you implying the plane was sabotaged? That someone was trying to assassinate you?"

"I'm not implying it, I'm telling you."

"Who?"

"I'm not exactly sure—although I do have a few suspects and a few theories."

"Mossad?"

Charles frowned at her. "Why do you mention Israeli intelligence?"

"Philip suggested that the Falcon might have been blown up by them—that *they* could have been after you."

He was silent.

"I didn't say anything to your mother or Philip, Charles. I never mentioned our meeting in Madrid. I was also extremely careful in my reaction to Philip's news." She took a deep breath. "You see, I thought you were alive all along. I *believed* you were. I just knew you weren't dead, and so there was no way I would have put you in jeopardy. Put your life at risk."

Still he said nothing.

Nicky hurried on, "Philip told me something very odd, Charles."

"What was that?" he asked, raising a brow.

"He said the person who gave him the information on Monday morning—about your death in Madrid—also implied that you were a terrorist."

Charles sat perfectly still in the chair, a thoughtful expression settling on his face again. Finally, he gave her a very direct look and said, "One man's terrorist is another man's freedom fighter."

Nicky shook her head. "Sorry, but I'm not sure I understand what you're getting at."

"It depends on your point of view, doesn't it?"

"That's what I thought you meant." She stared at him for the longest moment, and then said, "Are you telling me you *are* a terrorist?"

"Of course I'm not a terrorist!"

With a smile of relief she exclaimed, "No, you're a British agent who has gone undercover. You're a British mole who has *infiltrated* a terrorist organization based in the Middle East. Right?"

"No, I'm not."

"You're not a British agent?"

"No, and I never have been. Nor am I a mole."

"You lied to me in Madrid?"

"I did."

"Why?"

"Because I didn't want to tell you the truth."

"What is the truth?"

"I *am* involved with a Middle East organization, Nicky."

"What is it called?"

"Al Awad—it means The Return."

"I know what it means," she cried, shifting in the chair, staring at him aghast. "It means the return to the homeland—Palestine." She leaned forward and added with intensity, "And it is a terrorist organization. A Palestinian terrorist organization, to be exact. I've heard of it, even though it's not quite as high-profile as Abu Nidal and some of the other groups."

"It's not a terrorist organization," he snapped.

"Oh, come off it! And what do you do for them?" she demanded, her voice rising. "Kill little children and women, innocent people?"

Charles said, "I told you, I'm not a terrorist. I handle the money, the financial matters."

She glared at him, and cried, "You may not tote a Kalashnikov or a Beretta, but you're still a terrorist. The money you handle finances barbaric acts, terrorism!"

"Nicky, Nicky, do you think the British Secret Intelligence Service, the CIA, Mossad, or the French DST are any different? They're all the same the world over. Everyone lies, cheats, kills, dies, and for what? *Patriotism,* they say. The Palestine freedom fighters are also patriotic."

"Oh boy, do you have your rhetoric down pat!" she exploded angrily, scarcely believing what she was hearing. Charles Devereaux involved with Palestinians was the most unlikely thing she had ever heard. Now she took total control of herself, realizing that she must not let her past relationship with Charles or her feelings of anger and outrage get in the way. Emotion must not cloud judgment. Think with your head, she cautioned herself, and ask a few more leading questions, get to the bottom of this. Solve the enigma of Charles Devereaux once and for all.

She said, "And why are you doing this—for money? Or what?"

He recoiled, a look of contempt on his face, and he said bitingly, "How little you know me, Nicky, if you think I can be bought. I work for the group because I believe in it, and in its aims."

"You believe in its aims!" Nicky's eyes narrowed dangerously. "Are you saying that you believe in its ideology? Is that it?"

"Yes, I am saying that."

"*Why?* Why *you*? An Englishman, an aristocrat. I just don't get it."

"Do you really want to know?"

"That's a pretty stupid question—of course I do."

Charles leaned back in the chair, crossed his legs and stared at her.

Nicky suddenly realized he was wearing the brown contact lenses. They did make a difference, added to the change in his appearance. He suddenly seemed less than ever like the Charles she had once loved.

After a few seconds of contemplation, he said, "It was a man I loved—"

"A man!"

"Ah, no, Nicky, it's not what you think." With a faint smile he murmured, "To continue, it was a man I loved, and the love that that man felt for me, which brought me to Al Awad and the Palestinian cause. His love, his influence over me, his greatness as a man, all of those things induced me to adopt his beliefs, and follow in his footsteps."

"He's a Palestinian, correct?"

"He was."

"He's dead?"

"Sadly, yes."

"Who was he?"

There was only the merest hesitation on his part before he said, "My father. He was my father."

Nicky was thunderstruck. After a second, she managed to say, "Are you telling me that Henry Devereaux was not your father?"

"I am."

"Did Anne adopt you?"

"No, she didn't. Anne is my mother."

"Your *biological* mother?"

"Yes. Just as Nayef Al Kabil was my biological father."

"Anne Devereaux had an affair with a Palestinian?" Nicky's voice echoed with incredulity.

"Yes, she did. But that's my mother's story, not mine, and I'm not going to tell it. If you want to know more, you must ask her."

"But you were born and brought up in England, educated in England, at Eton and Oxford. How did all this come about? How did you become involved—become involved with your father?"

"My mother thought I should know him."

"When did you meet him?"

"When I was a little boy—six years old, actually."

"And is that when your indoctrination started?"

"No, later, when I was older, when I could understand everything properly. But *I* wouldn't call it indoctrination. It was his legacy to me. I have his blood in my veins! I am his son!"

"Your father's bloodline is more important to you than your mother's? Is that what you're telling me?"

"I am more of an Al Kabil than a Clifford, I suppose. That's what it comes down to in the end. I am my father's son."

"When did your father die?"

"He was killed in 1981. In southern Lebanon, during the hostilities there."

"Is that when you became involved with his cause?"

"No, about two years before that, in 1979. That was when he asked me to help with the group's finances. He had started Al Awad in 1958, and for what it's worth, he was a moderate. He believed in moderation, violence was not his way, Nicky. He believed in the conference table."

Nicky ignored these comments. She said, "So you were part of the group when we met?"

"Yes."

"Then why did you ever get involved with me in the first place?" she demanded, staring hard at him.

There was a hesitation, and then he said quietly, "It was a sexual attraction at first. I wanted you—I wanted to have an affair with you. But I made the same mistake as my father."

"What does that mean?"

"He fell in love with a beautiful English-woman. I fell in love with a beautiful American. I hadn't intended our relationship to go that far, Nicky. Then when I did get emotionally entangled with you, I thought I could handle it, handle you, and my involvement with my father's group, and our marriage as well."

"And you changed your mind?"

"No, not really."

"Then why did you decide to vanish into thin air three years ago?"

"Not actually because of you, although you were starting to become something of a problem. I thought certain foreign intelligence agencies were on my trail, were about to take me out."

"Which ones?"

"The CIA. And Mossad."

"Why was I becoming a problem?"

"As I told you, my father was killed in 1981. His second in command, who took over after his death, relied on me rather heavily, more than my father had, in some ways. I was getting really sucked in, and more so than I had intended, although I did believe in my father's cause. Nevertheless—"

"You wanted to lead your life in London as well, isn't that so?"

He nodded. "Yes. By 1986, just after we became engaged, I realized that it wasn't going to work. That you were a problem after all. I also realized that I wasn't being fair to you, I didn't want to put you in any kind of danger. And that, combined with my worry that agents *were* tracking me, convinced me I should disappear. So I did."

"And your mother never knew anything?"

"*Never.* My father didn't want her to know, and neither did I."

"Why are you telling me all this?"

"Because there's no reason you shouldn't know."

"Are you going to have me killed?"

"Don't be ridiculous, Nicky!"

"I could expose you."

"It wouldn't matter if you did. Not anymore."

"Why not?"

"I'm leaving today for the Middle East. I won't be returning to Europe. I shall live there for the rest of my life."

"Why?"

"It's too dangerous for me here now. And there are other reasons, which I can't go into."

"Are you going to Lebanon?"

"I can't tell you where I'm going, surely you know that."

There was a sudden knock on the door. Charles looked toward it and said, "Come in."

Pierre, the man who had searched her suite in Madrid, was standing there. "The car is downstairs," he said.

Charles nodded and stood up. Turning to Nicky, he said, "I have to go. I have a plane waiting at Le Bourget."

Nicky also stood. "I won't tell your mother anything or mention our meeting today, you know."

He nodded. "No, it would only hurt her even more."

Nicky glared at him, the anger so close to the surface flaring for a split second, and then she bit it back to take hold of herself. "She wept bitter tears for you the other day," she said.

"I love her—but . . ." He left his sentence unfinished, picked up his briefcase and went out into the hallway. Nicky followed him.

Opening the front door, Pierre lifted the two suitcases standing there and hurried down the short flight of stairs out into the street.

When Nicky and Charles reached the bottom of the staircase, he turned to her in the little vestibule and said, "This is finally good-bye, Nicky."

She nodded. "In case you think I was doing a story on you, I wasn't."

"I know. You love my mother far too much, you'd never hurt her in that way."

They were outside on the pavement. "Small world, isn't it?" Charles said suddenly. "The way you ran into me today in Belleville."

"Yes."

"Can I give you a lift?"

"No, thanks, I prefer to walk," she said.

He smiled at her faintly. "Good-bye, Nicky."

"Good-bye, Charles."

Pierre had stowed the luggage, and after Charles got into the backseat he went and sat next to the driver. The car slid smoothly down the narrow street.

Nicky turned away and began to walk in the direction of the boulevard de Courcelles, with so many thoughts whirling in her mind.

The blast from the explosion was so forceful it threw her forward onto the pavement. For a split second she was dazed and then a strangled cry escaped her throat as she struggled to her knees and turned her head. The car Charles had been traveling in had exploded about eighty feet away. She gaped at it in horror, and pushed herself up onto her feet. The air was filled with smoke and the smell of burning, the street littered with bits of metal, broken glass and shreds of clothing. From the Parc Monceau across the street a policeman who had been on duty and several passersby were rushing toward her.

Still shaking, Nicky leaned against the wall of the building and closed her eyes. There was no chance that he was alive. Not in that inferno. And it was his car that had exploded. There was no other vehicle on the rue Georges Berger.

37

The two women sat on the old stone bench at the top of Sweetheart Hill. It was Sunday afternoon, sunny and warm, and a light breeze rustled through the trees, sent the white clouds scudding across the arch of the shining blue sky. It was a perfect September day.

Neither woman noticed the weather. They sat with their arms around each other, their blond heads close together, sharing a moment of quiet after a long and frequently painful conversation, one that had lasted well over an hour.

It was Nicky who now pulled slightly away, looked into Anne's eyes and said, "That's it.

I've told you the whole truth, and I've left nothing out. Now you know everything, Anne."

Anne nodded and squeezed her hand, then she reached into her jacket pocket and pulled out a handkerchief to dry her eyes.

"So, my son is dead." She shook her head sorrowfully. "It's funny, you know, I just don't think I can weep any more tears after today. There are none left. I've grieved for Charles for three years, I don't think I can grieve all over again."

"No, you can't. You must go forward, Anne. You must get on with your life—your life with Philip."

"Yes, darling, you're absolutely right." Anne smiled and continued, "A moment ago you said that I knew everything, and thanks to you, I do. But *you* don't know everything, Nicky. You don't know my side of the story. I think I should tell you about Nayef Al Kabil, and what happened forty-one years ago."

"Only if you really want to tell me, Anne."

"I'd like to, yes. And I shall tell Philip later. He has a right to know as well."

Anne stared into the distance, her face still, her eyes pensive, and it was a few minutes before she began to speak.

At last, she said, "I remember every moment as if it were only yesterday, each nu-

ance as clear to me now as it was then. My
father, Julian Clifford, was a renowned
statesman in his day, Nicky. He was frequently associated with that very great man
Winston Churchill, especially during the Second World War and at the end of it; they were
political allies. My father became involved
with the creation of the State of Israel in
1948. He and I were rather close at this time;
he was a widower—my mother had died during the war. Anyway, my father took me with
him to Palestine, as it still was then, in 1947.
He liked to have me with him when he traveled abroad or stayed away for long periods.
In January of 1948 I met Nayef. He was from
an old, very good Palestinian family, a promi-
nent family, who came from Gaza. They
owned land, orange groves, and were well
established in the area, respected. Nayef
was only a few years older than I was, and
we fell in love."

Unexpectedly Anne fell silent.

Nicky looked at her, squeezed her hand,
but said nothing, and she noticed then that
the other woman was trying to compose herself.

Anne picked up her story again. "We were
very much in love, Nicky. We were the first
for each other, and you know what first love
is like. We were blind to everything except

ourselves. He was so handsome, a slender young man, not all that tall, but very fair, with the most beautiful light green eyes, so clear and innocent. He was kind to me, very loving and devoted, and we became inseparable. In May of 1948, just after my seventeenth birthday, I discovered I was pregnant."

Anne paused once more, and looked at Nicky pointedly. "Things were very different in those days. There was nothing I could do, even if I'd wanted to, which I didn't. Naturally, I was distressed and frightened. Nayef and I told my father together, and then Nayef explained how much he loved me, said that he wanted to marry me. And I told my father that I felt the same way about Nayef. My father reacted badly. He was horrified, furious. He took me home to England immediately. I was heartbroken. And it was seven years before I saw Nayef again."

"Oh, Anne darling, how sad. You were so young, just a child."

"Yes, we both were. And inexperienced in so many ways. As it happened, my father's oldest and dearest friend was Henry Devereaux, the British industrialist. Henry had known me all my life, and loved me. Since he was a widower and childless, he agreed to marry me at my father's request. Our marriage was in September of 1948. Imagine my horror, being torn from Nayef, carrying his child, and marrying a man I hardly knew, except as my father's friend. I was in agony of mind and spirit, but there was nothing I could do except obey my father. Actually, Henry knew he had Hodgkin's disease, cancer of the lymph nodes, by that time, was aware that he did not have long to live. Since he had no family, other than a distant cousin, and because he had always cared for me, he was excited about our marriage. It pleased him to have someone to care for, and also to have a young companion for the last few years of his life. I must say he was good to me, and he did love Charles. But I was not happy with him. How could I be? Our marriage was a mockery. But I suppose, looking back, that I didn't make much of an effort. He seemed like an old man to me. He was, being a contemporary of my father."

"And naturally you yearned for Nayef," Nicky murmured, reaching out, taking hold of her hand again.

"Oh yes, Nicky, how I yearned for him! But there was nothing I could do. Also, I did have my beautiful child—Charles. Nayef's child. I loved my son to distraction, and he did help to heal the hole in my heart. And eventually I adjusted—one always does, you know. Charles had been born in February of 1949, but it wasn't until he was six years old that I decided he ought to meet Nayef, his real father. Things were much easier for me by then, inasmuch as Henry and my father had both died. So in 1955 I took Charles to the South of France, to Nice, to meet Nayef."

"And from that time on he saw his father on a regular basis over the years. Charles explained that to me in Paris."

Anne nodded. "Very regularly. I'd told him it was a secret, that no one must know about Nayef—I was worried about my brother, Geoffrey, you see. I must say, Charles was very good. He kept the secret. He loved Nayef, and Nayef loved him. Little did I know he was brainwashing our child." She paused, took a deep breath, then added, "But I couldn't have stopped that. Once Charles was eighteen, he came and went as he pleased, and he was always strong-willed, independent. But to tell you the truth, Nicky, I had no idea how strong the bond was between them, how much the relationship had grown, until you told me today. Charles was very secretive about that—I suppose he had to be."

"Did *you* continue your relationship with Nayef?"

"No, I didn't. Well, that's not strictly true. I did for a couple of years, between 1955 and

1957. We picked up where we had left off. But it was never quite the same—it never is—and then it ended by mutual consent. It wasn't feasible, darling. He was living in Lebanon, and I was here at Pullenbrook, and by then he was starting to become involved in politics, was consumed by his beliefs. I think he was already deeply committed to the cause."

"Charles told me his father was a moderate. Do you believe that?"

"*Absolutely.* Nayef wasn't a man who would ever condone violence, or resort to it. He always believed that peace could be achieved by other means."

"Did he ever marry? Have other children?"

"No, he didn't marry. Nor did he have children—not to my knowledge, anyway. Perhaps that's one of the reasons why Charles was so important to him. He was his only son, and he claimed him for himself, didn't he?"

Nicky said softly, "Yes, he did. And Charles allowed himself to be claimed. He did have a choice."

Anne sighed heavily and looked at her. She said slowly, "It's all my fault, Nicky—if I had not become involved with Nayef when I was a young girl, none of this would have happened. . . ."

"But you wouldn't have had Charles either."

"That's true." Anne forced a small smile and murmured, "Well, darling, perhaps we'd better go inside for a while. You and Clee will have to leave for the airport soon. Also, Philip and I have something to tell you. And I have something to show you."

The two women stood. In the distance, the great Tudor house gleamed under the brilliant sky, ancient, unchanging, everlasting. Together they walked down the hill toward it, their arms linked.

Philip and Clee were in the library talking when Anne and Nicky came in a few minutes later.

Philip exclaimed, "There you are! I was about to come looking for you. Inez will be bringing tea shortly. I'm sure you'd both like a cup."

"Thanks, I would," Nicky said.

Anne merely nodded, walked over to the desk and took an envelope out of a drawer.

Nicky looked across at Clee and smiled. It was such a comfort to have him here, and over lunch he had seemed to make everyone feel more relaxed. He was not only warm and understanding, but sane and down-to-earth, and you knew where you stood with him. It pleased Nicky that Anne had responded so well to him, was comfortable around him. She had been so uptight when they had arrived from Paris late last night.

Clee led Nicky to one of the Chesterfield sofas near the fireplace and they sat down together. Anne handed Nicky the envelope she had taken out of the desk. "I think you should read this, Nicky. It arrived last Thursday morning."

Nicky took it from her, and when she saw Charles's handwriting she flinched. The letter had arrived at Pullenbrook the day he had died. Shaking off the sudden chill she felt, she looked more carefully at the envelope. It was postmarked Tuesday, September 5, and it had been mailed in Paris. Slipping the letter out of the envelope, she read it slowly.

Paris   Monday evening, September 4, 1989
Dear Mother:

Three years ago I allowed you to believe I had committed suicide. I could not take you into my confidence, because if my suicide was to be effective, you above all had to believe it. This was a cruel thing to do to you, I know, but I was certain my life was in danger. I had to slip off the face of the earth, become someone else if I was going to live.

I was being sought by intelligence agents from various foreign countries. You see, unbeknownst to you, I had adopted my father's cause long ago and I had been active in his organization since 1979.

My father, whom I loved very much, was a moderate man, as you well know. And so am I. Sadly, there are those in the group he founded, The Return, who have not held to those principles. There is a faction within it now that is embracing violence. I cannot and will not condone that. I have spoken up many times in the past year, made my feelings clear. In consequence of this I know that once again my life is in danger—this time from within my own organization. They tried to eliminate me last week by blowing up my plane at Madrid airport.

There has been too much killing in the Middle East over the years. It must come to an end. Palestinians and Israelis must learn to live together. And in peace. Terrorism is foul. It must be outlawed, once and for all.

I know my time is limited now, a few weeks, a couple of months at the most. And before I die there is something I must do to help the innocents in the Middle East. Arab and Jew alike. For the past ten years I have managed the financial affairs of my father's organization, and brilliantly, if I say so myself. Today the funds belonging to the group total three hundred million U.S. dollars. That money is deposited in a numbered account in a bank in Zurich. I want that money used for the good of the Middle East, not for killing and mayhem. Only I know the number of the account and which bank it is in. This is the International Bank of Zurich. You will also know the number of my account if you think of my favorite childhood toy. The name of that toy is the number. I want you and Philip to go to Zurich the day you receive this letter. Take the money out of the International Bank of Zurich and deposit it in another Swiss bank, using a numbered account again. Invent your own number.

I want you and Philip to use that money to help the children of the Middle East, to help ease their suffering. And it must be used for all children, no matter their race, creed or color.

I know you can never forgive me, Mother, but I do hope you will think more kindly of me one day. I have always loved you.

Charles

Nicky held the letter in her hand, and looked across at Anne. "May Clee read it?"

"Of course, I would like him to."

Clee did so, and then silently handed the letter back to Nicky, who quietly sat holding it. Finally she said, "Did you remember the favorite childhood toy, Anne?"

"Of course I did. His rocking horse. It's still upstairs in the old nursery. Charles called the horse Foxy. If you take the letters that make up the name and give each one a number, working on the principle that the letter A is number one, then you have 6152425."

"Did you go to Zurich?" Nicky asked.

"Oh yes, that very day. I drove up to London immediately. Philip and I took an afternoon flight, and we visited the bank on Friday morning."

"Was the number correct?" Nicky knew the answer from the look on Anne's face.

"Yes," Anne said.

Philip now explained, "We withdrew the money from the account, received a cashier's check for the three hundred million U.S. dollars and went to another bank, where we opened an account and deposited the check. We want to create a fund with it, and we plan to build hospitals, canteens and schools for the children of the Middle East, just as Charles wanted. Yes, you can be damned sure it's going to be done."

Nicky turned to Anne. "It was an act of redemption on Charles's part, wasn't it?"

"Yes, it was, Nicky."

"Can you ever forgive him?"

"I think so . . . perhaps . . . in time."

· · ·

Later, after tea, Nicky and Clee went upstairs to the lavender-and-gray bedroom where they had slept last night.

As she packed the few items of clothing they had brought with them she said to Clee, "Thanks for coming with me. You've been wonderful."

"You *are* glad you came now, aren't you, Nick?"

She zipped the bag, lifted it off the bed and took it to the door. "Yes, I am," she said. "And I'm grateful to you for making me. I almost lost my nerve at the last minute."

He stood up from his chair and placed his hands on her shoulders. "Nicky Wells lose her nerve. Never!"

She smiled. "But I did. You gave me the courage to face Anne, to tell her that Charles was dead."

"You owed her that, Nicky, in view of the relationship you have with her, all she had meant to you, still means, and the kind of woman she is—a wonderful woman."

And then he added, a little ruefully, "God knows if we'll ever get to Provence at this rate—there's always something preventing us from going down there. Problems at my office, Yoyo arriving, and now all this."

"Oh, don't let's worry about Provence," she murmured, looking into his eyes. "We've got the rest of our lives to go to the farm."

A huge smile spread across his face. "Does that mean you're saying yes?"

"Yes, I'm saying yes."

He hugged her, then held her away from him. His smile grew bigger, and he exclaimed, "But if you marry me you'll be living in Paris. What about your big career in American television?"

She laughed, and shrugged her shoulders lightly. "I'm going to let Arch worry about that. He'll find a way to work it all out."

Clee bent forward and kissed her. "I promise you I'll be the best husband."

"That means a lot, coming from a man who's a bachelor at heart, like you."

"Not anymore I'm not. Come on, let's go!"

Downstairs, Anne and Philip were waiting for them in the small entrance hall, and Anne said, "Your car just arrived, but you've plenty of time to get to Heathrow, so don't worry, you won't miss your plane."

"Thanks for everything, Anne," Nicky said, embracing her. Against her hair, she murmured, "I'm going to marry Clee."

Anne gently extricated herself from Nicky's arms and looked deep into her bright blue eyes. Her own, so similar in color, filled with sudden tears. She smiled through them and said, "I'm so happy for you, Nicky darling. And it's I who should be thanking you for being such a good friend—"

Philip said, "I couldn't help but hear what you said, Nicky. Congratulations to both of you." He shook Clee's hand, and then opening his arms to Nicky, he said, "Thank you for caring enough to come and tell us everything, Nicky."

"It was the only thing I could do."

The four of them went outside and said their good-byes, and Nicky and Clee got into the car. The driver turned on the ignition and they rolled slowly down the gravel driveway, heading for the huge front gates. When they came to the bend in the corner, Nicky looked back. Anne and Philip were still standing on the steps, waving, and behind them, glimmering in the fading afternoon light, was Pullenbrook. The first time I came here, Nicky thought, I fell in love with a fascinating man, an extraordinary woman and a great house, which might have been my home one day. I thought my life was going to be here with them. It was not meant to be, and I'll probably never come back. But I'm leaving a little bit of my heart here, and I'll always remember . . . everything.

BARBARA TAYLOR BRADFORD was born in Leeds, Yorkshire, and was a reporter for *The Yorkshire Evening Post* at sixteen. By the age of twenty she had graduated to London's Fleet Street as both editor and columnist. In 1979 she wrote her first novel, *A Woman of Substance,* and that enduring best-seller was followed by five others: *Voice of the Heart, Hold the Dream, Act of Will, To Be the Best,* and *The Women in His Life.* The first five have been made into television miniseries. Her novels have been published in eighty-two countries and twenty-four languages, with more than thirty-five million copies in print. Mrs. Bradford lives in New York City with her husband, film producer Robert Bradford.

15.00

LT FIC
Bradford, Barbara Taylor.
Remember.